the
SEARED
LANDS

DEBORAH A. WOLF

the
SEARED
LANDS

TITAN BOOKS

THE SEARED LANDS
Paperback edition ISBN: 9781785651144
Electronic edition ISBN: 9781785651151

Published by Titan Books
A division of Titan Publishing Group Ltd
144 Southwark St, London SE1 0UP
www.titanbooks.com

First edition: April 2020
2 4 6 8 10 9 7 5 3 1

A CIP catalogue record for this title is available from the British Library.

Printed and bound in the United States

This book is dedicated to

MY MOM

—who read me stories,

MY DAD

—who took me hunting.

TABLE OF CONTENTS

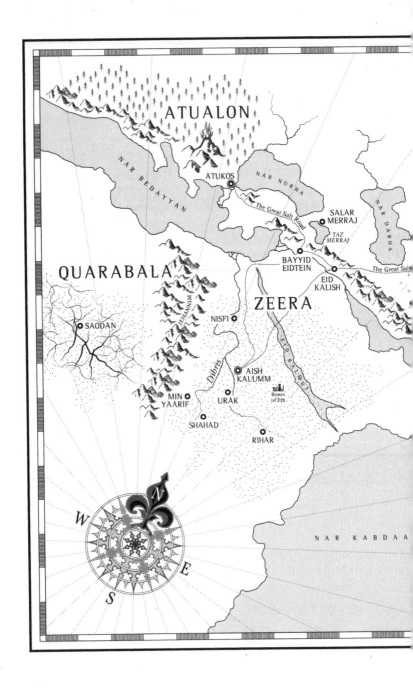

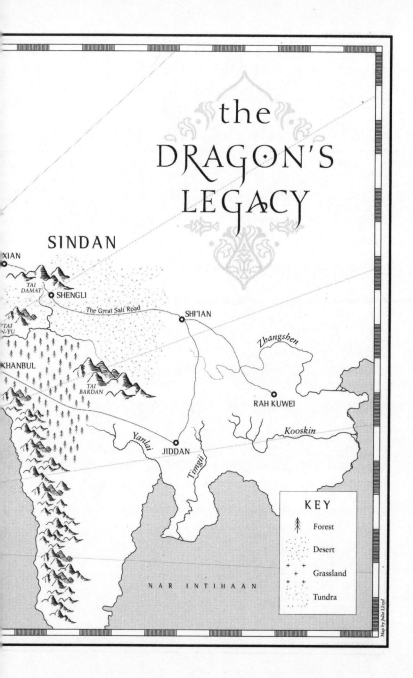

DRAMATIS PERSONAE

Ani (Istaza Ani): Youthmistress of the Zeerani prides. Though she has no children of her own, she loves her young charges fiercely.

Daru: A young Zeerani orphan, apprenticed to Hafsa Azeina. Born a weakling, Daru is keenly aware of the thin line that separates life from death.

Hafsa Azeina: Former queen consort of Atualon, mother of Sulema an Wyvernus ne Atu, and foremost dreamshifter of the Zeeranim.

Hannei: Expatriate Ja'Akari, Hannei Two-Blades is known in Min Yaarif as the esteemed pit fighting slave Kishah.

Ismai: A Zeerani youth who once wished to break tradition and become Ja'Akari, now held in unofficial thrall to the Mah'zula leader Ishtaset. Ismai is the last surviving son of Nurati, First Mother among the Zeeranim, of the line of Zula Din.

Jian: A Daechen prince and Sen-Baradam of Sindan.

Kal ne Mur: Lich King of Eid Kalmut, and a former Dragon King of Atualon.

Leviathus: Son of Ka Atu, the Dragon King, brother to Sulema Ja'Akari, Leviathus was born *surdus*, deaf to the magic of Atualon and thus unable to inherit his father's throne.

Maika: Kentakuyan a'o Maika i Kaka'ahuana li'i, last of the Kentakuyan, traditional rulers of Quarabala, Yaela's niece, and newly confirmed queen in Saodan.

Sulema Ja'Akari: Ja'Akari warrior, daughter of Zeerani dreamshifter Hafsa Azeina and Ka Atu, the Dragon King of Atualon. Considered by some to be the rightful Dragon Queen of Atualon, by others nothing more than the daughter of a usurper.

3

ILLINDRA'S WEB

Born of salt and laughter and love of the long, slow night, the wind danced down the streets of yesterday. It sang as it danced, painting pale stone with dried-blood dust. It was a small magic and sly, power enough to raise a little army of shadows best left dead and gone but not to keep them.

Shadows thus summoned, feckless and fell, found themselves caught in the sticky web of time and death and infinite thought. They faded away as they had come, weeping lullabies of apathy and rage.

Fainter than memory, pale as filtered sunlight from the world high above, the mistral capered and laughed between the shining strands of an Araid's lair, hung with traps and songs and dreams of fresh blood. The spider slept, as the shadows slept, dreaming of the day it would rise and feast upon the bodies of men.

Soon, soon.

Not today.

Aasah the Illindrist's apprentice lifted his face to feel the breeze, breathed deep its song of blood dust and salt dust and the sorrow of lost mates, and smiled in gratitude as it caressed his skin, drying the fear-sour sweat.

If I die today, I die, he thought, *but the wind will live on.*

It was a comfort.

The song in the wind beguiled his heart, fanning the embers of youth. The dust beneath his bare feet was cool, here in the belly of the world. The bone walls and ventricular halls of the long dead sea-thing into which his ancestors had carved this city were as cold and still as any forgotten thing,

Yet the stirring air spoke to him of life, and hope, and *a'a pua'a oneho*—the heart of a dragon at the heart of the world.

He turned his face toward the dreamed-of surface, closed his eyes and smiled, imagining what must it be like to gaze upon a world of sunlight and rain, breath and bone and blood, in days before things were cursed? Thus dreaming, so blind, he let his feet choose his way in blessed darkness.

The breeze lifted its voice in prayer, and his heart beat *tha-rum tha-rumble*, and his bare feet *shushhh-shushhhed* along the pounded sand, and joy lifted him up. It cajoled his limbs to dance, raised the breath from his lungs and up, up through his chest, his throat, his singer's mask, till he was a note in the song, a twirl in the dance of life. Thus did Aasah the Illindrist's apprentice, on this day of his naming—this day of his death—dance blind down a road best left forgotten, down and out of the world of man, down and out of now and here.

Into the Web of Illindra.

He sang and danced, for he was a two-soul man. Male and female, *sa* and *ka*. Gifted and cursed, he sang and danced, laughing as the tears coursed down his dusted cheeks. Clothed in courage and terror he leapt, chanting an exaltation of life even as he left life behind. Aasah stepped once, twice, three times into the footprints of his own ancestor who had fled in terror from the very thing he sought—

Seeks, would seek, had sought, he thought, as his master had taught him. For every thing, every action exists in all times and all places at once.

Infinite and bold as a dragon, infinitesimal as dust he flew—

flies, would fly, had flown

—and in the end, as both dragon and dust are wont, he was—

is, would be, had been

—caught.

❖

6

Long he hung in the spider's web, a sacrifice come to the knife. He had been raised for this, trained and anointed and blessed for this. Every mouthful of food he had consumed, every breath sighed, every kiss denied, had been a step in the dance that had brought him here, a note in the long song of his people's atonement. The sins of his ancestors had led him here, and he would accept with a grateful heart whatever may be.

Or so he thought, until the web began to tremble.

A great weight descended from above, a heaviness in time and space, mind and heart. The web that stung and held him to this time and place shivered, sending ripples of chillflesh along his bare and hairless skin. Aasah had dreamed of this since the night he first slept alone, had thought himself prepared.

I know, he thought—

knows, will know, had known

—nothing.

It took all the strength he had, heart, body and mind, to remain still and willing as the thing crept nearer. The web swayed and then shook till his bones rattled and his head whipped back and forth. Blood poured red and molten through the stone caverns of his heart, heat enough to burn himself free, should he so choose. The wind swept his arms, his legs, pulling at his hands and feet, promising to show him the way to escape, should he so choose. He could abandon this mad and futile quest, give his people over as sacrifice in his place, should he so choose.

The world went still and the thing stood over him, legs as long as three men laid head to foot stretching up to the stars. Clusters of eyes like wicked stars glittering with their own pale light all turned toward his pliant form, fangs like polished dragonglass curving out and down as it prepared to strike. He had seen this—in every dream he had seen this, and in every dream he had been faced with the choice. Live, or die?

7

Life, or death? sang a voice in his mind, his heart, his bones. *Life, or death?* sang his ancestors. *Life, or death?* sang the shadows. *Choose, choose, choose.*

He chose—

chooses, would choose, had chosen

—death.

—and life.

Aasah stared straight into the eyes of death and life and all things in between. He hung suspended from one ankle in the Araid's web, a model of the Illindriverse so vast his mind could not conceive its scope, so small his soul could not find it. At each joining of this web hung a glistening, shimmering drop of atulfah—pure magic, dragon's song manifest. In the act of falling into this web, Aasah saw, he had torn the fabric of time and space, had rent an ugly wound in the flesh of the everything.

Ah, he thought.

Thus seeing, thus knowing at the last, Aasah made his choice.

He flung his arms wide, so that they stuck fast to the strands. The web burned as it touched his skin, branded him traitor and sacrifice, betrayer and hope. Aasah flung his head back to scream, but a song came out instead as the Araid waved its vast forelegs over his human flesh. Once it passed over him, sending a cold chill through his blood. Twice again it passed over, and his soul quailed. Thrice, and Aasah let out his final breath in a long, slow hymn, begging and granting forgiveness for the pain he had caused—

causes, would cause, had caused

The spider's myriad eyes flashed, its forelegs stilled, and drops of venom formed on the needle tips of its curved fangs. Though he had come as a willing sacrifice, though every step down the path of his life had led him to this meeting of webs, Aasah trembled beneath the enormity of his own death, and dread burned through him in a thrill akin to lust. Fear smote the self his training had not fully eradicated and brought with it the final revelation any man needs in order to survive his own death, and become wise.

Oh, he thought—

thinks, would think, had thought

Oh.

A drop of venom fell, as a star might fall through the midsummer sky, and as it fell it burned. Aasah opened his eyes wide, so as not to miss a moment of what was to come. Opened his arms wide, and his heart.

"Yes," he whispered to the spider, "for my people. Yes."

Swifter than grief the Araid struck, fangs sinking into his flesh. Aasah opened his mouth to scream but nothing came out. There was no air, there was no time, there was—

is, would be, had been

Nothing.

BITTERSWEET

"Sssssst," Etana held out a hand, blue and gold and glittering against the soft night sky. The small caravan behind her halted. Someone at the back of the line coughed—a youth, no doubt, unaccustomed to choking on the red salt dust of Quarabala's hard-baked surface. "Sssst!" she hissed again, viperish and sharp. She had neither the time nor the patience for soft-footed fools new to the run.

Long ago the fires of Akari had destroyed the grand cities of Quarabala, so that the people had been forced to shelter far underground in the rifts and rents in the earth made by Sajani's attempts to wake. When the days of the Sundering had passed, the Quarabalese had found themselves isolated from the rest of the world by a road made practically impassable by the deadly heat. As they recovered, the people had made a life for themselves far from Akari's wrath. They fashioned cities from the bones of the world, far less grand than those they had lost, but not without grace and beauty, and mined the mineral-rich red salt which sustained all life and which could be found nowhere else in the world. Eventually they learned to travel overland in small groups, shielded from the sun by shadowmancer magic, though such travel was risky at best and only undertaken by small groups of individuals driven by need or greed.

As the population of Quarabala grew, their fertility rates buoyed by easy access to red salt and at a safe distance from the wars that ravaged the far green lands, settlements pushed farther and farther from the queen's city of Saodan. These settlements served a noble purpose, as well; they served as a defense against the Araids, great spiders who had dwelt in caverns below the world's surface and to whom the priests of Eth paid foul homage.

But Araids were not the only danger, here at the heart of the world.

Amalua's fingers drummed against her arm in a quick tattoo, runner's code for those times when silence meant life.

Hear something? the younger woman asked.

Etana reached out and made her reply against her companion's taut flesh.

No. Feel something. Close. Close.

Run? Amalua asked, with two fingers pressed hard.

Proximity to any settlement meant predators, and the recent earthquakes which had brought them to check on the outer bastions would have roused some of the nastier ones from their deep homes. Etana had no desire to become a runner who had *almost* made it to her journey's end.

No, she answered. *Wait. Listen.*

The travelers stood for a long while, quiet as deep shadows. Etana and her swift companion were beacons against the endless dark, painted as they were with whirls and sworls of glow paste in shades of green and blue. The palms of their hands and soles of their feet had been smeared with a thick paste of honey and gold dust—and other, less pleasant, things.

Such brilliance marked them out to one another as they made their way from city to settlement and back again. It warned lesser predators that they were dangerous—or at least unpleasant to taste—and gave greater predators easier targets than the salt caravans or settlers whose lives they were sworn to protect. They were the Iponui, swift-footed, stout-hearted warriors of the Quarabala, marked out as the lights that would one night guide their people home.

One night, but not this night.

On this night, Etana let her ka flow light as a mother's song, searching for bright, hot life against the burned-out husk of their world. Prickly-sharp she could feel the bright souls of the small knot of salt guildsmen and healers who traveled in her wake, and sharper still the soul of the shadowmancer who trailed them, ready to give magical assistance if it were needed. Etana fervently hoped it would not be needed—a shadowmancer's fees, were she required to perform, would be astronomical.

Beyond the shadowmancer, she felt nothing.

In the shallow crevasses that mocked the true path, nothing. But high above their heads, faint and fluttery as a new babe's cry, she could feel a hundred tiny lives hungering, hungering. Etana let out her breath in a laugh, though she kept it silent. More than one of the greater predators knew how to mask their soul-scent from one such as she. Still, it was a relief to find that the disturbance she had felt posed no danger to them.

"It is nothing but a flock of hali'i," Amalua whispered, and her voice was thick with suppressed mirth, as well. "Shall I tell the others that my mother is frightened of birds?"

"Impertinent brat," she laughed. "Would you prefer to make the return trip by yourself?" Etana squeezed her arm affectionately and let her hand fall away.

"Shall I run on ahead?" Amalua said.

"You just wish an excuse to stretch those long legs of yours."

"That I do." White teeth flashed. The night was loosening her cool grip on the Seared Lands. "I hate crawling along with these soft-feet. Morning is near, and I have no wish to burst into flame."

"Run then, and tell them we are coming. We will be there soon."

"As you wish, Mother." Amalua bowed, deeply and with no hint of her usual teasing, and then she was gone, a streak of blue and green, leaving gold-dust footprints for those who would follow.

Etana shook her head, smiling inside her heart. "Come," she whispered to her charges. It was as loud as a shout after the long, slow silence of their journey. "Come quick. We are nearly there. Food waits for us, and baths, and bed."

"And profits!" one of the healers shot back, eliciting a chorus of soft chuckles.

"And warm bodies!"

"Your bodies will be warming the bellies of a bintshi if you do not hurry your soft asses along," she scolded, though her heart was not in it. For she was at the end of the road—this road, at any rate—and Etana dearly longed for the delights of the flesh that would be her reward. Bath, and food, and bed...

Paleha.

"Sweet as manna wine, bitter as black salt."

These were the words the poet Saouda had used to define love, and described perfectly this final meeting between old friends. Etana stepped down the cool and shallow steps and onto the red sand floor, smiling in delight and irony at the grandeur of Paleha's rooms.

"You have done well for yourself."

The stout figure in the middle of the room turned slowly, slowly, absorbing the shock of this unexpected visitor so that by the time she faced Etana only the whites of her eyes showed her surprise. Tiny bare feet peeked from beneath robes as red as the sand floor, and a large seer's bag hung at her waist. Dragon's-eye lanterns hung all about the room. Tiny hands stretched toward her in greeting and supplication.

"Etana," she whispered, as if horrified. Eyes round and pale as golden moons glistened with unshed tears. "On this day, of all days, why did you have to come to Mawai?"

It stung. "Our new queen sent us with her greetings, and to see whether those of you in the far settlements needed Saodan's

13

assistance after the recent earthquakes. But if our presence is unwelcome..." She turned to leave. After all they had been through together, this was the greeting she had earned?

"No, no, you do not understand. How could you?" Paleha drew nearer, so near that the warrior could smell book dust and salt dust and the woman's own musk. "How could you know?" she continued. "But it is cruel, too cruel even for this world."

"You still speak in riddles." Etana snorted but allowed her hand to be taken. Paleha's grip was not as strong or as sure as she remembered. She pulled away, frowning. "Are you not the least bit happy to see me?"

Tears spilled down Paleha's round cheeks, like stars fallen from grace.

"A moon ago, I would have been happy to see you. Had you arrived yesterday, I would have fallen at your feet and kissed them. But today?" She shook her head as tears welled and flowed, welled and flowed. "Today it breaks my heart. Come, I will show you."

She turned and Etana followed. Silence and dread stretched between them like the darkness between candles.

Paleha had a shrine to Illindra, as was usual and proper for those who had answered the call to priesthood. Hers was set in an alcove nearly large enough to be considered a room, floored with soft red sand denoting her high caste, tiled in red salt and black glass and beaten gold. The room was bare save for a pedestal of black glass lit from within, and upon this pedestal rested an Illindrist's threefold loom.

Etana shuddered at the sight of it. She had never understood the seer's craft and, like many warriors, feared magic more than she feared death. Death she understood—predators, raiders, monsters, these things she knew how to fight—but how, she had wondered before, could she fight

14

that which she could not see, or smell, or touch?

The Illindrist reached toward the closest petal of the loom. Gems set like stars in her dark skin glittered in the dim light.

"This is *was*," she said, which explained nothing. "You see how the web is full and shining? This is our path, this is Quarabala in the long ago, when we were young and strong, and the world was good." Indeed, the web was shining and full, a breathtaking tapestry spun of silver and starslight. Tiny beads of magic hung suspended here and there, constellations which spoke volumes to one such as Paleha, though to Etana they were just a pretty design.

"I remember being young and strong," she tried to joke, "but I do not remember a time when the world was good."

"Do you not?" A quick smile, quickly hidden, and Etana felt her face heat with a girlish blush.

Ah, she thought, *she* does *remember.*

"This world was before your lifetime, or mine, or even that of our grandmothers' grandmothers," she explained. "By 'we' I mean 'we the people,' the Quarabalese. Before the—the Night of Sorrows—" here her voice faltered, "—before the Sundering, even. In the long ago."

"I... see." Etana shrugged. "But what does this have to do with us, now? The past is the past, dead and gone. It is dust." She slapped her thigh, raising a small cloud of red salt dust for emphasis. "The past cannot touch us now."

"Can it not?" Paleha shook her head. "You know better. See this? This strand right here." She reached out and pointed at a single strand of the web, which glowed silverish in response. "This strand is *is*—"

"Your hand," Etana whispered in horror. Only now did she see that the fingers which had once been so deft and strong were gnarled as manna roots, thickened at the joints, twisting back upon themselves. Her own hand twitched in sympathy. "What happened?"

15

"What happened?" Paleha smiled wryly. "What happened is that against all odds I survived my foolish youth. As have you. I notice that you, yourself, favor the left knee."

Etana stared for a moment and then stuck out her tongue. They shared a girls' laugh, which echoed oddly beautiful among the golden tiles and spider's web. For a moment in time the world was, indeed, good.

Paleha looked at her with eyes of sorrow, of regret.

"There is no time," she whispered.

"Did you not once tell me that now is all time?" Etana said. "If now is all time, we have all the time in the world."

"Still the impertinent brat," Paleha said, and Etana smiled at the words. "You are right, of course, but even so we are bound to the web. For us, in the here and now, the road has come to an end." Paleha gestured to the middle petal of the threefold loom. This web was a sad shadow of the first, a very few irresolute strands clinging to the edge of the wooden structure. It was still lovely, but where the first web was lively and bright and strong, this one held the translucent beauty of a dying child.

"You asked how then affects now, which is—forgive me—a stupid question. Then is now, in more ways than one. See here..." She pointed a knotted finger, and yet again one strand was illuminated.

Etana pursed her lips. "That is the same strand as in the first web."

"Yes, and no," Paleha said. "Same, not same, then, now—it is all one. And look—"

Etana gasped as Paleha rotated the loom's third petal to the fore. This web was tattered and dead, as if some monstrous thing had torn through it with malicious intent.

At the bottom of the tray, curled upon herself like a skeletal brown fist, lay the spider who had been Paleha's companion since she was a child. O'oraids were known to live exactly as long as their human seers, and Etana's heart stopped cold at the sight.

"Is this…" Her voice trailed off.

"This is *will be*."

Etana's breath caught in her throat. "Did the quakes…"

"She died before the quakes," Paleha said in a rough voice. A single tear rolled down her cheek. "Just before. I fear that Sajani's stirrings—you know this is the cause of these disturbances, do not pretend as if it is not so—have rent the defenses we have spent so long building. That Araids are coming with their foul priests and their hungry reavers. It is over, for us."

Silence hung between them, dull as the dead magic in this third web. Somewhere in that silence, Etana came to understand that they had no moments left to waste.

She was pleased to note that her hand did not shake. *After all*, she reminded herself, *Death is a warrior's only true lover*.

"There are no tomorrows," Paleha continued, "not for us, at any rate. This is why I wish—" Her voice broke.

Etana turned to Paleha and gathered the small, warm, soft woman into a tight hug.

"I am glad I have come," she whispered into the fluff of graying hair. "I am glad."

Soft arms crept around her waist and squeezed back. "Well, you are a warrior," Paleha said finally, voice muffled in Etana's robes. "And warriors are known to be mad."

"Is there nothing we can do?" Etana asked.

"There is one thing we can do. One thing we *must* do. Though I wished you would not come, I dreamed that you would, and so I made ready." She reached into the seer's bag and drew forth a package wrapped in precious spidersilk, blue as the daytime sky, green as the grass in stories.

"Paleha!" Etana gasped, shocked by the sight of the heavy bundle.

"It is necessary, and it is time." Paleha thrust the bundle at Etana, who took it unwillingly, and turned back to her trifold loom. "See here—" She rotated the three petals so they lined up perfectly, one behind the other—*is*, *was*, and *will be*. The strand she had caused to illuminate in each web shone like a beacon, and Etana imagined she could hear, very far away, the first notes of a travelers' song.

She knew a map when she saw one. "This is us, here in Mawai!" she exclaimed, pointing to a tiny globe of magesilver. Her finger traveled further down the illuminated strand, not quite touching it. "This is the Huanoha settlement, which was our last stop before this one. Here is Epaha, and A'apela, and…" She described the path with a wave. "There, that big one, that can be none other than—"

"Saodan," Paleha agreed. "The City of Queens."

"I have never been," Etana said in a hushed voice.

"Nor I." Paleha sounded as wistful. "We should have gone. It would have been—"

"—glorious." Etana shook her head, clearing away the cobwebs of regret. "You mean for us to take this…" She clutched the bundle to her breast as if it were a girl child. "…to Saodan, and then to the lands beyond?" The shining path continued past the City of Queens, to some mysterious destination beyond the limits of her imagination.

"No," Paleha said. "Not us. I am old, and fat, and slow." She held up a hand to forestall an argument. "Ah, now, it is true," she scolded. "You are, well, you are not so old as I, but you are still slow."

Etana grimaced, and a twinge in her knee seemed to mock her.

"For you and me, beloved, there are no tomorrows." Paleha tapped the edge of the third loom, and the dead web trembled. "But your daughter—"

"Our daughter," Etana whispered, and was rewarded with a smile so brilliant that Akari Sun Dragon himself might have fallen in love.

"Our daughter," the Illindrist allowed, "if she succeeds at this, if she lives, might weave a new web of tomorrows for our people."

"The last road." Etana stared at the web, at the fragile illuminated path, scarce daring to breathe lest she shatter the delicate strands.

"Our last hope."

Amalua fidgeted irritably as Etana again checked the straps that bound the precious bundle to her back.

"They are fine, First Runner. You fuss so much one would think I had a child strapped to my body. I am good! *Ow!*" She shrugged the lingering hands away, laughing good-naturedly.

"You have water enough?" Paleha fretted.

"Illindrist," Amalua replied. "I have one mother, thank you, and she is quite enough. I hardly need two of you fussing at me." She smiled to take the sting from her words. "This is not my first run, you know."

Paleha ignored this. "You remember the map? You know the way?"

Amalua rolled her eyes. "What is in this pack, anyway?" She shrugged at the straps that ran across her shoulders, across her back and chest, and beneath her breasts. "Salt bricks? It is so heavy."

"Not so heavy that my daughter cannot carry it." Etana's voice was thick with hidden emotion, and with pride. Amalua peered at her, suspicious at last.

"Why am I leaving before the caravan... and before you?" she asked. "What is so important that you would have me run all the way to Saodan, by myself, and without stopping?" She stopped her fidgeting and stared straight into her mother's eyes. "Answer me true, First Runner. What is this burden I carry?"

Paleha smiled. "It is—"

"The Mask of Sajani." Etana ignored the Illindrist's angry gasp. "She carries the hope of our people, Paleha. She has the right to know."

Amalua's eyes went round as the moons. Etana took advantage of her daughter's shock to grab her by the shoulders and kiss her soundly on each cheek. "Run well, my sweet. A mother's blessings upon you."

"And a daughter's upon you," Amalua answered. Her mouth trembled, but her voice remained steady. "Will I never see you again?"

Etana would not end this day with a lie.

"We are runners. Swift as the sunlight."

"Silent as the night," Amalua answered. She dropped to the ground, kneeling, and kissed her mother's feet. Tears fell fat and warm upon her skin; a powerful magic. Then she leapt to her feet and was gone, the gold dust on her soles and the blue-green glow of her runner's camouflage painting a mural of courage against the night.

"Run well!" Etana called, breaking tradition and drawing a few disapproving stares from those few passers-by who had risen before the sun was fully down.

At her side Paleha sighed heavily. "I wish—"

The still air was rent by a shriek of despair.

"Reavers!" a man screamed, somewhere high above them. "Reav—" The scream cut short, horribly so. Etana gripped her spear and set her jaw.

"There is no more time," Paleha mourned. "There is no hope. We cannot stop them."

More screams, nearer, as people woke to death and horror.

"We cannot stop them," Etana answered, voice grim. "But we can slow them down."

Paleha clutched at her robes. "I am glad you are here," she said. Etana turned and looked down, surprised to see her friend smiling through the tears. "Despite everything, I am glad."

Etana loosed a breath that she had been holding in for a lifetime. "How long has it been," she said by way of reply, "since we have faced an enemy together?" With that she smiled, and that smile lifted her spirit up, up through the city, through the webs of rope and magic and dreams that for so long had held this place safe, up over the seared flesh of the world and into the sky, where it startled a late-hunting nighthawk.

"Too long," Paleha answered. Gnarled fingers tightened on her Illindrist's staff. "Shall we join the dance, my love?"

"Yes," Etana breathed, "but first—" She drew Paleha close and bent her face down. Their mouths met, light as a hummingbird kissing a flower.

Was was gone, and *will be* would never come, not for them.

But they had *now*, and it was beautiful.

O N E

"The ancestors will show us the way."

Night fell sweet and mild. A cool breeze, carrying the faint notes of jasmine and dragonmint, caressed Maika's upturned face. The wind had been wild once, a howling, killing thing. Quarabalese engineers had caught it in their wind-traps, caressed and beat it into submission with their tunnels and cunning blades until it was a lesser, gentler version of its true self.

It was not, she thought, unlike the process by which an unruly girl might be bent to the will of her people and molded to serve their needs.

Maika hesitated at the bottom step, savoring the moment, and let the tamed breeze lave the nervous sweat from her brow. She urged her features to solemnity as befit the serious nature of this outing—a young runner had nearly died to bring her a message from the outer bastions—but the yet-untamed girl at her core wanted to run and shout with delight. Surrounded as she was by an entourage of counselors, guards and wise women, still she walked at their head rather than in their midst. As princess and heir to the Kentakuyan throne, she had spent her waking hours trapped in a prison of well-meaning shoulders and backs. On this day, having experienced her first moons-blood and having been deemed ready by the oracles, she walked at their fore as queen.

It seemed a silly and arbitrary measure to Maika—as if a woman's blood had anything to do with governance!—but this thought she kept to herself. It would not do to give the counselors any reason to stuff her back into the protective cocoon, just as she might break free.

It was a short trek across a wide road, between the brightly painted doors and sculpture gardens of Saodan's elite families, and the worst danger—that Maika might stub a slippered toe upon a cobblestone—did not come to pass, but it felt like an adventure all the same. She wished that they had timed this visit during the morning or evening hours, so that she might have seen more citizens going about their mysterious daily lives, but chided herself for this selfish thought. It was not as if the Iponui had chosen to arrive at midday, after all.

Midday. Maika paused at the wide red gates before the healers' tunnels and shuddered at the thought of her own skin exposed to raw sunlight. Her life—and the lives of her people as far back as the history books remembered—had been lived far underground, safe from the wrath of Akari Sun Dragon. This runner must have been driven insane by the sun, as the rumors said, to risk death by immolation. Maika *hoped* it was sun-sickness. Because if the messenger was not mad, the message she bore must be dreadful.

The gates were hauled open, and Maika stepped through them. A healer's apprentice in a red and white apron bowed low, eyes cast down and away from her magnificence, then spun on her heels and led them along a narrow corridor that smelled of bitter herbs and sorrow.

The runner they had come to see had first been taken to the priests for emergency healing. She had been "burnt to salt," as the saying went, so lost to exhaustion and dehydration that she had not been expected to survive the night. Yet the Iponui were known to be as tough as manna roots, and this one seemed to be no exception. She had lived and was aware enough to insist on delivering her message to the queen.

The apprentice rapped on a white-painted door, which swung inward to reveal a thickly bandaged woman reclining on a healer's cot. Her limbs were long and thin, her glow-painted skin raw and blistered, her head wrapped in layers of fine gauze soaked in ointments and herbs so that everything above her nose was covered. They had said that she was fortunate not to have lost her eyes. Maika winced in sympathy. What burden could be so important, she wondered, that this woman would give her eyes to bear it?

The runner lay with one arm protectively curled about a bundle as large as her own head, wrapped in blue-green spidersilk as fine as the robes of state. Maika ignored Counselorwoman Haoki's hissed warning and hurried forward as the stricken warrior tried and failed to raise a mug to her cracked and bleeding lips.

"Here," she said as she steadied the woman's hands. The mug was cool and the water smelled strongly of herbs. "Let me help you."

"My thanks," the runner whispered in a voice as cracked and blistered as her skin. She drank but a little, and then pushed the mug away, settling back into the pillows with an exhausted sigh. "Are you another healer? I do not recognize your voice."

"No..." Maika began a bit awkwardly.

"You have the honor of addressing your queen, Kentakuyan a'o Maika i Kaka'ahuana li'i," Counselorwoman Lehaila informed the runner.

The runner attempted to rise. Precious water sloshed over the mug's rim, wetting her hands and Maika's. "Your Magnificence!" she gasped. "Forgive me—"

"Nonsense," Maika protested, trying to press the woman back down again without causing further pain. Despite the splendor of her new robes of state, she did not feel particularly magnificent. Next to this heroic runner, she felt positively dull. "Nonsense. Lie back now, at your ease, and tell me why you have come."

Awkward, she thought, and she scolded herself, but the runner lay back with a sigh.

"Magnificence," the runner said. "Forgive me."

"Forgive you?"

"Forgive me," she repeated, "for I come bearing terrible news, and a heavy burden. Our outer strongholds and settlements have fallen. The Araids have mounted an attack, and we could not... we could not withstand them." Red-tinged tears slipped from beneath the gauze, leaving tracks in the runner's streaked glow paint. "I ran as fast as I could, but I—" Her voice broke, and her breathing became ragged. "I fear I have come too late. You must flee, sweet queen, you and all our people must leave the Seared Lands. We must go now. I will show you the way. I know the way, I have seen it—"

The runner would have attempted to rise again, but a healer stepped forward and pressed her back, scowling at the queen.

"She needs rest," the healer snapped.

"I need to tell you—" the runner gasped. "I need to give you—" She groped for the bundle at her side, fretting and pushing at it until Maika reached across her body to pick it up. Whatever it was, it was heavy.

"Who sent you?" Counselorman Kekeo asked. "Who sends us these words?"

"My mother," the runner replied in a broken voice. Now that she had passed her burden on to the queen, she seemed to shrink in upon herself, to grow weak and thin before their eyes. "My mother, First Runner Etana, and Illindrist Paleha of Mawai. You must leave now," she insisted, as another wash of tears streamed down her face. "There is no time for talk. I know the way; I will lead you—"

"Nonsense." The counselorman frowned, staring at the runner's bound face as if he sought the truth in her eyes. "We cannot just cease our daily lives and run, as greenlanders might. Even if we were to convince all our people to leave the Seared Lands, and ushered them all to the Edge, what then? It is a three-day run from Min Yahtamu at the very edge of the Edge to Min Yaarif in the green lands, and that is assuming a strong young runner with a shadowmancer to assist. What of our children, our infirm, our elders? How could we possibly cross the shadowed road? There are not enough shadowmancers to shield our people from the dreadful heat of Akari's wrath; many of the people would die at first sunrise. Would you sacrifice many, many lives in an attempt to save a few, based on the words of one sun-sick Iponui? It is impossible. Impossible."

Once again Maika's counselors talked over her head as if she were a child, playing with her dolls while they made decisions for her. She only half listened, however, as she tugged loose the cords that held the bundle together and began to unwind the silk. The wrappings fell away to reveal a magnificence of gemstones and precious metals, and she choked on an indrawn breath that was nearly a sob. She held, in her too-young and insufficiently powerful hands, the dreaded treasure of her people—the Mask of Sajani. If they had sent this to her, it could mean only one thing.

The Araids had breached their outer defenses. The spiders and their horrid priests would be moving upon Saodan—Quarabala would fall.

Maika's heart sank.

"Impossible," Kekeo said. "Even if what this runner says is true, and even if she has been shown the way, none can expect our people to simply abandon our cities and take to this unknown path. Few runners, even with the aid of shadowmancers, are strong enough to reach Min Yaarif, and that is the closest greenlander city. What of the elders, the children?"

"Nevertheless…" Lehaila stroked her face, and her eyes were troubled. "First Runner Etana is known to many of us here, and she would not send such news lightly. If, indeed, this is the counsel of Illindrist Paleha, as well, we must consider taking some action to defend ourselves. We should gather the council and take these matters into serious deliberation."

Kekeo nodded. "Yes, yes, we must convene—"

Maika stepped forward, and held up the mask, letting the light play upon the faceted gems. Instantly, the counselors fell silent.

She took a deep breath and held it, closing her eyes. When she opened them again, when she breathed the dry hot air, she had set the last of her childhood aside.

"First Runner Etana and Illindrist Paleha have sent us the Mask of Sajani," she said. "*The Mask of Sajani.* They send word that the outer defenses are failing, that we need to leave or we will all die, and this is exactly what we are going to do." She kept her voice steady, and the heavy mask in her hands, though her heart fluttered wildly as if it wished to fly away without her.

"Your Magnificence," Kekeo protested, "we cannot simply—"

"*Mana'ule o ka enna i ka pau,*" Maika snapped. Aasah himself had taught her how to speak with force, and it worked. The small crowd fell silent. "I invoke my authority as queen." Her heart pounded. Would they listen to her? Could one turn overnight from girl to queen merely by bleeding between her legs? It seemed utterly ridiculous.

The counselors and chiefs went to their knees, though some moved less quickly than others. Kekeo was slowest of them all.

"What is your will, Magnificence?" he asked, as if the words tasted bitter.

"The people of Saodan—of all the Quarabala," she amended, "must leave immediately. It is time for us to abandon the Seared Lands and seek a new home for our people." Even as she said the words, Maika felt the enormity of them falling from her lips. "We must work quickly, and save as many people as we can." *As many people as we can—but not all.* The unspoken words hung heavy in the air between them.

Please stop me, she wanted to beg the assembled leaders. *Tell me I am wrong, send me to bed with a story, let me wake up to find this has all been a terrible dream.*

The mask in her hands seemed to mock her. *What kind of queen leads her people into certain death?* it might have asked.

"Leave our homes?" someone said harshly. "Leave our homes and go where? How are we to cross the Seared Lands, and the Jehannim, as well? There are not enough shadowmancers to protect us, and we are not all runners. We do not know the way!"

Maika closed her eyes. She knew the way by heart, though never in her worst dreams had she imagined that she, herself, might one day take it. The traders' road ran, like the blood vessels in a human body, from the life-giving red salt mines deep in the heart of Quarabala, up through the tunnels and rifts which had shielded the people from Akari's wrath for a millennia, across the deadly shadowed roads and the equally hazardous Jehannim, and finally into the hostile city of Min Yaarif. A trained runner or salt merchant might take this road once in a lifetime, with only the dream of wealth and a life in the green lands urging her feet to fly. For an entire people to attempt such a journey was utter madness.

And their only hope.

"There is only one choice open to us. We must take the traders' route to the Edge, and from there over the Jehannim and into Min Yaarif. The ancestors will show us the way," Maika answered, with more assurance than she felt. It was the right thing to say. "Our Iponui will guide us to the green lands, and they in turn will be guided by the ancestors."

Lehaila nodded slowly, glancing at her fellow counselors from the corners of her eyes as if gauging their reactions. "The ancestors will show us the way to a new home."

"A new home." Maika smiled and nodded, holding up the Mask of Sajani for all to see. "A *better* home. We will see the sun rise upon our people at last."

A murmur of assent rose among those assembled, though no few of her counselors exchanged doubtful looks. Maika, clutching the dreadful mask so tightly her knuckles had gone pale, took a deep breath, looking at each face, trying to commit them all to memory.

These are my people, she thought, *more precious to me than my own life. I pray to the ancestors that I have not just condemned them all to death.*

TWO

Akari Sun Dragon soared high above Atualon, bathing the city in golden splendor so that the walls of the meanest hovel sparkled like salt, and colored windows winked like jewels. Children laughed as they chased one another in the narrow alleys between buildings, heedless of the shadows that nipped at their heels; bakers piled high their rounds of soft white bread, never guessing at the source of heat for their ovens. Sunlight poured as sticky sweet as spilled mead across the land and people laughed as they lapped it up, bawling and dumb as golden calves fattened for the slaughter.

Yet Atukos rose frowning above the city. The Dragon King's fortress, named for the living mountain from which it had been carved, crouched brooding and cold. Call as he might, the sun dragon in all his glory could not warm the walls as Atukos mourned her dead king.

Neither could he reach the king's daughter.

She who had once been a Ja'Akari warrior, who had ridden and fought and loved beneath the gold-scaled belly, lay stiff as a corpse on the cold dead stone even as her father the king had lain, broken and defeated. Her fox-head staff had been broken and burned, her sword fed to the forge; even her warrior's braids had been shorn away. Sulema lingered in the dark, sinking into the bed of lies her elders had laid down, and waited to die as voices rolled over her like thunder.

"Is there nothing more you can do?"

"She will not eat. She will not drink. She will not wake—if, indeed, she is truly asleep. No, Meissati, there is nothing more I can do for her."

"Just as well, I suppose. If she cannot properly wield atulfah, and if she is no virgin—"

"She is known to have bedded Mattu Halfmask." This last was whispered, as if the speaker did not wish to be overheard.

"Then she is of no use to us."

"Shall I...?"

"No!" The reply was quick. "No, she is bound to the fortress. Spilling her blood here would be... unfortunate. No, if the girl is willing herself to die, let her do so. There is another who can take her place. A bit young, but—"

An indrawn breath. "Abomination!"

"For you and me, perhaps. For a king, who can say? The powerful are not bound by the same rules as lesser folks. Would you tell Pythos Ka Atu that he cannot do as he wishes?"

"No, not I."

"Nor I." There was a long pause. "Pythos wishes to be rid of this one, quietly and without bloodshed. So. Have this cell bricked up and forget about her. Go back to your family and die in bed as a physician should, with a skin of wine in one hand and a woman in the other."

"It is a pity. Such a beautiful girl."

"Fire is beautiful, too," the first voice reminded. "Let us snuff this one out before it burns us all."

"As you say," the physician said, his voice becoming softer as they departed. "Oh, speaking of the false king's get, do you know whether they have found Leviathus, or..." Sandals scuffed against the stone floor, shuffled away, and left her in silence.

A rat or some other poor creature skittered across the floor. Closer it crept, closer, till its whiskers brushed Sulema's calf. The little beast let out a thin squeak and fled.

Some time later, the stonemasons came.

The harsh light of torches and scrape of stone against stone, the smells of men and smoke and mortar, assaulted the outer shell of she who had been a warrior, but even these things could not reach her spirit. What little of the world as was left to her—torchlight and lantern light, the sighs and cries of other prisoners, the faint redolence of bread and old water and urine—retreated from her senses as a stone wall was raised into place.

Eventually the rough voices and noise of work ceased, and she was left finally, blessedly, alone.

In the dark.

To die.

After an age had come and gone, long after Akari had abandoned his attempts to rouse his love, after dinners were eaten and dishes washed, after lullabies and lovemaking and the last oil lamp burned low, Sulema opened her eyes and regarded the long, slow night. Though her eyes could not pierce the gloom, she knew that her stare was met and answered by the cold golden eyes of the portrait her father had commissioned, the one that showed her as a princess of Atualon, lovely and serene.

Those painted eyes had watched impassive as her mother and father had been slaughtered, and as she had been forced to confess to their murders. Beneath the painting's surface, concealed by the artist's magic, lay another image, this one truer to its subject. That hidden Sulema was a warrior, a true daughter of the Zeera.

"Life is pain," her mother had said. *"Only death comes easy."*

"But I am Ja'Akari, am I not?" Sulema asked, though it was now and forever too late to seek her mother's advice. "A warrior is no easy meat. They expect me to die here, quiet and neat, and make their lives easier."

She smiled in the dark.

"Fuck *that*," she said.

THREE

The wind was born of a long-dead king, singing forgotten songs. His name, which once had rolled across these lands as thunder, was lost to memory, robes and jewels and fine horses long gone to dust and bone and the tattered pages of history books.

He sang, and the song was still the same, however, pouring down from the heart of Akari Sun Dragon as a blessing, welling up from the dreams of Sajani Earth Dragon, sweet as well water.

The song swirled deep in his heart, this beating borrowed heart of a Zeerani youth. It swept around and through him, rousing him to life. Through him also rose the hordes of living dead, those who in life had foolishly loved their liege more than they loved their souls, and who had pledged to him fealty beyond the Lonely Road. They stirred now in his mind: loyal monsters, doom's companions, his to command. All he had to do was stretch forth his hand and whisper words of command and intent.

And yet...

Long he had lingered in the dark of the moonsless cavern, presiding over an endless feast of souls, ever hungering and thirsting and lusting for life. This life was his, now—this flesh, these desires, the hot blood racing through the veins of one willingly come. A vessel filled and overwhelmed by the dark passions of the dark lord. A new life, a new world to command, his for the taking, ripe and sweet as a low-hanging fig.

And yet...

The Lich King sat cross-legged by the banks of Ghana Kalmut, wearing the body of Ismai, son of Nurati. The river's song accompanied his own, and in it he heard the slow, sweet refrain of death, of ease, songs of hope's end and a surcease of sorrow. For an age, and an age after that, he had bidden his time—

Life was his once again.

He was not sure he wanted it.

Perhaps, he thought, *my time has passed.* Might he not, after all, choose instead to slip free of this human body as one might shed a robe, to leave it crumpled and abandoned at the river's edge and decide instead to set foot upon the Lonely Road? For surely the road had been singing to him, too, of passings-on and passings-over and adventure in strange new worlds. This world was dying, and all the dead knew it. Sajani Earth Dragon stirred in her sleep even now, restless with the need to wake, to fly, to break free and seek solace in her mate's embrace.

The world would not survive the dragon's ascendance any more than this broken body would survive his abandonment. Why choose this—this dying earth, this dying body—when he, king of kings, could instead elect to master death? Surely that was the only realm he had yet to conquer.

His blood boiled at the thought.

Even as he sang, as he called the wind and the rain and the sand, as he called death to life, the song mocked him. He had journeyed across the face of the world, had stretched forth his bare hands and bade Atukos rise from the living stone, had soothed Sajani to sleep and roused Akari to smite his enemies. He had bound the warrior mages of the Baidun Daiel and thrown back the fell sorceries of his enemies. He had known the world and every living thing in it by name, and in knowing, he had owned it.

Now, sitting at his ease beside the untroubled waters, he heard the strains of a strange new song, smelled the dust of an unfamiliar road—

The Lich King frowned.

"What troubles you, Father?"

She was a flash of sunlight on dark waters, his Naar-Ahnet, sweet and deadly as mad honey. The years had tainted her, the pain had poisoned her, he knew, but the fault was his, and she was his sweetest love.

"Death," he answered honestly, and she laughed.

"Death?" she said. "After all this, you fear death?" She sat beside him, rested her head on his shoulder, and her small hand found its way to his. "You have mastered death. You are death's king." She squeezed his fingers. "And mine, Father."

"I do not fear death," he said, frowning again at the youthful sound of his voice. "But neither have I mastered it. Death is as yet unknown to me. It might be… peaceful…"

"And it might not," she finished, guessing his mind.

"True. Why would death be any more peaceful than life?" he said. "Why would the dreams experienced in death be any less horrific than those of the living? Why should the roads be any easier, any less… lonely?"

"You miss her."

"I miss her."

"You loved her so." Naara snuggled close. The story of her mother's passion for her father, and his for her, had ever been a favorite.

"I love her still," he said, wrapping an arm about her small form. "Ahsen-sa Ruh a'Zeera was the most maddening, the most skilled—"

"The most beautiful—" she urged.

"The most beautiful and the most beloved of all the Zeera's daughters. 'Spirit of the desert wind' she was named, and from the moment I first laid eyes on her…" His voice trailed off. An image came to him, unbidden, of a flame-haired girl with skin too pale, too freckled to ever be his Ahsen-sa, a girl with eyes of gold and a wide, troublesome smile.

"When you first laid eyes on her?"

35

"You favor her, you know," he said. Kal ne Mur turned his face and kissed the top of his daughter's hair. She smelled of deathblooms and grave dust and other, less pleasant things.

"I do not, and you know it," she said, "but I thank you."

Sulema, he thought, *her name is... Sulema*. He shook his head, trying to clear his mind, and shoved the boy Ismai deeper into the shadows of their shared mind. "Your time is done," he said irritably.

"Will you take it up?" Naara said, playing with his fingers. "Take up your crown, reclaim what is yours..."

"You would see me raise my faithful, and wage war upon whomever dares call himself Ka Atu now. To ride down the people of this land and seize that damned throne, but why? For a thousand years I have thought about how I might have lived my life differently. We all have," he added, waving his free hand toward the caverns, the canyon, the thousands upon thousands of undead. "Never would one more war have made my life better, let alone the world. The people of Atualon do not wish for the return of a long-forgotten king... any more than that king wishes to return."

"You do not wish to return?" Her fingers dug into his arm, and Naara's voice grew very soft. "To claim what is yours?"

"Many asses have parked themselves on the Dragon Throne while mine sat here and grew dusty," he answered. The wind played a short riff across the dead waves, causing the spirits trapped beneath the waters to moan. "Many men have called themselves Ka Atu and forgotten their own names, even as the world has forgotten mine. Shall the pages of the book turn backward, then? I have no wish to return to the land of the living, any more than I wish to join the trek of the dead. My faithful do not wish to be disturbed. They cry out against it, in their sleep."

"You wish neither to live nor to die," she said. "What, then, do you want, Father?" In Naara's voice he could hear the dry fire that was Char, guardian of Eid Kalmut, and he smiled into her hair. She was very much his daughter, after all.

"I do not know," he confessed.

"I know what I want."

"What is that, beloved?"

"Vengeance," she told him. "They killed my mother. They… hurt me. They took in vain the name of Zula Din and perverted her warriors, the Mah'zula. They killed Sammai, and Ismai's mother, and they hurt Ismai—" Her voice rose as a litany of hurts became a chant, a song almost, and this tugged at his borrowed heart. Surely the youth Ismai had cared for Char, though he had not known what she was. And the name Mah'zula had kindled the embers of his soul to fury. "I want justice," she said. "I want *revenge*."

"The Mah'zula," Kal ne Mur repeated, tasting the name as if savoring a dish long forgotten. "The men of Atualon. Upon whom would you have me unleash my wrath, little one?"

"All of them," she replied in a choked voice. "All of them." She was crying. They had hurt his little girl, had turned her into this monster—and now they had made her cry.

A dirge, low and slow and full of ill omen, rose from the depths of the Lich King's soul, and flared in his heart. He gathered his daughter up in his arms and held her against his chest.

"I can do that," he said.

Kal ne Mur sang again. This song was born of a dragon's love and tuned to the heart of a boy. Its rhythm was the bridge of a spider's web, a chorus of stories, a sorcerer's verse, and at its climax…

Death.

The web unraveled, the song was sung, the story told as the Lich King stood knee-deep in the Ghana Kalmut and raised his voice in command. The magic was his, pouring through his veins like sweet water, like sunlight, like mead. From the cavern behind him, the canyon walls around and above him, came the cries of the wakening dead. The sounds of rocks falling, of swords unsheathed...

Of sobbing. Though the Lich King hesitated in the face of death, his fell hordes felt no such compunction. They longed for death, they *wept* for death, with every ragged indrawn breath they begged for the release that only he could give them. And with every note dredged up from the bottom of his sorry soul, he denied them.

The magic, the atulfah, swirled about his feet like sand-dae. The sa and ka beat with the rhythm of his heart and carried the dragon's canticle up, up, from the heart of the world to the breath of the heavens, in and out like the tides, waxing and waning as the moons, deep as the darkness between stars.

Come, he sang.

Wake, he sang.

And they obeyed.

By the tens, by the hundreds they came, his faithful dead. Fell they were, nightmares made flesh, flesh made whole. Sinews knotted and knitted along long white bones, muscles grew fat and red and were covered with sleek, pliant skin. Eyes blinked, mouths worked, shattered limbs were made whole again as the horde drew near their king.

Kal ne Mur did not look upon them, but he knew they were there—he could feel them. Feel their despair and their pain, their horror as he dragged them back from the Lonely Road to serve once more at his pleasure. The atulfah he could summon here, in the Valley of the Dead, was a weak thing compared to the power he had once commanded. A shadow of the power he might wield were he in possession of the Mask of Akari.

Still it was enough to unmake this world, as once it had unmade him.

Live for me, he commanded, and they did. They would die for him, as well, again and again until the dragon woke, or until he died, and with his death released them.

He opened his eyes.

Ah, he thought as he beheld his terrible host of the undead. They knelt before him, heads bowed. Some were naked, some in tattered and tarnished armor, still others in finery or funereal rags. All were whole, and all were his.

Deep within him, Ismai son of Nurati cried out in fury and in horror, beating against the prison of his own flesh like a bird in a cage made of bone. Far above a vash'ai sang of loneliness, and fury, and defeat.

A fitting tribute, Kal ne Mur thought, as he surveyed his monstrous horde. This was a small force, compared to the massive armies he had once commanded.

But it was a beginning.

FOUR

Bonesingerrrrrr...

Istaza Ani sat cross-legged with her back against a large rock, eyes closed, face turned up to the sun. Many times she had sat just so, while guarding her adopted people or their flocks or their children. Ever the bones of the earth, the bones of the dead and living, had whispered to her, their voices entreating her, begging her to listen, listen.

Always before she had disregarded them, but it had taken great force of will, knowing full well that some paths, once chosen, can never be unchosen. The path of vengeance was one such, the path of magic another, and the path of the dead most especially so. Once a soul had set foot upon the Lonely Road, those steps could never, *must* never be retraced.

Such laws were written upon the bones of the earth and stars. Life and death were to be immutable, the distinction between them sacrosanct. The living lived, the dead remained so, and only the foulest of sorcerers would dare to challenge the way of things. Any who broke the laws would become a necromancer, a lich.

A bonesinger.

Bonesingerrrrrrrrrr...

She ignored the voice, a low rumble that trembled up through the ground, and resisted the urge to conjure the speaker. It would be easy to do and so very, very gratifying. After a lifetime of denying her own nature, of turning from the magic that was her birthright, would it be so wrong just this once—

Stop.

40

Without opening her eyes or moving so much as a finger, Ani thrust aside the compulsion. Whether it came from within, or—as she suspected—from some ancient bonelord was immaterial. Often in the past she had enjoined the younglings under her command to think before they moved, to avoid stepping into a dark hole before determining whether it contained snakes or vipers. This particular hole was filled with foul and venomous things, and she would not give in to foul temptation.

Not for anything would she—

Not even for Sulema? Daughter of your friend, the daughter of your heart? Would you not do this thing for her?

Ani hesitated, and the voice laughed.

Tell me, then, she commanded the speaker. *Or show me, if you would. What is this great disturbance of which you howl; what danger is so great that I should disregard the peril to face it? And what*, she asked most eagerly and most reluctantly, *do you know of Sulema's fate?*

Sssssssulemaaaaaa, the voice hissed, a sound like a cavern full of serpents and old bones. By this sound, Ani knew she had guessed correctly. It was an ancient bonelord, powerful and wicked and hers to command. *Come, Bonesingerrrrrr, come, I will sssshow you...*

Ani sighed, and gave in to the bonesinger's wheedling, to the song that whispered like sand deep within her body, to the sound of sunlight on stones, and set foot upon the wild and reckless path.

When at last Ani returned to her own bones, her own body, she found herself slumped in a tangle of limbs and hair, and her mouth tasted foul. She sat up painfully, rolling stiff shoulders and grimacing at the fire in her spine. Her neck was stiff, her ass numb.

The hot stink of carrion breath swept over her, and she froze.

Hrrrrrrrrh hrrrrrrrrh, came a low grumble, along with another wave of wet heat. Carefully Ani opened her eyes, blinking away crusted sand and worse, and found herself staring down the throat of death. Broken-tusked, old as a mountain's roots, as filled with dark secrets as the river's dreaming.

You are weak, Inna'hael snarled in her head. *Weak and thoughtless as others of your kind. I should kill you now.*

Though they were not bonded—by his choice, not hers— the words stung. She ignored the thread and stretched, rolling her head and waving away the stink of his breath.

You have been rolling in carrion, she accused.

And you *have been running with a bonelord*, the vash'ai countered, wrinkling black lips back from his tusks in a show of disgust. *You reek of filth and maggots. Reckless—*

There is singing in Eid Kalmut tonight, she told him gently.

The massive feline closed his mouth and regarded her with slow yellow eyes.

Bonelords lie.

Bones do not, she insisted. *They cannot. They have shown me Eid Kalmut; they have shown me the armies of restless dead. Even now they march from the Valley of Death, and Kal ne Mur rides at their head.*

She did not add that the face of the Lich King, ruined as it was now, was more familiar to her than her own. Her heart wept for Ismai—he had been a good boy, and this fate was ill-deserved.

Inna'hael was silent for a long while. When he spoke, his mind's voice was subdued.

So. Perhaps you are not as stupid as some others of your kind. By vash'ai standards, it was an apology. *Long have your kind been foolish, worse than cubs pawing at a hornet's nest in search of honey. Now the world reaps what you have long sown. No longer, human. It is time for my kind to put an end to this foolishness, however we may.*

Ani's blood ran cold.

She did not know what strength the wild vash'ai had kept hidden, or upon what powers the kahanna—vash'ai sorcerers like Inna'hael—could call, but she had the distinct impression that they might, if they so chose, bring about an end to humankind. Many kithren bonded to human companions, but she suspected they were only a small faction among the vash'ai, a quiet voice calling for peace among the roars of war.

"Sulema will fix this," Ani said, as if hearing the words aloud would make them ring with truth, *ehuani*. "And Hannei, and Daru—if he yet lives—our cubs will succeed where we have failed. Sajani will be soothed back to restful dreams, and the magic of atulfah tamed," she continued. *I will help them*, she added silently, *whatever the cost to my own soul*.

Beg your dragons to make it so, Inna'hael warned softly. His voice was not without pity, but his resolution was absolute. *Because if you humans do not clean up this mess you have made, we will clean it up for you*. He turned and sauntered away, the black-tufted tip of his tail twitching back and forth. Only then did Ani see what the massive paws had been hiding from her, the gift he had brought to lay at her feet.

A human skull, fresh and white in the sunlight, lay staring up at the midsun sky. Tusks had pierced the forehead and one eye socket, and most of the flesh had been torn from bone, leaving only a bit of scalp, a scrap of skin, and a cluster of warrior's braids drying in the wind.

F I V E

Home.

Despite the weight of his armor, the dragging weariness in his limbs, Jian's heart lifted at the sight of Dal Moragheirthi rising like a jeweled mountain above the pale trees. Delderrion picked up the pace, and Jian leaned forward to stroke the gelding's dark neck.

"*Innu bar nederiach, Delderrion*," he whispered. "We are nearly there, my friend." While not strictly true—here in the Twilight Lands, his father's castle could be seen from many leagues' distance, and they should not expect to arrive for a couple more days—it was as close to home as the army had been for nearly five years, as men reckoned time. Jian sent up a silent prayer of thanks.

"General!"

He turned at the voice and smiled at the sight of Telloren trotting up on his fat little horse. Lifting his demon's-face visor, he addressed the bard.

"Hai, Tello! What news from the rear?"

Telloren pulled a face. "That is a loaded question, Highness, considering that I have been subsisting on a soldier's rations since we ran out of goats." So saying, the little man leaned to one side and farted loudly enough to spook Jian's horse.

"Augh! Tello!" the nearest soldiers yelled in unison. Tello laughed and brought his placid beast up alongside Delderrion. The gelding eyed Tello with some trepidation, doubtless wondering whether the Dae's hindquarters might resume bellowing.

"What news?" Jian asked again in a quiet voice, guessing that the bard's antics were a ruse to get near the prince.

44

Telloren still wore a fool's grin, but his eyes were serious.

"Your father wishes you to make all haste to the palace, Highness." The morning's peace melted away like visions in a mere.

"Did he say why?"

"Somewhat. A delegation of your people has come to the ocean's edge, and they demand to speak with you."

"To speak with me?" Jian said. "Surely they intend to speak with my father."

"No, Highness. They asked specifically for you. They called you Prince of the Red Tides."

"Ah." Jian smiled grimly. For five years he had been leading his bloodsworn against the troops of Daeshen Tiachu, emperor of Sindan. His handful of followers had swollen into a respectable-sized army, of which this contingent was a small number.

Most of his soldiers were youths born into the Twilight Lands by Dae mothers who had taken human lovers during Moonstide, and who had withheld their children from the lands of men. Such a thing was, strictly speaking, a breach of treaty. Within the laws of the Dae, however, mothers governed all the matters of their children's upbringing until they reached maturity at fifty-six years of age. None among the twilight lords, not even the king himself, dared challenge the mothers in their own land.

Mixed in among the twilight-born, however—and growing in number—were those who, like Jian himself, had been born in the lands of men and who had chosen to forsake their homelands to join the army of their fathers. These tended to be among the fiercest of his troops. Having pledged themselves to treason, they gave no quarter and asked none. As Jian mounted his campaign against Sindan, more and more daeborn youths were found by the sea-side, waiting for their chance to join him. No few of his troops were former Daechen soldiers and officers who had defected during battle.

The twilight lords, being bound to their land, could not themselves wage war upon Sindan. But the daeborn, having signed no treaties and with the ability to walk in either world, fell under no such constraints. They came from the farms and fishing villages, from cities and shanty towns, and from the Forbidden City itself, ready to swear their blood and their lives to Jian as it became clear that his intention was to overthrow the ruling parties of Sindan, and free the daeborn from the emperor's tyranny.

Jian had not been able to save his wife or their child, and so he had vowed to bring to its knees the empire which had stolen them from him.

Telloren was Dae, not daeborn, and a lord at that, but he had sired a daughter one Moonstide, and the girl had been slain during the winnowing of her sixteenth year. A high bard with dreadful power at his command, he rode in Jian's train as if he were some lowly camp follower. Jian did not know how he could have managed without him.

"What does my father say of this?" he asked. "Did he promise that I would meet with these people, or tell them to go piss up a mountain?"

"The king," Tello replied with a meaningful glance at Jian's other followers, "told the delegation that Tsun-ju Jian de Allyr is a grown man and no longer needs his father to speak for him. They await your pleasure, Highness."

Jian's throat clenched and he stared skyward lest surprised tears fall from his eyes. "In that case," he said finally, voice a little rough, "we should continue without stopping. Tell the troops that we will not camp this night. If the wounded need to stop and rest they may, and the medics with them, but those of us who can, will ride on."

"Your will, Highness." Telloren's eyes flashed bright blue with approval, and his smile was wider and sharper-toothed than a human man's would have been. He wheeled his stout gray horse and rode back to give the captains their orders.

"Tsun-ju Jian de Allyr is a grown man and no longer needs his father to speak for him." It seemed that some time in the past five years, during which Jian had endured countless battles, terrible injuries, and the loss of beloved friends, his father had grown to trust and respect him.

He lifted his face to the morning mist, let it kiss away his fatigue and tears. A new day, a red day, and his doom had come to call at last.

In the end, they had not ridden to the palace; the palace had ridden to meet them. They came with lutes and dancing boys, with banners and horns and laughter—

—most importantly, they came with food.

The Sea King himself came, splendid in his moonscale armor, with a crown like starlight and his arms held wide to receive his son. He showered the daeborn with words of praise and with gifts both magical and practical—six-legged horses from the Nether Isles, swords and halberds bound with glyphs of luck and warding, mail armor and black arrows and scrying glasses. Those soldiers who were newly come from the lands of men and had never experienced the splendors of the Twilight Lands were wide-eyed and stupefied. Those who were hardened campaigners rushed through the ceremonies and fell upon the food train like starvelings, knowing that a king's true wealth is kept in his kitchens.

Thus feted, fed, and hastily bathed, Jian rode with his father grim-faced at the head of a massive and formidable force down to the sea's edge.

On this side of the veil the sea was darker and, to Jian's mind, more beautiful than it appeared upon the shores of man. It glistened not with the sun's light—for Akari Sun Dragon did not venture into those gray skies—but with starslight and moonslight and magic.

The stars were different from those that lingered in the skies above Sindan. There were more of them, brighter and more colorful, clustered together in constellations so detailed they might have been paintings. Yet the moons were the same, hanging low and lovely in the never-bright, never-dark skies. During Moonstide, which lasted one night only in the human world, the waters seemed darker and angrier than ever.

The Sea King signaled his armies to a halt. He and Jian dismounted, and signaled that their troops should remain as they were.

This created an outcry. Though the Dae and daeborn were loyal to the death, this did not translate into cowed deference, as it might among men.

"Nonsense!" Hounds milling about her feet, the Huntress's dark horse pushed through the wall of cavalry and she glared down at the king and his son. "You would go alone to face these honorless rats on their own soil, and not expect treachery? This stinks of a trap!"

"Of course it is a trap," Jian's father replied, expression unperturbed but eyes gone as gray as the storming sea. "We are going to see what kind of trap it might be."

The Huntress was joined by Maug, whose pied crest was raised in agitation and whose birdlike black eyes glittered as she glared at the king. Her wings were folded and dragged on the ground behind her like a glossy black robe.

"And if you do not return, brother, what then?" the Huntress demanded. "Who will lead the ladies and lords, when your blood has been sucked up by the dry lands?"

"Dear sister," the king said, laughing, "*you* will lead them, of course!" Many of the host laughed. The worst-kept secret in this kingdom of gossips was that the king's sister feared nothing so much as the thought of being forced to rule.

"If you get yourself killed," she rasped, "my crows and I will peck out your eyes and hang your head to rot upon the Gates of Yosh."

"I love you too," he said, and he winked. "Come, Jian. Telloren, if you would?"

Telloren dismounted as well, pulling an urchin's-bone flute from its leather case.

"Majesty," he said, and his eyes flashed scarlet.

The Sea King and his son, the Prince of Red Tides, walked slowly along the moonlight path, over the foaming waves. Bard Telloren played a sad song, a mad song, firming and calming the waves so that the waters did not so much as lick the soles of their feet as they walked across the water to the veil and, beyond that, to the shores of men.

Jian reached the distant shore sooner than he had expected, though that in itself was hardly surprising. The moons-path sometimes took weeks to traverse, but other times only a few strides, and there was no predicting the length of a particular journey. Suddenly the night sky was too bright, the air too thin and filled with the stink of dying things.

"Jian," his father warned as they neared the pale shore, "do not leave the sea. Stand in the shallows."

"Yes, Father," Jian answered, bowing his head.

When they were still some distance from landfall, he could see that there was, indeed, a delegation from the emperor waiting for them. It was a large enough party to be called respectful, though not so large that it might be threatening. Colored silks and threads of gold winked like saucy stars in the moonslight, and a constellation of cookfires sent up a savory smell that recalled to Jian memories of his own childhood. Unless his nose deceived him, they were preparing the special hot-sweet spiced goat stew that was a specialty of Jian's province, fragrant cinnamon rice, and goose-heart dumplings.

"Ugh." The Sea King wrinkled his nose. "They are ruining good meat."

"Humans like their food cooked and spiced," Jian said, without mentioning that his mouth was watering at the thought of stew and potatoes. He had come to appreciate the savor of tender, raw flesh, but human fare still appealed to him.

"And their women veiled?"

"No, why... oh."

As they halted near the water's edge, Jian could see that among the throng there were indeed two women, both veiled, one in white and the other in a dark blue that rivaled the midnight sky for its beauty. A new fashion, perhaps. The one in white stiffened as if she had seen them, then bent hurriedly toward the other woman, who also went still.

Curious, Jian thought. *I wonder who...*

The notion died unfinished as one of the cookfires blazed suddenly bright, revealing the white armor and antlered brow of a man Jian had known well.

"Mardoni," he whispered. "What is he doing here?"

"The Sen-Baradam of whom you spoke?" The Sea King frowned, and frothing waves pulled at their feet. "I thought you said he was one of those who wished to diminish the emperor's power? What would he be doing here, with the imperial troops?"

"I do not know," Jian answered, "but we are about to find out."

Horns sounded up and down the beach as their presence became known to the emperor's delegation. Mardoni rose from his seat by the fire and strode toward them, bathed in moonlight and firelight, looking for all the world like some felldae from a hearth tale.

"Jian?" the figure called as he came closer, arms out-stretched to show that he bore no weapon. "Daechen Jian? Praise the emperor, it is you! Welcome home, my old friend!"

"Home," Jian's father snorted.

"Old friend," Jian echoed, every bit as skeptical. "We will see."

"It is good to see you, Daechen Jian," Mardoni said, his voice as hearty and bold as if they were village youths challenging each other to a drinking game, not seasoned veterans of forces at odds with one another. "You have been missed."

"Is it?" Jian asked. "Have I?"

"Do not use the title 'Daechen.'" Jian's father spoke in a voice like sea rocks, hard and unforgiving. "There are no half-children, only Dae and others." His tone left little doubt as to which group he believed Mardoni belonged.

The general brushed it off. "Forgive me, your Majesty," he said, bowing deeply, "but that is not entirely correct. Certainly there are the Dae, and then there are humans. I would not argue this point with you. However," he added, standing proud and straight once again, "there are 'others,' and it is to these outsiders we should turn our minds and swords."

"You speak of Atualon," Jian guessed.

"I do," Mardoni agreed, and his face was as earnest as any suitor's. "Come, sit with us by the fire, and we will speak of these things."

"Yes," the Sea King said, "we will do this." Jian lifted an eyebrow in surprise. Behind them, Telloren's flute raised in pitch like an angry mother's voice, warning them away from danger.

"It is all right, Tello," Jian called over his shoulder, even as he stepped from sea to shore. "If they try anything, I will kill them all." His father chuckled. They walked some way toward the fire, and Mardoni turned.

"Do you really think you could defeat all of us, Daechen Jian? I have over a hundred men here, and more within earshot were we to blow our horns." He seemed curious, not threatening, but Jian's hackles rose at the suggestion of treachery. He stopped, held Mardoni's eyes, and allowed himself a long, slow smile.

"If you tried to betray me, I would kill you all," he said, "and I would eat some of you afterward. Starting

51

with you... 'old friend.'" Mardoni looked shocked for a moment, but then shrugged it off and resumed walking toward the fire.

"It is a good thing I do not intend to betray you, then," he said. "My wife would be very disappointed."

The son of the Sea King and the Voice of the Emperor— so Mardoni styled himself—sat upon logs near a fire on the beach, swatting at ants and slurping goat stew.

"I did not think I would like this," Mardoni confided. "Simple village fare is so..."

"Simple?" Jian said.

"Yes," Mardoni agreed, "but filling, too. Wholesome, I guess." He grinned. "Like village girls, I suppose."

The Sea King snorted and shook his head.

Jian did not take the bait. The night was becoming long, and Telloren, though powerful, could not hold the moonspath open for them forever.

"Say what you have brought us here to say, and we will be gone."

Mardoni raised his eyebrows in surprise and glanced at the Sea King, who paid him no mind. This was his son's world, his son's war.

"As you will," the general said at last. "The emperor has a gift for you, Dae... Jian, and a proposition. Which would you like first?"

"A gift and a proposition." Jian glanced at him from the corner of one eye, but Mardoni's slight smile betrayed nothing. "Which would you take first, I wonder?"

"Well," Mardoni answered cheerfully as if he had been expecting the question, "when I was a small boy, I used to take my medicine first, and then the spoonful of honey. But we are not boys anymore, so," he shrugged, "it is up to you to decide, I guess."

Jian pursed his lips. He did not glance at his father, though he would have given much to know the older man's thoughts. Neither did he look again at the Sen-Baradam—it seemed to him that Mardoni was playing some kind of riddle game, and Jian had not been told the rules. Then again, even as a child Jian had known that life was not fair.

He was no longer a boy, either.

"Both at once," he decided.

"Both at… hm, interesting choice. Very well." Mardoni held up a hand and gestured. The two veiled women strode toward them unhurriedly. "The Red Tide Prince wishes to have both offers presented to him at once," Mardoni told them, "so I guess it is up to you to figure it out."

The white-robed woman moved first, drawing back her veil so that Jian could see her face. He nearly gasped with surprise when he recognized Giella the White Nightingale, looking as if she had not aged a day since last he had seen her.

Of course she does, he scolded himself. *Time moves differently for them than it does in the Twilight Lands. Years have passed for me, while here they have seen but a few moons roll by.* He had used this to forward his campaign of terror against the forces of Daeshen Tiachu, letting Jian and his armies seem to be attacking everywhere at once.

"You look well," he said, composing himself quickly.

She snorted. "I look like gull's shit," she countered. "I did not have time for a proper bath before this son of a goat—*herder*—dragged me from my rooms and told me that I could either deliver a message to you or lose my head."

"Ah." Jian shot a dark look at Mardoni, who shrugged.

"Have you ever tried to hurry this woman from her bath?" he asked. "Our kingdoms might have crumbled to dust before that happened."

"What is your message?" Jian asked. He tried not to stare too curiously at the second woman, the one covered head-to-toe in dark blue. *What gift does she bear?* he wondered.

53

"The emperor wishes to strike a new treaty with the twilight lords," Giella answered.

"A new treaty?" he asked, and he suppressed a laugh. "Why would the Twilight Lands sign a treaty to end a war when we are winning? Unless Tiachu wishes to surrender his throne to us, we do not wish to hear what he has to say." He made as if to rise.

"Wait," the White Nightingale said, her voice so urgent it gave Jian pause. Why did she care, when she had been forced to deliver this message in the first place?

If *she has been forced*, a voice whispered in his mind, but he would not believe that she had been untrue to him. Besides Perri, this girl had been the closest thing he had to a friend in the lands of men.

Even if she was an assassin.

"There is a new king in Atualon," she told him, "and rumors of others besides him who can wield the power of dragonsong. If they raise an army of gold-masks and march upon Sindan... it might be better, Jian, for you to set aside what differences you have with the emperor. Side with him instead, so that we might stop this new threat before it takes hold. Daeshen Tiachu is offering to cease all hostilities with the Dae, and put an end to the winnowing, if you and the twilight lords will join with him and throw your combined might against the fortress of the Dragon King."

"They would stop the winnowing." Jian sank back down. Staring into the fire, he saw not flames, but wagons loaded with dead boys like so many lengths of firewood. It was not a believable offer, and yet—

"If we march upon Atualon while the country is embroiled in internal war, and seize the power of atulfah from the Dragon King, we might rejoin our two lands as one," Mardoni added, leaning forward as if by sheer force of will he could persuade the young prince to believe his words. "Wielding the power of atulfah and of the Twilight Lands, the emperor of Sindan would be as bright and glorious as Akari Sun Dragon himself, exalted above all others in history. Join us… join me," he coaxed. "I have put aside my grievances with the emperor—so have all the Sen-Baradam—as we face this new threat from the west. Are we not brothers? Should we not unite against our common enemy in Atualon?"

"What exactly does the emperor want from me?" Jian asked bluntly. "Simply to cease hostilities against Sindan? Or does he expect me to urge the twilight lords and ladies to cross the veil and spawn a bigger army of daeborn for the emperor? The Twilight Lands are not Sindan—I cannot simply tell the people what to do, and expect them to bow and obey me.

"Nor would I, if I could."

"The emperor wishes to have you at his side, Jian. You would be his advisor and honored guest—a high warlord, set above all the Sen-Baradam. Moreover, as the emperor has not yet been blessed with a living child, he has sworn that, should you aid him thus in destroying our enemy in the west, he will name you as heir to the Forbidden City. In time, you might unite three lands—Sindan, the Twilight Lands, and Atualon—and usher in an age of peace. Is this not a thing worth setting aside our differences? Is this not a thing worth dying for? Such a world we could leave to our children—"

"Our children." With those words Jian was dragged back to reality, and to his decision. He stood up abruptly. "You side with Tiachu, who killed my wife and our child, and speak to me of *our children*?" Such was the fury in his voice that Mardoni moved away from him. Even the White Nightingale stepped back.

The woman in the dark veil, however, did not. She strode forward as Jian spun to leave, blocking his path.

"You have heard the emperor's offer," she said, soft voice wounding him as no sword of man ever could. "Will you accept his gift?"

The voice was one which sang to him in his dreams. With one slender hand she drew back her veil. Eyes round as Jian's, deep as the seas, looked into his. Teeth white and sharp as a sea-bear's smiled up at him. Tsali'gei stood before him with her feet planted wide apart as a warrior's, a daring gleam in her eye—

A tiny infant, black-haired and beautiful, was asleep in her arms.

Jian fell to his knees.

The trap snapped shut.

SIX

Think, girl, think. Mother escaped from this shitforsaken place before she was a dreamshifter. Before she was anything, really—how did she do it?

Hunger gnawed a hollow in her belly, but she had been hungry before. Thirst scoured her throat, as well, but she had been thirsty before. The bite in her shoulder and not-quite-healed bones in her arm throbbed and itched, but she had felt pain before. These things were nothing to a warrior, and it was high time that Sulema Ja'Akari remembered who—and what—she was.

What she had never been, not for a day in her life, was alone. Her mother, her youthmistress, her friends, her pride had always been there, infuriating in their meddling, stifling in their interest. Even when she had faced the lionsnake, she had not been truly alone. First Warrior had known where she was, after all, and Sulema had known in the depths of her heart that if she needed them, if she wished for them, her people would come. But now—

Tears are not rain, her mother's voice scolded. *They will not cause the desert to bloom.*

Sulema stood, as best she could judge, in the center of her walled-up cell.

Think!

The air was still but not stifling. Small cracks and holes in the dragonstone let the air and the rats come and go, yet she was neither air nor a rat, so there was no escape for her that way. Nor did the newly laid stone wall give beneath her hands, push though she might.

If I had my staff, maybe I could—but no, her mother had

not wanted to teach her to dreamshift, any more than Sulema had wanted to learn. *If I had learned more about wielding atulfah, perhaps—*

If I had armies to command, they could storm the castle and set me free. She shook her head and grunted a laugh. Strangely enough, that made her feel better. *"If you can still laugh,"* Ani would say, *"there is yet hope."*

She is laughing.

A woman's voice.

Why is she laughing? Is she mad?

The voice was soft and smooth and strong. Sulema froze as the words whispered through her cell, faint as footprints upon the Lonely Road, thin as shadows in the deep of night. Had she imagined it? *Was* she mad?

No, not mad, a man answered. *Not yet, at any rate—no more than any other of the Zeeranim, who are all a touch insane. Too much time spent under the sun; it bakes their brains.*

Sulema's mouth dropped open, and she spun about, as if turning circles in the dark might help matters.

"Who is there?"

There... there... there...

Her voice echoed, and Sulema thought she heard a response, deep in the heart of Atukos. Now that she was aware of them, the voices were clearer.

They should have killed her, the first voice said. *It is foolish of Pythos to leave such a weapon lying about, where I might pick it up and use it.*

A weapon he may yet bring to bear against you, my queen, the male voice replied. *Better to kill the girl and be done with it than take this foolish risk.*

I am no fool, ta. The woman's voice rang cold and hard with power. Sulema thought she must be a warrior. *Neither am I your queen. We will not kill the girl today—to do so would tear a hole in the web big enough for Eth to crawl through. I have seen it. I would pick up this weapon and wield it. She is her mother's daughter, and her father's. She can be a powerful ally.*

As you wish. Remember, however, that this is the City of Lies. An ally made here is surely doomed to become your enemy. As for its usefulness, perhaps this sword is less than the sum of hilt and blade. The girl is afraid to confront her potential. She is weak, and a weak weapon may be worse than no weapon at all.

"Het, het!" Sulema shouted a challenge into the dark. She tensed, expecting an attack. "Show yourself, you goatfucking coward. I am Ja'Akari, and I am no easy meat!"

In each possibility where I choose to aid the girl, the woman continued, unfazed, *she returns from Quarabala with Maika. My Maika, alive and well.*

Do not let the yearnings of your heart blind you to reality. We both know this is impossible.

You forget yourself, Illindrist. I have seen it. Do you doubt me?

Sulema controlled her anger in the dark and waited for these voices to decide her fate. She knew to whom the voices belonged now, and they possessed the power to snuff her life as easily as she might pinch the flame from a candle.

If you are no queen, I am no Illindrist. Do as you will, then, my… apprentice, but if the girl becomes a threat to you, know this. I will kill her myself.

I would expect nothing less… Master.

Safe travels, then, little one. I will go to the new Dragon King and make some excuse for your absence. It should not be difficult. The man is an idiot.

Sulema knew then that she was alone again, straining eyes and ears to no avail. Alone in her cell in the belly of Atukos, where there was only silence, and darkness, and the occasional hopeless rat.

"Hello?" she called, and again Atukos answered with an echo.

Hello… hello… hello.

"Well, fuck!"

"My *akamu* always said that a foul mouth is a sign of a weak mind. Do you have a weak mind, girl?"

Sulema spun, half crouching as a light flickered, flickered, flared to life. Once again she could see the details of the room, including the painting on the wall. There, in one corner of her cell, stood the Illindrist's apprentice. She held a glass oil lamp in one hand, a small glass bottle in the other. She was clad in robes the color of road dust, had a pack slung over one shoulder, and on her face she wore the most disapproving frown Sulema had seen since leaving home.

Her name is Yaela, she remembered. Sulema bared her teeth as if the other had challenged her to a fight. "I do not have a weak anything, *girl*. I am Ja'Akari."

"Good." Yaela nodded, strange eyes slit against the faint illumination. "You promised that if I were to help you escape Atukos, you would travel to the Seared Lands and bring to me my little niece. Did you speak truth?"

"I am Ja'Akari," Sulema said again, standing straight so that she towered above the newcomer. "My words speak only truth, *ehuani*. I will do this thing…" She hesitated, and because there was beauty in truth, she added, "or I will die trying. I am no Zula Din."

"No, you are not," the sorcerer's apprentice agreed. "It is not possible for you to do this thing."

I have no wish to do this thing, Sulema thought. Still, she stiffened at the insult. "Impossible for an outlander, perhaps. For one who is Ja'Akari—"

"Impossible," Yaela insisted, unmoved. "I have seen the scars you bear from fighting a single lionsnake. You were nearly broken beyond repair in the course of a single day, Ja'Akari, and in your own lands at that.

"There are worse things in the Jehannim than snakes and spider-men," the apprentice continued. "Bonelords, mymyc,

60

and bintshi are only the beginning. The mountains would chew you up and spit you out like a handful of your pemmican long before you could ever dream of reaching Quarabala. You are no shadowmancer, able to weave shadows into protection from the sun and walk the Seared Lands, nor do you have the salt to hire one. You are no bonesinger, to sing the bones upon the shadowed roads into quiescence. You are not even a dreamshifter, as your mother was.

"You are just… just a girl." Yaela sighed.

"If I am so weak," Sulema asked, jaw so tight with affront that she could scarcely force the words out between her teeth, "then why do you ask me to do this thing?"

"You are no Zula Din," Yaela answered after a long pause, "but you are what I have. Here." She held out the bottle. Sulema eyed it suspiciously, even as she took it and brought it close to her face. A familiar stench wafted to greet her, and she wrinkled her nose.

"Did you get this from Mattu?" She tried not to feel anything as she said his name. Tried, and failed.

"I stole it from Rothfaust's quarters. There were only a few bottles left, and I took them all. I thought to ask the loremaster to make more, but he is nowhere to be found. Many people besides your brother and your mother's small apprentice have gone missing since Pythos has returned— Rothfaust is probably dead in a pit somewhere with the rest of them." She shrugged. "This will help against the reaver venom, but I do not know for how long."

Sulema froze, with the bottle against her lips.

"You know about the reaver venom?"

Yaela rolled her eyes. "This is Atualon. Everybody knows everything."

Sulema wrinkled her nose, held her breath, and swallowed the contents of the bottle. The loremaster had refined his medicines—or so he had assured her—but it still tasted like churra piss. Maybe worse.

"Gaaaah," she said, and she spat. "Surely turning into a reaver cannot be worse than drinking this shit."

"Oh," Yaela said, "but it is. Worse than you can know, child of the sunlight." Every word as slow and dark as a stone dropped into a well.

"You have seen a reaver?" Sulema had not believed that they existed, not really, until that day at the Bones of Eth—

Her mind fled from the thought.

"I was a child," Yaela answered, "a little child, on the Night of Sorrows."

"The Night of Sorrows?"

For a moment, Sulema thought that Yaela's little oil lamp had flared like the sun. When she realized that the shadows had fled the room in terror, all the hairs on her arms stood up.

The sorcerer's apprentice, she thought, *is more than she seems*.

"Forgive my ignorance," she said. "The shadows flee your wrath, and my... my father's shadowmancer... calls you 'queen.' Why do you not simply return to Quarabala and retrieve your niece yourself? Why send someone unfamiliar with the land, someone who—as you say—is no Zula Din?"

"I cannot," Yaela answered, her face smooth and hard as stones in the river. "I have run from the edge of the Seared Lands to Min Yaarif three times. Three—when no other living shadowmancer had passed the shadowed roads more than once and lived to tell the tale. Shadowmancy leaves a trail, a smell of sorts, and that scent draws all manner of... unpleasant attention."

"Ah." Sulema remembered something Leviathus had told her. "Like the magic slick left upon the Dibris by the Baidun Daiel? That was why they had to take me overland to Atualon, rather than taking the shorter river route."

"Much like," Yaela agreed. "Each shadowmancer has a unique... scent, I suppose you could say. Travel the road once, and if you survive you have left a taste of yourself. Attempt a second pass, and…" She shook her head.

"Yet you have made that journey three times? Why not a fourth?"

The fleetest of smiles crossed Yaela's face, there and gone again.

"I am very fast, but a fourth time?" She shook her head. "I survived my third run by the thinnest of luck and do not dare another attempt. Another shadowmancer will have to shield your path into the heart of Quarabala, one who has escaped the Seared Lands without using his own magic. There is one such I know of. His name is Keoki. He lives in Min Yaarif and has let it be known that he is willing to provide escort… for a price."

"So." It was Sulema's turn to smile. "I can choose to die horribly here, or I can die horribly in Jehannim, in a futile attempt at an impossible quest."

"Sometimes a death of our choosing is the best for which we can hope. But I offer you more than certain death, Ja'Akari. The thinnest hope, less than a mouthful of water to a woman dying of thirst."

Sulema swallowed. She had almost forgotten how dry she was, and how hungry.

"I am listening."

Yaela swung her traveler's pack to the fore, unfastened the flap, and rummaged about inside. After a moment she pulled out a round bundle bigger than a man's fist and handed this to Sulema as if it were of little note. Curious, Sulema let the wrappings fall away, and gasped to see the rose-rock globe her father had shown her in Atualon. Veined in lapis and set with jewels, the globe, as Ka Atu had explained, was a miniature of their world; anything which affected the land might be reflected upon the stone's surface. It was possible, he had added, that damage to this artifact might in turn wreak havoc upon their lives.

"This..." She breathed. "My father said it was too powerful for me to handle."

"Your father is dead," Yaela said, sharp and short. "This is my offer to you, should you return from the Seared Lands with my Maika."

"You offer me... this globe?" Sulema wanted to laugh, but she remembered how the shadows had fled Yaela's presence. "You have already given it to me."

"I offer you the world, Sulema Ja'Akari. I offer you freedom."

"But... how?" Sulema stared longingly at the globe. *Freedom*. "Even if I was not locked in a dungeon—which I am—I am bound to Atualon by blood and honor, and I am bound to weakness by the reaver's magic, as well. How can I ever be free?"

"I can use shadowmancy and the magic in Cassandre's painting to free you from this place. That is a simple matter. Crafting a medicine that will cure you of the reaver's venom for good will cost me a great deal more, and the risk will be... considerable. If I am to perform such a dangerous task for you, you must repay me in kind. As for the ties of blood and honor, you will have to learn to sever or live with them yourself, just as we all do. I am an Illindrist's apprentice, not Illindra herself.

"Here is my offer, then. Agree to bring to me my little niece, my Maika, daughter of my twin who died birthing her, and I will give you, Sulema Ja'Akari ne Atu, the greatest treasure any person can hope for—a chance at freedom. Freedom from Atualon, from the reaver's venom, to become again who you once were. A warrior blessed to ride the desert sands, beneath the gaze of Akari."

Free of the Dragon's Legacy at last, Sulema thought. *Is such a thing possible?* She knew only that she had to try.

"Yes," Sulema said simply. "Yes. Show me the way."

Yaela rocked back on her heels and let out a long, low

breath. Shadows flowed back into the room like the river after spring rains.

"That is the easy part," she said. "You already know the way, truly. Here, touch this, here…" she moved Sulema's finger to a tiny jagged chip like blackened bone upon the globe, not far from the gem that was Min Yaarif. "Yes, just like that. Now, look at the painting Cassandre made of you. The *real* painting. Close your waking eyes, open your dreaming ones, and look." Even as she spoke, Yaela struck a dancer's pose, one arm above her head, hand twisting like leaves in a summer wind. Her spine arched, and she flowed like dark water. "*Look!*"

Sulema closed her waking eyes, just as her mother had taught her, back when the world was sweet and Hafsa Azeina immortal. She drew in a long, slow breath and as she let it out again allowed it to resonate through the singer's bone deep within her face that Aasah had been teaching her to use, the one he had referred to as her hidden mask.

"*Ohnnnnn*," she sang, feeling a bit foolish. "*Ohnnnnnn…*"

Her dreaming eyes opened slowly, slowly. Shadows writhed like snakes in every corner; they dripped like black blood down the walls. Yaela was, oh, she was beautiful, and how she danced—

The painting Cassandre had presented to the dragon court, of Sulema as an Atualonian princess, wavered and fled like a mirage. The true image, hidden by the artist's magic, flowed from the canvas hot and real as the desert sun. She gazed upon herself as she had been, as she would be again. Sulema Ja'Akari, true daughter of the desert, fierce and free. It seemed almost as if she could reach up and tug at the warrior's braids that she had worn, which had been cut away from her to mark her shame.

A hot wind caressed her shorn scalp—

The dunes were so cunningly, so lovingly depicted it seemed as if she could almost hear them singing. Sand burned gold beneath Akari's gaze.

Her feet burned—

The river, the sweet Dibris, was a shining ribbon of blue in the distance; she could all but smell it.

Somewhere in the distance a serpent sang, sweet and low, and was answered by another. Its mate perhaps, or a sister, welcoming the lost one home.

"Sulema. Sulema! Wake. Wake now, *aiwa*! We are here!"

There was joy in the young shadowmancer's voice, and it startled Sulema so that she opened her eyes. Opened them and blinked against the hot blue sky. When had she fallen asleep? And how?

She pressed her hand against the ground and came up with a handful of sand. How—

A shadow fell across her. It was Yaela, face split in two with the most beautiful, most brilliant smile Sulema had ever seen.

"I did it!" The shadowmancer's apprentice exulted. She threw her head back and laughed. "It worked!"

"What?" Sulema sat up, faint from long captivity and from shock. "What?"

She was sitting upon the sand, beneath a hot blue sky, in the shadow of a twist of standing stones like and not like the Bones of Eth. In the distance she could see the shining blue Dibris as it snaked across the Zeera, with a belly full of life, a belly full of death. A harsh wind stroked the dunes and they curled upon themselves like waves, roused to dance and to song.

Sulema closed her eyes and her heart broke at the sound of the desert singing. Singing her home.

SEVEN

The Great Salt Road began at the heart of the world and went on forever, glittering with the sung bones of heroes, cobbled with the unsung bones of ordinary people, bitter with the red salt dust.

Born in the aortic tunnels of the red salt mines of Quarabala, it flowed through the land like blood through a person's body, bringing the life-sustaining red salt to every corner of the known world. From the deepest mines and canyons in the subterranean queendom of Quarabala to the easternmost reaches of the Sindanese empire and beyond it rang with the hooves of mounted warriors, sang with the voices of merchants, and bound them all together even as Illindra's web bound all worlds.

A book had been placed in Maika's hands before she could walk, and she had spent her childhood with a coterie of tutors whose collective goal was to stuff every bit of Saodan's massive libraries into the stuff between her ears. She knew that the Great Salt Road led up through the shallow cracks in the earth that marked the Edge of Quarabala, across the seared flesh of the earth on a portion of the route known as the shadowed roads, through the once-thriving merchant city Min Yahtamu, through the Jehannim and to the green world beyond. She knew the names of the engineers who had delved deep and wrought the road from living rock, could recount its history and the value of trade goods that followed Quarabalese shadowmancers into the green lands and back again. Yet knowing *of* the road was not the same thing as understanding its perils.

Only now, as they ran from the Araids and their fell priests and toward the surface lands with their surfeit of wicked creatures or wickeder men, was Maika beginning to understand that this thing of wonder was also a thing to fear. And even if they survived the road, what then? Where would her people lay their heads at night, name their babies, make their music? Would the greenlanders welcome a people with no home? Maika was a student of history; she knew the ways of queens and kings. And she thought not.

A bit of something beside her foot caught Maika's eye. She stooped and picked it up, glad for the distraction. *Bone*, she thought, though it glittered in the torchlight like mica-filled rock.

"What is this?" she asked Akamaia, holding it up near her tutor's face. The woman peered nearsightedly through the shadowmancers' gloom and pursed her lips.

"It is a proximal phalange," she replied, wiggling her own thumbs at the young queen. "Human." *Leave me in peace*, her eyes added, *I am tired*.

Maika stared at the bone as she walked, trying to imagine the person to whom it had once belonged. *Had it been a woman or a man?* she wondered. *Bandit or bard?* It glittered like a precious thing; someone had sung this person's story into their bones. Whoever this bone belonged to had been loved, then, and had died long ago when Dzirani bonesingers still walked the world. She wondered who had loved this person, whether they had a good heart or bad, and whether they might have written a book she had read or painted a mural she had seen.

She wondered how many of the people she had led here would leave their thumb bones to lie forgotten for a thousand years, and if hers might be among them.

Eventually she tossed the bone aside, and then rather wished she had not. Was it disrespectful to the dead, to so casually discard a piece of their body? Or would it have been worse to keep it? She would have liked to ask Akamaia, but the Illindrist had turned aside. The old woman was weary and in pain, and Maika did not want to bother her any further. She turned instead to Tamimeha.

"Tell me, Grand Princess" she asked, "have you walked to the Edge before?" Tamimeha frowned, and the glow-paste of a high-caste warrior frowned with her.

"No."

Maika waited for more, but Tamimeha strode on, glaring around them as if some mother or grandmother might suddenly decide to assassinate their queen. So Maika sighed and turned with reluctance to Amalua, the young Iponui who had brought them the Mask of Sajani. The young queen thought she would have liked the runner, but the young woman's eyes were full of horrors and shadows, and she never smiled. Ever. Rumor had it that runners were full of salt and mischief, but this one had a face and a heart hard enough to break rocks.

"We are drawing near the innermost boundaries of the Edge," Maika said, eager to show this youth that her queen was not ignorant of the world. "Are we likely to be attacked?" As she said this, she fingered the hilt of a long, sharp knife Tamimeha had bidden her wear at her hip. Maika had never been armed before.

"Perhaps," the runner said with only the briefest of glances. "I would very much like to kill something." Though Amalua's face, shiny with healers' ointments and fresh scar tissue, was half-healed from the terrible burns she had suffered, the grief in her eyes ran too deeply to ever truly mend.

It had taken them two full moons to leave Saodan. Half of her counselors moaned that this was not enough time to gather all the people together, while the other half— notably those of the outermost bastions, most pressed by the Araid threat—shouted at them to hurry, hurry. For her part, Maika had leaned her hopes against the pillars of Tamimeha and Akamaia. She trusted that they would know what best to do, and wished that she could share their combined confidence and experience.

Far beneath the scorched surface of the Seared Lands the people of Quarabala crawled like a thick black snake through tunnels and along the bottom of rifts that had been hewn and cobbled and worn smooth over the course of a thousand years. Woman, man, child, elder—all of the people who could walk, be carried, be pushed in a cart. There had been a few souls foolish enough to remain behind and clutch at their worldly possessions. Maika had wanted even those few rounded up and forced to march.

"My people are my people," she had insisted through tears, "even the stupid ones." But Tamimeha just shook her head.

"They would only slow us down," she had said as gently as she was able, "and we must make haste. Three more runners have come in with reports of Araid incursions." The warrior had not wanted to bring along those people who could not walk on their own, viewing their lives as an acceptable sacrifice to speed, but Maika had invoked her privilege as queen.

"We will not bring the prisoners," Tamimeha had insisted, "and that *is* within my authority to decide. Those who have broken the queen's law have forfeited the queen's protection."

"Besides," Akamaia had added—sweet, gentle Akamaia who wept when she fed moths to her o'oraid—"they will slow the reavers down, when our pursuers break through the walls and into the city." Akamaia's favorite husband had been murdered, years and years ago. She had no pity in her heart for criminals.

The black snake rattled with wagon wheels and hand carts. It wept with the voices of children and scolded with the voices of mothers. But mostly it sang the song of Quarabala, the Seared Lands—of love and regret, of leavings and homecomings, of weariness and wonder and hope. This song sustained Maika as no food or drink ever could; it kept her moving forward after her second pair of sandals fell apart and she grew so tired of spitting red sand that she just gave up and let it cake upon her lips and teeth.

If I make it through this alive, Maika promised herself for the thousandth time, *I will never take another walk as long as I live. I will remain at home in a palace, eating sweetmeats, and growing fat upon my throne. I will change my clothes twice a day, and take twice as many baths. Pshew, I stink!*

She had hoped that once the people were convinced to leave they might have finished their journey in a moons' time. But it had been a full two-moon since they had left Saodan and they were just now coming to the innermost boundaries of the Edge, those lawless lands where the strong preyed upon the weak and the sky was so close you could see it. She had walked through three pairs of sturdy sandals, lost a great deal of weight, and lost more than a few of her people too as they slipped away by twos and threes and whole families during each midday rest, preferring the possibility of reavers and Araids to the very real struggles of walking day after day after miserable day.

Four times during that two-moon span, Maika was called upon to give her blessings over the body of someone whose spirit had chosen to take the Lonely Road instead. The third was an infant who had been born too soon and whose grieving mother refused to look her queen in the eye. Maika had returned to her travel tent after that one and had cried until she threw up. The bodies were burned, as there was no time to bury them properly and nobody wanted to leave them for the reavers.

For the first time in her short life, Maika knew despair. This journey seemed as wretched as any tale she could remember hearing about the Night of Sorrows, and they had not even made it to the surface yet, nor faced the enemy from which they fled. How, then, did she dare hope that any of them would survive the shadowed road?

The great black snake made of people had wound its slow way through the greater and lesser towns of the Quarabala—Oloulou, Ameha, and Leakala, Ehana, Ia'u, and Ni'ipau—past the empty merchants' stalls and alleyways thick with vermin. It grew bloated as stragglers joined the whole, more than making up for those who fell away. They slept through the heat of day and every night traveled under the glow of lanterns and starslight and the carved faces of the ancestors, until finally they had reached the border between the civilized lands of Quarabala and the Edge, marked by the Starfell Gates.

Fashioned in days of old by the Hammerfall Smiths, forged of stars-fallen metal and precious gems, the gate glittered like the heavens above, reminding the people of Quarabala of the ancestors' promise: that some sweet day in the far-off, they would once more walk beneath the night sky and the day, with water and sand beneath their feet, and the wide sky overhead.

Today is that day, Maika thought, and her heart pounded hard against her ribs. *I am not afraid*. Yet her hands shook as she walked forward on trembling legs to hand the queen's key to the gatekeeper. This gate had not been opened since the Night of Sorrows, and on that night—

No, Maika told herself firmly. *I will not invite black luck into the night by entertaining such thoughts*. She breathed deep to banish the trembling from her limbs, the trepidation in her spirit, and forced a smile as she handed over the heavy, cold key. On this night of all nights, her people needed her to be strong.

The gatekeeper, a woman as broad and strong-backed and possibly as old as the gate itself, bowed to Maika and pressed the key to her reverent sunken mouth. Her starsilk robes flowed about her thick ankles as she made her slow way up the last steps, thrust the key home, and turned once.

Twice.

Three times.

For a moment nothing happened, and Maika wondered if perhaps the gate had died of dust and hopelessness. Then came a coruscation of tiny, glittering lights as a thousand miniature spiders, cunningly crafted of silvery metal and each set with a single precious stone, dropped from holes concealed all along the top of the gate like stars falling from the heavens. They darted this way and that across the face of the gate trailing strands of precious magesilver, each a wonder of color, so that within moments the gate was veiled in an intricate weaving of light and magic.

Their task finished, the spiders scurried back up the webs and into their holes again, for all the world like living things.

Brilliance rippled across the gate, glowing brighter with each wave, until Maika's eyes watered to look upon it. She raised a hand to shield her face from the glare, but the gate gave one final, massive burst of brilliance.

Then winked out.

Maika sighed, and the people sighed with her, in the absence of beauty. She opened her mouth to ask the gatekeeper to turn the key again and bring back the light, but a soft glow began to emanate from the gate, and this was not so kind. A great spiders' web glowed blue and cold. At each meeting of strands hung a silvery globe as big as a man's fist, and each of these held the image of a different face. Dark faces and fair, women and men, slaves and queens, alike only in their expressions of agony—these were the enemies of Quarabala, caught in the moments of death, a warning to those who would oppose her queens.

A warning to my *enemies*, Maika realized. It was a frightening thought… and satisfying. Each of these screaming, dying people had been a threat to the ancestors of her line, to the people whom she had been bred and born to lead, and she was glad—suddenly, fiercely glad—that they had suffered.

A hand settled warm and heavy on her shoulder; Maika started and nearly yelped out loud.

"Do not be afraid." It was only Tamimeha, looking down at her with grave concern. Maika rolled her eyes and shrugged off the warrior's hand.

"I am not afraid," she insisted. "I am a queen."

"So you are." The old warrior's lips twitched into a rare smile. She inclined her head. The dreadful web flared bright as moonslight, then a darkness fell upon them so swift and terrible that it hurt their eyes, and the Starfell Gates swung outward.

"It is time," Akamaia whispered. "Time for us to leave our home. Have courage, my child."

Maika did not need to be told twice—nor, she realized, did she need courage. She simply needed to do her duty. She tilted her face upward, let the pride of her ancestors fall upon her like stardust. Then she led her people through the Starfell Gates and out of Quarabala forever.

EIGHT

They were no more than a half-day's slow walk into the Edge when a commotion near the front of the line brought them all to a standstill. Warriors' spears bristled round Maika and she strained to peer over them, to see what was happening.

There was a runner, an Iponui who was almost as short as Maika herself. The runner was followed by a man. A raggedy, rough, low-caste man with missing teeth, brought into the presence of his queen. This was the first Edgelander Maika had ever seen, and she could not help but feel a twinge of disappointment. She half expected to see a giant, wild-eyed and with his teeth filed for tearing at human flesh; instead she found herself entirely too close to a low-caste ragtag who smelled of piss and whose unkempt mop of hair made her itch just looking at it.

The Iponui dropped to one knee, bowing so low her nose almost touched her thigh. "Your Magnificence," she said through a veil of spears and hard-faced warriors. "This man begs audience of his queen. He would ask—"

"Makune does not beg," the man said. "Especially some little *buta* thinks she queen, eh?" A low hiss ran through the warriors, but he just laughed, showing a mouth full of rot. "Makune demands."

He probably thinks himself brave, Maika thought. *But I think he is just stupid. Tamimeha is ready to knock his head off.* Indeed, the older woman's eyes narrowed with hard contempt.

"Demands." Tamimeha frowned. "You make demands of your queen?"

"Not my queen," the man said, setting his feet shoulder-width apart and throwing his chest out in a belligerent manner. "I am Edgelander, and this is my kingdom."

"A charming kingdom it is, too," Maika said in the chilliest voice she could muster. She did not like the way this man stared at Tamimeha's tits, even though the warrior could beat him to death using nothing more than her sandals. "You wish to speak with me? Speak. Do so quickly, before I have my *buta* poke you full of holes and let all the shit out."

The Seared Lands fell into a shocked silence.

Well, Maika thought, *that was effective.*

The coarse man burst into coarse laughter. "Ah! Ah! You got balls, little buta. Maybe you are queen after all? Maybe after you grow some *mamouleh*." He cupped both hands over his chest and leered. "You want to be part of my nag?"

Maika opened her mouth to answer, but Amalua stepped in front of her, somehow making that a gesture of respect for her queen, contempt for the man facing them, and a threat, all in one smooth movement.

"Speak to my queen like that one more time," she said softly, "and you die." A promise, not a threat.

The man's smile faded, and he shrugged. "Just talk," he said in a petulant voice. "Just man talk is all."

Maika pursed her lips and waited. Her first meeting with an Edgelander was proving disappointing. She very much wanted to ask the man why he had come, then she wanted him gone.

Be patient, she told herself, taking a long, slow breath. She knew that the first to speak in a parley ceded power to the other. *Be patient*. In the end, the low-caste man spoke first, and Maika felt as if she had a victory.

"We have built a barricade," he said, puffing his chest out again. "You cannot pass."

Maika breathed through flared nostrils, refusing to speak or bite her lips or clench her fists, any of these things her body urged her to do. The man went on in a petulant voice, obviously frustrated by her lack of reaction.

"You cannot pass unless you pay."

"And what is your price?" Akamaia demanded, coming up behind Maika and sounding badly out of breath. This journey had been hard on the Illindrist, not least because she had insisted on bringing with her every book in the Queens' Library. "What price for safe passage by your queen through her own lands?" Her voice was hard and clenched as a fist.

"Her lands." The man laughed. "The Edge is no man's land, no girl's neither. This land"—he spat—"is for those who are strong enough to take it. You strong enough, girl?"

Maika strove to ignore the man's taunts, and the threat that lurked behind his words. Were they strong enough? Every Illindrist would be needed if they hoped to provide what shade and safety they could to the evacuees; they could not afford a battle, not now. This journey would stretch the sorcerers to their breaking point, some to the point of death, and every moment wasted was a moment more than they could spare. She judged that they were strong enough to take this land, and that doing so would be the end of them all.

"We are strong enough to take this land," she assured the Edgelander, "but we do not want it. We seek merely to pass through these parts unhindered. Pass through, and never return."

"Never return, hey." The man's eyes flashed in the gloom. "Saodan is empty?" he craned his neck and looked down the river of people.

"We have left Saodan," she said. The memory of those few who had been left behind was a stone dragging at her heart. Honor bid her add, "But it is not safe for you to go there. The Araids come, with their Arachnists and hordes of reavers. You should follow us, those who may, lest your lands are overrun as well."

"Safe." The man stared at her for a moment, lip twisted upward in an ugly sneer. "Safe is for queens. Not for the likes of us out here, living on the Edge." He spat. "Not for the likes of us."

"Then what is your price?" She repeated Akamaia's question. "I will not ask again. Tell me what it will cost for us to pass through this—kingdom—of yours unmolested, or we will raise spears against you and take what is mine to begin with. You say this is the Edge, and that these lands are yours. I say this is Quarabala, and these lands are mine. But in the interest of making haste, I will listen to you, and I will decide whether to play your silly game." She pulled herself up to her full, if unimpressive, height, mustering all the dignity she could. "Or to have my spears thrust through your stupid bellies and leave you for reaver food."

Tamimeha grunted surprise. Amalua thumped her spear down once, twice, three times in respect, and in the next moment the ground was shaking as warriors drummed their approval of this fierce young queen.

The man bristled at her insulting words, but spears bristled back at him, and finally he backed down with an ugly laugh.

"Not worth the fight, you," he said. "Little girls and old women not fit for my nag. When you are gone, I will shit in your bed and eat your food."

Maika imagined an Araid wrapping this man up in spidersilk, and smiled.

"The price for passage is—" He looked around him, at the people, the warriors, the counselors, and licked his lips. "Sweet water, and red meat, and your nubile women."

"Unacceptable." As Akamaia had taught, Maika did not elaborate or allow outrage to show in her voice, but merely waited for his counteroffer. *I should let my nubile women kick his ass*, she seethed. *As if I would buy my safety with the bodies of my people.*

"Girl children—" he began again. Maika raised her hand and cut him off.

"No," she told him. "Not one woman, nor man nor child. Name another price. You try my patience."

Makune hit her with a black scowl. "Sweet water," he growled. "Red meat, and—" He glanced at Akamaia with greedy eyes. "An Illindrist. Make magic for us. Keep safe."

The seer sucked breath in through her teeth with a sharp whistle, and Tamimeha's grip tightened on her spear. Maika held up her hand again, and pitched her voice to carry.

"Manna water," she offered, "not sweet. Dried meat, as much as you alone can carry. Not a single Illindrist or shadowmancer, but"—she ignored Akamaia's hot, hard glare—"my own Illindrist will cast a blessing on you and yours, a protection against reavers. That is my offer. That is my *only* offer."

The words hung between them like a body in a spider's web, and the man remained silent for what seemed like an eternity. Finally he shrugged, face unreadable.

"Manna water, dried meat—packed tight, no cheat—and magic blessing for me and my chiefs against our enemies."

"Against reavers," Maika corrected.

"Against reavers," the man agreed, and a sly smile stole across his face. "What other enemies do we have out here on the Edge, hah? Surely not *you*. You are our queen." He laughed, his hard round belly shaking as if they were the cleverest words ever uttered.

Maika let her hands drop to her side, resisting the urge to rub at her throbbing temples.

A headache, she thought ruefully. *Now I really do feel like a queen.*

After the queen's ransom had been delivered, the people of Quarabala resumed their slow and wretched exodus.

Tamimeha and her strong women encouraged them to move as quickly as they were able, and for a time the pace quickened, spurred on by the Iponui's shouts and deep-seated fear of the Edgelanders, but soon the weariness which clung to them all tight as clothes dragged at their feet. Somewhere nearby a child sobbed, a thin, hopeless sound that wrung tears from Maika's eyes. She despaired that even the fittest citizens would be hard pressed to keep up the pace, and that the frailest would soon be lost.

"My queen," Amalua murmured to her, "you must understand—some of these people will die. Perhaps many of them will die, but if you survive this journey, and a greater portion of our people as well, you will have succeeded. We have our books, our songs, our seers—you will have saved the heart of Quarabala, if not our cities."

The horrifically scarred runner had shadowed Maika since the day she had faced down the Edgeland leader, sleeping curled at the edge of Maika's bedroll as she slept, even insisting on tasting food and drink before it passed the queen's lips. Maika suspected that the young Iponui felt as if she had failed to save those at the outer bastion, and wished for a chance to redeem herself.

She nodded reluctantly.

"I know," the young queen said. "I just wish—I wish I could save everyone."

"You cannot," Amalua answered, and a cold wind blew through her words. "I cannot. No one can."

They had been moving quickly for some nights' time, sleeping during the hours of heat so that the shadowmancers could rest in preparation for working their magics when they reached the shadowed roads. These lands had been the outer bastions when Maika's grandmother had been a queen, and they had been part of the inner city in her grandmother's grandmother's time. Now it was the Edge, the half-dead shallows of a sea of salt and blood and frightened people drying and dying under the wrathful eyes of Akari.

This land has been shrinking in on us all along, she thought, *like a spider's web unraveling at the edges, till nothing is left but the spider and a few sad strands. Had we remained, we would have died anyway, in my time or my daughter's, perhaps. It is good we left when we did—perhaps I have saved my people, after all.*

Or perhaps, whispered the dark voice of doubt, *you have simply hastened their deaths.*

"How do I know?" she whispered, anguished. "How do I know?"

"How do you know what?" Akamaia asked, not as lost in thought as Maika had guessed.

"How do I know if I have done the right thing, leading my people from their homeland? What if we all die here? What if we die when we are on the naked earth, and Akari flies above us? What if—"

"You will never know," Akamaia interrupted gently, laying a hand on her shoulder. "Not until the historians write the books of these times and the ink dries, not until you are old as dust and your name is used to bore a schoolgirl to tears. Maybe not even then."

"Yet you know," Maika insisted. "You with your eyes of Pelang and your o'oraid, you can see the future."

Akamaia shook her head. "I can see a short way," she amended. "It is like staring into a clouded pool: you see a fish flashing by, maybe, or a bit of moonslight shining upon the water. Mostly you see your own face reflected up at you, puzzled and confused and lost."

"You said the Araids are coming," Maika said, "that they would overrun Quarabala and kill us all if we remained."

"I did, and they are," the seer agreed. "Likely the Araids rule in Saodan now, and would be feasting on our flesh had we remained. Yet I cannot tell you with certainty whether we survive this journey, or this day, even this hour. That which is seen does not always come to pass, and that which comes to pass is not always seen. This is why we have sa and ka—to sense the land about us, the song of earth and sky and wind. It is also why we have Iponui and warriors, and our own strong eyes." She patted Maika's arm. "And strong, smart young queens who question everything. With these tools, we may have hope."

"It is not much."

"No, it is not," Akamaia agreed. "But it is something. And it may be—if we are lucky, and smart, and brave—it may be enough."

They walked on in silence after that. Maika listened to the *shushhh-shushhh* of the warriors' feet padding along the path, to the crunch and whisper of bone and dust beneath them. To the dry hot wind that sucked through the rifts like the air through an angry old woman's lips. They were closer to the surface than Maika had ever been, so close the path and the walls were hot to touch, though the shadowmancers strove to shade and cool their steps. She strained her eyes upward, hoping—though she knew better—to catch a quick, far-off glimpse of this sun dragon who had banished her people to lives of exile and darkness.

Bright as gold, they said of the sun, hot as fire. Though it was folly to look upon the sun here, in the Seared Lands, to have one's flesh melted away and bones crisped to dust. Maika had always longed to turn her face to the sun's warmth, just once, to look upon the dreadful splendor of Akari Sun Dragon.

To ride beneath the sun, as those horse-warriors of legend, she thought, closing her eyes and walking blind, *must be glorious.*

Urged by Akamaia's words, she unfurled her ka up toward the seared surface of the earth, let the tongues of sa taste the wind. She sensed the moving body of her people like a great mass of life and light and brilliance, a lovely low chorus of vibrance defying the silence of rock and dust. They burned bright as stars, the souls of her people, like hearth-fires on a cold night, or—

Above them, in the cold faces of a forgotten city, bright lights winked and shone. They moved furtively, in twos and threes, above and before the seething mass of humanity, closing in from all sides. Maika's eyes flew open and she gasped.

"Ware!" she shouted, breathless, pointing up and up into the canyon walls above. She could not see them with her eyes open, but she knew they were there: enemies, armed enemies, waiting in the dark. "Ware! We are betrayed!" For she had no doubt that this had been the Edgelanders' plan all along; to lure them into this quiet place and kill them all.

Makune ducked away from the warriors and would have run, but Amalua caught him by the hair. She dragged him down to the ground at her feet, and without a word or a glance at her queen she drew a long knife and stabbed him in the eye with it. The Edgelander screamed, horribly, heels drumming against the sung bones of heroes, raising the dust and shadows of the dead as his soul flew to join them.

Maika stared. She had seen animals butchered, had attended executions of prisoners, but she had never seen death like this. Raw and ugly and stinking, spraying blood and eye fluids as it went. Amalua wrenched her knife free and wiped it on the Edgelander's filthy robes even as he gasped in the dirt.

"Araids take him," she said, spitting upon his ruined face. "I knew he was a liar."

Maika opened her mouth—to say what, she had no idea—and laughter bubbled out; loud, clear laughter like a child's. She clapped both hands over her face.

A man died, she told herself. *His blood is on my feet! And I am laughing—*

83

Even that thought was torn from her as, in the next moment, men swarmed down the cliff face, screaming, blades flashing in the dim light. She drew her knife and held it before her, trembling like a moth in a spider's web.

A queen is not afraid, she told herself. *A queen is not afraid.*

"Spears!" Tamimeha cried, and warriors clustered thick around their queen, bristling outward, grim-faced and ready to die. "We are betrayed!"

And then there was no more time for fear.

The Edgelanders attacked the shadowmancers first, and the women with children next. Perhaps they wanted to take them as prisoners, or perhaps they guessed—rightly—that the warriors of Quarabala would not resist the urge to protect the most vulnerable, at any cost to themselves.

Men poured down the sides of the canyon like the spiders of Starfell Gates. They were armed mostly with clubs, knives, and crude spears, but what they lacked in weapons and training they made up for in numbers and sheer savagery. Maika watched in horror as one of these low-caste men threw himself upon Tamimeha, teeth snapping like a reaver as he tried to bite her throat. He was cast off, and the next as well, but looking up at the swarm of Edgelanders and listening to the screams of her people, Maika knew they would be overwhelmed. She gripped her knife with a trembling hand, drew a breath, and prepared to die.

There was an odd whistling noise, like the wind in a narrow canyon, and Maika's first thought was that it might be bats, or birds. Then something brushed across the top of her head, as if death itself had reached a hand from Eid Kalmut to ruffle her hair, and she let out an involuntary squeak of fright.

"Archers!" she cried. "Ware archers!"

Another arrow whispered overhead, not so close this time but still terrifying, and Amalua shouted as a third landed with a soft clatter at her feet.

"My queen!" she shouted. "To my queen! *Ulukau i ka Peleha o'e!*" So saying, she scooped Maika up in her strong arms—knife, mask and all—and began to run toward an overhang in the rock.

Perhaps her shouts had drawn the attention of the archers, or perhaps they knew to look for a young girl who had the foolish arrogance to have been born a Kentakuyan queen. Maika would never know. Arrows fell about them thick as secrets as Amalua ran for their lives. Maika clung to the Iponui and felt the woman's shoulders jerk, her footsteps falter, felt the body jerk again, but she did not stop or slow her pace until they had reached scant shelter. Even then she curled protectively around the queen, shielding her body. Her arms tightened, and she breathed into Maika's ear in long, shuddering, warm gasps.

"Mother," Amalua whispered. "Tell my mother—oh, my queen—tell her—"

And then there was nothing but the gentle fall of arrows, the singing screams of the wounded and dying, the long empty silence between the breath that was and the breath that would never be.

"She is here! I have found her!"

The voice came from far away. The world shifted and a weight, a great and heavy cold weight, was lifted from her shoulders.

I will die now, Maika thought. *They have discovered me.* She shivered in the cold and dark, waiting for these crude men to hack her into pieces, or worse. In the end, it was her own warriors who had found her.

The Edgelanders had been defeated, beaten back, chased to their mean camps and put to the spear. Akamaia had lived through the attack, though one arm had been badly broken, and her trifold loom smashed to pieces. Tamimeha had survived as well, without suffering so much as a torn fingernail, much to her shame. Too many of their own citizens had been killed in the attack, but they had lost a great many more warriors.

Their greatest loss was the loss of hope. The shadowmancers had been hit first and hardest, their sparse numbers decimated. Only four remained alive—four, when two dozen had scarcely been enough to protect the people in their exile and exodus. Four surviving, their scent now carried in the winds and wounded flesh of the Seared Lands, a lure to shadows and greater predators of the worst sort.

It was the death of all hope. The hopeless men of the Edge had not hoped to gain anything through their actions so much as they desired to drag the lives of others down into the same miserable pit they had dug for themselves.

Maika trembled and wept as the body of her faithful Iponui was dragged off her. Beautiful, bright Amalua had died protecting her queen. When they rolled her over, Maika could see her eyes, flat and dry and blind, staring up toward the sky.

A low wail rose from the bottom of the young queen's soul. It wound its way like a dark snake through her gut, her heart, her lungs, and finally burst through her mouth into the dangerous world. She screamed, and screamed again, jaw cracking and chest heaving as she could not force the utter wrongness of what she was feeling out and away from her body fast enough.

"Hush, sweet girl, hush, my queen," Tamimeha murmured as she helped Maika to her feet. She glanced around them and leaned in to whisper. "Be still. Have courage. The people need to see you alive and well and confident. We will survive this. We will. Have no fear, my queen."

Maika closed her mouth and clenched her teeth hard, so hard her jaw ached, in an effort to hold the screams back. A shudder shook her thin frame and tears rolled like thunder down her face as she stared into the empty eyes of the Iponui. Amalua, she thought, would have understood. It was not fear she felt, not for her person or even for the fate of her people.

It was rage.

NINE

The sand beneath her bare feet was white as bones, and softer than the sands of home. The wind that swept down from the peaks of the Jehannim to the foothills where she stood whispered of early berries and sage and wyverns' eyries. The mountains' passions were clutched in stony fists and held up to the sun, not buried and secret like the heart of the desert or locked away in dark places like the daughters of dragons.

Sulema wiggled her toes, luxuriating in the sensations on her unclothed body, of wind and sunlight and freedom. It was not home, but neither was it a dungeon.

"I thank you," she said, and meant it. "Had I remained in Atukos, likely I would have died of thirst. I might have worked out a way to escape"—she thought specifically of the Dreaming Lands— "but I thank you."

"If you had remained in Atualon, you would have been dead before tomorrow's dawn," Yaela said. She dug through her bag and pulled out articles of clothing to toss to Sulema. "Bashaba plans to have poisoned gasses pumped into your cell through the drain-holes. Here, you cannot go naked into the mountains. I did not rescue you from the Dragon King's dungeons to lose you to sun-sickness."

"Bashaba. I do not even know the woman. How can she hate me enough to want me dead?" Then Sulema looked, really looked at the clothing Yaela had tossed at her feet. "My vest! You brought my vest! How did you...?" She turned her face away, to hide shameful tears.

"Bashaba does not hate you. You are a threat to her son, and she would see you eliminated. Surely the daughter of Hafsa Azeina understands this." Yaela rolled her eyes at Sulema's stupidity. "Cassandre still had your clothing from the last time she painted you, and I thought you would prefer them than slippers and gowns, or a golden crown." Her lips twitched. "Certainly they are more sensible."

"Ah, my thanks, this is *much* better." Sulema wriggled with delight as she laced up her vest. It felt like home. She hoped that she would not have to bare her breasts on this day. She wanted a meal, and sleep, and another meal before she was forced to fight so much as a stray thought. "Cassandre knows of this?"

"When the magic in her painting is discovered—and it will be discovered—her life will be forfeit. She and all who loved you in Atualon will fall under suspicion, and if Bashaba has her way, they will fall under the sword, as well."

Sulema's breath caught in her throat, and she shut her eyes against an upwelling of grief and shame. That sweet, bright, joyous Cassandre would die because of her was unthinkable; that she would not be the first to die for her was horrifying. *What about me is worth dying for?* she asked herself. *Nothing. Nothing.* She had grown up Ja'Akari, and knew a true thought when it came to her.

She thought of Daru, her mother's little apprentice who had gone missing and was almost certainly dead, and of her brother Leviathus. Of Saskia, and others of the Ja'Akari whose bones lay unburned in foreign lands because of her birth or her folly. She could not yet face those deaths which lay so near to her heart, and which could arguably be laid at her feet: those of her mother and father. Too close, too new. Neither did she mention aloud the name of Mattu Halfmask, her lover and the younger son of Bashaba. Sulema refused to think of him, that ten-faced bastard, or give a damn whether he lived or died. And she most certainly did not miss him.

But Sulema had grown up Ja'Akari, and knew a false thought when it came to her.

"Will your master Aasah be in danger?" she asked, more to take her mind off her own grief than out of real concern. She had studied under the man but had never really known him, and had not particularly liked what she knew.

Yaela's mouth twisted as if she had bitten something bitter. "Aasah," she said, "can take care of himself. As can your lover."

I do not give a dead goat's ass what happens to Mattu Halfmask, Sulema thought fiercely, but she knew that to be another lie. "My *former* lover," she said aloud, "can go piss on an itch bush, for all I care."

"Your *former* lover," Yaela mocked, "is the one who told Aasah of Bashaba's plans, and fortunately for both of us, my master saw fit to tell me."

Sulema slumped, weary of it all. Her head hurt, her arm hurt, and her heart hurt most of all, but she would not admit any of this to a woman she hardly knew. Yaela had saved her life, but she was hardly a sword-sister. Sulema shook the weakness from her mind and body as a horse shed sand after a long roll.

"Men," she declared, "whether they are lovers or liars, sorcerers or kings, are all a pain in the ass." Then she asked, "Do you have water in that pack of yours? Or food?"

"Neither," Yaela said with a shrug, "but I have salt to buy both for our journey, and there is a good watering hole not far from here." She turned and walked away from the twisted stones, and Sulema followed.

The air smelled sweet, if Sulema herself did not. It had been long since she had bathed. Her skin itched, her scalp itched where the hair was growing back, and her teeth felt sticky and abominable.

"How big is this watering hole? Big enough to bathe in?"

Yaela glanced over her shoulder, a look that said *idiot*.

"Bathe in a watering hole? As if this were an Atualonian pleasure hunt in the spring sunshine." She rolled her eyes. "What do you know of the Jehannim, Ja'Akari?"

"Not much," Sulema admitted. "I know the winds blow so hot and dry it can be dangerous, and I know that wyverns nest in the heights. Other than that..." She shrugged. "We Zeeranim do not venture often into the mountains. There are too many slavers prowling between the pridelands and the peaks, and there is no desire in our hearts to travel through them, much less into Quarabala. The Seared Lands are not fit for woman or beast, so there is no reason for us to ride west at all."

"No," Yaela agreed after a long pause, "I suppose there is not."

"I do not mean to offend."

"You cannot offend. You speak in ignorance."

Sulema opened her mouth to argue, but in that moment, she was too weary and heartsore to bother.

The watering hole was indeed big enough to bathe in—big enough for a fist of warriors to bathe in all at once. Sulema took her cue from Yaela's alert stance—and her own senses, which sang in her blood like shofarot along the riverbanks—and kept her clothes on. She crouched on her heels at the water's edge and scooped handfuls of sweet, cool water to her mouth.

It was good. Good beyond taste, or smell, or even the sensation of cold liquid in her parched mouth. It was good in that she was free, with the wide world about her, road dust on her feet, and a song in her heart. It was—

It *was* a song, she realized, a sweet slow canticle like the earth rousing to the rain after a long dry winter, or a warrior rousing from her sickbed long after she had been given up for dead. Water dribbled between Sulema's fingers back into the still pond. She stared, fascinated by the ripples and whorls that disturbed the water's surface, dancing to the aria that wound through her sa and ka, black-thorned tendrils delicate and deadly tearing her to pieces with its loveliness.

The ripples spread from the heart of the pond outward and small pebbles capered at the water's edge as the ground beneath her feet heaved and shuddered.

Earthquake, Sulema thought, and a cold frisson of terror dribbled between the song's lovely notes to chill her heart. *Sajani! Sajani stirs!*

The song stopped abruptly, and with it the trembling of the earth, but not Sulema's fear. All the little games of her life—the struggle between her desire to be Ja'Akari and her dread of dreamshifting, the tangled knot of anger and grief that was all she had left of her mother, love and lust, even her imprisonment and escape—were no more important than a game of aklashi in the face of this absolute threat. Sajani was waking; she could hear the dragon's thoughts in the stillness of the earth, could feel Akari's anticipation in the warmth of the air.

"Ja'Akari?" Yaela sounded breathless; as good as a shriek of terror from any other woman. "Was that—"

Nearby, a woman screamed.

Sulema froze, a new terror rising in her heart as she remembered every frightening story ever told to her about Jehannim.

"Yaela," it was her turn to ask, "what was—"

"*Ssst!*" Yaela hissed. She stood poised on the balls of her feet. Her face was calm, but her slit pupils had gone wide, giving her a feral look that set Sulema's nerves even more on edge. The scream was answered by another call to the north, and a third to the north-northwest. Neither of these sounded remotely human.

"Mymyc," Yaela said calmly as if she had not just declared both of their lives forfeit. She pivoted with such grace and beauty that it took Sulema's breath away, tucked her chin in to her chest, and ran.

"Escaped a dungeon to be eaten by mymyc," she muttered bitterly, leaping awkwardly to her feet. "Unless the dragon wakes and kills us all first. Story of my life."

Where there is life, there is yet hope, whispered a voice cold with the winds of the Lonely Road. *Run, Kithren, Run!*

The woman screamed again. Though Sulema knew beyond a shadow of a doubt that this was a greater predator's mimicry, it still sounded like a woman, which made it somehow even more horrible. Sulema dropped her horror, the dragonsong enchantment, the sick-weak feeling of having been imprisoned away from the sun, and ran.

Yaela was a woman of Quarabala. Though Sulema had heard little of those Seared Lands, sun-cursed and deadly, she knew this: to be aboveground at first light was to die a horrible death. The Quarabalese people were known, therefore, for their ability to outrun even the dawn.

Knowing and *knowing* were two very different things.

Though less time passed than it took to drop a handful of sand, already Sulema caught only the barest glimpse of the shadowmancer's apprentice as she ran down the hilly path. Swift as the wind she raced, seeming unhindered by the heavy bag slung over her shoulder or the pale sand that rose behind her in soft little puffs.

She does not have to outrun the mymyc, after all, Sulema thought. *She just has to outrun me.*

Even as she followed, Sulema could hear the predators calling behind her, yelping and cackling and screaming. Sometimes one of their voices would mimic a human's scream, or a horse's whinny, or the low fluting call of a wyvern. Mymyc, it was said, had no song of their own, and so had to steal the voices of those they killed.

And mymyc would kill anything. Not even wyverns or bintshi were safe from a pack of the creatures. Judging from the sounds closing in at her heels, they would soon be singing with the voice of a Ja'Akari who was too stupid to stay in the desert.

It is only trouble if you get caught... Sulema thought, as her legs screamed and her lungs burned *...and it seems I am well and truly caught. If I get out of this alive, I am going to run all the way to Aish Kalumm, and never look back.*

She had always wanted to see mymyc. It was said that, from a distance, they appeared as beautiful black horses. Only when a traveler was too close might she discover that they were fanged and clawed as any greater predator, and that they were covered in iridescent black scales. As if knowing her thoughts, claws scrabbled behind her, and a low coughing laugh spurred Sulema to even greater speed.

Guts and goatfuckery, she thought in a rising panic, *I am about to see what a mymyc looks like on the* inside.

The path took a steep dip and turn to the right and ended among twisted stones that reminded her of the Bones of Eth. Sulema dodged into the small circle as a hare might take cover under a tangle of blackthorn, knowing the shelter was insufficient but clinging desperately to hope. As she passed between the stones, shadows roiled up from the ground and engulfed her. She yelped, and the sound was swallowed by the darkness.

"Stop."

It was Yaela's voice, soft and low, and it seemed to come from every direction in the dark.

"Stop, little warrior. Stay still."

Sulema skidded to a halt, arms windmilling, afraid that she was going to bash her head into one of the rocks before the mymyc could eat her. Or before she could catch fire and die screaming in the Seared Lands—or die in the mountains, or in the hold of a slaver's ship, or—

Guts and goatfuckery, she thought again as she caught her balance. *The entire world competes to see which horror can kill me first.*

The shadows roiled into a sinuous solid shape that coiled itself protectively around her and the shadowmancer's apprentice. Yaela was dancing, arms outflung and feet pounding the sand, a soft little tattoo that seduced the heart and ensnared the soul. Hips swiveling, feet pounding, head thrown back and face suffused in joy, she was lost in her magic in a way Sulema could only envy.

That, she thought, *is the soul of ehuani.*

The shadows heeded Yaela's commands. They joined into a serpentine whole and reared over the women's heads, hissing, red eyes glowing, smokelike plumes rising in a crest above a lionsnake made of shadows and fear. It was huge, impossibly so, many times bigger than the old grandmother bitch that had almost killed her, and Sulema found herself paralyzed with fear as it loomed above her.

The mymyc felt no such terror.

Sulema could see them through the shadow-snake. A pack of five or more, they were indeed horselike in appearance, but a second glance was all it took to dispel the illusion. Bigger than horses and more thickly muscled, their iridescent black hides shone in the sunlight. They moved with a quick, reptilian grace, fanged mouths open and tongues lolling as they called to one another in borrowed voices, and lizardlike tails whipped behind them as they swarmed down the path, intent on eating these humans who had dared invade their territory. No illusory snake, it seemed, would deny them their rightful prey.

Sulema grabbed a fist-sized rock and held it high. *I am no easy meat*, she reminded herself. *It is a good day to die.* She knew that the lionsnake, frightening though it looked, was shadow and illusion; it could not—

The lionsnake struck, snapping the lead mymyc up in its jaws. It thrashed its head back and forth like a vash'ai with a pig. The predator squealed, a terrible grating sound that made Sulema drop her rock and clap both hands over her ears, and then its neck broke with an audible snap and it went limp. The illusory reptile tossed its head back, unhinged its jaw, and swallowed the mymyc whole before whipping back around and striking at the rest of the pack.

The remaining mymyc spun about and fled, wailing, into the foothills.

The lionsnake twisted around and regarded the two women who were neatly trapped inside its coils. Shadow-claws curled into the sand, and its shadow-plume stood out in a stiff mane as it swayed in the air above them, preparing to strike.

The sight froze Sulema's heart. It did not seem to her that the magical beast was under Yaela's control, not by half.

"Enough," Yaela said. She brought her dance to an end, one leg pointed before her in almost a fighter's pose, arms raised above her head, wrists poised in the air so gracefully she looked to Sulema like a poem come to life.

The lionsnake opened its mouth, venom sacs bulging, and hissed.

"Enough!" Yaela cried, and her voice was a thunder that rolled across the low hills, echoing in the world of Shehannam, as well. The lionsnake bowed its head in submission and faded away like black mist.

I can hear echoes of the Dreaming Lands while I am awake, Sulema thought. *That is interesting. Terrifying, but interesting.* She did not mention this to the shadowmancer's apprentice, however. To Yaela she said only, "I thought that your shadowmancy was illusion."

"It is real if you believe it so," Yaela said. She brought her arms down and swayed where she stood, as if exhausted beyond caring.

"But it—it ate that mymyc."

"The mymyc believed it was real." Yaela smiled, an unpleasant little smile that had Sulema taking half a step back. "Remember this, Ja'Akari, if you think to betray me, or break your vow."

"Ja'Akari do not break their vows." Sulema scowled so hard it hurt.

"Everyone breaks their vows, eventually," Yaela said. "Even you. Even I—" And then those brilliant jade eyes went dull and blank and she fell to the ground, senseless.

Sulema regarded the still form at her feet for a long moment. She thought of earthquakes, and lionsnakes, of kings and consorts, of a world delicate as eggshell and a dragon singing herself awake. *It is a good day to die*, she thought, *but let me not die here in these cursed mountains, or among the sung bones on the road to Quarabala. Let me die Ja'Akari, shoulder to shoulder with my sword-sisters, protecting my people until my last breath. I want to go home. I want to go home!*

From the deepest well of dark wishes in her heart, Sajani's voice whispered forth, *I want to go home. Let me wake. Let me live. Let me go, Dreamsinger!*

Sulema stamped the voice from her heart as she might stamp out a campfire that had grown too wild.

I want to go home. Her wish, or the dragon's? Sulema decided that it did not matter. She had given her word to Yaela; but what beauty remained in honor, in *ehuani*, when all the beauty of the world was about to end?

"I wonder," she said at last to the unconscious Yaela, "if you have any weapons in that bag of yours, sorcerer." Her voice was strange in her ears, as if she, like the mymyc, had stolen it from another. It was, she thought, the voice of a woman who could lie, or steal, or break a vow. The voice of a woman who could murder another in cold blood, and run from the scene of her dishonor, run without stopping, without looking back.

All the way to the Zeera.

TEN

I want to go home.

Ismai froze as he was, crouched beside the river of the dead, cupped hands halfway to his mouth. It had happened again—one moment he had been trapped inside the Lich King, fighting to get out, and the next moment he was himself again.

More or less.

The earth had trembled, and then the river had spoken to him with Sulema's voice, sure as he lived—

Well, perhaps *lived* was not the word he wanted. Ismai plunged both hands into the turgid waters, grasping, groping, as if his lost friend were a fish and he could pull her out alive. It seemed to him that if he could find her, she could in turn find him, and they might indeed go home.

Home. I want to go home.

"What are you doing?"

It was the warrior Sudduth, tall and lissome, she who had been so feared and celebrated in life that upon her death, he had bound her to him—

Not I, Ismai reminded himself. *That was Kal ne Mur. I am Ismai, son of Nurati. I am Ismai!*

"I thought I heard the voice of… a friend," he said. "Singing." He rose, feeling more than a little foolish, and tried to wipe his wet hands on his touar only to remember that he was wearing the Lich King's armor. He grimaced and settled for shaking the drops from his fingertips. "It was only the river, I guess."

"Perhaps not, your Arrogance. The Ghana Kalmut sometimes sings with the voices of the dead, and the nearly dead. Perhaps your—friend—is in mortal danger." Sudduth did not look as if she particularly cared. She knelt in the black mud, cradling something carefully against her belly.

"What are you doing?" Ismai said, echoing her question of moments before. The woman narrowed her milk-dead eyes at him, pursed her lips, and shrugged.

"I found some cacao beans in my tomb. I thought to wash them and see if they were still edible." She opened her hands, revealing five smallish, oddly shaped dark beans. Shriveled things they were, as dead as Sudduth herself had been just days before. "Not enough to make chocolate, but I thought perhaps a drink…"

"Chocolate? What is that?" Ismai wrinkled his nose at the sight of the dead things. "They do not look good to eat or drink. Maybe you should just throw them away."

I am talking to a dead woman, he realized, and sighed. How strange his life had become that this was normal. His head itched and he raised a hand to scratch at it, wondering whether Kal ne Mur had ever had to deal with head lice.

Sudduth froze. Her dead eyes widened, and she stared upon him with horror.

"What is *chocolate*?" she asked, voice rising as if he had uttered blasphemy. "Chocolate is everything! Chocolate is *life*." She turned and called out, "Naara!"

"Yes?" Naara—Charon—was there, flush and whole as any healthy young girl just risen from a long night's sleep. Ismai resisted the urge to run. *Daughter*, he had called her, Naar-Ahnet, and so his heart named her. He had considered her a friend, and perhaps she was… but she was also a monster.

"You claim this… this *boy*… must be our king, and yet he does not know anything. The fool does not even know what chocolate is." Scorn dripped from her words as the river water had dripped from Ismai's hands. "Explain!"

"Oh." Naara sighed. "There is no chocolate, not anymore."

99

"What." Sudduth's milk eyes, Ismai noted with some alarm, began to glow red at the very center, where a pupil should be. "What did you say." She cradled the seeds to her belly, as if to shield them from such blasphemy.

"There has been no chocolate for generations, not since the Sundering," Naara explained. "Those beans that were buried with you are likely all that remains—"

Sudduth threw her head back and howled, which was especially unfortunate as she had had her throat slit from ear to ear, and Ismai could see the ululations in her exposed throat. He supposed he was not afraid—being, as Naara had said, more than half undead himself—but it was disconcerting at the very least. And more than a little bit gross.

The warrior's anguished rage drew the attention of several of her companions. Uruk, Fatheema, Amraz, and several others whose names Ismai had not yet learned, shuffled over to stand with their companion. Uruk put his hand on Sudduth's shoulder and his eyes gleamed bright and bloody as he glared at their commander.

"What have you done?" he grated. His other hand, as big around as Ismai's thigh, tightened upon the haft of his spiked war hammer. Ismai swallowed.

I am not afraid of the undead, he reminded himself. *I am their king. I think.* He shook his head, which made his scalp itch again. "Nothing," he assured the fur-clad hulk of rage. "Naara told her there was no chocolate. I do not even know what that is, but I guess it was important to her."

"No chocolate?" Uruk gaped at him and squeezed Sudduth's shoulder in sympathy. "You raised her into a world with no chocolate? Are you *mad*, boy?"

Sudduth's howl grew louder and more strident. More of the undead were gathering, and all of them faced Ismai now, ember-eyed and indignant.

"Help her," Naara hissed between gritted teeth. "Fix this."

"Fix this? Fix it how?" Ismai moved toward the keening

warrior. Her wails of agony were as hooks in his heart, dragging him to her side, demanding his attention. "What can I do? I—"

As abruptly as Sudduth's cries had begun, so they stopped.

"Make them live," she whispered, voice hoarse. She held out both hands to him, dead seeds cradled in them as if she held her beating heart. "Make them live, my king... make them live. Please. I lived for you, I have died for you, and I will do so again. Only... only do not expect me to abide in a world where there is no chocolate.

"Please."

It was that *please*, the brokenness of it, that was Ismai's undoing. The despair and sorrow in her voice, the lost pleading in her dead eyes, and the abrupt realization that she had sat here in dust and emptiness, caught between death and undeath, just so that she could be dragged into the harsh light of day and denied even this simple comfort.

All for Kal ne Mur.

For me.

Can we help her? Ismai closed his own dead eyes and reached deep into the shards of his shattered soul. When he opened them again, the undead host—all save Sudduth—drew back with a sigh of reverence, and he knew that he was not Ismai.

"My king," Sudduth murmured.

"My beauty," he replied in a deep voice, a voice accustomed to being heard. He reached out and brushed the backs of her knuckles, feeling the harsh rasp of calluses grown in his service, seeing the ragged edges of her wounds. "Sweet Sudduth who died for me. I am here. Live. Live." He cupped her hands between his, and breathed deep, pulling the living air into his seared lungs. Her faded beauty was a testament to his power, and a remonstrance.

See what I have done, he said to Ismai. *What I have wrought. And now see what I can do, little warden.*

He let the air become a fire in his belly, let the fire become a dragon, and then Kal ne Mur, once and future king of Atualon, lifted his face to Akari and sang.

Had the body he rode been his own, had the life he had lived not been cut short—or had he the Mask of Akari—such magic as he wove would have been a grand thing, a great work. Forcing the bodies of those who had sworn their blood and souls to him was easy, as easy as pumping blood through his own veins, air into his own lungs. These seeds, however, small and shriveled and dead as they were, owed him no fealty. Their small lives were woven into a new song, small sparks long gone dark and cold, and they resisted his call, his pull.

Yet he was Kal ne Mur, the Dragon King, the Lich King, and he would not be denied. They were dead, and the dead belonged to him. He sang, he commanded, and eventually...

angrily...

reluctantly...

they obeyed.

Kal ne Mur let the song fade from his lips, the fire from his heart. When he released Sudduth's hands again her skin was brown and pliant as a young girl's, the slash at her throat had been mended, and her eyes sparkled wide and brown. She unclasped her hands and fell to her knees before him.

"Oh," she cried in a voice as soft and sweet as a nightingale's. "Oh, oh, my king." She bent her head and wept, live tears falling from living eyes upon the soft green of new leaves; the boon she had asked had been granted. All five of the beans she held cupped in her palms had sprouted.

"You gave me your life, ages and ages ago," he told her. "In this I hope I have repaid a small portion of that debt."

A wind rose then in the heart of Eid Kalmut, born from the tears of the grateful dead.

"Kal ne Mur," one whispered, then another, then another.

"Kal ne Mur."

"Kal ne Mur."

"Father!" Charon cried. Naara, his beloved child. "It is I! It is you! You have returned to us, at last!"

And so he had.

Ismai tried to wake from the dream, tried to reclaim his body, and found with rising terror that he could not. As he began to panic, to fight, to scream, his arms were raised high, his mouth formed into a smile by a will not his own.

Sulema, he cried, reaching out to the river. *Help me! Find me!* But Sulema did not answer. From the Ghana Kalmut came only the voices of the dead, raised in a hymn to the glory of their king.

The voice that issued from his mouth now was not his own, and never again would be.

"Who am I?" he cried, low and ringing as a call to battle. "My friends, my faithful soldiers... who am I?"

As one, the host of the undead went to their knees and raised dry voices in exultation:

"Kal ne Mur!" they cried, they howled. "KAL NE MUR!"

"Indeed," he answered. Ismai opened his mouth to scream, but Kal ne Mur smiled upon his faithful instead.

Kithren, Ruh'ayya wailed, far away and helpless. *Kithren, come back, come back to me.*

I cannot, Ismai answered. *I—*

"I am home," said Kal ne Mur, and smiled with Ismai's face.

"I have no wish to go to war."

Ibna sud Barach stood before him, tall and proud and straight as the blood-iron spear he bore. In life he had been Iponui, one of the running warriors of Quarabala. Deadly with spear and sword, able to outrun a horse—many a soldier had made a small fortune betting on Ibna's legs, or lost one betting against him—and with a laugh like healing rain. He had never been one to back away from a fight.

Until now.

"I have raised you to fight for me." Kal ne Mur rubbed a hand over his aching dead eyes. "And you say to me now that you have no wish for war. What, then, do you wish to do with this life I have given you?"

"I will fight for you, my king, and die for you. Again." Ibna's face was smooth and devoid of emotion. "But my heart is no longer in the fight. I wish, if I would—"

"Yes? You would what? You might as well say it." Ibna was not the first of his soldiers to approach him this day, to express both undying loyalty and a wish for something—anything—other than warfare. "Husna wishes to be a farmer. Aydna would like to spend an eternity fishing. What would you do with your time, pray tell me?"

"I would make things. Beautiful things, with my hands. I would shape clay, or rock, or perhaps wood... I would like to make beautiful things, instead of dead things." Ibna clenched his jaw. "If I had your leave to go."

"You do not have my leave to go," Kal ne Mur replied. *Any more than you do, Ismai son of Nurati*, he said to the screaming boy who shared this body. "You wish to make something beautiful, Ibna? Then help me retake this world, and we will make it over in our image. We will reclaim the Zeera and teach these false Mah'zula their place. We will take the river, and Min Yaarif, and send word to our allies in Quarabala. Together we will raise Atukos over all the world, and these kings and emperors of loving men will bend the knee to us. That will be your thing of beauty, my friend."

"War." Ibna spat. "War does not make the world beautiful, your Radiance."

"I know," Kal ne Mur answered. "But war is what we do."

ELEVEN

The day was long, and the way was long, and Sulema was half dead before it began. But she was warrior-trained, warrior-born and bred. Half dead was simply a reminder that she was wholly, fully, fiercely alive.

The wind had shifted, bringing word of places where the mountains met the rivers and serpents sang in the flowering shallows, of dark shadows, deep hidey holes, of land held up to the gaze of Akari Sun Dragon like a handful of jewels. Ahead lay a town. The sand beneath her feet was slippery-soft and that was good, because it made her slow down, placing each foot with deliberation, and not think too much about the pain in her neck and shoulders.

And arms.

And back.

No, she mused, *I am not thinking of the pain at all.* She laughed silently at herself, alive and free once more under the sun. *Ehuani*, it was a good day *not* to die in the bowels of her enemy's prisons.

The way to Min Yaarif was not difficult to see. Faint paths became clearer and more frequently used as they wound their way down the foothills and toward the wide Dibris. All roads—Istaza Ani had been fond of saying—led to Min Yaarif, as all strands led to the center of a spider's web. Sulema wondered if this was true, and why, and what lay in wait for her at the center of this web.

She also wondered how someone who looked so small and fragile could be so dragon-blasted heavy.

Yaela groaned, and her weight shifted so that Sulema nearly lost her footing.

"Wake up," she suggested, less than sweetly. "Walk your own self down the mountain. I am tired of carrying you, and your tits in my face make it difficult to look for snakes."

Yaela groaned again, kicking feebly as Daru used to during one of his fits. Sulema stopped in the middle of the path, bent beneath the weight of her companion.

"Are you awake?"

"*Uhhh*," Yaela answered.

"Good." Sulema dipped one shoulder, ducked her head, and dumped Yaela unceremoniously, bag and all, into the sand on the side of the road. Her legs threatened to buckle beneath her, but she forced them to be still, and her back to straighten, and shook the weariness from her arms. *Not dead yet.*

Yaela curled into a tight ball, arms cradling her head as if protecting herself against an assault, and a single soft whimper escaped before she went still and limp. Then she straightened, yawning and stretching, opened her eyes, and scrunched her face against the late sun.

"Whaaaat…?" she said, yawning again before rolling into a seated position. She looked up at Sulema and frowned. "Where are we? And why are you still here?"

"We are almost to Min Yaarif, by my best guess," Sulema snapped, turning on her heel as if to continue alone. *Ungrateful whelp.* She rolled her shoulders. "And I am still here because I am Ja'Akari. A warrior does not break her vow, even if it means carrying your fat arse down a mountain."

"Fat arse." Yaela's voice was flat and hard. After a surly silence, she added, "Thank you. I did not expect—" She groaned. Sulema stopped and glanced over her shoulder to see Yaela pushing herself upright. The woman swayed where she stood, and her face had a gray cast to it.

"You thought I would kill you, take what you carry," she said, "and run all the way home to the Zeera without looking back."

Yaela stared straight at her, unblinking.

"Yes."

Sulema snorted. "That speaks to *your* honor, not mine. Come, we need to get to shelter before the sun goes down. I hear that mymyc are excellent night hunters." She rolled her shoulders again—they ached, but it was a good ache, she decided, free from the burn of reaver's venom—and walked the rest of the way down from the hills toward a town that lay waiting for them crouched beside the river.

Like a giant spider.

She did not look back.

"Is stealing not dishonorable?" Yaela asked around a mouth full of dates. "You are going to get us both in trouble. I have salt enough to pay for food."

"It is not *stealing* to take food if you are hungry," Sulema protested. "That law is older than the Zeera. And I *am* hungry." She shrugged, unconcerned. "Also I thought it best that we avoid talking to people when we can. I would rather our whereabouts not become common knowledge. Besides, it is only trouble if you get—"

"*You!*" a voice roared from the other end of the alley.

"—caught," Sulema finished. "Ah, horse shit."

"Do not run," Yaela cautioned. "If you do, they will catch you anyway, and kill you before you can fulfill your vow to me. At best they would cast us both naked from the walls of Min Yaarif, where we would be eaten by the great desert cats, and we have yet to find the shadowmancer Keoki."

"Vash'ai do not eat people." Sulema wrinkled her nose at the idea. Three men approached them, but they did not move like warriors. None of them were particularly impressive, so she dismissed them as a threat. "And I am no coward, to run from trouble. So we spend an afternoon cleaning churra pits or washing the vendor's soiled clothes—"

"What are you talking about? This is not the Zeera. In Min Yaarif, thieves do not pay the price of stolen goods by performing chores. Here, they cut off your hand. Or your foot. Or your head. Sometimes they sell you into slavery—you, and all your companions." For all her dire words, Yaela appeared more irritated than frightened. "*Au Illindra*, you desert crawlers have heads full of cobwebs. Shut up and let me do the talking."

Sulema opened her mouth to protest, or argue, or come up with some witty retort—*desert crawlers? Heads full of cobwebs?*—but Yaela turned to address the men who had come close, and the handful of curious onlookers who had followed, no doubt hoping for some entertainment.

"A heart welcomes you, good men," she called out. "How may we serve?"

"As prisoners," the man in front replied. He was the tallest of the three and, judging by the scowl on his face, he was the angriest as well. "That little bald shit stole food from my cart."

Yaela glanced back at Sulema and shook her head in exaggerated sorrow. "This one? She is an idiot, a foreigner, and cannot be held responsible for her actions. What is the value of the goods she took?" She touched the bag at her shoulder. "A handful of red salt?"

Sulema stared at her. The dates she had snatched had not been worth more than three pinches of white salt, never mind red.

The man frowned thoughtfully, and his companions looked to him.

"You can pay?"

"I can pay."

"In that case"—the man smirked, eyes crawling over Yaela and then Sulema in a manner that made her skin crawl—"how about you pay me with a handful of pussy?" He grabbed his crotch at them, and his companions laughed. It was an ugly sound.

A few in the crowd chuckled, as well. Others appeared uncomfortable at the exchange.

Sulema glanced at Yaela and was shocked at the naked fury on the other woman's face. Her eyes had gone wide and black, and she bared her teeth in a snarl that would make any vash'ai proud.

"Then I will fight you for it," the shadowmancer's apprentice said. Her voice was soft, soft as a killing wind, soft as poisoned honey and hungry shadows. She raised an arm in a delicate arc, cupped her hand before her face and blew. Shadows poured from between her fingers like smoke from an oil lamp.

She is bluffing, Sulema thought. The shadowmancer's apprentice trembled with the effort it cost her to summon even this small handful of shadow. *But two can play this game as easily as one.*

"Works for me," she agreed aloud, stepping into a fighting stance. Though it seemed a lot of fuss over a few dates, and though she was a three-day journey past exhaustion, it occurred to her that a good brawl might cleanse her heart of anger—and these shit-brained outlanders had just volunteered.

"Shadowmancer," one of the tall man's companions muttered loudly, tugging at his sleeve. "My friend, this fight is not worth it."

"A shadowmancer and a desert slut," the third man agreed, "shorn of her braids." He held up both hands and took a step back. "Not worth the risk, even for prime pussy like this."

That was enough for Sulema. "Desert slut?" her voice raised to an outraged squawk on the last word; she had been called *slut* by these men one time too many. She spat on the sand and yanked her vest open in a show of contempt. "I will teach you to mind your tongue, you—"

"*Geth! Geth!*" someone shouted, and the crowd of onlookers parted to let a woman through. She was tall and well-muscled, and reminded Sulema immediately of Sareta. She wore robes of pale yellow, and a pale yellow wrap at her brow emphasized the most beautiful cloud of black-and-silver hair Sulema had ever seen. Her dark eyes were wide, and almond-shaped, and filled with a hard expression that said there had been enough nonsense for one day. She was flanked by four enormous hard-faced men in yellow vests and white trousers.

Yaela curled her hand into a fist, and the shadow-smoke faded away. Sulema dropped her stance and bowed her head. She knew trouble when it had caught her.

"What is all this?" the woman snapped, mouth set in a firm line as she eyed the tall man. "Baoud, what do you do here?"

"These women stole from me," he said, his voice aggrieved. "I am simply trying to support my family, and they stole from me. I seek justice."

"Justice, hm." The woman glanced at Sulema, but addressed her words to Yaela. "Does Baoud speak true? Did you steal from him?"

"He speaks true in part," Yaela agreed. "My companion, being an idiot child who does not know the ways of this place, took a handful of dates to fill our empty bellies. I offered to pay this man in salt, but he thought to take payment in girl flesh instead." Her shadow-filled eyes glinted dangerously. "We refuse."

"She lies!" Baoud cried. "I would happily take salt—"

"No!" An older woman pushed her way to the front of the growing crowd. "Ayya, the girl speaks truth. She offered salt, and this pig's ass and his pig's ass friends made to attack them instead." She glared at the three men, who had all gone red-faced and silent. "Do not think your mothers will not hear about this, all three of you. *Shame!*"

"Shame," several bystanders muttered. Sulema noted, wryly, that none of these people had spoken up before the yellow-robed woman had appeared.

Ayya, if that was her name, pursed her lips.

"Did you steal from this man?"

"I did not *steal*," Sulema explained. "I took two handfuls of dates to eat, because I was hungry."

The woman shot her a sharp look at that, and then turned to Yaela. "And did you offer to pay in salt?"

"I did," Yaela said. "I offered a handful of red salt, as payment for the dates and for the insult."

Ayya stared hard at Baoud. "And did you and your companions think to attack these women, in an attempt to take flesh-price instead?"

The man's mouth worked as if he had bitten bitter fruit.

"I did. We did."

Several people in the crowd began to mutter. The woman in yellow clapped her hands together once, twice, three times, and they fell silent.

"This is my judgment," she said. "The Zeerani girl is guilty of theft. She is sentenced to five lashes with a cane"—several onlookers sucked in a breath—"to be given if and only if she offends any other law within a two-moon, as it is permissible to suspend punishment for one crime, one time only." She glared at Sulema. "The ways of Min Yaarif are not the ways of the Zeera. It is your responsibility to learn our laws and learn them quickly. Do you understand?"

"Yes," Sulema said. She bowed her head and felt her cheeks go hot with embarrassment. "I am sorry, *ehuani*. I have been an idiot."

"You have," Ayya agreed. "Again, did you offer to pay a handful of red salt?"

"I did," Yaela said.

"You will pay one half-handful of red salt to the merchants' guild, to pay for the dates and the insult, and one half-handful of red salt to the peacekeepers' guild, to pay for my time." Yaela nodded in agreement.

"What about *me*?" Baoud asked. "They stole from me!"

"You," Ayya said, "I find guilty of intended rape. I declare your merchandise forfeit to the merchants' guild, to disburse as they will. I further declare your dick forfeit, as you have used it to offend the peace of Min Yaarif." She pointed to one of Baoud's companions. "*You* will remove the offending member with a machete." Then she pointed to the other. "You will wear it around your neck for one week as a reminder to others that citizens and visitors to our fair city are not to be molested."

Baoud cried out and fell to his knees. The yellow-vested men surrounded him and his companions. They were seized and borne away, wailing and struggling to no avail.

Ayya stared hard at Yaela, and harder at Sulema.

"You are to go straight to the guilds and pay your fines. I trust that there will be no more trouble from either of you?"

"No," Yaela said.

"No," Sulema agreed. She met the woman's eyes, though it shamed her to do so. "I am truly sorry to have caused this much trouble. It will not happen again."

A corner of Ayya's mouth quirked. "Do not make a promise that you will be unable to keep, young Ja'Akari. Trouble follows your kind like night follows day. Oh, and, ladies?"

"Yes?" they said together.

"Welcome to Min Yaarif."

Half a fistful of Yaela's salt tablets bought them a bath and beds at an inn, and food fit for the festival of Jadi-Khai. Having bathed and eaten, the two women sat in a comfortable silence and watched the river turn red as Akari dipped his wings and dove beyond the mountains in search of his sleeping love.

Sulema could have slept, but she was in that comfortable state of being full and clean and in no immediate danger of being run through with a sword or torn into pieces by a pack of mymyc. It had been long since she had seen a sunset, so she lingered. River serpents sang to one another in the glooming, a sweet counterpart to the sound of the Zeera, so close Sulema's heart could taste sand upon the wind.

"They sound happy," she remarked.

"How can you tell?" Yaela glanced at her curiously over the lip of a water pipe, face wreathed in pinkish smoke.

"I... I am not sure. You just can, if you listen. Hear that?" She paused as a sweet trill pierced the darkening sky. "They do not sound like that when they are aroused or angry. Or when they are mating." She winced at the memory. "*That* sound will give you a headache for weeks."

"Hm." Yaela placed the end of the hose between her lips, and water gargled merrily. "Often I have listened to the song of serpents, but I never thought about them having moods. Perhaps you are more sensitive because you are echovete, able to hear atulfah?"

"Perhaps." Sulema's enjoyment of the serpents' singing paled at the reminder. "I do not know."

Bruise-purple darkness bled across the sky, and the lights of men leapt up in tiny, futile attempts to keep it at bay. So many people packed into one place—hundreds and hundreds of them—made Sulema's skin crawl. She longed to ride across the singing dunes with her sweet Atemi, and Hannei, and no need at all for words or fire or... anything.

When this day began, I had been cast into a pit and left to die, she thought, scolding herself. *Ungrateful wretch.* But the thought did not stop her heart from longing.

"Home," Yaela remarked around the pipe's mouthpiece, and fumes curled from her mouth as if she was Sajani incarnate. "Never closer, never farther away. I could be home in three days if I started dancing now—"

"Dancing?"

"Dancing," Yaela affirmed. "As you have seen, this is my gift. In order to bind shadows to my bidding, I dance, and weave them into a veil of darkness so thick it shields me from Akari's wrath. If I stop, the shadows dissipate, and when the sun comes up—" She blew out a fat puff of smoke, "Poof! Just like that."

"Poof, just like what?"

"In the Seared Lands, if you are aboveground when the sun comes up, and have no spun shadows to protect you," Yaela blew another puff of smoke, this time directly into Sulema's face. "You burst into flame and burn away to ash. Poof!"

Sulema waved the smoke away with a grimace. "Not a good way to go."

"No." Yaela's teeth flashed white through the gloom and the smoke, a wicked smile as if she remembered some secret joke. "But it is better than being eaten by a bintshi. Faster, too. And less messy."

"There are not many bintshi on our side of the river. We have our share of greater predators, though. Na'iyeh, wyverns, bonelords, oujinn—"

"Dreamshifters," Yaela added softly. "Dream eaters. But those are monsters, not predators."

Sulema stiffened. *This sorcerer is not a friend*, she reminded herself. Standing abruptly, she said, "I am tired. It is time for me to go to bed."

"Stay. Please, stay." A woman's voice flowed from the near darkness, and her form followed. Startled, Sulema rocked onto the balls of her feet, the better to flee or to fight. Yaela just took another puff of her pipe, but her eyes illuminated by the glowing coals were wide and wary.

"I am sorry, I did not mean to startle you." The woman smiled disarmingly, dimly visible in the near-dark, spreading both hands wide to show that she bore no weapons. "I have been seeking the two of you all day and look! I have found you. May I?" Without waiting for an answer, she plopped her butt on the ground next to Yaela and reached for the water pipe. Yaela handed it over.

Peering through the gloom, Sulema studied the woman as she smoked. She was long-limbed and well-muscled, with the kind of thoughtless grace and the scarred forearms earned through a life of fighting. "Who are you? What do you want from us?"

"She is Rehaza Entanye," Yaela answered, taking her water pipe back from the woman.

It was the stranger's turn to be startled. "You know me?"

"I know of you," Yaela answered, and she set her pipe aside. She gestured, and Sulema crossed to sit reluctantly at her side.

I wish I knew half of what was going on.

"If you know of me, then you can guess why I have come." Gloom turned to darkness, so that Sulema had to squint to see the woman. She glanced at Yaela, whose eyes had begun to glow like jade held up before a fire.

I bet she can see just fine.

"You want us to fight in the pits," Yaela said. "We are not interested."

"Oh?" Sulema did not need eyes that could see in the dark to know that the woman was smiling. "I suppose you are going to tell me there is no price that could entice you."

"None." Yaela's voice was flat and hard.

"Neither of you?" she glanced at Sulema from the corner of her eyes.

Sulema snorted. "I am Ja'Akari. We fight for honor, not for outlanders."

"Ah, that is a pity. Especially when one considers tomorrow's prize—a war-bred asil mare. And look! One of you happens to be a Zeerani warrior without a horse."

Air hissed between Sulema's teeth before she could stop herself.

115

"Yet you would not be interested in this mare, in any case. She is golden as the Zeera—an unlucky color, I am sure—and a bit of a handful, having recently been held in captivity in the far-off and fabled land of Atualon. I am afraid that the Atualonians do not know how to properly care for such a creature. She is half-starved and mad from being beaten, but I am sure that whoever wins her will—"

Sulema exploded to her feet, and the night washed red as blood pumped behind her eyes.

"*Atemi!*"

"Sulema—" Yaela warned.

She spun about to face the glowing eyes.

"They have my Atemi!" She threw the words violently, beyond rage or reason.

"The mare is yours, you say?" The stranger's voice was thick with laughter. "What an odd bit of... luck. Convenient, to be sure."

"Atemi is *mine*," Sulema insisted. "And I will have her back. Or I will burn this place to the ground."

"As you say."

"We will not fight," Yaela insisted, but her voice lacked conviction. "We cannot—"

"Ah, I understand. Surely two young women such as yourselves are... what? Adventurers? Travelers? Heroes, come to Min Yaarif in search of a quest? Or perhaps you already have a quest in mind... *Kentakuyan*."

Yaela's eyes blazed against the night.

"One of royal blood such as yourself—forgive my presumption—is no doubt uninterested in such lowly treasure as a half-dead horse," Entanye continued. "Now, what prize might my mistress offer that would entice such a one as yourself?" She paused as if to think. "Hmmm..."

The night grew abruptly deeper, ink-dark, black as the pit of the belly of a beast. *Shadows*, Sulema realized, and chillflesh raised the hairs on her arms. Shadows flowed outward from the place where Yaela sat, as water would spill from the banks of the Dibris after a spring flood.

"Oh, I know!" Rehaza Entanye continued as if she had not noticed. "Surely you wish to return and visit your— homeland?—and all your friends and relatives. But in order to do that, you need a skilled shadowmancer. One not previously known to those who guard the ways. If at least one of you agrees to fight in the pits, my mistress offers as your prize the services of Shadowmancer Keoki, who finds himself in her employ."

A hissing sound rose about them, a rustling noise like the sound of scales, or bat's wings, or nightmares.

Shadows, Sulema realized, and shuddered. *Grown so real we can* hear *them.*

"You dare," Yaela said. Her voice was smooth and unruffled, but her eyes glowed bright as the moons.

"Three days," Rehaza Entanye said, and her voice had lost all trace of mirth. "The Fight of Champions will be held in three days, and I have been instructed to invite the two of you to compete. This is an unusual privilege, and I expect you to be properly grateful for the opportunity. No doubt you will beat the lesser competitors—the fighting has gone on now for nearly three months, and only the best are still alive, but still they should be no trouble for the likes of a— Ja'Akari, you say? And a shadowmancer's apprentice, by the looks of your unscarred skin? Indeed, only our champion might prove any real challenge to you, and it is this fight that my mistress most wishes to see."

"Who is your mistress?" Yaela asked.

"Who is this champion?" Sulema asked. She did not give two shits from a sick churra about this woman's mistress. She would win back her Atemi, and that would be that.

"My mistress is none of your business. Do not cast your net at a dragon, child. As for our champion." She chuckled. "You will have the honor of fighting Kishah Two-Blades herself."

"Kishah?" Sulema asked, intrigued despite herself. "That is a Zeerani word. It means—"

"Vengeance." The woman stood, her face lit by the pale green fire of Yaela's wrath, and smiled at them. "I will see you in three days, warrior." She walked away without bothering to look back.

Sulema and Yaela stared at each other, lit only by starslight and moonslight as the shadows dissipated and the apprentice's eyes returned to normal.

"I cannot fight in the pits." Yaela's voice was tight with an unspoken plea, her body tense. She would not meet Sulema's eyes. "I am forsworn."

"I will fight, then," Sulema said. "I have no choice."

"There is always a choice," Yaela said. "Just never any good ones."

TWELVE

"No," Hannei signed. "*No.*"

The pain in her heart felt worse than anything she had ever experienced. Worse than the pain of betrayal she had felt when Sareta sold her into slavery. Worse than the pain of having the tongue sliced from her mouth.

Worse than watching Tammas die?

She imagined a flutter deep within her belly and laid a protective hand over her thickening abdomen. No, not worse than that. She had died with Tammas, and lived now only for his child.

"Yes," Rehaza Entanye said. "You will do this thing, Kishah. Do I need to remind you of your pact with Sharmutai?"

No, Hannei thought, but this time she kept her hands as still as her face. The pitmistress had reminded her of her damn vow yesterday, tóday, and she would again tomorrow. *It is almost as if they do not trust me.* The notion brought a grim smile to her mouth. The two women stood facing each other across a table of silverwood, finely carved with scenes of battle and glory and inlaid with river pearls.

"Nothing is too good for my champion," Sharmutai had said, upon showing Hannei to her new quarters. *"I shall dress you in silks if you like, drown you in pleasure slaves and spiced wine. And when you die,"* she said as she kissed Hannei on the forehead as if she were a favored daughter, *"I will dress you in silks and commission poetry fit to make the sky weep."*

"I understand that you know this girl, this child warrior and pretender to the Dragon Throne. It may be that you were once friends—you are of an age, and you barbarians are a close knot. It is a vast land, the Zeera, but a small village all the same, am I right? A girl can hardly get laid without bumping into a cousin, as they say. But answer me this, Kishah Two-Blades, where was this fine friend of yours when that cunt warleader of yours was selling you to Ovreh? Off in her father's kingdom sitting upon a golden chair and being wooed by the world's finest assholes, I should think.

"Did she give up that golden chair and ride to your aid when you needed her? No? Then why should you give up your life to spare hers? Sharmutai has sent me here to tell you this, slave—kill this girl today, this last spawn of the dragon, and she will consider your contract fulfilled. You have only to do what you do best. Kill, and you will be free. Free to go wherever you like. You could remain in Min Yaarif and spend the rest of your days growing indolent with the rest of us. Or return to the Zeera and wreak bloody vengeance, as I know you want to. Or grow wings and fly to the fucking moons, for all I care.

"You can do anything you want, once you have killed this one little redheaded cunt. But you will kill her, Kishah, that I promise you."

Hannei watched as Rehaza Entanye poured the black wine known as dragon's blood into a goblet of glass and raised it in mock salute. She reached for the second goblet, but the pitmistress slapped her hand away.

"Now, now," she said, laughing, and her eyes as she looked upon Hannei were filled with an emotion too terrible to name. "Think of the *baby*."

THIRTEEN

The worst part of wearing another person's bones was how much they itched.

Istaza Ani wore the face and form of a dead man as she led her stallion Talieso through the gates and into the too-crowded streets of Min Yaarif, wrinkling her nose at the smell of so many humans packed armpit to armpit. She would think a city with so many public baths would smell better, but no. Gladly would she have shed this disguise and fled the sights, sounds, and smells of civilization. More gladly still would she have ridden back into the heart of the Zeera to pick up the life she had set aside.

Had she ever thought raising the children of the prides to be a thankless task? Had she ever considered her lover Askander Ja'Sajani the biggest pain in the arse this side of the Jehannim? She would have welcomed them now—but that life was lost to her. As much as the notes of a flute were lost to the wind. Fondly recalled, but beyond all hope of recovery.

Where there is life, there is yet hope, Theotara had said to her, and more than once. That was all well and good, but the old warrior had never considered the life of a bonesinger. As long as there were bones in this world, Ani could extend her existence until it was a song without tune, a story whose original intent was buried and forgotten in the pages of time. What hope could be left to her then, when all she knew was sand, and those she had loved were gone to dust and legend?

What use was a beating heart, when the one for whom her heart beat had turned his back on her?

Human, Inna'hael chided, *you bore me*.

I bore myself, she admitted, shaking off her self-indulgent mood as Talieso might shake off dried mud. She had come to find Sulema. All roads led to Min Yaarif, and the bones had told her that the girl had ridden this way. She would give Sulema what aid she could, but from a distance. The girl would not know her now, and Ani would not burden her with the curse of forbidden magic. It was the duty of every warrior to slay a bonesinger, and Ani had no wish to force the daughter of her heart to choose between duty and love.

You do not wish to know which way her blade would fall, Inna'hael observed.

It was not a lie.

The form Ani wore did not draw a second glance, save from the vendors who lined either side of the road. A nondescript Zeerani warrior leading an old gray stallion, this was nothing new or exotic, though she might prove an easy mark for a merchant's apprentice. Indeed, a young girl approached her now, bowing and smiling and offering spiced meats on a stick, sizzling hot from the fire. The scent reached Ani's nostrils, and her stomach began to gnaw at her. When was the last time she had eaten?

She could not recall.

Smiling at the waif she reached for the pouch at her waist. It was heavy with coins and salt tablets. Several of those whose bones she had worn in Atualon had been wealthy, and her needs had been few.

A young man walked by, dark-skinned and dark-eyed, and his smile was pure mischief, reminding her strongly of a young Askander. A different hunger rose in her and she smiled back, a baring of the teeth that sent the young man scurrying away from her in alarm, as any prey will which scents a greater predator.

The worst part of wearing another person's bones was how much they hungered.

❖

She melted beneath the old woman's hands, delighted to be wearing her own shape for a change, though her own body had grown so young and strong and free of scars that Ani hardly recognized it. Her belly was full of meat and cheese and bread, her head full of usca, and she had chosen this bathhouse because the woman who gave massages was as stringy as an old goat and half as attractive, therefore unlikely to arouse a bonesinger's more dangerous hungers. Warm oil and honey poured across her skin, warm and fragrant steams rose from the hot rocks near her feet, and she was for the moment content.

"What do you do here, Meissati?" the old woman asked as she kneaded two lifetimes' worth of anger from the flesh. Her voice was gorgeous, deep and sweet, giving lie to her frail features. "The Zeeranim do not deal in flesh, so your visit is unusual. Not unwelcome, mind you—desert warriors are always welcome in my house, so clean and so courteous— but unusual."

"Mmmmmf." Ani did not open her eyes. "I am come to make sure none of the asil are being sold by outsiders." A plausible lie. The prides' horses were valued above salt or rubies, and it was forbidden for any but the Zeeranim to own one—indeed, to touch one. For certain kinds of people, this was oftentimes more of a draw than a deterrent. Warriors had made asil raids on places such as Min Yaarif, and would do so again. "Have you heard of any such a one offered by the traders?"

There came a long pause, so long that Ani found herself holding her breath in anticipation of the woman's answer. Perhaps her lie had contained more truth in it than she had known. The idea of one of these outlanders riding an asil made her blood hot.

"I have," the woman whispered, leaning close to Ani's ear. "I will tell you what none other will—perhaps, though it is not a secret. One of your horses is to be awarded to the winner of a championship pit fight, three days from now."

Ani grunted and opened her eyes. The old woman drew back, hands held up in supplication.

"I only tell you what everyone knows!"

"I will not hurt you." Ani sat up and rolled her head from side to side. *Blessed Atu, that feels good.* "You are sure the horse is asil?"

"Yes, a golden mare, and the most beautiful I have ever seen. Though your own white stallion is very pretty," she added hastily.

Guts and goatfuckery; if the prides hear of this, Min Yaarif will be overrun with screaming warriors. "Tell me about this fight."

"It will be spectacular," the old woman breathed. Despite her fear, her eyes lit with anticipation, and she smiled a near-toothless smile. "Our own champion, Kishah, is to face one of your Zeerani warriors. They say she is Zeerani, anyhow, though I rather doubt it myself. Whoever has heard of a desert barbarian with hair like the setting sun? No doubt she is some Atualonian slave, bought and trained for the pits. Still, the whole city will be there to watch the fight, and not just because of the prize. Sharmutai only lets her pet fight the most exotic battles, and only the wealthiest will be able to afford seats near the front. Rumor has it that the pirate king himself will attend, the one who talks to river serpents! I will be there myself…"

The voice went on, but Ani stopped paying attention. A Zeerani warrior with hair like the setting sun? It could be no other.

"I will go see this fight," she said. "If the mare is indeed asil, as you have said, honor demands that I bring her home. I will buy her—"

"They will not sell her to you, Meissati," the woman said. Her smile dropped, and she wrung her hands. "Neither will they allow you to attend this fight. Oh! I should not have said anything."

"Well then," Ani said, "at least tell me of this champion of yours, this... Kishah." She smiled the gentlest smile she could manage and averted her eyes so that the old woman would not see her intent. She lowered herself back to the table, indicating that the massage should continue. "If I cannot watch the fight myself, perhaps I can imagine it through your words."

A long moment passed, and then the hands returned to Ani's shoulders. The touch was hesitant now, stiff, as if the woman was ready to flee at the slightest hint of danger.

"Kishah Two-Blades," she began, "Sharmutai's champion of champions, is the fiercest and deadliest fighter to enter the pits, at least in my lifetime. They say she has no tongue. Certainly she has no pity. They say that Sharmutai feeds her the flesh of those she has killed..."

Ani made a show of relaxing, of breathing deeply and murmuring at appropriate times. She only half-listened to the older woman's stories, though, waiting for her guard to drop. She already knew what she needed to know—

I will be there myself—

And the old woman had lived a full life, after all.

The very worst part of wearing another person's bones was the price she had to pay to obtain them.

The old woman passed between the gate-guards without challenge. They knew her as a woman who had been a famous courtesan in her youth, a whoremistress in middle age, and who now supplemented her retirement hoard by selling the skills and knowledge of a lifetime, serving the human body and all its needs. Doubtless they assumed that she had been hired to soothe the hurts of some favored pit fighter, or to limber tight muscles for an oncoming fight. She nodded at the guards over her herb basket, stopping only to pet a blue-crested raptorling on a golden chain.

"Pretty girl," she said, and offered it a dried fish from her basket. The young raptor hissed softly but accepted the bribe. It was not fooled by her stolen bones but felt no real loyalty to these men who had chained it for a life of servitude, and so did not screech an alarm.

Straightening, the bonesinger-in-disguise made her slow way down a smooth-cobbled path between rows of stone and salt-brick houses, past fountains and gardens and pools filled with colored fish. The bright moonslight cast sharp shadows. Some of the houses were lit from within. From a few came the sounds of merriment, or lovemaking, or fighting. Ani had noted more than once the similarity between those last two. Other houses were dark, brooding over their inhabitants' suffering, perhaps.

There was beauty here, the kind of beauty which could be purchased with gold or salt or blood, but there was little joy. This small fortress-like estate was a home for pit fighters, and the fighting pits of Min Yaarif—though the source of dark pleasure—was the death of all hope.

This one, she thought as an especially large and well-appointed house caught her eye. It was an elegant dwelling meant to house a single fighter, not one of the long dormitory types meant for those whose blood was more cheaply spilt. Though the dwelling was silent, a warm glow of candlelight came from within. *How does Vengeance spend her free time?* Ani wondered. *Drinking? Whoring? Reading a book, perhaps?* What would she do if her life was not otherwise occupied with dealing death?

What do you *do, indeed, Bonesinger?* Inna'hael asked. He was nearby—not within the walls of Min Yaarif, but not far, either. *Mostly you spend your waking hours mewling for your lost mate like a cub cries for its mother.*

Ani stiffened at this but masked her reaction with an old woman's naturally halting walk as she started up the steps to the salt-brick mansion.

That was not necessary, she answered.

None of this is necessary, Inna'hael sent. *We should just kill all your kind and be done with it.*

"Halt!"

Ani jumped half out of the old woman's skin, and it was not an act. So preoccupied had she been with her own thoughts and the kahanna's that she had not noticed the guards as they stood in the shadows. *Foolish, foolish.* The warriors she had raised would have laughed in astonishment to see their old teacher caught out in such ignominious fashion.

"You scared me!" she accused in a tremulous voice. It was not her own, any more than this face, this body, these bones were her own.

"Where do you think you are going?" The woman stepped forward into the moonlight. She was tall, dark as the shadowmancer Aasah and his little apprentice, though there were no stars in her skin and her eyes were dark and natural-looking.

"Where does it look like I am going?" she snapped, a wealthy old woman irritated by the presence of ignorant youth. "I am come to make Kishah ready for her forthcoming fight. Unless you would like to explain to your mistress why her pet was not given the services she paid for? I am very expensive." She sniffed, tottered the last few steps up to the door, and stood staring belligerently up at the young woman.

"Let her through." A second guard, this one a man, stepped forward and touched the first guard's shoulder. "It is only old Ulseth, and she *is* expensive. Excuse this one, Meissati, she is new."

Ani sniffed. "Very well—"

"No." The young woman shook off her companion's hand and shot him a hard glare. "Not until I see what you have in your basket, Meissati."

"Teatha—"

127

"Orders from Rehaza Entanye, Kaneh. Unless you would like to explain to her and to the mistress"—here she lowered her voice—"how we let an assassin walk past us? Every visitor is to be searched. No exceptions."

Kaneh sighed, but shrugged. "You are right. Hand over the basket, Grandmother."

Ani huffed but handed them the basket. The guards removed her bottles and bundles of herbs, treating them with respect. The former youthmistress found herself grudgingly approving of young Teatha, especially as she so carefully examined each bottle and bundle, sniffing and pinching and frowning in concentration.

"This is catbane," Teatha said at one point. "It can cause the kidneys to bleed and fail."

"It can," Ani agreed, "but only when given in great quantities, and fresh. A small amount of dried leaf, such as this, can help to purify and strengthen the blood. It is also useful for forcing water from a body—"

"A trick to help a fighter make weight." Kaneh chuckled. "Are you satisfied, Teatha?"

"I suppose." Yet the warrior still eyed Ani suspiciously.

"I cannot fault you for your diligence," Ani grumbled, repacking her herbs and bottles with contrived irritation, and returning Teatha's glare with one of her own. "It is the mark of a good guard, after all. And you know your herbs. Perhaps if you tire of working for Sharmutai, you could come work for me."

Teatha nodded but did not answer. Ani covered her basket once again and waited as the guards opened the doors for her.

"Thank you," she said, then, "you may leave us. This is private business." She shut the door in their faces and turned.

She found herself standing at one end of a wide, warm room. The walls and floors were honey-colored. There were only two small windows, set high and too small to allow entry to much more than an evening breeze and a little bit of light, though the far end of the chamber was taken up by a wide hearth, in which blazed a merry fire. It was sparsely furnished, nearly bare. In the center of this room was a low wooden table surrounded by cushions, desert-style, and a single figure reclined upon these. She was hooded, brown-skinned hands turning the pages of a book.

Ani waited. Though the pit fighter did not speak— perhaps she had no tongue, after all—or so much as move to acknowledge her presence, Ani could feel heat and fury rolling from the supine form, hotter than the fire upon the hearth. And deadlier. The bonesinger was reminded of a wild vash'ai, crouched and ready for the kill.

"Your mistress hired me," Ani said at last, "to bring potions and salves which will help ready you for the champion's fight." She reached into the basket for an ordinary-looking glass bottle, full of death. Death for the champion of Min Yaarif, and more likely than not death for the guards, as well. But why stop at a few more murders when she had come so far already?

Why, indeed? Inna'hael asked softly. *When have your kind ever stopped at murder?*

As if she had heard the vash'ai, the figure sat up abruptly. The silk hood fell back, exposing her face, and Ani gasped, dropping the bottle back into her basket.

Hannei, she thought, *oh my Hannei, oh my girl, what have they done to you?*

But she could not, dared not reveal herself, not even to this girl she loved. Hannei was Kishah now, Kishah Two-Blades, whose name was vengeance. And she—

I am no one, Ani thought, reaching for a different bottle. *I am a bonesinger—my bones are no longer my own, and my life is forfeit.*

The worst part of wearing another person's bones was... everything.

FOURTEEN

The Pit of Min Yaarif was neither as grand as the newmade Sulemnium in Atualon, nor as steeped in honor and tradition as the Madraj in Aish Kalumm. This was a simple hole in the ground, with one ramp leading down, and another on the far side leading back out for any who might survive the day's entertainments. The walls were red brick, made not with red salt, she had been told, but fashioned from the mud and sweat and tears of countless slaves sent here to die.

Sulema stood at the precipice and found herself smiling. She had been unable to grasp the politics of Atualon, unable to fight the dragonstone walls of Atukos. This she understood. This she could overcome. This was her world...

"Come on, girl, what are you waiting for?" One of the slave handlers put a hand in the middle of her back and shoved. Sulema sidestepped the pressure easily, turned and grabbed the man by the front of his robes. She dragged him so near she could have bitten his nose.

"Touch me again," she growled, "and I will kill you." She gave his face a light, contemptuous slap and tossed him aside. "I am no slave," she said, glaring at the gathering crowd. "I am Ja'Akari. Touch me at your peril." She brushed the sand from her vest, straightened her spine, and took her time walking to the down ramp. The people before her parted to let her through, many of them smiling or nodding their approval.

"Good, good," Rehaza Entanye murmured, close behind her. "Give the people a show before the show, whet their appetites."

"What show?" Sulema asked, dismissing the outlander woman as casually as she had thrown the man. "If any of you touch me, you will die. I am done being civilized." Leaving them all behind she walked down the wide ramp.

It was a fine day, bright and hot under the eyes of Akari, and the path was smooth and easy, having been pounded flat and hard by the feet of those who had gone before her. Some of them had died—perhaps most of them had died— some had lived, and Sulema thought in that moment that it did not matter. In the end, all would be bones bleached in the sunlight, pounded into sand and trodden under the feet of new generations of fools come to try their luck in the game of life.

It was a fine day to die.

It was a fine day to live.

It was a fine day to be a warrior. Sulema stopped halfway down the ramp, tilted her face up to the sun, raised both arms above her head, and laughed for the sheer joy of *saghaani*, of the beauty in youth. The people who clustered thickly about the mouth of the pit, come to watch her die, raised their own voices in a ragged cheer.

"Ja'Akari!" someone shouted. "True warrior!"

"*Ehuani!*" shouted another. "*Ehuani!*"

And the crowd took up this chant.

"*Ehuani!*"

"*Ehuani!*"

"*EHUANI!*"

Though they were outlanders, doubtless ignorant of the meaning of the word, Sulema grinned and waved at them and danced to the roar of their approbation as she ran the rest of the way.

Two male slaves stood in the middle of the pit, hooded but otherwise naked. Between them they held a rack of weapons for her consideration. These were of crude make, with the pointy ends wrapped in tarred rags, as if a weapon made for killing might be dissuaded from that purpose.

Stupid. Sulema snorted. The halberds and maces she dismissed outright, and a short sword in the Atualonian style drew a scowl. There were three blunted shamsi of indifferent make—those blades had been stolen by raiders, no doubt, ground dull and pressed into slavery along with their former owners. At last she chose a blackthorn staff. It was of better make than the rest of these weapons, smooth and unadorned, capped with black iron at either end.

"This," she said. The closest slave reached out to hand it to her but shrank back at the last moment.

"Take it," he whispered hoarsely. Perhaps a slave was not allowed to touch a weapon? Sulema shrugged and seized the staff, easily pulling it free of the rack. Indeed it was of fine make, better than she had thought, light and well-balanced, with the supple strength of a master-crafted weapon.

"Thank—" she began, but the slaves were already hurrying away, dragging the weapons rack between them.

"—you," she finished, perplexed. She shrugged away their odd behavior. *Outlanders are strange*, she told herself. *I should not be surprised when they behave strangely. I wonder if they will let me keep this staff when I am finished? I will have my mare, and a weapon, and a companion who can wield shadow magic.*

Not a bad start, for someone who is supposed to be dead.

She ran one hand up and down her new staff, familiarizing herself with the feel and weight of it, and her palm encountered an irregularity in the wood. She held it closer to her face, squinting against the sunlight, and when she saw the maker's mark her fingers tightened so that the knuckles turned white.

Jinchua. The face of a fennec laughed out at her, cunningly wrought into the wood's grain, as if it had grown there and been harvested just for this day. Would she never be free of the legacy of her mother's dreamshifting magic? The only way it would be worse would be if it bore the dragon's mark of her father as well.

No. Oh, Yosh *no.*

Her heart pounding harder than it had at the thought of dying in single combat, Sulema turned the staff end for end, sliding both palms up the smooth wood. There, where a second maker's mark might be, she found—

Nothing. Oh, thank Akari. But as she thumped the butt end of the staff against the ground, a bright flash caught her eye. Pressed into the iron cap at that end of the staff was the stylized image of the sun dragon's mask in hot, angry gold.

Sulema gripped the staff in both hands, held it up to the sun, and screamed in fury. Somewhere in Jehannim, she knew, Jinchua barked with laughter.

A voice boomed across the stadium.

"GENTLE PEOPLE OF MIN YAARIF! MERCHANTS AND MURDERERS, LOVERS AND LIARS! WHORES AND PIIIIIRATES!"

Sulema jumped half out of her skin as a voice boomed behind her. She spun to see a smallish man of indeterminate age. He was wearing a hat made of dead things and speaking through some sort of shofar-looking bronze object that made his voice roar out like a wyvern's.

"YOU SEE BEFORE YOU A DAUGHTER OF THE ZEERA. BEHOLD SULEMA THE MAGNIFICENT, JA'AKARI WARRIOR AND CHAMPION OF HER PEOPLE, SCOURGE OF RAIDERS, LOVER OF MEN AND WOMEN, WHO HAS SLAIN NOT ONE, NOT TWO, BUT THREE LIONSNAKES IN SINGLE COMBAT!"

"Guts and goatf—!" Sulema exclaimed, but the crowd's roar of approval drowned out her words. The booming man ignored her protestation and went on.

"THIS BEAUTIFUL BARBARIAN PRINCESS COMES TO MIN YAARIF IN SEARCH OF SUPPLIES AND ALLIES! SHE SEEKS NEITHER RICHES NOR LOVERS, BUT ADVENTURERS TO JOIN HER ON A NOBLE QUEST TO SAVE THE PEOPLE OF QUARABALA!"

"Noble quest?" Sulema stopped even trying and stood staring at him in open-mouthed shock. Was he insane? *"Allies?"*

"Beautiful barbarian princess?"

"I just want my horse!" she shouted, but nobody was listening.

"...SO DEDICATED TO THIS CAUSE, THIS OBSES-SION, THIS NOBLE QUEST, THAT SHE HAS CONSENTED TO A FIGHT AGAINST THE NASTIEST, THE DIRTIEST, THE DEADLIEST PIT CHAMPION EVER TO PISS UPON AN EN-EMY'S HEAD."

That, Sulema thought, *does not sound promising.*

"KIND CITIZENS, ROGUES, WHORES, PICKPOCK-ETS AND SCOUNDRELS, THE LOT OF YOU, I GIVE TO YOU THE SCOURGE OF MIN YAARIF, THE SLAYER, THE PUNISHER, THE AVENGER! I GIVE YOU BLOODY VENGE-ANCE AND THE SILENCE OF THE GRAVE! I GIVE YOU..."

The crowd drew its collective breath and went still.

"KISHAAAAAAAHHHHH TWO-BLADES!"

The loud little man pointed up, and Sulema followed his gesture in time to see a dark and sinister figure, tall and hooded in funereal gray and black, appear at the lip of the fighting pit. The newcomer strode down the ramp lightly, easily, a loose-hipped fighter's stance that said *I will win today, and not you. I will live today, and not you.* The hilts of two long, straight swords rose over the figure's shoulders.

Why do I think they should wield a shamsi? The hairs on Sulema's arms stood stiff. The slim brown ankles, the way the fighter moved, these things spoke to the marrow of her bones and the blood in her heart. *Why do I feel I should call her "Sister"?*

No. No. It is impossible.

The fighter reached the pit floor and strode silent as death to face Sulema. Strong brown hands reached up and pushed the hood back, and her heart shrieked to a stop.

"Hannei," she gasped. "Hannei!"

The face of her sword-sister turned toward her, and a stranger's soul stared out from behind an enemy's eyes. She raked Sulema from sandaled feet to shorn scalp with one long glance, curled her upper lip in contempt, and spat upon the sand between them.

Sulema's heart stuttered to life again when she saw Hannei's hands curled at her sides. In hunter-sign she was speaking to Sulema.

"Go. Home. Go. Home."

Sulema held her staff between them and stared into the face she loved more than her own.

"Cannot," she answered.

Some trick of the light then made it seem as if a sheen of tears washed across Hannei's eyes, there and gone again. She shrugged out of her black robe, revealing studded and padded leather armor as fine as Sulema had ever seen. A device was worked upon the chest; a fool's mask with its mouth opened wide in a grimace of pain, blood pouring out.

Hannei spat once more upon the ground, turned her back on Sulema, and walked the required five steps from the center of the fighting pit. There she reached up over her shoulders and unsheathed both swords. Those swords of black iron, Sulema saw, did not have the dull edge of a pit fighter's weapon. She looked from the death-sharpened blades to her sister's grim expression, and she knew.

She turned her back on Hannei and took five steps, half expecting a blade through the back. This was not meant to be a fair fight, after all, but an execution.

"Well, fuck it," she muttered. "I guess it is a good day to die, after all." She tightened her grip on the staff, imagining as she did so that she could hear Jinchua's barking laugh. She turned to face her childhood friend as the small man bellowed,

"LET THE GAME BEGIN!"

135

Where are you? Their eyes met, and Sulema searched that dark gaze for some sign of her sword-sister, wondering at the angry face before her. *Who are you? Where is my Hannei?*

"*Sister,*" she signed, and wished that a hunter's signals could convey more meaning than "*goats here*" or "*lionsnake there*" or "*danger, run.*"

"*Go,*" Hannei signed one last time. "*Go home. Run home.*" She still held her two swords, but her body was stiff.

She does not want this any more than I do, Sulema realized.

"*No,*" she answered. She was—they were—both bound to this fate, as surely as she was bound by the blackthorn vines in her dreams. "*Trapped. Ehuani.*"

Hannei crushed her eyes shut, and for a moment her face contorted with grief.

Then she shook herself, opened a stranger's eyes, and flowed into a fighter's stance. Hannei held her twin blades in front of her and pointed them both at Sulema. The fingers of her left hand curled inward, toward her heart.

"*Here. No truth. Only vengeance.*"

And then her sword hand, in a final message.

"*You die.*"

They circled each other warily, paying no attention to the little man, or the bloodthirsty crowd, or the sun pounding down overhead. Sulema watched Hannei move, studied the way she held two swords lightly, easily, how her center of gravity flowed, and her face emptied of all emotion. Her former sword-sister had grown more thickly muscled since they had ridden together just this spring—

A lifetime ago, she thought, *for both of us.*

—and stepped more surely upon the pounded sand. Hannei had ever been Sulema's peer when they trained as youngsters. One would excel at archery, the other at forms, but so closely matched in skill that they were considered true sisters, heart-sisters, the very ideal of *saghaani*.

This, Sulema realized as she watched Hannei advance, could no longer be said to be truth. She had spent months recuperating, and then confined, in the soft lying outlands. Hannei, it seemed, had suffered a fate perhaps harsher than her own. The hot stare of Akari, the merciless pounding of a hard land, had forged her into a blade meant for killing.

I might have beat Hannei in a fair fight, once, she thought. *But looking at her now...*

Use me, whispered a seductive male voice, deep and sweet. The Mask of Akari stamped into the end of her staff flared bright in her mind's eye. *Sa Atu. Sing the song of death, the song of my people, and you will taste victory with your enemy's blood.*

Jinchua barked a fox's laugh. *Use me*, she insisted. *Dreamshift. Close your waking eyes, and let the dreaming mind guide your hand, and you will fashion objects of power from your enemy's bones.*

Use me, use me, use me, the sun whispered, and the sand, and the desert wind. *Let us use you.*

Sulema stopped her pacing, threw back her head, and shouted in wordless fury at the world. Hannei stopped as well, and answered with a scream so ugly and blood-choked that the assembled crowd edged back from the fighting pit. It seemed in that moment that Akari Sun Dragon himself turned his face away from them in fear, that the world went dark...

And then the two warriors raised their weapons and charged.

The song of Hannei's dark blades became quickly apparent, as did the sting of their kiss. Half a dozen small bleeding mouths, like the ones on her opponent's breastplate, opened on Sulema's arms, her thigh, her back, as she twisted and tried to find some quarter from which to attack. Like the wind Hannei came on and on, like death, implacable and relentless. It was all Sulema could do to keep from being spitted like a tarbok.

Hannei did not play, as she had when they were young just a handful of moons ago. She did not smile, or dance back from the reach of Sulema's staff any more than was needed to deflect the blows, but came at her with a bold focus that would have drawn a nod of approval from Sareta herself.

Sulema swung her staff up, deflecting one blade, and its sister snuck beneath her guard to open another, wider smile along her ribs. She hissed in pain as she spun with the blow, scattering blood upon the packed earth, and brought her weapon to bear as she had intended, striking Hannei hard one-two first on one hip, then the other. Hannei grunted and staggered back, but turned away a third blow almost contemptuously—and she kept on coming.

I stepped into this pit without first checking for vipers, Sulema thought bitterly. *Ani would be disgusted with me...*

The dark sister-swords flicked toward her face and she spun away again, and again, and again, retreating from the onslaught so that it seemed she was running in circles around the pit, backward.

There was no sign of love on Hannei's face, in her eyes. Sulema had caught glimpses of scars, terrible scars, on the back of Hannei's arms and legs, her neck. What little flesh was exposed on her back was a horror, and there was something wrong with the way she held her mouth.

What have they done to you? she asked in her heart, as Hannei looked for an opening in her guard. The black blades flicked and swayed like serpents' tongues, hungry for another taste of her blood. Sulema's staff whipped out, striking first a blade and then Hannei's shoulder in quick succession. *What have they done to us?*

Then there was no further room for thought, or pity, or love, as the women stopped retreating and moved in for the kill.

It was a fight Sulema could not win. She had known from the first flurry of strikes that Hannei had every advantage. She was better trained, in better condition, better armored and armed. The most Sulema might have hoped for was a draw, and a favorable vote from the judges.

Hannei's first sword bit deeply into her staff. The second bit into her upper arm, just beneath the spider wound, slicking away a mouthful of flesh. Sulema cried out in pain as her weapon was wrenched from her grasp. A kick she never saw hit her midsection and she went down hard, rolling as she fell while the blades licked the air behind her, savoring her pain and terror.

I do not want to die, she realized. *Not like this. Not by my sister's hand.* She raised both arms in a vain attempt to ward off the killing blow—

The wind stopped.

If you did not want to die, a voice laughed, taking the place of the wind, *you should not have brought a staff to a sword fight.*

A low hum like rocks singing rose from the ground, the air, from everything. Sulema's bones itched as the sound grew in intensity. It came in waves. Hannei's swords fell to the ground and she clapped both hands over her ears, mouth open in a wordless yell so that her face matched the mask on her bloodied breastplate.

Sulema clapped her hands over her ears as well, though it did no good at all. The sound came from the middle of the world, from the middle of her very bones. Hannei dropped to her knees and Sulema curled into a ball as agony radiated from the half-healed wound in her shoulder.

"Bonesinger!" someone screamed from far away. "Bonesinger magic!"

Impossible, Sulema thought, *the Dziranim are long gone.* She found herself curling into a tighter ball, even as a whimper was forced from her throat. *It hurts...*

Shush, the laughing voice said. *Shhhhh*. The pain eased, ebbed, flowed away, then abruptly the hum ceased. The wind picked back up, tentatively, and stroked across Sulema's shorn scalp as if a hand were brushing hair from her eyes.

Be good, now. Sulema felt—she would have sworn it, *ehuani*—lips pressing against her forehead, a hand upon her cheek.

Istaza Ani? No one else in her life had ever touched her so, not even her own mother. Yet that was absurd, an even crazier thought than the existence of a bonesinger.

Hannei collapsed in the dirt near Sulema and lay on her back, arms out to the side and fingers digging into the sand. Sulema unfurled slowly, like a blackthorn flower uncertain of the sunlight. Her staff lay a short distance from her fingertips, but Sulema found that she had no desire to pick it up and wield it against Hannei, now or ever.

Whatever lies between us, the exhausted thought came, *we are still sisters. I will not bear weapons against her again.*

Hannei turned toward her, grimaced, and looked away again. She made no move toward her swords. The sun pressed down upon Sulema, the world pressed up, and the wind danced on her sweat-slick, blood-slick skin.

Those onlookers who had chosen to remain stirred, and a few began to cry out.

"*Fight! Fight!*"

Then a new cry rose up to drown the voices calling for blood. Not the painful, roaring hum of whatever magic had overtaken them before, but the joyful voices of dragon-kin raised in greeting.

The serpents were singing. And though Yaela had not been able to hear it, to Sulema the emotion in those ancient voices was clear as sun and sand. They were happy.

But why?

"Pirate king!" someone shouted. "The pirate king is come!"

Those who were left around the entrance grew agitated, then parted to admit the cloaked figure of a man, tall and imposing. He stood silhouetted against the sun, hands on hips, regarding the two women who lay on the ground. The pirate king, Sulema guessed, come to see blood spilled upon the sand.

Let him come, she thought, rolling reluctantly to all fours, and then forcing herself to stand upright. *I will fight the pirate king instead. No longer will I fight my sword-sister for the pleasure of these outlanders.*

Hannei gained her feet as well, and together they stood looking up at the tall man as he began his descent. Sulema took a warrior's stance, disdaining the dream-cursed, dragon-cursed staff.

Let him come, she thought again. *I will die, but it will be a death of my own choosing.*

As the man reached the floor of the pit, alone, he pushed back his hood and Sulema saw that his hair blazed blood-red in the sunlight. He extended both arms toward her, laughing as she gasped in shocked recognition. He grasped her shoulders in his strong hands and gave her a resounding kiss on each cheek.

"Sister!" Leviathus called out, loudly enough for all to hear. "Well met! Well met, indeed!"

"Leviathus!" Sulema leapt into his embrace, and they half crushed one another.

The crowd above fell silent, and then erupted in riotous cheers.

Hannei held both hands up before her mouth, dark eyes gone wide. Leviathus laughed again. Sulema grabbed her brother's shoulders and held him at an arm's distance, staring up into his handsome, laughing, sunburned face. It felt like a dream, like the best dream ever.

"Leviathus," she said. "What in the name of Zula Din's tits are you doing here?"

"You have not heard?" His grin was wide and beautiful as life under the sun. "While you have been lounging about in Atukos, growing fat and lazy, I have become the pirate king of Min Yaarif."

"The world has gone mad." She swayed on her feet, wearied beyond all hope of rest. "Completely mad."

Leviathus leaned in closer, face completely serious now, and whispered into her ear,

"You have no idea."

FIFTEEN

"To set sail upon the River of Life is perilous. Ever her currents draw you in, directing your course. No matter how strong the vessel upon which you embark, eventually Life will cast you into the arms of her lover, the great sea that is Fate; there your vessel will be broken and remade until it is strong enough to brave the storm's wrath, or until it breaks apart entirely, leaving you to drown or be cast out upon strange shores..."

—From the *Song of Illindra,* by Athalia sud San Drou, as translated by Loremaster Rothfaust in the Third Age of Atualon

Leviathus ap Wyvernus ne Atu stared across the rim of a salt-crusted goblet at the crowd gathered before him, wondering at the strange shores upon which the tides of Fate had cast him.

He had been to Min Yaarif before. As the surdus son of Wyvernus ne Atu he had been his father's proxy. Knowing that his backside would never warm the Dragon Throne had not kept the would-be wielders of power from pressing their lips to it—figuratively speaking, of course, though many would have done so literally had he welcomed such attention.

Min Yaarif, being a known den of iniquity, had long been the watering hole of choice of slavers, merchants, politicians, and other persons of dubious moral value. Leviathus had even been entertained in this very hall—by a former pirate king, no less, though that had been many years ago. The food had been terrible, and the place had reeked of terrified slaves and ill-gotten wealth.

The river pirates' current leader, having been reared somewhat more gently and educated most expensively, knew that good spidersilk lanterns sent a more welcoming message to guests than, say, severed and rotting heads.

More welcoming—but no less threatening.

Magical floating lamps of spidersilk from Sindan, red salt vessels from Quarabala, dragonglass goblets and a roast of blue goat from Atualon; these things spoke of immeasurable wealth and power.

"So," he said to his sister over the drink-induced din of the gathering, "the desert slut has decided to play at being queen."

The room went altogether still.

"Why now?" he continued. "I thought you wanted no part of our father's world. Certainly when we were together in Atualon, you could speak only of being healed and returning to your warrior's life in the Zeera. What has changed?"

Hannei, sitting to Sulema's left, set her drinking horn down with a soft and ominous clack. Sulema, at whom his comment had been directed, only shook her head and smiled at him as if she could see through the bright striped silks of a river pirate, through the knives and sword of a soldier son, through the dubious honor of having been born ne Atu, all the way down to his center. In this, and in many other ways, she reminded him of her mother.

Hafsa Azeina would see me as I truly am, he thought with a fresh pang of grief, *though I hardly know myself. She would crack my dreams open like an egg and suck out the gold of my soul.*

"I would rather be a desert slut than the Dragon Queen of Atualon," she answered, speaking to him as if they were alone in the room, or as if she did not give a horse's fart what anyone else thought of her. In this, also, she was like her mother. "Certainly it would be a more honest—and cleaner—way of life. But our father is... our father is dead."

She took a hurried swallow of mead to wash the roughness from her throat.

"The Dragon King is dead," she continued, "and Pythos has taken his place—along with the dragon mask. He has the blood of my people on his hands, and he threw me in a dungeon." Sulema scowled then, and her golden eyes flashed deadly bright. "He took my horse," she added, as if saving the most grievous crime for last. "And we *still* have not been reunited!"

"You will have her back soon enough," he said. "As for Pythos's list of crimes… though I grieve the loss of my father—*our* father—his death was not unexpected. Nor was it brought about by any machinations of Pythos, but by the hand of Hafsa Azeina." He held up a hand to still Sulema's protestations. "Or by his own folly, depending on your point of view. I share your sorrow, sister, but aside from leaving you to die and rot in a dungeon, which is a thing kings are wont to do, and aside from stealing your fine horse, it seems as if Pythos's only crime was to survive our father's attempts on his life, when we were all very young.

"Moreover, he is trained to wield atulfah, and you are not—as yet. Our father Wyvernus was a usurper, as he wrested the throne from Serpentus, Pythos's father. Is it not appropriate that Pythos be left to rule in Atukos, and to use the Mask of Akari to bind Sajani in her endless slumber? You could finish the task which has brought you to Min Yaarif and return to live out your days among the Zeeranim.

"Surely you would not trade the life of a warrior under the sun for the dark path of vengeance?" he concluded.

Hannei picked her goblet up and brought it down hard on the table again. She made a series of hand gestures which looked quite rude, and which caused Sulema to laugh.

"Yes," she agreed, "he did inherit our father's endless love of speech." She turned. "Leviathus, if only you were echovete, *you* could be king in Atualon—and talk the dragon to sleep—

and *I* could go back to riding my horse and hunting. I do not wish vengeance for its own sake, and neither do I particularly desire to be the Dragon Queen. Queens do not drink usca, or play aklashi, and they spend their days surrounded by windy old men who smell of cheese." Sulema wrinkled her freckled nose, and it made her look years younger.

I wish we had grown up together, he thought. *I wish we might do so now.* But he was no longer free to choose his own path. He had never been free: born the son of Ka Atu, he now sat in this hall as king-elect of the river pirates, chosen to represent their interests among the land-loving merchants and leaders of Min Yaarif. He had been chosen by the sea serpents as well, and they spoke to him even as vash'ai spoke to their bonded warriors. None of these were honors to which he had aspired or even earned, though he did his best to live up to them.

As does she, he realized. *My sister, in truth.*

"If you do not seek the Dragon Throne out of vengeance, or a desire to rule," he asked, "why, then, seek it at all?"

Sulema shifted in her seat, looking uncomfortable, though that might have been from the cuts and bruises she bore. She and Hannei had beaten the juice out of each other, to be sure.

"You cannot hear it, can you?" she asked in a soft voice. "None of you can hear it. Sajani is rousing—that is the reason behind these recent earthquakes, mild though they have been. I believe that is the reason the mymyc attacked us, and probably the reason that the sea serpents have decided to speak to you, when so far as we know they have never spoken to any human. Istaza Ani once told me that such odd things happened before, when the sun dragon's attempts to wake Sajani—and the magic of Kal ne Mur as he attempted to bind her in sleep—sundered our world. The song of Sajani grows in strength, as does the song of Akari. They seek each other, and I fear she will wake this time.

We here, all of us, *everything*"—Sulema lifted both hands, palms up—"we are nothing more than a dream to Sajani. She will wake and break free from this world so that she can join her lover. Then none of this will matter; not you, not me, not vengeance. There will be no horses, no usca, no brothers." She looked at Hannei. "No sisters. Nothing."

As she spoke, Leviathus thought he understood. "Pythos is echovete, and was trained by his father. Surely he…"

"Pythos has the Mask of Akari, yes, and he is trained to use atulfah. He could continue the work of the Dragon Kings and keep Sajani asleep, I think, if he so chose. But I think, I feel…" She closed her eyes and frowned, as if listening to the discordant notes of a far-off song. "That is not his intent. I can hear the song of Ka Atu, I can feel the dream of Sajani, and they are… wrong." When she opened her eyes again, they were dark with worry. "I do not think Pythos is singing Sajani to sleep, as our father was. His song is different. I think Pythos is trying to *wake* the dragon."

"Why would he do such a thing?" a woman in the crowd said, speaking unexpectedly. "The Dragon Kings have always mucked about with our lives, but why end the world? Surely he must know that it would mean his death as well." It was the whoremistress Sharmutai, whose hatred of the Dragon Kings was one of Min Yaarif's worst-kept secrets. Sulema looked at the woman, curled her lip as a cat might if it had smelled something particularly vile, and directed her answer to Leviathus.

"I do not know. Outlander ways are strange, but this makes no sense to me, either. Perhaps he thinks somehow to survive Sajani's waking… or perhaps he is mad." She bit her lip and scowled. "I suppose 'why' does not matter, so much as the knowledge that we *must* stop him. If we do not, we are all dead, and our petty quarrels mean nothing."

"You wish to dethrone Pythos out of the pureness of your heart, then, and not for love of power, or vengeance?" The whoremistress did not conceal her disbelief. "The ne Atu are not known for their honor."

"I am ne Atu." Sulema smiled a grim little smile. It had taken no less than the imminent end of the world to break through her stubbornness and wrest this admission from her. "But I am Ja'Akari as well. I will do as I must, as honor demands. I will go to Quarabala and retrieve the child for Yaela, as promised, and I will retrieve the Mask of Sajani of which she has spoken, so that I might throw down Pythos and sing Sajani to sleep, because no one else can." She sighed, picked up her goblet, found it empty, and sighed again. "Because it is my duty."

Hannei touched Sulema's shoulder and made a sign. Sulema nodded.

"Yes," she agreed. "*Mutaani*. There is beauty in an honorable death. I will do this, or I will die trying."

My sister, thought Leviathus, though his throat was so tight the words would not form, *refused to be named champion of her people, and will now become champion of the world.*

"I will help you, as I can," Yaela spoke up. The shadowmancer's apprentice sat in a far corner of the room, wreathed in shadow and mystery and her own impossible beauty, and Leviathus—as usual—tried his best not to stare at her.

Yaela is beyond you, he reminded himself. *Especially since Mariza—*

He drowned the thought with spiced rum, refilled his goblet, and raised it toward his sister. "If, as you say, Sajani is truly waking, and if Pythos is doing nothing to stop her—or, worse, if he is actively trying to rouse her—then, Sulema an Wyvernus ne Atu, sister of my heart, would-be queen of Atualon, you have my support." He waved his hand to sweep the room. "Mine and that of my people... pending a vote, of course."

Sulema froze with her refilled goblet half raised to her lips.

"Vote?"

"I am a king, to be sure," he said. "But I am not a Dragon King. I am a king of pirates, and we are a *civilized* folk."

The hall erupted in cheers and laughter loud enough to wake the dead.

Loud enough to wake a dragon.

Yet not nearly loud enough to wake his stone-dead heart.

"The king is dead. Long live the king."

Mahmouta came to stand beside him. Leviathus did not turn his face from the river, so beautiful in the light of the dying sun, silver and gold and pearl. Azhorus the serpent was stirring beneath the water—he preferred to sleep in the dark and deep during the hottest hours of day, and to hunt and sing under the moons.

Even in his half-slumber, their bond heightened Leviathus's senses to a near painful edge. He could hear a lizard's belly scraping across the sand half a league away, he could taste the dying breath of a man murdered in a dark alley, he could smell blood that had not yet been spilled.

"Long live the king, indeed." He laughed, despite the chill in his bones and the foreboding in his heart, despite the trembling awkward state that Yaela's presence always incited, despite the lateness and strangeness of the hour. He laughed despite everything, and because of it, and because there was no king of pirates once they left land for the sweet, clear truth of water. It was a joke older than Atualon, and perhaps the only true secret ever to be held in Min Yaarif.

Mahmouta, whom the world thought had been queen of pirates before Leviathus came along, took his hand and squeezed. He would not consent to be her twenty-first husband, but their friendship ran deep as the swift Dibris.

"Is it true?" she asked. "What the girl says about Sajani?"

"Yes," he told her, "it is true." He did not have to wait for Azhorus to wake. Now that he knew what name to put to it, Leviathus could hear the song of Sajani as she rose up from the sea of dreams. It was a beautiful song, lovely as life, dark as the void between stars. Now that he knew its source, Leviathus found the song terrifying as the end of all stories.

She let out a long breath. "Can you not wield the Mask of Akari yourself?"

"No. Neither can anyone else, to my knowledge. There were always whispers that Pythos had sired a child upon this or that concubine of Serpentus, and occasionally a rumor that a child might be able to wield atulfah. I have always made a point of tracking such stories down, and that is all any of them ever proved to be. Stories. If Sulema's suspicions are right—if Pythos is trying to wake Sajani—Sulema is our only real hope."

"It will not break your heart," she pointed out, "to have a valid excuse to revenge yourself upon the usurper of your father's throne."

"It will not," he admitted, "though Pythos might no doubt say the same. Had Wyvernus not overthrown Serpentus, perhaps we would not be facing such perilous times as these. Which of us has the right of it, do you suppose?"

"There is no right. There is no wrong. We are pirates, remember? Right and wrong are beyond the likes of us." She squeezed his hand again. "In a pirate's life there is only power… and profit."

Leviathus squeezed back, glad for the comforting strength of her grip, wishing that she were strong enough to pull him from the depth of his despair. Not even Azhorus had been able to do that, and the serpent loved him more deeply than the stars were high.

"I suppose you are right," he agreed. "And I suppose you are here to tell me that we must help my sister save us all."

"Of course I am," she said, "and of course we must." Her hand was warm in the swiftly cooling air. "There is no profit to be made in a dead world."

SIXTEEN

He had hoped it would be easy to slip back into the world of men, as easy as slipping into an old robe. It seemed as if he should be able to just shrug his shoulders and feel the world settle around him again, light and comfortable as wormsilk and as easily forgotten.

Yet as he rode with an entourage toward Sindan, Jian found himself shaking his head at his own naivety. It was not for the first time, he realized... and probably not for the last time, either.

Jian had accepted the emperor's offer, false though it might be. In truth, though he had made a show of conferring with his father and weighing every consideration, he had made up his mind well before Mardoni's lips had stopped moving. Though his campaign against the emperor's might had provided great satisfaction, the dark pearl Jian had long clutched to his heart had been a desire to return to the world of men, wreak vengeance for the deaths of his family, and to topple the rulers of Sindan.

When those he loved were returned to him, as if fetched from the Lonely Road, the shock had served to enflame his desire to end a reign which kept an entire population bound in servitude, where daeborn children such as he were sacrificed to the emperor's war machine. If those in power thought they could avert the wrath of the sea-bear prince, they were deeply mistaken.

Jian had every intention of delivering the empire to his father. It was, he had decided, a dream worth dying for.

He was dressed in sea-silks and silver. A circlet of silver set with moonstones and mother-of-pearl graced his brow, and at his waist he wore the sword his father had given him, the blade of bitter tears. The hilt was chased in silver and bound with sharkskin, the tang was red steel and the blade had been fashioned from sky-iron which had fallen into the ocean long ago. It shone like moonslight on dark water, rippling and changing in the light of day. Jian could hear it whispering to him of long songs and deep water. It wanted war, this blade; the world that had birthed the sky-iron must have been a warlike place, torn asunder when its own dragon had woken.

This blade loved nothing more than the dance of death.

Soon enough, Jian thought, *but not today.*

Riding beneath the baleful eye of Akari, he blinked in the harsh light and grimaced at the jolting walk of the four-legged horse he was forced to endure. He missed his sleek and smooth-gaited palantallomir, the misted skies, the cool air of the Twilight Lands. Even the halfbreed Daechen looked too alike here, a sharp and dreary contrast to the varied faces and forms of those who comprised the Twilight Court.

Still, he would not have traded this moment in time for any other. Tsali'gei rested in the carriage that jolted down the road ahead of him, with their son at her side. He would endure anything the world might offer, for their sakes.

He would end the world, for their sakes.

"Tell me, de Allyr," a soft voice sang at his side, "about the world of our mothers and fathers. Tell me about the Twilight Lands."

Jian turned his head fractionally to smile at Giella. She was as beautiful as he had remembered—more, for being real—fierce and intense as her mother.

"*Wei xun yu*," he said, "the Twilight Lands. What have you heard of them?"

"Only the stuff of children's tales," she replied wistfully. "Talking bears and eight-legged horses. People with antlers and horns and feathers." She touched the spray of bright red feathers at her own temple. "Others who can shift their shapes to become animals. Never-ending hunts, never-ending feasts. Poems that were begun before the first human took her first breath, and which have not yet reached their endings." Her smile was a little self-mocking. "As I said, the stuff of children's tales."

"All of it is true," he said to her in a voice hardly more than a murmur, moving his four-legged horse closer to hers for privacy. "And more. More. It is so beautiful it will break your heart. There are rivers of mist so thick you can swim in them, so wide you cannot see the far shores. Music so deep it pierces rock and bone. Colors too fierce to name, and the stars..." His voice trailed off, and he dashed a sleeve across wet eyes.

"The stars?"

"When this is over, I will bring you home with me," he told her in answer, "with me and Tsali'gei. Then you will see for yourself. Your place is there, not here"—he indicated the land around them—"in the world of men. Your mother waits for you. In your absence, she has amassed an arsenal of weapons for you." He grinned. "She is *sha-rai*, you know, a warrior of great renown. When all this is over, we will all go home. You will always be welcome in our house."

"Your house," the White Nightingale murmured, glancing at the carriage. "Of course." Eyes sharpening, she leaned across her saddle and whispered, "When all this is over? What do you mean?"

Jian regretted saying even that much. "Oh, you know," he said, "my time as the emperor's general. Surely he cannot mean for me to remain in the Forbidden City forever." His eyes told her a different story, however, a deeper truth.

When all this is ours, he thought fiercely, *and our two lands made one.*

Giella smiled a sharp smile, a raptor's smile—her mother's smile. Satisfied, she leaned back into her saddle and nodded.

"Of course," she agreed. "I look forward to it."

They arrived on foot at the Gate of the Iron Fist as the sun was setting—a fitting omen, Jian thought with a grim smile. The city was smaller and less grand than his memory had made it, the Wall of Swords more tawdry than impressive, the waters of the moat clogged with offal. He stared up at the faces of the two giant warriors and frowned.

"Do they look different to you?" he asked Tsali'gei.

"No, why?" She looked up from the small, fussing bundle she held clutched to her breast, and frowned. "They are stone. How can they be different?"

Jian averted his gaze from the monumental warriors, lest his interest draw scrutiny. "Never mind," he told her. "My memory must be playing tricks on me. You have seen them every day, after all, while for me it has been years."

"I still do not understand how it is that years pass in the Twilight Lands, while here it has only been a few months since you left. I suppose I should be grateful that you remembered us at all—ow!" She yelped, turning her attention back to the babe. "He bit me! Little beast! I do not look forward to his first teeth."

Her delighted face was the most beautiful thing Jian had ever seen, and the music of her laugh sweeter than the most ancient of poems.

"Remember you?" he said under his breath, too softly for even Tsali'gei's sharp ears to catch. "Not a day went by that I did not mourn you, my love. Not a day went by that I did not burn to avenge your death. I returned to your grave, only to find you alive and well. What would I not do to keep you so?"

They passed through the gates beneath the stone giants. His memory was true; they had changed. The golden one stood with his arm upraised in victory. The red giant, however, though he still knelt bareheaded upon the grass, no longer had tears upon his face, and his eyes were fixed upon the face of his enemy. The fallen warrior bided his time, Jian knew, waiting for the moment to rise up and strike the other down.

As he walked down the Path of Righteousness, Jian trod again upon the skulls of the fallen, and found that it no longer bothered him. They had had their chance, after all, the defeated ones. Their attempts to challenge Daeshen Tiachu, the White Bull of Khanbul, had left only swords and skulls to crumble into dust.

It is my time now, he told the restless spirits who resided there. *I am Tsun-ju Jian de Allyr, son of Tsun-ju Tiungpei and Allyr de Devranallenai. I will succeed where you have failed.* He glanced back, and in the light of the dying day it seemed as if the red stone giant peered at him... and smiled.

SEVENTEEN

Counselors were wise and learned—every child in Quarabala was taught this. Warriors were brave and strong. Illindrists were elevated, all-seeing, and queens—
Queens were infallible.

The line of Kentakuyan had been sent to Sajani Earth Dragon as a dream and breathed to life through her by the First Woman, Zula Din, she who was the huntress, the trickster, the lover, and the mother all at once. Skin dark as the night sky between stars, she was so closely bound to the web that it was not uncommon for the children, especially girl children, to be born with eyes of Pelang. Eyes which could see the world as it was, as it had been, as it might yet be. No girl born with the cursed gift could ever be queen, of course—to bind heavens and earth in such a manner was to invite the dragon's waking. It was a mark of Illindra's favor, nevertheless.

These things were set in the bones of the people, these truths, these songs and stories of knowing. Deeper than words engraved in rock—for rock could be shattered—this knowledge had been a truth known to Maika before she learned to speak her own name.

Counselors were wise.
Warriors were strong.
Queens were infallible.

Why, then, had her counselors not known this would happen? Why had her warriors not been able to stop the murder of her people? Why—
Why—
Why have I failed my people?

Maika sat upon the dusty ground that served as her throne now, paying little mind to the words swirling about her head like storm dust, or the sad travelers' fare that had been set forth to tempt her appetite. How could she eat, when Amalua could not? How might she enjoy even the thin comforts of manna water and dried meat, when children—her children, her responsibility, her failure—lay dead and bloating among the sung bones of heroes?

The pain was beyond understanding.

Why have I failed my people?

"We have no hope now of reaching the greenlands if we all journey together," Counselorwoman Lehaila said. Her face was properly grave, her words measured as she tried yet again to condemn Maika's people to death. "With the loss of Su'umara, we have left to us no more than three shadowmancers and six apprentices, one of whom is little more than a child. With rest, these shadowmancers would be able to protect a few of us against the heat of the Seared Lands just long enough for us to make it to the Jehannim, if we move with extreme haste.

"We must carry only that which we need," she continued, "and—though it grieves my heart to say it—leave behind those who cannot hope to keep the pace. Perhaps, once we reach the cool green lands, we might send back help."

That elicited a cry of outrage from many of those assembled.

Many—but not all. Maika was shocked and disheartened to note that too many of the Quarabalese were willing to listen to Lehaila's cold words.

"Perhaps the Araids will see fit to grant us mercy, rather than the long, slow death of a reaver's venom," Akamaia said in a voice that was nearly a shout. "You say your heart is grieved, but would you so easily abandon our elders, our children? Would you so easily abandon me, old friend? You say, 'once we reach the cool green lands,' but by 'we' you mean 'I.'"

Counselorwoman Lehaila stiffened her spine, face darkening with embarrassment, and she could not meet Akamaia's eyes.

"If we are to save any small part of Quarabala," she protested, "sacrifices will need to be made—"

"Oh, but *we* will be making those sacrifices, will we not? Not you. What are you willing to sacrifice, Counselorwoman? One of your husbands? A daughter, perhaps? Surely Puanale is too young to—"

"*Enough.*" Maika slapped her hands on the dusty ground and stood. Had her hands been bigger, or her legs longer, it might have felt more impressive, but it was all she had to work with.

"Your Magnificence—" Lehaila began.

"*Mana'ule o ka enna i ka pau,*" Maika intoned with power, channeling her impotent fury into the words. "*Paleha ia'u, e pau ia'u!* I am finished listening to your traitorous words, all of them. We will not abandon the least of my people to these foul sorcerers or their spider-masters. We will not, not as long as I am queen, not as long as I breathe. By the ancestors, by the blood in my veins, I swear it!"

The stone around them rang with the sincerity of her words, and the counselors fell silent. For a common woman to swear upon the ancestors was sacrosanct. For a queen—

"I am finished," Maika said, controlling her breath as Aasah himself had taught her, so that the words were calm and even. A storm of fire and shadows raged in her soul, but she was a queen—curse the ancestors for it—and the least she could do was pretend to be infallible. "Return to your duties. Tend my people. Tend them as carefully as you would your own families. We will leave here together, or we will die here together."

Turning on her heel Maika left them to stare after her. Her heart fluttered like a caged beast, eyes burned with tears that she could not, *would not* shed.

Ancestors hear me, she prayed, and the words seared into her very bones. *Help me find a way to save my people, and I will pay any price you ask. Any price at all.*

From the halls of her ancestors, buried deep in the shadows of memories in her blood, she imagined that she heard a reply:

If you wish to find the way, child, a cold, dark voice whispered, *you must first learn to see.*

EIGHTEEN

The world of the living had long ago shunned and forgotten Kal ne Mur. He wore the body of a young man clothed in the ancient armor of a dead king. The dead were his only companions, and his mouth full of dust.

"War is what we do," he had told Ibna, and this was true. There would always be war, and those too foolish to cease fighting. *When all roads lead to war*, he thought, stepping out onto the burning sands of the Zeera, *one might as well go down fighting*. His horde of ungrateful dead had lost their taste for war—*ehuani*, perhaps he had as well—but when the heart has gone to char and grave ash, its song is easily silenced.

He sang as he walked, though it pained his borrowed burnt lungs and cracked lips. This voice was still so ill-fit, the throat untrained. A song of fire and poetry, of life and lust, of blood and mead. The dead came shuffling behind him, drawn by his song and their foolish vows. The sad truth was that they had nothing better to do than wage war and kill and die.

And die.

And die.

Ismai, whose body this was, would have set Ibna free from his vows that he might create beautiful things. Yet such a kindness might doom them all, and so Kal ne Mur bound his undying legions with the song of ages past. With his ka he found them, with his sa he bound them, with atulfah he bade them obey.

Those who had sworn to him in life came as women and men, warriors and wardens, soldiers and runners. As they drew near to their king, they grew ever more lifelike in appearance and manner so that if one did not look too closely—especially at the eyes—they might be mistaken for living people, though curiously dressed.

Those who had not sworn to him in life answered to him in death, as well, and theirs was a less perfect union. They came to him as a penitent comes to punishment, groaning in pain and fear as their souls were dragged back from the Lonely Road and stuffed into bodies that had long forgotten them. Milk-dead eyes glowed a sullen red, in those faces as had eyes at all. In the others, empty sockets blazed like the fires of Yosh, and bones whispered together of vengeance in the thin night air. Kal ne Mur gazed upon the dead without regret or pity and urged Ismai within to do the same.

We are one, he told the boy whose life he had stolen. *Your body is too damaged to live without my power, and I cannot be free without this living flesh. It will be easier for us to do what must be done if we work together.* In truth, the boy might still cast him out of the body they now shared, to the detriment of them both. *See, I have brought you an old friend to be a comfort in these dark times…*

The boy's eyes caught sight of her, staggering among the throngs of wailing dead, and his spirit thrashed so that it was nearly wrenched from the Lich King's grasp.

"Ehuani," he gasped, and it hurt everywhere. "Ehuani."

She came to him, his beloved, his beauty in truth, stumbling and struggling and blind. Her eyes had been pecked out, her face was shrunken tight against her skull, and her hide burned away in patches where the snake-priestess's venom had struck. Her left shoulder was stained red with the blood that Hadid had spilt to free him.

Hadid died to free me, Ismai thought, *and Ehuani died to bring me here.* Pain swelled his heart; it overflowed and watered the gardens of hatred, of anger and fury. *Now it is the Mah'zula's turn to die.*

In this we are agreed, Kal ne Mur whispered from the dark wells of his heart. *They have slain your family, your friends—they have slain your very world. Indeed, they have slain you, for would you not die, were I to do as you wish and depart this body? Is this not enough? Will you not join me now and repay those who have wronged you, a hundred times over?*

The flames of hatred leapt in Ismai's heart, fanned by the Lich King's bloodlust, and then fell away to ash. He had never been a killer. *Leave me alone*, he thought miserably. He reached out to touch Ehuani's shoulder, the dull gray hide which had once shone like molten silver and pulsed with life. She stood still at his touch, dead and still and uncaring, and all the emptiness of nothing pooled in her eyes.

If I leave you, you die, the Lich King said.

So I die. There are worse things than death.

There are better things than death, too, young warden. The chance to save a friend... Jasin yet lives, does he not? And Hannei? And... Sulema?

Sulema.

Ismai shook his head. "They are beyond my help," he said aloud, "certainly beyond my reach."

Perhaps. Perhaps not. Perhaps they have all perished, in which case there is the sweetest fruit of all. When the tree of life has withered and all hope is lost, there is yet one black fruit of which you may eat, and that is... kishah.

Vengeance.

Kishah, Ismai thought, tasting that ancient and fell word for the first time. *Kishah.* It was a bitter conceit, and yet Ismai realized he had never tasted anything sweeter.

What say you, beautiful youth? Will you cast me out and die, or will you take up my sword and use it to strike down our enemies?

Kishah.

The dead turned their incurious faces toward him as if they, too, awaited his decision. A stray breeze played through

Ehuani's lank and knotted mane, stirring it—though not to life. Never again to life.

"My beauty," he said to her, and his voice broke. "My beauty in truth. My friend. My friend." He pressed his face into her cold and stinking neck, wishing that he had eyes left that could cry, for surely she had been worth a river of tears. He pressed the flat of the Lich King's sword against her shoulder—he had drawn it, unthinking. And yet—

"Yes," he said, and his whole being flooded with relief as he let go his reluctance to do harm. It was right, it was good. He pressed a kiss into Ehuani's mane and turned his head to press another against the heartless steel. Sharp as pain the blade was, after all these years, and by this he knew that the pain of loss would never dull.

"Yes," he said again, and "yes" a third time, as the Lich King rose within him, filling him like blood, like sweet water, like passion. Ehuani quickened beneath his hands, for she had in her way been sworn to him. Her dull silver hide turned to right shadow, to soot, to obsidian; she shone like a star without a heart. She tossed her head, eyes glowing a dull red as she struck the sand with a sharp hoof, impatient to be off.

Ismai took a half-step back and the song of atulfah caught in his throat at the sight of her. She was sleek as a dream, deep-chested as the west wind, and her eyes were stars, cold and distant and bright. Her hide shone like water over black rocks, save her left shoulder upon which Hadid had died, and which was stained a deep and abiding red. So beautiful, his Ehuani—

"No," he said to her. "No. There is no beauty in truth, only in death. I name you Mutaani."

Mutaani reared at the sound of her name, screaming, and the dead flinched back.

"Yes, my lovely girl," the Lich King said to his dark mare. "Let us ride, let us ride now to the land of our enemies, these false Mah'zula, and bend them to our will." He leapt onto her back and laughed as she reared again. "To the pridelands!" he shouted to his fell host, sheathing his sword and digging heels into Mutaani's sides. "To vengeance!"

From ten thousand throats came a cry, hungry and despairing.

"VENGEANCE!"

They flowed across the desert beneath the cold eyes of the moon, as a shadow within a shadow within a dream.

The wind was born of an undead king, and it had a name.

Kishah.

NINETEEN

"Ai, lovely girl!" she said. "Ai, my bright love."

Sulema stood at Atemi's shoulder, one arm draped across her mare's withers. As she had since she was a gangly child of eleven, she pressed her nose against her horse's neck and dried unwanted tears in the coarse mane. Atemi made silly faces, twisting her soft nose this way and that, exposing her gums, and generally giving lie to the dignified nature of asil horses.

Finally letting go, Sulema inspected her mare. Atemi's hooves needed trimming by someone who knew what to do with the bottom half of a horse. She needed to lose weight, and some goat-assed outlander had chopped her forelock short.

The important thing, however, was that they were together again. Atemi had forgiven her for taking them so far from home and showed little sign that she was bothered at all by their recent adventures. It was more than Sulema could say of herself. Her shoulder ached, itching and burning, and her ears rang with the constant presence of the dragon's song. She had been trained to hear the song, but not to control it, and she could not shut it out of her head.

Her heart hurt, as well, and with this reunion her emotions threatened to overwhelm her. In a short space of time she had gained and lost a father, lost her mother, and watched friends die. Because of her. *All* because of her. She had never asked for this thing, but there was no escaping the truth that if she had never abandoned her people for Atualon, lives that had been shattered would still be whole.

Her world would still be whole.

Sulema worked her hand into a pouch tied at her waist until her fingers found and tightened on the rose-rock sandstone globe. When she was not holding the globe, it seemed to her that it might be lost. When she was holding it, she was plagued with fear of dropping the thing. She drew the globe forth and breathed a shaky sigh of relief. If changes in the world showed as physical changes in the stone, as Ka Atu had taught her, how could she be sure that damage to the stone would not likewise influence the world? She had no father to ask and would not care to find out by destroying some far-off country with her clumsiness. She had ruined enough lives already.

Hannei.

Saskia.

Daru.

Mother...

It was a litany of guilt played over and over in her mind, a dirge sung in counterpart to the constant hum of atulfah, the relentless drumming of her heart, an endless canticle of wishing herself back into a life that was gone, long gone.

All because of me.

It seemed then that the wind spoke with the voice of her old youthmistress. Dear Ani, lost like Daru or dead like her mother no doubt, because she had been too foolish to stay with her sisters and live an ordinary life.

Such power you claim, to have unleashed massive destruction upon the world. In that moment the voice of Ani mocked, both gentle and sharp. *And so much of it while you slept. For one so mighty, you seem to be spending much of your time wallowing in self-pity.*

Sulema straightened, wiping her face and looking around. Surely that voice was a shadow in her mind only. Istaza Ani was gone.

She is right, though, Sulema thought to herself. *Even though she may walk the Lonely Road, Istaza Ani shows me the way.* For a moment, standing beside the river with her father's sorcerous globe, her good mare, and a heart full of ghosts, Sulema felt less alone in the world.

Perhaps Ani is not dead, she mused. *Leviathus said that she was alive, last time he saw her, in the company of those false Mah'zula.* She brushed away the rage that swept over her at the thought of how her brother had been abused by those false warriors. Then she peered at the globe. *I wonder... could this be used to find a person? To see things as they are happening? Perhaps I might see how the people fare. I might find Ani... or Daru.*

Sulema used both hands to bring the globe close to her face. It was dusty from long travel, so she blew upon it, and it seemed to her that the Zeera glowed faint gold in answer. She held the globe so close and stared so hard her eyes crossed and hurt a little.

Probably wishful thinking, she decided at last. *I long to go home, so—*

But no, this close she could see that there *had* been changes. Parts of the Zeera, where she had blown away the dust, indeed gleamed in the rising light of dawn. Other parts, especially at the junction of the Dibris where lay Aish Kalumm, seemed to lie in shadow. Sections of the globe also seemed troubled. The Valley of Death emitted a faint, ugly light, and even—she sniffed—a whiff of corruption.

A strange dull haze lay over the far-off country of Sindan. Sulema touched it, and marveled that her fingertips felt cold and wet, as if they had been thrust into a mist. These things, combined with Leviathus's description of the Mah'zula, gave her a pang of disquiet. If she left now for Quarabala, would she be turning her back on the people when they most needed a warrior?

If I do not, I am turning my back on a vow, she thought. *How, then, could I ever again call myself Ja'Akari? Can a warrior who is no warrior serve her people?*

A dull headache began to pound between her eyes, in time to the world's endless insistence that she be this, do that, come here, go there. Sulema wished she might leap onto Atemi's back and ride... but where, exactly? Which path might lead her to peace, when the whole world seemed to have gone mad?

The only peaceful road is the Lonely Road, and I am not yet ready to die.

Then live, Ani's imagined voice replied. *Do what needs to be done and stop whining.*

Sulema snorted a laugh. If Ani was, indeed, dead, perhaps this was the youthmistress's spirit, showing her no mercy. And Ani or no, the voice was right. She might as well pull up her warrior's trousers and get on with it. There would be no peace for her until she did so.

Sulema gave the globe a final longing glance. *Ehuani*, there would be no peace for her anywhere until she had fulfilled her duty. A true warrior could not simply set aside the burden of her obligation—not until she had breathed her last. Probably not even then.

I wanted to be a warrior more than anything else.

And do you still? the youthmistress asked in her imagination. *Knowing more of life, understanding the weight of duty, do you still choose the way of Ja'Akari?*

Yes, Sulema realized, *I do. I would not choose another road, truly, even if it were the path to peace and ease for myself.*

Now, my girl, Ani's voice came, fading but full of pride, *you are truly a warrior.*

Though she knew it was but the faded ghost of memories, Sulema smiled for the first time in a long while. She tucked the globe carefully back into its pouch and gathered up Atemi's lead. Her mare came away from the sparse river grass with no show of reluctance. Indeed, her ears pricked forward, and her huge soft eyes shone with eagerness.

"Are you ready for a new journey?" Sulema asked, and she grinned at Atemi's answering snort as the golden mare danced in place, eager to be moving. "We will be riding over mountains thick with wyverns and mymyc and worse, and then straight into the Seared Lands themselves. Yet you do not care which road we take, do you, my love? As long as there is adventure at either end, and danger in the middle. So bold, my sweet girl. So beautiful." Sulema kissed Atemi's nose and thought she could do worse than emulate her horse.

She will ride into danger and never look back.
I will do no less.

TWENTY

*N*ow, *my girl*, she whispered to Sulema, *you are truly a warrior.*

Ani watched with her mind's eye as the daughter of her heart shook her head and smiled, no doubt believing that the voice in her head was nothing more than a memory. Nevertheless the seed was planted. How many times had she given one of her girls such a gentle nudge? How many times had she advised Hafsa Azeina thus, with a rough-edged tongue and a too-soft heart?

As many times as there are stars in the sky, she thought, *as many times as there are worlds in Illindra's web.* She liked to believe that not all her advice had fallen on deaf ears, that not all of her tears had been shed in vain.

Letting the vision fade away she grimaced at the pain. Her skull felt as if there were a dragon inside it, trying to get out. *I wonder if the world hurts like this*, she thought, *as Sajani fights to wake?*

The ground beneath her feet rumbled in answer as an aftershock sent small pebbles tumbling.

A cool breeze rose from the river and caressed her sweat-beaded forehead, played with her hair. She sank to her knees and then twisted to sit cross-legged upon the river's edge, listening to the song of the Dibris. How like the Lonely Road it must be, going on and on, ever changing, never resting, never returning to the lands or lives it once had touched.

A soft whicker sounded behind her, and she was shoved half over as Talieso nudged her shoulder.

"You know me, eh, my love?" she said, reaching up to stroke his silk-soft muzzle. "True friend. Though I hardly know myself, these days." It was true. The hand that reached up to touch her horse was a stranger's hand, the dark braids whipping into her face were glossy-black without the slightest hint of her hard-earned gray. Gone were her scars, marks of struggle and honor. Gone were the laugh lines and frown lines given to her by her many students.

Just as Askander was gone...

For one so mighty, you seem to be spending much of your time wallowing in self-pity.

You throw my words back at me? she growled at Inna'hael.

I mirror your truth, just as the Web of Illindra shows all truths, the feline answered, unperturbed, *even those truths which are lies we tell ourselves.*

You speak in riddles, she told him. *You would have gotten along very well with Hafsa Azeina.* The memory of her lost friend brought tears unbidden to her stranger's eyes, and she dashed them away with the back of one hand.

The dreamshifter and I were... acquainted, he said in an odd tone. *And I am not wrong.*

Are you ever wrong? she asked. There was a long silence, and at last he answered in a voice as strange and sad as any she had heard.

Yes. Yes, I have been very wrong... but not in your life-time, little huntress. The grief in his words echoed the grief in her heart, so she did not press. Besides, there was work yet to be done.

The girls' fight in the pit had passed without either of them killing the other, thanks in some small part to her meddling in their skulls, but in every future the bones whispered to her that one would kill the other. Some fates were preordained, her father had insisted, fixed as stars in the night sky.

She would have none of that. She had never believed, as a good Dzirani might, that there were songs written into a person's bones which could not be unsung. Ani was as stubborn as the desert is hot, as Askander was fond of saying,

172

and not even bones were immutable to a bonesinger. Any path might be abandoned, once one realized it led to dark places. She closed her eyes, drew a deep breath, and thought of Hannei.

It was a simple thing, to picture the girl in her mind's eye. She drew from the deep well of her memories: Hannei as a fat-cheeked cub, cutting her first teeth. Hannei as an angry new orphan, come to live with the youthmistress and those of her year-mates whose mothers had died or, like Hafsa Azeina, declined to raise their own children. Hannei with her arm in a splint after some foolery with Sulema. Ani pictured herself standing next to the girl, laying a hand on that arm and speaking to those broken bones, so long knit, stronger now than the surrounding tissue but never perfectly straight. It was a break, a discontinuum, a doorway—

A doorway through which the bonesinger entered, unbidden, forbidden. Ani found herself in a dark, warm, alien place surrounded by the song which was Hannei, and let herself spread out like drops of blood in the river, or like drops of poison in a lover's cup.

Hannei, or Kishah as she was called now, had been cold-faced and silent when Ani had seen her. She had accepted the basket of salves and harmless apothecaries, though one nondescript bottle had been discreetly tucked back into a fold of Ani's robe; the poison meant for Sulema's rival would not, on this day, end Hannei's life. Hannei had received the medicines silently and without so much as a flicker of recognition. Had she not raised the girl herself, Ani would have thought her a still pool, unruffled by the wind.

On the inside, where her bones held the truth, Hannei was a raging storm. The red song of heart's blood, of fury; the black of betrayal. Little was left of the song of Hannei, soft-hearted warrior girl of the Zeera. All that remained was what could be seen on the outside, a scarred and broken shell of a woman fit only for killing things.

Oh, Ani thought, her own heart breaking again. *Oh, my poor girl*. A second heartbeat thrummed along with the first, fast as a hummingbird's, soft as spidersilk, bright and lovely and very, very small. It flitted round the storm that was Hannei, wings caught and tattered in the tumult of her wrath, breaking itself against the hard edges of her heart. A child, its life scarcely more than a candle lit against vast darkness, trying to win its mother's love, and failing utterly.

Not again. The thought came from that part of Ani that could, as Askander would say, outstubborn a rock. *Never again. I will not make the same mistake Hafsa Azeina made, to turn aside from a child in the pursuit of pain. I failed her in this... but I will not fail you*.

Softly she began to sing a canticle, a hymn, a lullaby for bones. She sang of long days on horseback, of fighting-drills and mead, sandstorms and giggling girls. She sang of *saghaani*, and *mutaani*, and *ehuani*.

Kishahani, Hannei sang back. *The only beauty is in vengeance*.

Still Ani went on. She sang of the river in springtime, of stallions and mares, of mothers and babies and handsome young men. She sang of sword-sisters and lionsnake whelps, and spiders' eggs, and courage. She sang of Hannei Ja'Akari, champion of the people, as true a friend as any woman could ask for.

Remember who you are, girl, she coaxed. *You are Hannei Ja'Akari, daughter of Deaara and of Mazuk Ja'Sajani. The blood of queens flows hot in your veins and your bones sing of honor. Remember*.

I am no one, Hannei replied, wroth and aggrieved, heart's voice black and ragged. *I am nothing. I am Kishah, and my heart is hollow*.

You are Hannei, Ani soothed, gentle and implacable as any Mother. *You are beloved*.

The tiny heartbeat flared in agreement, so bright and sweet and pure that for a moment Hannei's attention was turned from the source of her own pain. She looked toward the child's bright light. For a moment the storm stopped raging, the voices stopped screaming. In her mind's eye Ani saw her as a young girl standing naked and alone in the desert, surrounded by enemies—and night was falling.

Come, Ani said to her, holding out a hand. *Come. Let me help you. Let us love you.*

I cannot, Hannei answered. *I cannot*. She turned her face and thrust Ani and the child both away from her. Ani fell from the song of Hannei into darkness, into the soft cold well of her own being, but not before she saw hot tears on the girl's frozen cheeks.

Well? thought Inna'hael, as she returned to herself—as much of herself as remained, in any case. *Have you convinced them not to kill each other?*

It was a start. She curled forward and held her head in both hands. *Ai yeh*, the pain. *I showed my girls the path of love. It is up to them to walk it. There is yet hope.*

Foolish little huntress, Inna'hael chided, though not without fondness. *You and your little human dreams. While you were tracking tarbok, you missed the scat of the greater predator.*

What? What are you talking about?

Only this, he answered. *Come see.*

Abruptly Ani cried out as teeth seemed to close on her neck and yank her backward. They pulled free her spirit form, and she watched her body slump into the dirt as her essence was carried away as if she were an errant cub.

Let me go!

Inna'hael ignored her cries and struggles—perhaps he laughed a little, catlike—dragging her helpless ka over the city and the river, along the trade road and across the singing dunes toward Aish Kalumm. Even from this distance she could smell the savor of burnt bones, hear the weeping dead seeking, seeking the lives they had known.

Please, she begged, *please no. Not there. I cannot—*

But he was not taking her to Aish Kalumm.

Inna'hael's spirit form stopped high in the air above a small oasis, midway between the Nisfim herdgrounds and the Valley of Death. Once a great lake favored by herders and hunters, it was now barely more than a muddy pit. A force was gathering there, armed and armored, ten thousand strong or more, or she was no battle-mistress.

Atualon invades the Zeera! she thought, and redoubled her efforts to break free. *Let me go! I must warn—*

Bonesinger, he snarled around a mouthful of her spirit. *You are not stupid. Neither are you blind, or deaf. What do your eyes tell you? What do the bones tell you?*

Ani stopped fighting, stopped being stupid, and looked again. Really looked this time, with the eyes of one who had walked too near the Lonely Road. She listened, as well, so that she could hear the bones. For where there had been war there were always bones. The bones were singing to her. They sang, as always, of mortality, of breath cut short and stillborn dreams. They sang to her of their own deaths, those of their beloveds, deaths to come.

Ani stared at the dark mass of warlike figures far below. One of them stood above the others, armored and with an antlered helm, his arm draped about the shoulders of a young girl. As if he sensed her presence, this man turned his face up to the sky. Ani saw him clearly, and her soul froze in horror. She knew this boy, burned face or no, dead eyes or no. The last time she had seen this youth, he was trying to convince Sareta to allow him to ride as a warrior.

Ismai, she thought dismayed. *Ismai, what is this madness?*

The bones sang to Ani, enjoining her to share their delight.

The king is risen, they rejoiced. *The king is dead. Long live the king.*

TWENTY-ONE

"A beautiful sight, is it not?" The Zeerani warrior and her horse, glowing in the sunlight as they prepare for a great quest. She does not have the braids for it, of course, but they will grow back.

"Unlike your tongue."

Hannei tensed beneath the hand that was laid on her shoulder in a false show of sympathy. Sharmutai laughed and went on.

"They say that little golden mare was one that had been taken from her? How touching, and how fortunate for your pretty friend. I do not suppose you will ever see your own horses again, your weapons and leathers, those things you barbarians hold so dear. Certainly you will never again gaze deep into the eyes of—oh, you never told me his name, did you? The father of your brat? So much has been taken from you, my poor little pit slave. I know how you feel."

Anger rose in Hannei's gut with every word that fell from the whoremistress's rouged lips. She jerked her shoulder from the touch, risking a beating. Sharmutai laughed again at Hannei's broken growl. The laugh was a beautiful sound of honey and venom.

"Oh, but I *do* know how you feel, little pet. I know just how you feel. To have everything you love stripped from you, to have your body savaged and torn for the amusement of men."

Sulema stood with Atemi by the river, oblivious to all the world. Hannei turned from the sight of her onetime sword-sister and stared with surprise at Sharmutai. She had a mymyc's voice—now soft and low, then seductive, then harsh, but always dripping with deceit. Never had Hannei detected the faintest ring of truth from this woman, but she heard it now.

"Yes, even so," the whoremistress said. "I was not always as you see me now, you know. Powerful, wealthy beyond imagining, untouchable…" She raised her hands high, salt-stained blue silk shivering in the hot wind, and fixed her eyes on the sky. "No. I was young once, and I was owned even as I own you. In my case, however, I was not sold. I *gave* myself away, and freely." Her beautiful face stilled into a mask of perfect hatred. "I gave myself to a king's son, body and heart, sa and ka. I walked in his footsteps as if he were the sun and I no more than his adoring shadow. When I was scarcely more than a child myself, I grew round as the moons with his child. My child." She lowered her arms, her eyes, and smiled such a smile that Hannei recoiled.

"Nnnnh," she said, cupping one hand protectively over her abdomen. *Please. Please. It is all I have left.*

"Round as the moons," Sharmutai repeated, ignoring her garbled plea. "The child grew and slept in my belly, beneath my heart, even as Sajani sleeps and grows in the belly of the earth. He loved me, or said he did, and I was happy."

"Nnnnnhhh." *Please.*

"His name was Pythos ap Serpentus ne Atu, and he was the son of the Dragon King of Atualon. He was so handsome—he could be an ass, of course, but he was very handsome, and he was kind to me. Our child would grow to be a king, or a queen, and *I was happy.*

"Do you know what they do to the prince's mistress, little slave, when a new king takes the throne and replaces the old? Do you know what they do to the child in her belly? Would you like to see the scars?" Her face twisted, terrible with wrath and old sorrow long gone to poison.

Hannei dared not move, dared not even breathe. Would Sharmutai kill her babe, then, as some sort of twisted revenge?

Or would she allow Hannei to bear Tammas's child, only to claim it as her own?

Sharmutai stilled then, gone all to cold stone draped in fluttering silks, with eyes hard and shining as river stones. Terrible was the grief that poured from her, a bitter wind that had seared the land of her soul till nothing could ever grow there that was good or true.

"I see you, Kishah," she said at last, in a voice Hannei had never heard from her. It was low, and ragged with grief, and unlovely, but it was the woman's true voice at last. "I see myself in you. I might save you, if I could. Return your life to you, and hope, and love, but I have no hope or love left to me. Do you understand? None. They killed it when they killed my little one. All that is left for me in this world is vengeance, and I will have it. So I will give you what I never had. I will give you a chance.

"They left me to bleed and die in the rag pits, holding my dead babe in my arms. She was a girl child, you know, a little daughter. I named her Tatiana, and gathered up her little torn... her little torn... I..." Sharmutai closed her eyes and drew a ragged breath, long and slow. When she opened them again, she was once more the whoremistress of Min Yaarif. "I made a little cairn for her on the slopes of Atukos. I vowed that I would live, and I vowed revenge. One of those promises I have kept quite nicely. The other..."

She stepped close and laid a small, hard hand on Hannei's cheek. She was trembling with fury.

"...the other promise I will achieve now, and you will help me. You will journey into Quarabala with this pretty friend of yours, my vengeance, my Kishah. The Seared Lands will be as nothing after my fighting pits." She laughed. "Go on this quest, help your friends here to achieve their goals. Save the shadowmancer's brat, by all means. Save every miserable person in the Seared Lands, if that is your wish, only help find this Mask of Sajani and return it to Min Yaarif—to me.

This, and do one other thing." Her lips curled into a cruel smile and she stared pointedly at Sulema.

Hannei's heart died in her chest. *No*, she whispered, deep in the part of her that still believed in love and truth and happy endings. *No.*

It seemed to her that she stood at the heart of a storm, the sands of time and vicious regret stripping flesh from bone till there was nothing left but bitterness. Then the gentle sound of Ani's voice came to her on the winds.

Remember who you are, girl, it said. *You are Hannei Ja'Akari, daughter of Deaara and of Mazuk Ja'Sajani. The blood of queens flows hot in your veins and your bones sing of honor. Remember.*

I am no one, Hannei replied to the ghost-voice, and spat bitterness upon the sand. *I am nothing. I am Kishah, and my heart is hollow.*

Sharmutai continued, unaware of the storm that raged. "That mask should have belonged to my daughter, the daughter of Pythos, son of the true Dragon King. It would have been her birthright, so I claim it as her blood price. The mask—"

Sulema stood with her arms around Atemi's neck, her face buried in the mare's wind-whipped dark mane.

"—and the heart's blood of Sulema an Wyvernus ne Atu. Wyvernus who killed my child has escaped my vengeance, so I will have the life of his daughter just as he took the life of mine."

She turned again to Hannei. "I give you this gift of a second chance at life, Kishah-whose-name-is-lost. I can see your heart, and I know you do not wish to do this thing. You will betray me, if you can. I respect that." She smiled. "I will send Rehaza Entanye with you, to make sure that you do not. You are still Ja'Akari in your heart, still bound by honor and *ehuani*. You promised obedience to me in return for the life of your child. Obey me now. Fulfill your promise, your purpose, and regain your life. Return to me with the Mask of Sajani, and the blood of the spawn of the dragon upon your swords. Then you and your child will be free."

Even as these words settled like a shroud upon her heart, Hannei watched as Sulema leapt upon Atemi's back and leaned forward, urging her horse to fly, laughing as the golden mare broke into a joyful run that carried them both away. Sulema never looked back at the one she had called "sister." She had not seen her standing there, wearing a cold iron collar and the swords of a pit slave.

Sulema sees only herself, Hannei thought bitterly. *She would make a fine Dragon Queen, after all.*

Sharmutai reached out and affectionately tousled Hannei's short curls. "You are a smart girl, Kishah," she said. "I trust you to make the right decision." She turned and walked away, silk robes fluttering like the wings of a bird.

TWENTY-TWO

Sunlight poured across the Zeera, sweet and warm as mead poured from a pitcher of gold. A playful wind laughed before the ebony mare Mutaani, kicking up little sand-dae and erasing the tracks of a herd of tarbok.

It seemed to Ismai that the desert was ageless as the sky, ever-changing never-changing as the stars, and that he was nothing more than a character in one of his mother's stories, soon to be forgotten by sand and sun and time.

The sand will fill my mouth, my eyes, he thought. *My bones will dry and crack; they will be ground down to sand beneath the hooves of the next journeying hero...*

...or perhaps a villain.

He glanced behind him. The host was, to his dead eyes, clearer and perhaps more beautiful than anything in the land of the living. Here and there at the fringes of this great force the desert's skin rippled and split. When the Lich King called, those bits and pieces of dead things which were too destroyed to be of real use would sometimes join and create a new, foul creature. Never sleeping, ever hungering, these newborn bonelords swam just beneath the sand's surface and followed the army, eager to devour the spoils of war.

My children, Ismai thought. *The only children I will ever have, now.* Had his eyes not been dead, had his heart been more than cold stone, he might have wept.

Nor were the undead Ismai's only followers. He could feel Ruh'ayya trailing them to the south and east. Through his connection with her he could feel, as well, the presence of other vash'ai. Their number and intentions were hidden from him—hidden, he thought, by his own bond mate.

Kithren, he remonstrated, *what is this? I have been betrayed by the prides, my heroes, by the very blood in my veins. Surely you do not turn against me as well?*

I, Kithren? Her mind's voice was haughty as only a cat could be, and he imagined the tip of her tail twitching. *I have betrayed nothing. It is you who brought this abomination into our lives, and I will save you, if I must—*

If you must... what?

There was no answer. Whatever his Ruh'ayya and the other vash'ai were planning, he would not be privy to their counsel. Ismai looked about him. There was Char—Naara—erstwhile friend, sometimes daughter, staring at him with brown eyes wide and innocent as his sisters' had been. Warriors and sorcerers and revenants dragged back from peaceful death through their bond with the Lich King. He knew in his own bones they would turn on him the moment that bond was severed.

There is no loyalty here, Ismai thought to himself. *No fidelity, no honor, only fear and mutual need. Certainly there is no love—not here, perhaps nowhere in the world.* The foundation upon which he had built his life, he knew now, was a lie. How had he ever believed that the world was a good place, and just? That warriors were honorable and such a one as he could love and be loved in return? *We are all monsters, every one.* Even Sudduth, the companion of Kal ne Mur's childhood, who in life had burned so bright and clear.

Ismai pursed his lips thoughtfully as he looked at the woman who strode beside his horse. She was tall and lovely and strong as any Zeerani warrior. Kal ne Mur recalled, and Ismai had no reason to disbelieve, that this woman had once been famed for her temper and was known to have fought the least imagined insult to her honor. In life she had been a stone-cold killer, and death had not made her warmer.

And yet, as she walked, Sudduth crooned over the clay pot in which she had planted her precious cacao sprouts, and which she held close to her heart as if they were little green children. The sprouts were thriving under her care, and Sudduth demanded that they stop at every oasis and well and watering-hole so that she might tend them.

There, Ismai thought, *there is honor. There is fidelity, and love.* Those little sprouts had nothing to offer Sudduth; the chocolate she recalled so fondly would be harvested years from now, if ever, and if any of them survived so long. Watching her stroke a tender leaf with one long finger, he smiled. *Sulema would like her.*

Sudduth looked up, caught his expression, and frowned. "My king?"

"Nothing. Only... you remind me of a friend."

Sudduth's clouded eyes flashed red, reminding him of her true nature.

"I am beyond friendship," she said stiffly. "My king."

"Of course." He looked to the horizon and saw the wavering image of Aish Kalumm as it had been before the Mah'zula burned it, as it ever would be in his dreams. It was only a mirage, an illusion. "Forgive me."

"I cannot." There was no more regret in Sudduth's voice than there had been love. "I will fight for you, and die for you, and obey when you call me back from the peace of my grave yet again. But one must live in order to love, and one must love in order to forgive. These things are for the living, not for such as you or I."

Is this true? he wondered. *Am I unable to love?* Certainly Kal ne Mur, who shared and sometimes commanded his body, was corpse-cold and unfeeling. But he, Ismai, still felt the pain of betrayal, the weight of regret. Was that not part and parcel of love?

You yet live, Ruh'ayya interjected gently, though her voice was pricked through with pain and anger of her own. *You yet love. I will it so.*

I wish you would go, Ismai told her miserably. *I do not wish to hurt you.*

184

I know, she replied. *That is why I stay.*

Ismai closed his dead eyes, which changed nothing, and turned his face up to the sky. The sun was warm on his face, the wind still tugged at his cloak, and the shifting sands still sang their low, mournful song of ages. These things had not changed, the world had not changed.

"The world has not changed," Ismai said aloud. "It is I who have been sundered, I who no longer belong to the world of the living." *Or to the dead*, he added silently. Though perhaps it was best not to mention that in present company.

"Then we will remake the world in our image," Naara said. Ismai felt her small, warm hand touch his calf, and then pull away. "In your image."

"A world remade," Sudduth said. "A world where cacao grows."

"A world where I can make beautiful things," Ibna agreed.

Ismai opened his eyes. The mirage of Aish Kalumm had disappeared, but another image was forming in his mind, and a dangerous notion. The city of his youth rebuilt bigger, grander, stronger than it had been. His mother, his brother and sisters, brought back from the Lonely Road—

No, Ismai thought, pushing the vision aside, horrified at the turn his own thoughts had taken. No. It would be an abomination. He glanced again at Sudduth, who had brought the clay pot close to her face and was singing to her plants.

There is loyalty, Kal ne Mur whispered within him, *there is love, pure and good. If this is death, there is indeed beauty in it. What might your mother Nurati do, if given another chance? Or Tammas, Neptara, little Rudya? What beautiful world might we make together, you and I?*

First we must free the Zeera from these false Mah'zula. After that—

"*Mutaani*," Ismai said, "there is beauty in death. Might there not be beauty after death, as well?" He turned his most winning smile upon Sudduth. "We travel to Aish Kalumm. There we will find ships, left behind by the Dragon King's son when he came to lay claim to Sulema. These we will sail down the Dibris and across Nar Bedayyan to Atualon, where I will reclaim all that is mine. And when we have finished— when the false Mah'zula have been destroyed, and the usurper Pythos, when I rule in Atualon and once more sing the song of all times—then, my sweet ones, then you may live such a death as you might dream for yourselves.

"The Mothers had a grove of trees in Aish Kalumm, precious trees. Sandalwood and sant—we could replant them, when this is done. Your small plants would be safe among them. I see no reason to stop living just because we are dead. When all the world is mine again I will give these groves unto you to tend as you will, and none will ever dare to disturb you or your green children."

Sudduth looked up at him, and this time she smiled back.

"*Mutaani*," she agreed. "It is good."

Naara skipped ahead of them, singing.

As they neared the wardens' encampment, Ismai was neither surprised nor particularly pleased to find a small force of Mah'zula waiting for them, bright beneath the sun in their wyvern-scale armor. They would have been poor warriors and blind to have missed the signs of such a large force on the move. The presence of two of Thoth's priestesses he had also expected, though the sight of the snake-women caused a growl to rise from deep in his belly, a sound that was echoed in his mind by Ruh'ayya.

More surprising to him was the sight of a dreamshifter, hair in a mass of tangles and pale staff upraised so that for a moment Ismai thought Hafsa Azeina had returned from Atualon to smite him. The old guilt flushed through him— had that fearsome woman ever learned of his true feelings for her daughter, she would have tanned his hide for a dance drum. Closer inspection revealed this dreamshifter to be an older man, somewhat squat and unremarkable.

Besides, Ismai reminded himself, *Hafsa Azeina is dead.* As Lich King, he knew the list of newly dead as if he read the names from a book. Mastersmith Hadid's name was written upon those pages, and Tammas. Fat, sweet little Sammai who had been named for him. Rudya and Neptara, his sisters, and Nurati his mother. The book of dead read like the book of his life.

Hannei yet lives, Ruh'ayya reminded him. *Also Daru, and your Sulema.*

With great effort Ismai pushed her words aside. They made his heart leap, and this was not the time for feeling alive. He looked upon the golden warriors, the twisted and unclean perversion of his mother's stories. At the priestesses of Thoth with their snake faces and snake plumes, their bright bottles of venom. And the rage grew hot in his breast.

This, he thought as he felt Kal ne Mur rise within him, *this is a day for death.* Thus, when the Lich King came darkly into his mind, Ismai did not resist.

The dreamshifter and one of the snake-women rode closer, palms out in the traditional gesture of peace. They were accompanied by a handful of others. Ismai was relieved to note that they did not have bells braided into their hair. That small breach of Zeerani protocol, the refusal to declare themselves of peaceful intent, was excuse enough to forgive himself for what he was about to do.

He drew Mutaani to a halt. She tossed her head and snorted, dancing beneath him like a hot coal. Sudduth stepped closer, shrugging into the harness she had fashioned to snug the little clay pot securely between her shoulder blades. She would not abandon her plants, not even for war.

"They seek to treat with us," she said. Her eyes were glazed and red, knuckles pale on the hilt of her short sword. "What would you have us do?"

Let me do this thing, coaxed the Lich King. *Let us be one.*

Ismai, looking upon the Mah'zula, gave in to vengeance. *As you will.*

A shudder took him head to toe. When it had subsided, Ismai looked down upon his friend, and smiled Kal ne Mur's smile. Sudduth smiled back, a feral expression, and bared an inch of her sword. "My king."

"These women," he said, raising his voice so that it would carry, "these false Mah'zula defile the name of Zula Din, the memory of her warriors. These snake-women foul the memory of Thoth. What would I have you do?"

A jagged cheer rose from the ranks of the undead as the Lich King leaned down to caress Sudduth's cheek.

"I will listen to their words, and consider them wisely," he told her. "And then you will kill them all."

The snake-woman spoke first, as Kal ne Mur had expected. These women were not priestesses of Thoth as he remembered them from old, but humans greedy for power. Power was a language that was understood in every age and every tongue, and none had spoken it longer than he.

"Who are you," the priestess asked, "to ride into our lands girded and armed as if for war? A boy I see before me, mounted and dressed above his station, and he rides with... an abomination."

The abomination that was Sudduth chuckled and spun her sword. Before she had become his captain, Kal ne Mur remembered, she had been an acrobat in a troupe of fools, and fond of putting on a show.

"If my face is not familiar to you," he answered, forcing this youthful and untrained voice to be more than it was, "perhaps my name will be. I am Ismai son of Nurati." He had not meant to say that. "And I am Kal ne Mur, risen to ride among you once more."

"He is your king," Sudduth asserted in a voice as hard as the sword at her hip. "Kneel to him or die."

"There is no king in the Zeera," the false Mah'zula said. She looked as if she wished to spit but did not quite dare.

"Sweet golden child," Ismai purred. He was rewarded as she flinched from the death in his voice. "How short your memory, and how very wrong you are. Indeed there is a king in the Zeera, and always has been. You may not remember me, but as you can see"—he spread his arms, indicating his undead armies—"I do exist. Indeed, I have never left."

The dreamshifter stepped forward.

"A king you may be," he allowed in a quavering voice, "but you are no king to the living. The dead have no power here, unclean spirit. Begone!" Thus saying, he brought a small whistle to his lips and blew.

A sharp note thrilled through the air, sweet and commanding. Shadows fled before the dreamshifter's magic, shadows Ismai had not realized were there, and the day became terribly bright. It rose and fell in a song of warning and dismissal.

Had he indeed been a spirit, Kal ne Mur would have been obliged to return whence he had come. Had he been a living man, Ismai would have been terrified as the music tugged at his soul and threatened to tear it loose. But they were neither spirit nor flesh, living nor dead, and Ismai threw back his head and laughed. Then he reached out with one hand, seized the music, and *pulled*.

The dreamshifter stiffened all over and collapsed upon the sand, breathless and blue.

"The dead," Ismai informed the remaining suppliants, once he had stopped, "have power where *I say* they have power. As you will learn."

"No," the snake-woman whispered as she stared in horror at the corpse. "No!" She reached for the small bottles of venom strapped to her chest.

"Sudduth?" Ismai said casually. He stretched, enjoying the feel of sunlight on his shoulders. It had been too long.

"My king?" She all but danced beside Mutaani, and her eyes were rubies.

"Kill them for me."

"Yes, my king!" Sudduth raised her voice in a joyful ululation and charged forward.

"Papa?"

Ismai looked down, surprised. "Yes, Naara?"

The living began to scream as Sudduth and her sword danced among them.

"I want to kill them, too."

"There are hardly enough for Sudduth, let alone... oh, very well," he relented, seeing the disappointment on her sweet face. "I suppose you all want to play?"

A hungry roar rumbled all about him, and the Lich King sighed. He had never been very good at denying his children their hearts' desires. Raising his right hand, pointing to Akari, Ismai bid him witness the dawn of a new day. Then he brought it down, pointing to Sajani, that she might take the souls of the newly dead under her wing.

"As you will," he said. A howl rose round him, a shout, a canticle of death, and Ismai closed his eyes.

The world is made of music, he thought as the horde surged past, screaming for blood, *and never have I heard a song as sweet as this.*

The false Mah'zula died well, Ismai would grant them that much. In the end, however, it meant no more than footprints in the sand. They were grievously outnumbered—would have been so, *ehuani*, had they faced Sudduth alone. The bloodlust was upon the horde, so the golden warriors were swept up and away in the killing wind, leaving behind nothing more than memories and the sharp smell of blood.

The remaining snake-woman was a hindrance. She had bound to her three young lionsnakes, and these rushed forward shrieking, spitting venom, and slashing the Lich King's forces with wicked claws. Three of his warriors went down beneath their assault, white bone and red meat exposed to sun by the burning venom. These would have to be raised again, Ismai knew, and they would not be best pleased.

He raised his hands to call his forces back, grimacing as Sudduth strode toward the bright monsters. Her face was enfilthed with her enemies' gore and she was laughing, but Kal ne Mur's memories bade him be wary. If *this* one died and had to be raised again, she would be in a foul mood for moons, and not even his status as her king would be proof against the sharp side of her tongue.

One of the lionsnakes struck. Sudduth danced to one side and slashed at it, drawing an agonized bellow and a face full of acid. She shrieked, and the Lich King raised both hands, prepared to end the thing himself. Then he hesitated. Interfering with a fight Sudduth had chosen may well piss her off more than being killed again. Whichever choice he made—to save her life or give her another—it would likely be the wrong one.

Women, he thought. *Living or dead, I will never understand them.*

Before he could call upon atulfah, however, another king entered the fray. The singing sands vomited forth a monstrous tangle of bones, dead trees, and horror as Arushdemma rose from the sands between Ismai's fighting force and the lionsnakes, bellowing his bloodlust. With his great maw stretched wide, the bonelord whipped around fast as malice and snapped up two of the lionsnakes. A cluster of wicked eyes turned toward Sudduth and the third lionsnake, locked in mortal combat and oblivious to all else, and a foul gurgling laugh rose from his sulfurous depths.

"No!" Ismai shouted. "I forbid it!"

But it was too late. That toothed cavern gaped wide enough that three horses abreast might have ridden into that mouth and down the throat. Arushdemma undulated across the Zeera faster than a dead man could blink. He snatched up the lionsnake, and then he snatched up Sudduth for good measure, sinking away into the sands still gurgling with terrible laughter.

Again, a small hand touched his leg. Again, Ismai looked down upon the wide-eyed face of his only daughter, his fiercest love.

"Father," she said. "I am sorry."

"So am I," he sighed, closing his eyes. "Sudduth is going to be *so* angry."

After the incident with the bonelord, the undead army lost enough of its blood frenzy to be manageable. They marched on for another day and a half, never stopping to rest, until they encountered a fist of wardens that stood between the horde and the camp.

Stern-faced and proud, though with eyes showing big and white as those on spooked horses, they stood ready to die in defense of their people. One, a strapping young man still in the first flush of manhood, tugged at Kal ne Mur's memories. A descendent, perhaps, of an old acquaintance...

No, thought Ismai. *I know him. I know him from this life.*

"Jasin," he said. "Jasin Ja'Sajani."

"Ismai?" The young man stepped forward, his face a mask of fear and astonishment. "Ismai Ja'Sajani?"

"Ja'Sajani no more," Ismai answered. "Though Ismai was my name, once."

"Who are you?" an older warden called, no less frightened than Jasin, and no less determined to die. "What are you? What do you want from us?"

Your love, Ismai thought, *your loyalty*. The part of him that was Kal ne Mur pushed those emotions away and banished, too, the vash'ai whose passions threatened his control. *Silence*, he scolded. *This is war, and in war there is no time for love.*

"Only this," he answered the Zeeranim, smiling and holding both hands palm-up to show that he meant them no harm. Not today, at any rate. "I require no more than that you ride to the prides and bring them my message."

"What message would that be?" a third warden asked.

"Ride to Nisfi, to Urak and Shahad and Rihar." Naara stepped forward and raised her arms, letting the wind whip her robes around her skinny little figure and carry her voice. "Bring them glad words, for your king has returned."

"The Zeeranim have no king," Jasin objected, but his voice was unsure.

The Mah'zula rode out, Ismai thought, *and only the horde returned. Surely they know it is futile to resist. Do not resist, little warden. For the sake of your people, do not resist.*

"Here rides your king," Naara corrected him, gently, kindly. "Kal ne Mur, who once was your friend Ismai, and now is both. Bend your knee to him and share in his glory. Bend your knee to him, and let us remake this land, to raise up the Zeeranim into the glory of Akari once more. Bend your knee to him—

"—or die."

Kal ne Mur could feel the horde behind him gathering itself, could feel their misery and their weariness and their battle-lust. Above all, they longed for rest... but in the absence of rest, they longed to kill.

The wardens could feel it too, it seemed. One after another they sank to their knees in the sand. Jasin was not first, but neither was he last, and Ismai breathed a sigh of relief. He had not wanted to slay a friend.

"Ride now, my faithful," he called out to them, "ride forth in joy! Carry this news to every corner of the Zeera, and let the people rejoice. For unto them—unto you—the king is risen."

Kal ne Mur, the dead whispered. *Ismai, Kal ne Mur.*
The king is risen.

TWENTY-THREE

Sulema and Hannei sat at ease in Hannei's quarters, deep in the heart of one of Sharmutai's estates. Sulema could not help but stare at the walls, the pools, the slaves in their bright garments. Everything was red, the red of life-giving and precious salt from Quarabala. It seemed to her that the amount of salt used to dye a slave-boy's robes might have been enough to sweeten the water of a pride for a year.

She reached out and picked up the salt-clay mug one of the boys had set before her and took a polite sip of dragonmint tea.

Red salt clay for a mug, she thought, indignation rising, *when the prides go without sweet water. Red salt clay used to build slaves' houses, when we do not have enough in Aish Kalumm to preserve our meat so that the mothers might bear healthy children. How many lives were spent to make this mug?*

Still, she could not deny that the tea was delicious.

Scouts had been sent into the foothills, to spy out the best paths to take—or at least identify the worst paths, as Leviathus had said, laughing—and emissaries had been sent by him and by Hannei's owner, the whoremistress Sharmutai, to negotiate safer passage with the mountain clans. He had offered them the use of the pirate clans' palace while they waited. Sharmutai had refused to let Hannei spend so much as a night away from her until the day of their departure, and Sulema would not leave her friend alone, so they slept and ate and trained with Hannei's whoremistress and waited, and waited, and waited some more.

Hannei stared out the small round window. Sulema could not read her friend's expression, but she seemed neither content nor ill at ease in her surroundings. It seemed as if she was neither heartened by Sulema's presence, nor bothered by the slave's collar about her throat, nor excited at the prospect of adventure. Sulema burned to ask her about the scars on her back, about how she came to lose her tongue, about the alarming whispers she had heard in the market regarding goings-on in the Zeera, but Hannei had shut her out completely, declining even the crude hand-talk of hunters. She had locked herself away more effectively than if Sharmutai had shut her into a whore's room and thrown away the key.

Sharmutai, Sulema thought, and felt her lip curl in half a snarl. *Hannei's owner.* The thought of any Ja'Akari beaten, savaged, raped—enslaved—was a call to battle-fury worth dying for. That it had happened to Hannei was unmistakable. That it had happened to Hannei and Sulema, her sword-sister, had let so much time go by without avenging it was unthinkable.

Yet here they sat, sipping tea from red salt clay, waiting for someone else to tell them what they might or might not do with their lives. She set her cup down with such force that the cup chipped, throwing out shards of red clay. One of these struck Hannei high on the cheek, drawing blood.

Hannei turned her face fractionally, just enough to glance out of the corner of one eye, and for a moment Sulema saw a beast peering out at her, a deadly predator waiting for the cage doors to spring open. Just as quickly the impression was gone again, and Hannei looked back out the window. The last rays of a dying day glinted dully off her collar and caressed her face with golden light, shining on the blood that dripped down her cut cheek like a tear.

It was almost a small-moon before the scouts and emissaries returned, the trips to market were successfully completed, and they could finally be on their way. Sulema had reluctantly parted with her Atemi. Even if the mare had been able to traverse the mountain passes, Yaela had explained to her, the shadowed roads to the Edge and then the heart of Quarabala would be death for any horse. Sulema had found a girl from Uthrak, a newmade merchant's apprentice, who had vowed to care for the mare as a child until Sulema could return to claim her.

"If I die," Sulema told the fierce-eyed youth, "and Hannei as well, Atemi is to be given to Aamia, half-sister of Saskia, who died for me." The merchant's apprentice nodded her assent, and Sulema watched as the better half of her heart walked away.

Jai tu wai, she promised Atemi silently, caressing the hilt of the fine shamsi with which the Uthraki had gifted her. *We will ride together again, my love.*

The party gathered beneath the shade of an enormous tent, a riotous patchwork of colorful fabrics that came, Leviathus had told her, from ships the pirates had captured.

My brother is the pirate king and my sister is a slave, Sulema thought.

Yes, Jinchua barked in the back of her mind, *but who are* you?

Not a dreamshifter, Sulema barked back, and she slammed her mind's door on the Dreaming Lands. *Not ne Atu*, she thought to herself, shutting out the dragon's song as best she could—*and certainly no slave to the reaver's venom*. The pain in her shoulder had subsided to a dull ache, a cold spot scarcely as big as a thumbprint. Sulema pushed away, as well, the knowledge that Yaela's supply of medicine was nearly depleted. There was every likelihood that she would die before that ever became a problem.

Not far away Yaela spoke to Leviathus of the paths they might take through Jehannim, the supplies they had to hand, and the dangers of sun-sickness, mountain-sickness, and the likelihood of being eaten by greater predators. It seemed to

Sulema that the sorcerer's apprentice, whose mad quest this was to begin with, had absented herself too much from these preparations until Leviathus had appeared. Leviathus, for his part, argued that they were under-supplied and under-prepared. To Sulema, who was used to riding out into the desert with nothing besides a weapon, some water, and her horse, their preparations seemed endless. And she was weary of watching the two of them fighting their too-obvious mutual attraction.

I wish Sareta was here, she thought. *Or Istaza Ani. Or my mother. Or—*

They had no seasoned warriors, no dreamshifter, nobody here who could lead them safely to Saodan and back again.

I will just have to pretend that I am such a leader and take charge of this goatfuckery. Otherwise we will be standing here until the dragon wakes, still arguing about whether we have enough rope.

"Is it true," she said, interrupting their endless debate, "that the mountain clans have been paid not to interfere with our passage?"

"Yes," Leviathus said, "but you will still need—"

"We have purchased weapons? Water? Pemmican?"

Her brother and Yaela both made faces at that. Let them. Nobody liked pemmican, but taste was beside the point.

"Yes, but—"

"Good," Sulema said, holding up a hand to fend off any further discussion. "Let us go to the merchants' house, retrieve our supplies, and be off at latesun." Leviathus opened his mouth to argue, but Sulema scowled him into silence.

"My quest," she reminded him, "my rules. We are going to the Seared Lands to retrieve one young girl, not riding to Atualon to wage war upon Pythos. The fewer mouths we must feed, the less equipment we have to carry, the better. We are not churrim. Let us stop chewing our cuds and go."

The pirates who flanked Leviathus grumbled a bit at this,

but Leviathus waved them to silence. Even so he did not look happy about it. Hannei pursed her mouth and nodded approval.

"*Good,*" she signed. "*We go.*"

Sulema let out a long breath. Her heart pounded in her ears as if she had been running. She had seized control of the group, and they had accepted her command. They had a plan, such as it was, and Leviathus would no doubt pack enough supplies for them to survive an apocalypse of the risen dead.

Then why did it taste like the kiss of doom?

Sulema shook her head at the size of their party. A fist of pirates had insisted upon providing an honor guard for their king, Sharmutai had sent a handful of slaves to keep an eye on Hannei, and three white-cloaked Salarian merchants had somehow convinced somebody that they should tag along as if this was a journey to procure salt and other rare goods from the Seared Lands. There were slaves to bear their packs, others to tend their beasts, a painted boy gifted to them by the whoremistress to tend to their clothes and makeup.

"No," she said firmly, though the last caused her a pang. Surely the boy reminded her of her mother's lost apprentice, Daru, and would have been better off with them than he had been in the comfort house. "The mountains are no place for merchants, or softlanders, or children. So large a group will attract bandits and greater predators. No. We will number only as many as are needed—myself and Yaela, Hannei, Leviathus, and the shadowmancer Keoki. We will take one churra, and only as many provisions as we can carry ourselves."

Sharmutai was not pleased, and it looked as if she was not used to hearing the word "no."

"You must at least take Rehaza Entanye," she insisted. "Or I will not allow you to take my Hannei."

"Agreed," Sulema said. "Another fighter will be welcome, but no more. No more." She held up a hand to forestall the dozen arguments that bloomed around her like flowers after a rain. "A small group has better chance of success."

Better than one bloated by incompetents, she thought.

Leviathus puffed out his cheeks, no more used to being thwarted than the whoremistress.

"You have never crossed the Jehannim," he pointed out. "You could hardly find them on a map."

"No," Sulema agreed, "but while you were learning to read maps, I was learning to survive in harsh conditions. We were," she added, indicating Hannei, who nodded. "This is our world more than yours, ne Atu."

"I am no more the dragon's son these days than you are the dragon's daughter," he replied, mouth twisted unhappily, "but perhaps you are right."

"I am right," Sulema said firmly, wishing she was half as confident as she sounded. "Six of us, and no more."

"Still—"

Hannei clapped her hands loudly, forestalling further argument, and pointed. Sulema turned her head and smiled.

"Oh, good," she said, happy for the interruption. "Our supplies are here."

Indeed they were. The merchants' guild had been as good as their word to Sharmutai. Slaves arrived leading three very fine churrim of a type Sulema had never seen, brown as coffee on top, white as river sand underneath, shorter-legged and heavier-built than those she was used to.

They look like goats, she thought, *though I suppose that will be helpful in the mountains. They do look hardy, at that.*

"We will take these three animals," she said, "and let us see what supplies they—"

A low growl from Hannei stopped her short. Sulema looked at her, startled, then followed her sister's stare toward the fat little merchant who stood chatting amiably with the whoremistress.

"Hannei—" Sulema touched her friend's shoulder. The other warrior was so stiff with outrage that she was trembling. "That man—was he one of those who hurt you?"

Hannei shied away violently, baring her teeth in a rictus snarl and never once looking away from the merchant.

"Ah," Sulema said, soft as the singing desert. "Ah." She turned her back on her shaking sister and walked to where the slave-merchants stood.

"You," she said, addressing the man. "Who are you? What is your name?"

"My name is Ovreh," the little man answered, puffing himself up in an attempt to meet her height. "I—"

Sulema drew her shamsi and ran it through his middle, using all the strength in her arms and back to push it through skin and innards and muscle. She twisted the blade and wrenched it from his belly with a sharp sideways slash, spilling his stinking guts upon the ground. The man's eyes went wide and he screamed, clutching at his own steaming entrails and falling heavily to his knees. He screamed again, and Sulema swept him sideways with one foot, then slashed his throat wide open.

The smell of death blossomed in the hot air, sweet as flowers.

"I am Sulema Ja'Akari," she said, kicking him in the face for good measure. "You touched my sister. For this you die." She unfastened the fine silken cloak which he had worn fashionably over one shoulder and which was free of blood and gore. This she used as a rag to clean her face and hands, and her befouled shamsi.

"What—" Sharmutai gasped. "What?"

Sulema glanced up, locked eyes with the whoremistress. The woman's face paled and she took a quick step back, slipping and nearly falling in the dying man's blood. "Take your collar from Hannei's neck," she told the woman in a soft, low voice. "Do it now."

The woman moved to Hannei' side, lifting the large ring of keys she wore upon her belt. "You cannot do this," she gasped, even as the collar dropped from Hannei's throat. "This is my property. The law—"

"I do not give a rat's ass about your laws," Sulema told her. She continued wiping her blade on the fallen man's robes as he twitched his last, and tried to hide the shaking in her hands. Moments before, this had been a living man, and now he was a pile of meat and stinking offal. *My hands did this.* Hannei reached up and touched her own bare throat, face unreadable.

My hands did that, too, Sulema thought. *I helped my sister be free. It is good.* She let out a long breath. "To touch a Ja'Akari is to die. That is the only law I need. Best you remember it as well."

A crowd had gathered to gape at the dead man, the travelers, the barbarian warrior sheathing her barbarian sword. Sulema ignored them all, breathing deeply and feeling better than she had in many moons. She finished cleaning her blade, sheathed it, and dropped the man's cloak atop his head. Finally she gathered the lead rope of the nearest churra and tossed it to Keoki, who stood gaping at her with eyes as wide as a tarbok's.

Sulema turned from the sight and smell of death and looked up at the mountains.

"Well," she said to her companions, "what are you waiting for? We have mountains to cross, and an impossible quest before us. Like as not we will all be dead before dawn— but it will be an interesting death, at least."

Hannei made an odd, strangled noise. Sulema looked at her sword-sister, at her bared teeth and the tears rolling down her cheeks, and realized that she was laughing.

❖

The scouts for which Yaela's salt had paid advised against going south. Some failure of nature or magic was causing water to sour in the Zeera, and it seemed to worsen in that direction. Besides, the mountain folk held those lands sacred.

They consulted the salt merchants, and Leviathus's maps—and Yaela gazed long into a spider's web, though Sulema saw nothing there besides a dead bug—and a way into the Jehannim was at last decided upon.

If only, Sulema wished, *the way back might be so easily foreseen*. Yet *"If wishes were water,"* Ani had been fond of saying, *"the desert would bloom."*

Ani was the one person in all the world she might have added to their expedition. Sulema missed the youthmistress terribly—her sharp tongue and sharper wit would have been a welcome change from this gloomy group. Wherever in the world she might be, Sulema hoped she was happy.

They loaded their gear into the churrim's packs and set off, leaving the good people of Min Yaarif to clean up the mess she had made of the slavemaster. It would be good for them, she thought, to remember what happened to those who tried to enslave a warrior.

Indeed, she was happy to be clad once again in a warrior's garb: a warrior's vest and trousers, and a shamsi at her hip. She missed her long braids bitterly and kept running her hand over the strip of scalp where her hair was growing back, as if she could hurry it along. Leviathus strode by her side wearing an odd assemblage of loose, bright clothing which flapped in the hot wind like the sails of one of his boats. He bore an Atualonian-style short sword at his hip, a long knife strapped to his thigh, short knives strapped to either forearm, and in sheaths on his tall boots as well. Sulema shook her head at him.

"A sword and five knives! How many blades does one man need?"

Leviathus glanced at her, grinned, and winked. "Ah," he told her, "those weapons are only the ones you can see."

She laughed. "I have missed you."

"And I you. Family should stick together. Even," he added in a whisper, "if they are heading off to certain death."

"Especially then," she agreed. "It is good to be with you."

Finding her brother again helped, a little, to ease the sting of losing Hannei. Her sword-sister was avoiding her, choosing to walk at the back of the pack instead of at her side. It was not the same Hannei she had left behind just a few short years ago.

Two warriors; a soft Atualonian prince—a pirate, now, and able to talk to sea serpents, but a soft outlander all the same. A slave trainer no doubt loyal to the whoremistress, and two Quarabalese sorcerers. Surely Akari himself has never seen such a mismatched band of travelers. All we need to complete this spectacle is Mattu Halfmask, his odd sister, and maybe her troupe of fools.

It was a torrid day at the peak of summer. The land around them lay still under the gaze of Akari, still as a hare beneath the hawk's gaze. A dry and fevered wind breathed down upon them from the mountaintops, abjuring their desires. The Jehannim were so severe, so hostile to human life, that their peaks were sometimes referred to as an earthly level of Yosh. Few were those travelers so foolhardy as to attempt this crossing, and fewer still by far those who lived to tell the tale.

A motley troupe of fools indeed, and they were perhaps following the greatest fool of all. Despite her earlier actions, Sulema knew herself to be too inexperienced, unprepared to lead such an undertaking. Unprepared and unfit, as the pain in her arm and shoulder reminded her. Her foolishness with the lionsnake had all but gotten her killed. This mad gamble was likely to end all their stories, and badly.

Sulema gazed up toward the peaks of the Jehannim, knowing all of this, knowing the mountains mocked her absurd human striving, and knowing as well that the whisper of wisdom that was trying to make itself heard would not be enough to stop her.

Surely I am casting my fishing net at a dragon, she thought to herself, and felt her lips curl in a grim little smile. *But just watch me catch the damned thing.*

After several days' journey through the foothills and ruins of abandoned towns, they reached the head of the upward path upon which they had decided. Days spent swatting gnats, sweating, and cursing the day she had ever left the tedious safety of childhood.

I would rather muck a thousand churra pits than endure another day of this, Sulema thought, slapping at one of the bloodsucking bugs and leaving a smear of red on her upper arm. *I would rather wash dishes for the Mothers for the rest of my life. I would rather watch over a horde of toddlers—*

Well, no, she had to admit. *Maybe not toddlers.*

The spare dark trees of the sere foothills gave way to sere brush and jagged red rock which cut at leather boots and turned treacherously underfoot. Game was scant; hares and rockbirds, ochre-tailed lizards with big glaring eyes, or the occasional hawk might be seen, but not much else. On their second morning a handful of scrawny goats bounced along the steep face of a far cliff as if gravity held no sway over them; Sulema laughed at their antics, but would have been glad of the fresh meat had they been within range.

They turned sharply westward at the Cairn of the First Men, a necropolis marked by pillars of stone and bone. This was the site of a great battle—or slaughter, depending on which story she believed—around which had been built a wall of red salt and white. There was wealth enough in those bricks to have sustained life in the Zeera for generations.

The dead had never held much dread for Sulema, young as she was and unsure of her own mortality, but there was no desire in her heart to take so much as a chip from that precious wall, much less peek over it. Flags of colorful cloth had been tied to sticks and left to flap in the wind, a warding and a warning against wicked shades, but these hung lifeless. The very air held its breath and tiptoed around that place. Such a pall hung over the Cairn that it was almost a relief to set foot upon the stone road that wound its silent, steady way toward the looming peaks.

Almost.

The churrim snorted and gnashed their short tusks at the presence, and did not seem much happier to be heading higher into the mountains. Neither was Sulema's heart lifted, though she tried to tell herself that the sooner this journey was started, the sooner it would be finished. She could not help but think she was stepping into a viper's pit with two bare feet.

Yaela, however, stepped so lightly and with such good cheer that her little feet danced *pitter-pat pitter-pat* upon the flat stones, and shadows cavorted in her wake.

"You seem in a fine mood," Sulema said to her finally, trying without much success not to sound like a petulant child. Their food sacks were growing too light too quickly, and she was already tired of pemmican.

The shadowmancer's apprentice glanced over her shoulder. She was not smiling, but her eyes were soft and wide, and seemed lit from within as if by delight.

"I do not expect you to understand."

"You are happy to be going home," Sulema guessed. She herself was homesick enough that the smell of horse shit would have been welcome. "But you are not returning to Quarabala, not really." The plan was for Yaela to remain at the other side of the mountains, just shy of the Edge of the Seared Lands, with the churrim and their gear and whomever of their party would not be capable of the three-day run to Saodan.

Yaela shrugged, and the movement became part of her dance.

"You do not understand," she said again. "I am closer to home than I have been in years. Years and years. So close I can taste it." She stuck out her tongue and crossed her jade eyes at Sulema, who was so shocked at this display of playfulness she stopped dead in her tracks, and Leviathus trod upon her heels.

"Sorry." Sulema looked up and into her brother's dawn-blushed cheeks. The shadowmancer's apprentice chuckled, a breathy little almost-laugh. Leviathus watched her twirl away, and his eyes were filled with a wistful hunger.

"As well love a rock as love that one," she said to him. "Yaela is hard as the stone at the bottom of a well, and as cold."

"You are hot as a new-forged sword," he retorted, reaching out to ruffle the short fuzz of her hair, "and twice as sharp. But I love you."

Their quick laughter was swallowed by the mountains. Sulema hoped it would give them indigestion.

The first two days of climbing were an uneventful slog of tedium, burning leg muscles, and wrestling with unwilling pack beasts.

The third day started out usual enough. Breakfast was a handful of cold pemmican, three swallows of tepid water. Sulema was so hungry she would have attempted to eat the stinking cheeses of Atualon.

"If these goatfucking churrim do not cooperate," she said between gritted teeth as she heaved at a lead rope, "I will eat one of them, as a warning to the others. They act as if—"

A roar from the rocks overhead cut her short. The lead rope was yanked from Sulema's grasp and the lead animal bolted back down the path, dragging its companions behind.

Sulema might have turned to chase them, or drawn her sword, or shouted for help, but she did none of these things. The timbre and depth of that roar gripped her very bones, and she could no more move than if she had been turned into mountain stone.

Lionsnake, she thought, and her mind went cold with terror.

Indeed it was a lionsnake, though not like any she had ever seen. The beast which hauled itself down the path toward them was a smallish, lumpy, gray-scaled and ugly thing with stubby legs and a thick wattled neck. Instead of the bright blue and red plumes of a Zeerani beast, this one had a bright yellow crest that rose high above its blunt head as it hissed at them, venom sacks swelling, reptilian eyes fastened greedily on Sulema.

If Sulema could have breathed, she would have screamed. Images flashed through her mind, *flick-flick-flick* like a bad dream. Azra'hael, snarling and broken. The grandmother bitch lionsnake rearing above her. A... a man... a man with a spider...

"Your father will be so disappointed."

Shadows devoured the edges of her vision. She dropped to her knees, sword-arm dangling limply at her side.

Someone shoved her roughly aside. As she dropped to all fours, Sulema caught a glimpse of rough linen trousers, bare brown feet, brown eyes bitter-dark with contempt. Hannei's dark blades hissed like iron in the fire as they left their sheaths and she sprang upon the predator, silent as wrath, quick as death. The beast snapped at her, but it hardly had time to blink in surprise as the shadow-blades hacked through the bone and gristle of its neck.

Blood fountained through the air, stinking, glowing like a handful of gems in the last rays of sunlight, as Hannei painted the story of its death upon the gray mountain rocks. Within instants the lionsnake lay still. She looked down upon this masterpiece of gore, frowning as if the fight had been too quick for her liking, and then shot Sulema such a look of contempt that for a moment she could not breathe.

For a moment, she did not *want* to breathe.

That my sister should look at me so, her wounded heart cried, *after all we have been to one another.*

The lionsnake finished dying, and the sun finished setting, and Sulema swayed to her feet as the rest of their group gathered and Hannei wiped her blades clean. Leviathus had caught the churrim before they could get far, and no one had been harmed.

"Well," Keoki said, after taking a good long look at the dead creature, "this could have been worse. Do you mind if I—" he gestured toward the sagging yellow plumes.

Hannei shrugged and turned away.

Yaela grimaced as she stepped over the knobbled gray tail. "This was hardly more than a whelp. There are likely to be others nearby, and much bigger." She glanced at Sulema. "Are you hurt?"

"No," Sulema answered. Almost to herself, she added, "I hardly know her at all. Back home, we were close as sisters. Closer."

Yaela watched Hannei's retreating back and shrugged.

"You are not in the Zeera."

No, Sulema agreed silently as Keoki strode past, whistling, with yellow feathers in his hair. *We are not in the Zeera.*

TWENTY-FOUR

The road to the Palace of Flowers, the emperor's grand residence at the heart of the Forbidden City of Khanbul, was said to have the heart of a river. Though human lives might sail across it, the road itself was untouched and untroubled.

The azure bricks beneath Jian's bootheels gave off a pleasant ringing tone as he strode beside Mardoni. They were said to be made of a secret mixture of clay, powdered sapphire, rice water, and the cremated remains of tens of thousands of soldiers who had volunteered to protect the emperors of Sindan from the afterlife. Shaped like the scales of Sajani, the bricks were polished clean as a new-hatched dragon.

Though the walls of every other building within the palace complex were tiled in yellow and deep gold which darkened to crimson as the buildings reached up into the sky, the Palace of Flowers itself was the deepest red of heart's blood. In this way the palace was meant to symbolize a unity of earth and heaven through the intercession of its daeborn emperor.

The complex was vast enough to have swallowed Bizhan several times over, and teemed with vibrant life. Though he knew ordinary citizens of Sindan were not permitted to remain in Khanbul past dusk, such a place required the same foodstuffs, goods, and services as any village, though on a grander scale.

Merchants and artisans, couriers, priests, and scribes bobbed along in the road's current like colorful little boats, making way for and swept up by the power of Jian's entourage. Straw hats fell like petals from the branches of flowering trees as the procession was noticed and people dropped to their knees in its wake, lowering their white and frightened faces lest they accidentally catch the eye of a Sen-Baradam or, worse, a member of the royal court.

Jian had never been in the midst of such a throng. As he passed a squad of yellow Daechen, who bowed before him like wheat in a storm, he reflected that never in his life had he felt so alone.

"They honor you," Mardoni remarked.

"Mmmm," Jian grunted, though he thought, *This honor looks too much like fear*. In his experience fear was a path which, like the deep river, flowed only in one direction—toward death. In observing the interactions between Dae, human, and daeborn he had concluded that it is in the nature of man to fear that which he does not understand, and to kill that which he fears.

He strode through the people of Khanbul like a farmer through the fields, fingering his scythe and considering where and when he should begin the harvest. Though on some level he pitied the people of Sindan, no longer did he love them. His love was reserved for those of his kin in the Twilight Lands, and for his little family here—Tsali'gei and their son. Everyone else he considered a threat to him and to those he loved.

Save your compassion for those who can do you no harm, his father Allyr had advised him. *And understand this: only a dead enemy can do you no harm*. Allyr's heart was as cold as the sea which had birthed them, and as true. His words had become Jian's law.

No weakness, he reminded himself as they passed a group of children playing hoop-toss and chanting as the colored circles flew through the air among them.

> *When the Dragon wakes at last,*
> *Who will rise and who will fall?*

211

Shaman, sorcerer, lover, liar,
Who will rise and rule them all?

No quarter, he thought further, hardening his heart as he watched a young merchant's apprentice scramble to hide behind a food cart. *No mercy.*

At last they reached the palace.

Though Jian had spent five long years in the Twilight Lands, surrounded by magic and beauty and grace unthinkable in the lands of men, still he caught his breath at the sight up close of the Palace of Flowers. It shone beneath the tourmaline sky like a crimson lotus blossoming in still waters, serene and beautiful. The golden-tiled roof rivaled Akari's gaze in its brilliance, and the many-colored windows dazzled even eyes grown accustomed to wonder.

Flowering trees—tended and twisted by dedicated gardeners whose tongues and eyes had been put out so that they might live only for their precious charges—lined the wide, steep steps that led up to the palace. The way was illuminated by magical lanterns of wormsilk and spidersilk, and as they mounted the stairs soft petals were crushed beneath the feet, fresh-cut flowers by the tens of thousands sending up a fragrant dying prayer.

Lashai of a kind Jian had never seen—red-clad servants with faces pale and beautiful as candles—opened the massive gold doors, and a score or more of young women and men, naked and exquisite, emerged from the palace bearing wide woven baskets. Laughing silently, they flung yet more petals before Jian's feet. Their smiles were wide and perfect, and their eyes shone dark and lovely and empty as obsidian.

As Jian crossed the threshold at Mardoni's side, white light bloomed around them painfully bright and pure. The doors closed behind them with a soft, deep, mournful sound like an enormous golden bell, tolling the empire's doom.

❖

Jian squinted against the brilliance of the luminists who lined the long hall and the steps up to the dais of the emperor's throne, but he never slowed his stride. Neither did he bow head or bend knee in the emperor's presence. He was the daeborn son of the Sea King, and the sea bowed to no man.

Daeshen Tiachu sat upon a massive throne, higher than the tallest man's head. It was carved of blackthorn and polished till it gleamed like a live thing. The symbol of the white bull rose over his head, wrought so cunningly—of human bone, it was said—that it seemed the beast would break free and trample them all underfoot. More luminists clustered about the throne like brilliant flowering trees, clad in sunlight, stern-faced and sun-eyed, each of them beautiful as a faceted gemstone, deadlier than a thousand swords.

The emperor himself was imposing even by daeborn standards: broad-shouldered and with the bull's neck of a fighting man, with dark eyes shadowed by a pair of massive bull's horns. He made no move to stand and did not address them as they approached.

Mardoni stopped at the foot of the dais and dropped to one knee, then bent so low that his forehead touched the bottom step. Jian merely inclined his head, drawing an angry hiss from some.

"Your Illumination," he said, in a voice meant to carry to the far corners of the wide hall. "I have come as you asked."

Daeshen Tiachu sat still and silent for many long moments, staring down at Jian and the rest of the entourage. His face showed no more emotion than a dancer's mask, and his eyes showed less than that.

"So," he said finally in a voice like soft blue thunder, "the sea has come to the mountain. Come, Tsun-ju Jian, son of the Sea King. Sit. We have much to discuss." He indicated a place at his side.

Jian took a deep breath and set one foot upon the lowest step, feeling that the moments of his life till this one had been raindrops in a river, and that this was the sea.

The emperor proposed, through Mardoni's mouth, that the problems of Sindan be laid neither at the feet of the Daechen nor the twilight folk—for were they not kindred?

"It is the self-proclaimed Dragon Kings and Queens, who would style themselves as leaders of the world," the emperor's proxy argued, and the other Sen-Baradam muttered agreement. "The Dragon King claims to sacrifice his very life to keep Sajani asleep lest she wake and destroy us all, yet who is to say the atulfah could not be wielded as well—or *better*—by his Illumination? Surely the wisdom of Khanbul is better suited to the civilized use of magic than the barbaric singing of some western king."

The greatest threat, he pressed, was Atualon itself, long gripped by internal wars of succession, and this eternal bickering threatened to destroy all the lands, not just those in the north.

"It is the duty of the Sindan daeborn," Mardoni said, "spawned man and magic, to take charge of this holy duty."

Not a word was spoken of coastal raids, or the winnowing of daeborn youths, or of wives and children held hostage. These unspoken words threatened to drown out all other arguments in Jian's mind.

In the end he agreed, however, as he and his father had intended, to set aside the difference between Dae and daeborn and humankind, for the good of the empire and the peoples of the world. An illuminated scroll was presented and described to those present. Written in ink and iron, it was a treaty between the Sindanese empire and the twilight lords.

Those in the hall held their collective breath, like a man dying on the battlefield not ready to let go of hope, as Jian dipped a bear's-hair brush into ink mixed with his blood, and the emperor's, and the light of Illumination.

He signed the document.

> *Tsun-ju Jian de Allyr*
> *Son of Tiungpei the pearl diver of Bizhan*
> *and*
> *Allyr the Sea King*
> *In this year of Illumination*

The emperor smiled at last and wrote his own name with a flourish. Tiachu leaned back into the hard back of his throne and raised a massive hand above Jian's head.

"It is done," he intoned. "Let there be light." The illuminists in the hallway glowed with their emperor's satisfaction, highlighting the bloodthirst of those assembled.

What he also meant was: *Let there be war.*

Jian saw that it was good. And it was terrible.

After the treaty had been signed, the doors were opened and a festival commenced. Gifts were presented first to his Illumination the emperor, and then to Jian. Practical gifts of horses, swords, books, even a full set of exquisite raptor-hide armor, presented by a young woman whose face was vaguely familiar, and who was introduced to Jian as a commander of one of the empire's new battalions of raptor fighters.

Most interesting was a torque of gold and red iron given to him by a pair of young daeborn who had walked all the way from Salar Merraj. Sea-bear's eyes, faceted bits of dragonglass, glittered at the ends of the torque. It was not a practical thing, but it was beautiful. One of the sea-bears, he thought, looked female, where the other was decidedly masculine. It reminded him of Tsali'gei. He smiled at the antlered young girl as she placed it around his neck.

"Who are you?" he asked.

"I am no one," she answered in a hollow voice, lifting her chin in an arrogant manner.

"We are Kanati," the youth who had accompanied her said, a bright-eyed young man. "And Awitsu." Though his voice and manner were soft, almost apologetic, the hairs on the back of Jian's neck prickled when their glances met. Son of the Sea King or no, Sen-Baradam or no, he had the distinct impression that were he to raise a hand against the girl, this youth would tear him flesh from bone.

More than you appear, are you? He favored the lad with the sharp-toothed smile of a predator. *You are not alone in this, youngling.*

The boy met him stare for stare, and a small smile formed at the corners of his mouth. He nodded, and the two backed away, bowing in the proper manner of emissaries.

Overhead the moons and stars could be seen through panes of colored glass, and the hours swam by like silvery fish. When an emissary from some far province was in the middle of a long speech—about honeybees, Jian thought, but perhaps it was meant to be a metaphor of some sort—the emperor raised his hand again, and the gathering went silent. Even the candles seemed to cease sputtering, the shadows to hold their breaths.

"Enough," Tiachu said. With no further explanation, he rose to his feet, and every person in the room fell bonelessly to the floor.

All save Jian. He stood, ruefully figuring that it would be a breach of etiquette to rub his numb-tingling hindquarters and wondering what sort of obeisance—if any—he should make. Groveling was out of the question, but as he had agreed to limited service under the emperor, perhaps he should at least take a knee? Never would Allyr bend, he was certain of it, but Jian was his father's son, and not a Sea King himself.

Not yet, anyway.

Just as he had settled on a deep nod of respect and a slight bend at the waist—enough to indicate honor without servility—the emperor turned to him. As he stepped closer, Jian was forced to look up, up, up to meet those too-bright, too-knowing, too-old eyes.

"You are tired," the emperor said. "It is time for you to rest."

Jian stifled a yawn, suddenly and completely fatigued. Was it magic of some kind, he wondered, or just the late hour? In the end it did not matter. The emperor's dark gaze swept across the room, sending the crowd tumbling backward through the door. When they had all gone—all save Mardoni, still on his knees at the foot of the dais—the emperor turned away from Jian, dismissing him as a man might a glove dropped and forgotten beside a muddy road, there to be trampled in the empire's march to war.

"Well," Tsali'gei said when he returned to their chambers, "I can see that the emperor has not had you killed yet." And then she proceeded to kiss him half to death. Jian began to wonder whether she had it in mind to conceive a second child then and there when a soft sound drew his attention. He turned toward it, and his heart stopped short as he all but dropped his beloved on her pretty little butt.

"Mother," he breathed.

Tiungpei stood poised in the doorway to an adjoining room, one hand on the half-open door and the other pressed over her heart as if to keep it from flying away at the sight of him. She was smaller than he remembered, older, more bent, and more frail, but in her eyes and the proud way she held her head lay the strength of a woman who had loved the sea.

"Jian," she said, and her voice cracked his heart.

"Mother," he answered, his voice the small echo of a seabird calling to the waves. "I have come back to you. I did not forget."

Tiungpei loosed her hold on the door and moved quickly across the room. Jian held out his arm and enfolded her, enfolded both of them, clinging to his lost ones and filling his heart with their presence.

In that moment, he knew, the fate of the world was sealed.

At the end of his third day in the Palace of Flowers—three days filled with assemblages, and decrees, and false jeweled smiles—Giella, the White Nightingale, flew to land at his side.

She seemed to him to have flown in truth. The feathered print of her red robes, hiked up and tied at the waist to display red silk pants, the crest of feathers at her temples, even the bright laughing intelligence in her strange eyes gave the impression that she could spread her arms and take flight. That she had left the wild skies to come to him filled Jian with a foreboding kind of pleasure.

Birdlike, too, was her stance as she perched on the delicate rail of the balcony upon which he stood. Balanced on one foot, arms outstretched, long red sleeves fluttering in the evening breeze.

"That seems risky," he commented, leaning upon the railing and pretending to himself that he was not trying to steal a peek as the wind plastered the silk robes close to her body. The White Nightingale laughed, her pale throat arched against the indigo-bleeding sky.

"What, this?" she teased, hopping from foot to foot light as a wish. "Or the color of my robes? Or our meeting here, now?"

"All of these and more," he said. "If you were seen wearing the emperor's colors—"

"If I am seen in the city at all, it will be my head," she chided softly. "No comfort girl is allowed in Khanbul at all after dark, and a comfort girl who is also a trained assassin?" She sat back on her haunches, paying no mind to the cliff-sheer drop beneath her, and waggled a finger in his face. "My being here would likely cause both of our heads to roll, O Son of the Sea King."

"Why have you come, then?"

"Because I can," she quipped. "Who is this emperor"— she made a rude noise with her tongue— "to tell me where I may and may not go? What colors I may or may not wear? I am Giella, daughter of the Twilight Court. As I was promised to this world, so was this world promised to me. It is mine, to travel where I will, wearing what I will, and…" She leaned close, so close her red lips brushed Jian's ear and made him shiver. "…loving whomsoever I choose to love."

"Giella—"

"Also," she went on, ignoring him, "I have come to warn you about Mardoni. He is not your friend, Jian. He smiles to your face, while sharpening his knife for your back. Rumors are cropping up in Khanbul and in Sindan beyond, falsehoods he has planted like mushrooms in his dark and shit-filled mind, that you seek to set yourself on a level with the emperor. Already it is known that you refused to bow before the throne of the White Bull. Many of the Sen-Baradam whisper in dark corners that your intent is to make the bull bow before you."

"Ah." Jian sighed. "I wish I could say that I was surprised."

"Let me grant your wish, then!" Giella said with a girlish laugh. She sprang down from the balustrade and before Jian knew it, kissed him full on the mouth.

He kissed her back. Knowing he would regret it later, regretting it even then. He wrapped his arms around the White Nightingale and drew her close, reveling in her bright heat and lithe body, the dangerous strangeness of her, the intoxicating scent of Daezhu.

"Now you can say you are surprised," she murmured against his chest. "I have granted your wish."

"Giella," he said too late, drawing back just enough to pretend that he was resisting, yet not far enough to be believable. "I cannot. Tsali'gei—"

"Is your wife and your true love," she finished, placing a finger upon his mouth. "I know this. I am just—" She looked up and into him, then changed what she had been about to say. "Just here to tell you to be careful. It would be safest for you to take Tsali'gei and the child back to the Twilight Lands, and forget the world of men."

"Would that I could," he answered, and he meant it. "But the oracles have spoken, and they all say the same thing. That Sajani is indeed waking, threatening the Twilight Lands as well as this one. The chance to unite all lands—Twilight, Sindan, and Atualon—under a single power is simply too great an opportunity to pass up. Besides, the ink has not yet faded on the treaty. Were I to be harmed while here in the Forbidden City, the armies of twilight would fall upon them like iron rain."

"All lands united under a single banner, hm?" Her lips brushed his again, and then she pulled away. Jian let her go, reluctantly. "Under whose banner, I wonder. The white bull? Your father's silver seashells? Or perhaps you think to unite the world beneath the banner of the blue bear?"

"Hush," he scolded, watching with some regret as she leapt gracefully back to the knife's edge of the balustrade. "Your mouth is too big to speak of such things. I do not care what banner the world chooses to march beneath, so long as it is united and kept safe for us. For all of us," he added, thinking not only of himself and the other daeborn, but of the Twilight Lands, the common village folk. Even the peoples of Atualon, he supposed, deserved a chance to raise their children in peace.

"Hush," she mocked, "your mouth is too pretty to speak of such grand dreams." And she leapt backward into the night sky, laughing.

With a cry Jian leaned out over the railing, but she was gone. Only her laughter, the scent of her hair, and the warmth of her kiss upon his lips lingered as proof she had ever been there.

TWENTY-FIVE

Morning burst upon the Edge hot and dry, with a hint of spice in the dusted air that mocked the refugees with memories of hearth-bread and pies. Maika worried as she climbed the wide stone steps to the rooms into which her counselors had insisted upon settling her—she did not want the bakers to be digging new hearths in this place; she did not want her people to get comfortable and attempt to resume some semblance of their former lives. As terrifying as she found the prospect of leading a doomed march aboveground with too few shadowmancers to shield them from the deadly sun, Maika knew that to remain here was folly. Even now, runners returned from scouting missions with wounded from an encounter with a greater predator, or with a voice shakily recounting tales of reavers hunting the road behind them.

Sometimes the scouts set out and did not return at all, or they returned bitten and were put down by their sisters and brothers before the change could take them.

The lives we had are over. There is no hope for us now but to leave the Seared Lands forever.

She knew this, felt it in her bones and fingertips, heard it in the empty wailing wind through the passageways. *If we brave the shadowed roads, many of my people will perish— but if we attempt to remain here, we will all die.* But how to convince her people of this truth, when they had followed in her footsteps the first time and had come so near to ruin at the hands of mere Edgelanders? How could she make her own counselors see the naked truth, when she herself did not yet reach past any of their chins?

That very afternoon Counselorwoman Lehaila had been caught trying to bolt with the remaining three shadowmancers, and Maika had had no choice but to call for her execution. Now she must, as was her duty, bear witness to the death of a woman whose greatest crime was giving into the fear they all shared. She could almost wish that the Araids would find and kill them all before she was forced to do this thing.

Counselorwoman Lehaila was dressed in the sky-blue and gold of one who was to be surrendered to Akari. A blue hood covered her head, and golden slippers graced her large feet. Those feet were splayed and strong, in the proud stance of a woman who had run miles in a youth spent in service to her people. In the end, she would have abandoned them, though, and such an offense no queen could pardon. Most especially in such dark days as they faced now. The woman had left her no choice.

No choice, she repeated firmly to herself as they bound Lehaila hand and foot to the red iron rings that had been set into a cobbled stone courtyard in ancient times, perhaps for this very purpose. She clenched her jaw and widened her eyes to keep them dry, lest the silent, grim crowd see her grief as doubt, and take tears for weakness. *I have no choice. She did this to herself, not I.*

Never, she knew, never would those words ring true. There was always a choice, though seldom, it seemed to her, much joy in the choosing.

When offerings of oil and meat, salt and manna water had been piled around the counselorwoman's feet, when Lehaila's weeping children had been led away, Maika took the last few steps to stand by her side. There, finally, she hesitated. She had been advised to give a grand and stirring speech—had been up all day and half the night composing it, in fact—about courage and sacrifice and remaining together as a people in the face of danger. Now that she saw the woman trembling in fear, Maika found she had no heart for queenly words or wise remonstrations.

Her eyes followed the thick manna-root rope that snaked up the rift walls all the way to the bare, burnt surface of her ancestral lands. Standing here in the Edge, the rifts and canyons and tunnels that made a world for them were much closer to the surface than those in Saodan; Maika could, if she raised her face to the sky, make out the stars high above and the faint bruise-purple edges of a dying night.

Unbidden a memory came to her of a day, not many years past, when she was small and alone. She had broken her arm in a fall down some stairs. She hurt, and she missed her auntie Yaela, and the nurses found her inconsolable. Counselorwoman Lehaila had come to her rooms, though she was a busy woman with duties to Quarabala and children of her own. Lehaila had brought sweets, and a doll carved of manna root, and a book written by the warrior-poet Maika, for whom she had been named.

"Forgive me," Maika whispered to the condemned woman, "I cannot do this."

"You must," Lehaila whispered back harshly. "You cannot turn back now, not if you are to lead our people. And you must lead them, you *must*. I was wrong and I knew it. It was wrong of me to—" She choked on the words, chest heaving. "Please just... just get it over with. My queen. I am sorry. I—"

Maika held up one hand, begging the woman to silence. Then she beckoned Tamimeha and her grim warriors forward and they came. The hood was drawn over Lehaila's weeping eyes, and the end of that long rope fashioned into a crude harness and tied about her torso. Finally Tamimeha kissed the counselorwoman on both cheeks, a formal farewell. She stepped back from Lehaila—they all did—and the rope went taut as unseen hands hauled at it. Like a bird in the stories Lehaila began to rise, slowly at first, twisting this way and that as they hauled her up to the surface of the world, and to her doom.

"Forgive me, my queen!" she wailed. "Forgive me!"

Maika made herself stand and watch as Lehaila rose to meet Akari, refusing her eyes the comfort of darkness, refusing her heart the comfort of a turned cheek. When Lehaila reached the surface she would be free to cut her bonds with the small knife tucked into her waistband and run, though it would do her no good; dawn would bring her death by fire. Or she could choose, as was more usual, to end her own life by the blade instead.

There is always a choice, Maika reminded herself. She clenched her fists till the nails dug into her palms, as if sharing the condemned woman's agony might somehow absolve some small portion of her crushing black guilt. *She made hers, just as I have.*

The crowd roared in horror as Lehaila made her choice: she plunged to the ground wailing, clawing at the air as if she might catch it, bright blade of her knife falling before her like an omen. She had chosen neither death by fire nor by the blade, but had sawed through the rope as it hauled her to the surface. She hit the ground with such a sound as would haunt Maika waking and sleeping for whatever time remained to her. Lehaila's bright life burst forth to spray upon the stones, splattering Maika's robes and staining her golden slippers a dull red. The horrified crowd of witnesses gasped, or wept, or turned away. Many of them glanced at their queen as they did so, with looks of respect, of awe, of fear or anger or a combination of the emotions of which human mouths are too small to speak or hearts to fully encompass.

Maika stood sick and stunned, whispering to Lehaila that of course she forgave her, that of course she would not do this terrible, unthinkable thing.

❖

The young queen did not return to her temporary rooms immediately after the execution, but wandered listlessly down the corridors of the ancient city, trailing her fingers along the gritty walls and sneezing at the stone dust. She was trailed by a handful of Iponui, their painted bodies glowing dully against the gloom. There were no torches here, no kitchens or dancing rooms; the Edgelanders seemed to lack the imagination necessary to build a life of comfort for themselves, preferring instead to leave the world as drear and joyless as they found it.

"Your Magnificence?" A warrior whom Maika did not know jogged up from the group.

"Yes?" Maika did not stop or turn her head to either side, but continued to stare straight down a long and narrow corridor half filled with the rubble of recent earthquakes. A chill wind caught at her ankles, and she suppressed a shudder.

"Are you... are you well, my queen? Would you not care to return to your rooms and rest? If you are unwell, I can send a... a healer, an Illindrist—"

They think me weak, Maika thought. *Too weak and too young to fulfill my duties as queen*. The idea saddened her, but her tutor Aasah would have said that the illusion of power *is* power, so she continued forward as if she knew where she was going.

"No," she said. "I wish only to commune with my ancestors, to be blessed and cleansed by their presence. You may leave me."

"But your—your Magnificence—surely some few of us should remain with you—"

"I said you may leave." Maika cut her eyes sideways at the woman and allowed her irritation to show. "Who would dare to attack me as I speak to the shades of those queens who have gone before me? Would you?" She shook her head fractionally and increased her pace, letting the woman fall behind her. *Let them whisper, let them think me mad.* Maika had no time for their political games. The Iponui drew back, muttering among themselves.

Maika turned a corner and was alone at last. She took a long, shuddering breath, finally allowing herself to feel the fear which had gnawed at her heart since Lehaila had been brought before her, and since she had sent the woman to her death. Though she had spoken of the ancestors only to rid herself of the warriors' presence—she truly wanted nothing more than to be left alone so that she could have a good cry—the desire rose in Maika to do just as she had said; to call upon the spirits of her ancestors, brave queens who had survived much worse than this, and beg their intercession. As the notion took hold of her, Maika's steps quickened till she was nearly running. She ran from the guilt and horror of Lehaila's execution, and ran, so it seemed to her, toward a desperate hope.

It did not occur to Maika, for she was still young and new to the ways of the world, to wonder whether she was following the desires of her own heart or the lure of a greater will.

My ancestors will know, she thought as she ducked beneath a low arch and wound her way through dust and rubble. The dawn had come, searing the land high above, and though unlit by torch or fire or magelight the path was clear enough for Maika to follow. *Surely they will know the way. Surely if I ask, help will be given.*

The others would perhaps assume that she had gone to the ancestors to seek forgiveness, but Maika told herself—again—that her soul bore no guilt. Lehaila had tried to save her own hide, and in so doing had imperiled not only those shadowmancers she had persuaded to flee, but whatever thin hope there was of saving her people.

Lehaila will be the last of us to die. I will save all *of my people*, she thought, *to the least and last of them, to the newest and weakest of suckling babes, to the tiniest white-haired grandmother*. This time, there would be none left behind. Whether they wished to join the exodus or no, whether Tamimeha attempted to forbid her or no, Maika was queen of Quarabala, and her will would become truth. *I will lead my people to safe lands*, she vowed in the halls of her ancestors, *or I will die trying. Die trying.*

Die trying.

Die trying.

A whisper stalked the narrow passageway like the echo of her own thoughts, or the laughter of some ancient and awful thing. It surprised Maika, jolting her from the tranced daze through which she had run and causing her to stop short, nearly tripping over her own feet. She stood bent at the waist, gasping for air and trembling as if she had run for hours.

When Maika came back to her senses she found herself staring at a wall inlaid with a silvery spider's web so bright that artisans might have laid it into the stone that very day. Beneath the symbol was etched a name: Na'eth. *Illindra's web*, she thought, studying the gleaming web. *This was a holy place, once.* Aasah had showed her such a symbol, when she was very young, and had told her what that name meant. Indeed, he had warded her eyes against the glamour which would have hidden it from ordinary folk and had instructed her as to what a queen might do, had she courage and a desperate need.

Her palm where it had touched the web stung, and her stomach felt queasy. There was magic here, dark and sticky; a deadly trap. Maika knew that she should turn back and run all the way back to the rooms in which she was housed, but her feet refused to move. She swallowed the bile of growing terror. Knowing the magic was there did not make it easier to withstand.

Touching her fingertips to thumbs she linked her hands together in the symbol of Illindra's unity and pressed them to the web's center. That portion of the wall into which the web had been set slid silently back a pace, the magic still fresh after these many years of men. Maika took a shuddering breath and then stepped forward, into a narrow passage, dark and deep and secret.

The passage led only one way, for a short distance, and ended in a smooth round chamber with a small arched doorway in the far wall. Directly before her, the thin and wavery light of an ancient mage-torch revealed the statue of a woman, stern-faced and lovely, with hair in tidy locks that extended nearly down to her feet. She was armored as if for war. At her belt she wore six knives, the hilt of each fashioned after some bird or animal the likes of which Maika had never seen. A lyre was strung across her shoulders, her booted feet were set shoulder-width apart, and both hands were held up, palms out toward Maika, in a clear warning.

Go back. Do not pass.

But pass she must; if Aasah's teachings were true, this sorcerer's path—for such ways were used only by those blessed of Illindra—might reveal to her some power or tool which would help lead her people to safety.

Maika edged around the statue of the ancient queen, wondering if perhaps this was some ancestor of hers whose name had been written in the dust of time. Drawing a long, shuddering breath, she hunched her shoulders forward and stepped through the narrow doorway, pausing only to snatch up the mage-torch. It brightened at her touch, giving off a wavering red light which did little to dispel her dread.

When he had told her of Illindra's silvery web and what might lie behind such a symbol, Aasah had given her a warning.

"Old ways lead to old things," he had told her, *"and many old things are best left undisturbed."*

Maika continued down a path trodden by who-knows-what and who-knows-whom in ages past, looking neither to the left nor the right. It grew narrow and wild, as the stone beneath her feet rough. The walls and arching ceiling closed in and the air was sharp with secrets and the spores of dark fungi. A sudden right, and then right again, and without warning the passageway opened into empty space over her, and under her, and to either side, as if some great thing had taken a big bite out of the flesh of the world and left a jagged void.

Maika paused on the threshold of a dark place. Her breathing was fast and raggedy, her heart bounced around inside her like a child's ball. Her voice trembled as she called out, "Na'eth, it is I." For so were named all the daughters of Illindra whose ancestors had fallen to this world from Illindra's web in time long lost, and with whom the Kentakuyan queens of Quarabala claimed ancient friendship.

For what seemed like a very long time there was no answer, no noise save the blood pounding in her ears, nothing to see save the dark and the trembling torchlight. Then came the wind whispering down the passageways, thin and dry as cobwebs. It rose in volume and passion, *shishhhing* and *shusssshing* and swirling with noises like words.

Closer, closer the wind howled, and Maika realized that the air was not moving; her torchlight never wavered but for the shaking of her hands. It was not the wind at all, but the whispering of Araids, and they were coming for her.

Maika shuddered as the light of her torch picked up a faint gleam, there and gone and there again. Glittering orbs bigger than her hand, her head, in clusters and rows and circles they appeared, steadied in the irresolute light, and approached. There was a noise like swords and knives clashing, and the gleam of light on cold metal as three lesser Araids crawled into her circle of light.

Monstrous they were, taller than many rooms, wider than doors, red-and-black striped legs gleaming metallic and hard with living armor. Their eyes twitched horribly as they focused on her, mouth parts moving as they considered the savor of her human flesh. Each had raised a pair of brass-haired legs and were rubbing these against their abdomens. This was the source of the not-wind sound she had heard.

The Araids spoke in whispers.

Whispers and death.

"It is I," Maika said, and it came out as a squeak, courage failing as it always did. This time, she knew, there would be no reprieve; this time she would be eaten by these spiders made of swords. "It is I, Maika, queen of Quarabala. I am come to speak to Na'eth."

At the mention of that name, the three monstrous forms rose up, forelegs waving madly, whispering and chittering. One of them, the largest and most fiercely striped, scuttled forward, needle fangs longer than her legs poised to strike—

"*Hisssst. Hissssssst.* Ach, my children, be still. Be gone. Na'eth would speak with this small beast."

The voice that rolled across the void was no wisp of wind, no hairy scratching, but a low rumbling growl like sweet water rushing over rocks. The three Araids froze as if they had been turned to stone, and then with a scuttle and a scrape and one last lingering glance backward they were gone.

Maika could not help it. She dropped to her knees, and then to her face in the dust, shaking from lock to toe in the grip of black terror. When the cold wind came, she cried out, and when one foreleg as big around as a child reached out to touch her hair, she wept.

"*Hisssst, hissst,* little humanling. Ach now, ai now, no need for that. Na'eth will not eat you." Laughter like fire through parchment. "Not this day. Not for many days, perhaps, perhaps."

Maika lay trembling in the dirt, unable to stand.

"Enough, humanling. Rise with courage and face me, if you would call yourself Kentakuyan. Tell me why you have come to tempt the hungers of my children, and why I should not let them eat you."

Maika dragged her knees across the rock, forced her splayed hands to push her body upright, and at last stood on shaking legs. "I have come," she said, "because I need to help my people. The Araids of the deep came for us with their Arachnists and reavers, so I have led my people here to the Edge. But we were attacked and now we are trapped. We do not have enough shadowmancers to lead all my people across the shadowed roads and into the green lands, and I... I have no power of my own."

Here her courage failed. What she thought to beg was forbidden, it was sacrilege. She screwed her eyes tightly shut.

"Ahhhhhh, humanling. I know what it is you would ask. You wish to *see*."

Maika drew a deep breath, the deepest she had ever taken. She stilled the shaking in her knees, the quivering of her heart, and reminded herself that she was a queen. She opened her eyes and looked up, up.

Up.

Up.

Into the face of a monster.

To call Na'eth a spider was to call a sword a knife, or to call death a respite. This was a being of stars and nightmares, fallen to the center of the earth and there to abide for all ages, a thing of black malice and bright laughter, whose children fed on human flesh and whose mercy might—just might— save an entire people.

"Yes, Na'eth," Maika said at last. "I come to beg the gift of Illindra's sight."

"Do you know what it is you ask, Kentakuyan?"

"I do."

"Do you know the cost of that which you ask? Such a gift is not granted without sacrifice. A terrible price, for one such as you." Maika imagined—surely, she imagined—that the nightmare thing spoke with pity.

Years ago, when Maika was very small and foolish, and trying to find her place in the hot, dark world, she had made her first decree, one which had set all the courtiers to laughing: that no spider might be smashed or harmed in any way. It was for this reason, perhaps, that the queen of spiders now granted the darkest wish of her heart.

Quicker than death, darker than shadows, Na'eth reared up. Her fangs glistened red and wet, and Maika froze in terror.

They will stab through me, she thought, *and I will die here in the dirt—*

Her mage-torch died, plunging them into darkness. A soft touch, gentle and loving as she had always imagined a mother's might be, brushed the nape of Maika's throat.

"Is that all?" she asked.

"Little queen," said Na'eth in a voice like dead things, "it is done."

Pain blossomed in her throat and raced through her veins like wildfire, weaving trails of searing agony across her skin and bones and blood. The Araid's icy fire consumed her.

She fell.

"You are bound now, child. You are bound to us."

It was her mother, who had died birthing her.

It was Yaela.

It was Aasah.

It was Na'eth, spinning her empty webs into the darkness and keeping the stars at bay. Of all the Araids, Na'eth had told her, only the great daughters of Illindra believed that humans were more than food, more than skin and blood and bile. When she herself was a spiderling, she had heard a human singing an old song, and it had warmed a corner of her sword-touched heart. It read her poetry and sang a child's rhymes in a dreadfully untrained voice, and showed her a child's drawings of home.

So she had not yet devoured the little humanling who came to her, in the dark place at dark times, bearing torchlight which hurt her eyes and food she could not eat, and allowed this small thing to ask a boon.

"Little Maika," the voice crooned, "you are bound to me. Wake. See."

Maika opened her eyes and would have screamed, but her mouth was bound. She hung suspended by a strand of web around her feet, head down, hair trailing back and forth across the cavern floor as the web sagged and trembled with Na'eth's weaving.

The great spider—if a sword is a knife—was moving with a delicate grace as she fastened tiny globes of magesilver to her web, weaving a grand design. Maika craned her neck to see, bound as she was, terrified as she was, because the web of forever was a thing of such beauty that it would be worth death to have experienced it.

Her breath caught in her chest as she saw at once that each globe held the image of a person's face. There was Aasah, and Yaela, and Tamimeha—there she was, Queen Maika, lovelier than she had ever seen herself, prouder and more regal. There was Lehaila, mouth and eyes open wide in death's agony. And there, before her face in a glowing orb twice the size of the others, she beheld a figure clad all in shadows, bright and terrifying. It threw back its hood, stared into her eyes, and laughed. "You see," Na'eth whispered, endlessly pitying. "You have paid the price, and now you can see."

I do not understand.

"Of course you do not understand," Na'eth snapped, a spider if death is but sleep. "I gave you vision, not the wisdom to understand what you are seeing. That is for you to earn, little humanling. I gave you what you asked for—I gave you sight. There is your savior; now you can see him. Only call, and you will be delivered from this land, you and yours."

Yes, Maika thought. *Of course.* It was what all the old stories called for—a hero in times of darkness, to lead the people forward into the light. She reached out, not with her hands, which were bound, but with sa and ka, the heart and breath of her soul, and touched the glowing orb. It burned— how it burned!—but it was a good pain, a true pain, the pain of a queen's sacrifice for her people.

The face in the orb smiled, a brilliant smile which brought her to tears, and winked out.

"You have seen, you have called," Na'eth said. "It is done."

Maika closed her eyes and prepared to die.

I am ready, she thought. *I will pay the price.*

"*Hissssst, hisssst*, silly humanling." Na'eth laughed like the clash of knives. "The price has been paid. You are free to go." She stretched one foreleg out and brushed the single strand that held Maika to the web. The strand broke.

Again, Maika fell...

Forever.

When the web-marked door slid back again and Maika stumbled forward into the light, Tamimeha was waiting for her. The warrior yelled with surprise and delight, dropping her torch and scooping her fainting queen up to cradle her in her arms like a child.

"Oh, my queen!" she cried, patting her hair and rocking. "Oh, my heart, where have you been? I feared you were—" Her voice broke.

"Tamimeha," Maika rasped. Her voice was raw from screaming, and she hurt everywhere. "There is no time. We must go. We must ready the people to leave this place."

"Hush now. Are you harmed?" Tamimeha stood Maika up and held her at half an arm's length, just far enough to search her with hungry, anxious eyes. "Your tracks led here, and no further. Where have you been? What happened to—

235

oh. Oh! Oh, my queen, your *eyes!*" The horror on her face broke Maika's heart all over again. "Pelang!"

"Gather your warriors," Maika repeated, softly so as not to hurt her raw throat or reveal the depth of her emotions. "A savior is coming to lead us all from the Seared Lands. I have seen it. You must gather your best warriors and meet her upon the shadowed roads, and bring her here to us."

"Eyes of Pelang!" Tamimeha wailed again, as if Maika had not spoken. "What have you done?"

"I needed to see into the future," Maika answered with quiet dignity. The horror on Tamimeha's face hurt; it took an effort of will for her not to hide her eyes from the sight. *I have nothing to be ashamed of*, she reminded herself. *I did only what I had to do.* "So that I might find a way to save my people. And I have seen it, I have found it. The price was mine to pay, and I have paid it."

"But, my queen—Maika—it is forbidden for one to hold the throne who has eyes of Pelang. It is too much power—this is forbidden by laws as old as time."

"Laws change." Maika smiled, though she was weary to the song in her bones. "Times change... I have *seen* it."

TWENTY-SIX

Killing the lionsnake had been easy. Hannei had faced her kind more than once in the fighting pits of Min Yaarif. They were slower and less cunning than their desert cousins. Their venom was milder. The trick was to kill the beasties before they could wrap those powerful coils around limb or midsection.

If heat and thin air and slow, stupid snakes are the worst these mountains have to throw at us, Hannei thought to herself, *this journey may prove easier than a day spent gathering spiders' eggs for the Mothers.*

Such good fortune was unlikely, she knew—would have been unlikely had she been riding with a fist of sisters, rather than this band of idiots, thieves, and pirates. So she kept her watch with as much vigilance as if she were guarding the pride's bachelor herds.

There was a new voice of the winds. The mountains had been laughing at them since first they set out—sometimes wheezing, sometimes howling with a thousand mad voices, even hissing like foul breath through rotten teeth—but since Hannei had been unable to talk, she had learned to listen better. Thus she was the first who noticed that the howl of mad laughter was not coming from one direction, as winds from on high, but from points all around them, above and below.

She roused Sulema, and the others. In haste they seized what weapons were to hand and piled their fire high with sage-brush and dead branches so that it blazed up into the night, sending a shower of sparks flying to meet the stars and warning the predators that this group of humans was no easy meat.

The mymyc came as a rush of dark water down the moonslit and cruel face of Avolk Tohn, first among the Jehannim in height and in wickedness. They also rose as a black mist from the foothills below, red-eyed and ravenous, rending the air with the cackling laughter they had stolen from men and which raised the chillflesh along Hannei's arms. From a distance they seemed as fine black horses, sleek and slender and lovely, but their movement was catlike, predatory, as they crept along the jagged rocks and the moonslight glinted off of scaled hides, revealing them as dragonkin.

One of them screamed like a human woman and the others laughed. Being predators, mymyc would hunt rabbits or goats or even a lone vash'ai, if they had to, but they took the greatest delight in the taste of manflesh.

Hannei stood naked but for her trousers and sister-swords, still and silent between Rehaza Entanye—who shifted impatiently from foot to foot, panting heavily in the thin, hot air—and Sulema, whose golden eyes glinted in the pale light, as hungry for this fight as the mymyc were for her bones.

She still loves the thrill of the hunt, Hannei thought, *because she still has a love of life and holds it precious.*

In that moment, Hannei hated her sister.

In the next the mymyc were upon them, and there was no time to ponder. One beast, larger and thicker with muscle than the rest and with a torn ear, wrinkled its lips back from long white teeth and growled in a tongue so human that it seemed to Hannei that she could almost understand it. Other mymyc crouched, dragonish eyes glowing red in the firelight, and as one they leapt, howling and screeching and laughing to frighten and confuse their prey.

Laughing her own mirthless, tongueless laugh—a scarred sound born of the cruelty of men and the betrayal of women—Hannei leapt to meet them. Her swords, forged of black iron by slaves and thrice quenched in blood-salted oil, did not throw back the fire's blaze but burned rather with their own dark fire, as if they drank deep of the night's sorrow and belched it forth as fresh death.

Azdafani, she had named one sword, a name which meant *beauty in sorrow*, and *Idbataani* the second, or *beauty in treachery*. With laughter the citizens of Min Yaarif had debated which was the lesser of two evils. The mymyc learned that, in the hands of Kishah, treachery was followed by sorrow and sorrow by pain and death. As she slashed and hacked her way through the snarling mass of claws and fangs and scaled hide that hungered for her flesh, there was little beauty there by the light of the fire, under the eyes of the moons.

Battle was who she was by then, killing was all of her—growling and grunting as if she were more of a beast than the mymyc, dark blades flashing till her shoulders and belly and back screamed with it. Her companions fought well, sword and spear and bludgeon sending sprays of blood to dance with the embers and the stars. Soon the corpses of mymyc were piled all about them, some twitching, all stinking of death and offal, but it was not enough.

There were too few of the humans, or too many of the foe, however you counted it.

We have come to the mountains to die, she thought, and was surprised that the thought did not aggrieve her. More, it was a comfort. She had vowed to kill her sword-sister in these mountains, and so buy her freedom. Here at the end of her life's road, Hannei Ja'Akari—who had named herself vengeance and killed without hesitation or pity—discovered too late that there was yet more honor in her heart than murder.

Blood sprayed into her eyes, and Hannei skipped back a two-step, shaking her head to clear her vision. A bright swirl of robes dazzled and confused her before she recognized Keoki, the shadowmancer from Quarabala.

"Ware!" he shouted to her. "Fire!" He bellowed something else, something she could not quite catch, as he shook a drinking horn at her, a drinking horn plugged at one end with scraps of red cloth. She had seen its like, once only, in the fighting pits...

Balefire!

Hannei turned and ran as the shadowmancer drew back his arm and tossed the horn into the heart of their campfire. She took two long strides toward Sulema, and another toward Rehaza Entanye. Grabbing them both by the shoulders, she bore them to the ground even as the mymyc closed in, laughing. Hannei covered their bodies with hers as best she could, even as claws tore into her shoulder and teeth tore a chunk of flesh from her ruined back.

Sulema went still, covering her head with both hands as they had been taught. Rehaza Entanye struggled to rise, fighting her hold even as Hannei squeezed her eyes shut and held her breath.

The world went red.

TWENTY-SEVEN

Balefire!

Even as he wrenched his short sword from the still-thrashing carcass of a mymyc, Leviathus shouted in alarm at the sight of a plugged horn tumbling through the air and into the bonfire they had built. He had seen its use before, once deep in the catacombs beneath Salar Merraj as the Salarians sought to open a new salt mine, another time by his father's imperators to collapse a colony of soldier beetles grown too close to the city.

It seemed as if a blast tore through his body before the horn had even completed its deadly arc, inspiring his legs to move more swiftly and strongly than ever before. As he bolted he caught a glimpse of silken robes and dark mystery, of wide green eyes sharp and deadly and beautiful as his sword.

"Yaela!" His shout was drowned in the blood and pain and tumult of battle, but not before it had reached her. The apprentice turned, her eyes widened, pupils dilated like shadows swallowing the moons. Spinning on her heel she fled into the dark, scrambling over rock and brush, clinging to the sheer face of the cruel mountain with Leviathus close behind.

The explosion was a dragon's roar, searing the backs of their heels and singeing Leviathus's hair as the flames sped past. The hot air was sucked from his lungs and he gasped, choking on ash and deafened by the terrible noise. Yaela's pale and fluttering robes were his only guide.

If the blast had frightened the mymyc they did not much show it. The greater predators chased their prey like hunting cats after a flushed hare. Claws scrabbled on the rocks so close behind that Leviathus expected every moment, every labored breath to be his last. He imagined those claws tearing into his back, those bright teeth rending the flesh as they tore mouthfuls of meat from his bones.

Yaela disappeared.

Leviathus stumbled in surprise and would have fallen, but a strong hand grabbed his shoulder and wrenched him sideways. Yaela dragged him through a narrow opening between two large rocks—nearly too narrow for his frame. He left most of his tunic and much of his skin behind as they tumbled together into a depression in the stone, almost a small cave.

The mymyc were still outside, just beyond the narrow passage that had scraped him raw, scrabbling at the entrance and snarling their frustration. The thin moonlight dimmed as one of the beasts sought to follow them, but its too-broad shoulders made passage impossible, and it withdrew, growling in its own fell tongue.

The son of Ka Atu sucked in ragged breaths of air, stale and thin, as a man dying of thirst might drink from a worm-riddled mudhole. Sweat poured from his body and was wicked away at once, leaving his skin dry and sticky with salt.

A fine seasoning for our pursuers, he thought with wry humor, *should they have their way with me.* The calls and howls and scrabbling at the cave entrance made it apparent that the night-skinned predators had not given up, not by any means.

A hand on his shoulder sent Leviathus jumping half out of his skin. *Yaela.* Her laughter floated round him, rich and warm and sweet.

"King's son," she said to him, "we need to make a fire. Build it big and hot, *ta*? Burn their eyes, singe their hides if they get in, turn their thoughts to softer prey."

"An excellent idea," he agreed. "Unfortunately for us, the mymyc are between us and our blaze. Unless you would like me to ask them politely to stand aside while I fetch a few embers?"

"Fortunately for us, I do not walk about the world unprepared," she answered. Her pale eyes gleamed soft in the night, jade lamps filled with starlight. Leviathus heard a sound of rustling, and of rocks, and she turned her face from him. Presently came a sharp *clack-clack* and a scattering of miniature stars burst forth on the cave floor.

"Flint?" he asked, astounded. "You have flint?"

"Yes," she answered. *Clack-clack*, more stars.

He tried, and failed, to stop his mind from guessing where she might have kept the flint concealed, and what else she might be hiding beneath those silk wraps.

"Also knives, a mirror, a bit of rope, and…" *Clack-clack*, a shower of tiny sparks, and a tiny ember came to life, breathing a tiny sigh of gray smoke. "…other such things as may come in handy. We have lived different lives, you and I." She breathed upon the ember, and it leapt dancing into bright flame under the glory of her attention.

"Different, yes," he said, "but surely that does not mean that—"

Whatever he had been about to say died in Leviathus's throat.

"Divines save us."

Yaela's tiny fire illuminated more than her comely face and alluring figure. As the shadows fled, a great hulking form was revealed at the back of their cave. Eyes each as big as his face blinked at them in the firelight, teeth longer than his sword revealed themselves as the monstrous beast yawned, flicking a scarlet tongue into the air.

"*Wyvern*," Yaela whispered. Her eyes were as frightened as Leviathus felt. She drew herself up into a dancer's pose, attention fixed on the creature as shadows pooled about her feet, eager to do her bidding.

A thrill of hot fear licked Leviathus's bones as the thing in the back of the cave unfurled itself. Scaled hide scraped audibly against stone as it loomed above them, and a carrion stench filled the air as it flared its nostrils and sucked in their scent.

"*Hass ish lurren hir?*" it hissed, head weaving back and forth even as behind them their pursuers laughed and scrabbled at the cave entrance.

Then he realized that the wyvern had spoken.

And that he could understand it.

"*Lurren hir,*" he hissed back, the dragonkin words strange and uncomfortable in his soft human mouth. "*Lurraith ish. Felsithoth ish kharrahen.*" *Humans are here. Two of us. We are being hunted by mymyc.*

The wyvern thrust its head toward him, paying no mind to the fire. Its tongue flicked out again, licking the air between them, and a curious cinnamon-musk scent filled the tight space.

"*Drach-alar,*" it named him. *Friend to dragonkin.*

Drach-alar, Azhorus agreed in the back of his mind. The king of leviathans was far away and concerned with other matters—eating, sleeping, and showing off for a beguiling young female—but the warmth of his affection washed over Leviathus like the ocean's caress.

The sound of falling rocks came from the cave's mouth. Leviathus spun, grabbing Yaela and thrusting her behind him—toward the wyvern, whether that was a good idea or not. A mymyc thrust its head and shoulders through the entrance. It screamed in victory, and then screamed again in an entirely different pitch as it saw the wyvern behind its intended prey. The beast's forward push became a desperate backward scramble as it sought to escape.

The wyvern narrowed its great luminous eyes and hummed low in its throat.

"*Kharnoch essa,*" it growled. "*Shukos, drach-alar.*" *Good hunting. My thanks, friend.* With that it pushed Leviathus and Yaela out of its way, sending them tumbling, and dragged itself across the cave floor, extinguishing their infant fire. Leviathus would not have believed that such an enormous creature would have been able to fit through that small passageway, but fit it did, squeezing and pushing like a snake through a too-small hole, scrabbling with wing and claw, its barbed tail thrashing at the last so that the humans had to dance out of the way.

Then it was gone hunting, bugling its delight at the prospect of mymyc for its dinner.

Something touched his leg in the darkness. Leviathus yelped, and then gave a shaky laugh when he realized it was just Yaela. He allowed her to help him to his feet and they stood shoulder to shoulder, pressed together against the shadow world.

"Well, king's son," she said at last, "*that* was a surprise. Have I died and gotten lost in the Dreaming Lands, or did you just speak to a wyvern and command it to go chase the mymyc?"

"I spoke with the wyvern in its own tongue," Leviathus admitted in an awed voice. "I suppose it has something to do with my bond to Azhorus. I assure you, however, that I commanded it to do nothing. Well is it said, 'Do not cast your fishing net at a dragon.' I would say the same of dragonkin. Their minds are... vast."

Far away, in the darkling sea, Azhorus laughed.

Yaela's hand found his in the dark and squeezed. "I will build another fire," she announced, "and then you are going to explain to me how it is that Leviathus ap Wyvernus ne Atu, magic-deaf son of the late king, just happens to be able to speak to wyverns."

Yaela's fire danced, sending shadows flickering about their cave, which did not seem so small now that it was not filled with wyvern. The smoke twisted itself into braids and curled lazily up to swirl and eddy about the roof.

They certainly did not need it for its warmth. Whereas night in the Zeera brought cool winds and relief, in the Jehannim there was no respite from the heat. The rocks themselves seemed to radiate, and bent their will to suck moisture and life from the air, as if the land were a forge and Akari meant to temper them within it.

It galled Leviathus not knowing what had happened to their companions, his sister. Yet there was nothing to do as long as the mymyc stalked the night. They would have to wait.

Yaela sat on her heels beside the fire, so close to Leviathus that he could feel the dark energy of her body shivering across his skin like the rhythm of an intoxicating song. She stared into the fire, never meeting his eyes. Still he could not help but feel that she was peering into his soul.

"So," she said, "you can speak to dragonkin."

"Yes," he admitted. "Some of them, at least. I was not able to speak to the mymyc—that I could tell—though they are kin. Others I have not tried, save the leviathans."

"The… leviathans? You mean serpents?"

"They prefer the name 'leviathan.'" The echo in his name had not escaped Leviathus's notice. His mother, like Hafsa Azeina, had come from the Seven Isles. When this current strife was ended—if he survived, and if Sajani did not destroy them all—he thought that he would like to seek out his mother's kin.

We prefer another term entirely, Azhorus informed him through their link, *but your ridiculous little human mouths are insufficient for pronouncing our words.*

Forgive me, o prince, for my inadequacies, Leviathus responded.

You are forgiven, the prince of serpents allowed magnanimously. *I like you.* With that, he was gone again. Leviathus shook his head. Whenever Azhorus spoke with him, it felt as if bubbles were creeping through his brain.

"Do you speak with them now?" Yaela cut her eyes at him. They were not slit as usual, but wide and glowing with their soft warm green.

"Just with Azhorus," he told her. "My... friend. We are bonded, he and I." Though "two made one" would have been more accurate. His link with the prince of deep waters had changed Leviathus on the inside every bit as much as Hafsa Azeina's link with Khurra'an had changed her, he supposed. His senses had sharpened, for one thing.

Yaela shifted, reaching out to the fire, and he was enveloped in a cloud of feminine musk. She turned to look at him over one shoulder, eyes both enormous and amused.

"Did you just *growl* at me?"

"I am so sorry—" he began, but Yaela turned to face him, and whatever he had been going to say dried to ash on his tongue. Backlit by the fire she was shadow and flame, moonslight and starslight and dawn. She was all things beautiful and unreachable. She was—

"Beautiful," she said, reaching out to touch his face. Strong fingers brushed the hair from his eyes, and her gaze was solemn. "I have always thought so."

"You what?" Leviathus stared. "But you... but I... I thought I was invisible to you."

"Of course you did." She laughed, and the shadows fled in terror. "You are male."

She is correct, Azhorus agreed, *as far as I can tell. Though you humans have such tiny—*

Leviathus shook his head again to clear it, with little success.

"I am so confused."

Yaela leaned forward, so that her weight was on her knees, and rested both hands on Leviathus's shoulders. They were small, and strong, and hot.

"It is a good start," she murmured, so close to his lips that the skin tingled. Then Yaela wrapped her arms around

Leviathus ap Wyvernus ne Atu, surdus son of the Dragon King of Atualon, king of pirates, friend to dragonkin, and kissed him.

She was all he had ever wanted.

Beautiful as the dawn, strong as a mountain's roots. He was not sure when he had known, exactly, only that the shadow she cast made all other women seem pale and insignificant. Leviathus leaned into that kiss and was lost as he had never been in the desert or upon the sea. Her tongue found his and they danced. Her arms wrapped about him and pulled him tight—

—tight, too tight, he could not breathe—

Heart pounding in his ears, Leviathus pushed Yaela away and fell to his hands on the cave floor, sucking air in jagged, gasping breaths. He could not stop shaking, and his mouth filled with the taste of Mariza and memories of her teeth, her tongue, her body. Leviathus hung his head, let his hair fall as a curtain about his shame, and wept.

After long moments he heard Yaela move, felt the dark energy of her closeness, but she did not touch him, for which he was pathetically grateful.

"Leviathus," she said at last, and her voice was soft sorrow.

"I am sorry." He wept, and could say no more.

"Fffft," she hissed. "Sorry does not belong on your tongue or in your heart. There is no sorry between us." She touched his shoulder, and he was comforted.

"I am broken," he whispered.

"You have suffered a great wound," she said, words falling like gentle rain, "and you will never be the same again. But you will heal, with time, and you will become stronger. It gets better."

His heart clenched so painfully that he almost cried out. Leviathus sat up, balancing in a hunter's crouch so that they faced each other, knees nearly touching. Yaela's face shone with tears, wet as his own, and he thought they must be as mirrors unto each other.

"You, too?" he asked.

"Yes," she answered simply. "I was... very young."

"I will find that man and kill him."

Yaela threw back her head and laughed. "Silly boy. Silly boy! Do you think that I would allow one such as he to live and gloat over his victory? No, no. I fed him to a bintshi." She wiped the tears from her face with the palm of her hand, still snorting with laughter. "But I thank you for the sweet thought."

Leviathus reached out, tentatively, and she met him halfway. Their hands clasped, fingers twined, and they remained like that for a long while. Finally he spoke.

"We should go before the wyvern returns. Friend to dragonkin or no, I do not wish to tempt his palate. We need to find Sulema and the others."

"What if we do not find them? I have braved the shadowed roads thrice already; I cannot set foot upon the Seared Lands, and do not mean to go further than the far foothills that lead toward Quarabala. Sulema and the others are meant to travel that road without me; if the others are lost to us, will you do the same?"

"No," he said without hesitation. "I will not travel to your people's lands without you, whether we find our companions or not." His fingers tightened on hers, and he felt the truth in his own words. *Ehuani*, his sister would have said. "I have no mind to travel anywhere without you, ever again."

"It is good," she said softly. "King's son, it is very good."

Hand in hand they squeezed through the narrow passage. The mountains were still blanketed with long shadows, though the moons had rolled far overhead, and the sky grew pale about the eastern edge. It was quiet. They began retracing their steps as best they could. In the moonslight Yaela could see nearly as well as during the day, so he followed her lead.

They had not gone far before they heard voices calling, calling his name.

"Leviathus!"

"Here!" he answered, and again. "We are here!"

They were joined in short order by a small group of his river pirates, two of whom were limping and looked ragged about the edges, though none seemed seriously hurt.

"Well met!" they called, and laughed upon finding him alive. "We thought you had been eaten by the mymyc, or by that wyvern. That was a bit of luck, to be sure—though whether good luck or bad remains to be seen. Still, we are not dead yet, and neither are you, it seems!" They did not comment on Yaela's presence, or that the two were still holding hands.

"You were supposed to await my return in Min Yaarif," Leviathus scolded halfheartedly. "Mamouteh had agreed to this."

"We are pirates, and pirates are notorious for being disobedient scoundrels," answered a young man by the name of Orunio. "Besides, we did not ask her permission. We simply went for a hike in the mountains and found you here. So fortuitous!" The others laughed.

"I cannot say that I am displeased to see you, at any rate. Where are the others of our party?" Leviathus asked, and braced himself for the answer.

"Alive, last we saw," Orunio answered. "They had used a rope to cross a chasm, and the mymyc chewed through it before we could cross." He shrugged. "The mymyc climbed down into the rift to escape a wyvern that came out of nowhere and began hunting them. We could see no other way to get across, so decided not to tempt fate any further and make our way back to Min Yaarif.

"Thank the Divines we have found you," he added, brightening. "None of us can remember the way back out of these mountains, and you are as good as a walking map." They all laughed.

Leviathus sighed. "Even if we could find another way across the chasm, we will never locate the others in this forsaken wasteland. And I will not leave Yaela. Indeed, our best path is back to Min Yaarif." His heart ached to say it, though. He had failed Hafsa Azeina, and her apprentice Daru, and now he was failing his sister, as well. Unless...

"If anyone can pull off this mad scheme," he said slowly as the thought occurred to him, "it is Sulema. The shadowmancer Keoki is with her, but he can only shield so many from the burning sun; our presence would be more hindrance to her than help."

"It is true," agreed Yaela.

"If she is successful in finding the Mask of Sajani," Leviathus continued, warming to the idea, "well, then she will return with the Quarabalese queen—not an insignificant ally—and the ability to wield atulfah using the mask. All she will need is an army, and a way to get them across the sea."

"She will, at that," Orunio agreed.

"We have little salt, less manners, and no common sense," Leviathus said, giving voice to an old pirate's joke. "What we do have are bodies, and..."

"Ships!" the pirates shouted in unison.

I have faith in you, sister, Leviathus thought fiercely, certain she was still alive. *And when you return, we will be prepared. We will see to it that your destiny is fulfilled. You will be the Dragon Queen of Atualon.* Feeling lighter of heart than he had for many moons, Leviathus brought Yaela's hand to his mouth and kissed her knuckles as he looked deep into her wide jade eyes.

"Let us make ready to receive your people," he said to her, "and then we will cross the wide sea and dethrone a king."

"Yes," she said, her face a mask of determination. "Let us do exactly that."

TWENTY-EIGHT

Deep silence rolled down upon them from the cruel peaks of the Jehannim, enshrouding Sulema and her three remaining companions in despair much as the song of the Zeera had once enfolded her in joy.

Hannei, Keoki, and Rehaza Entanye lay sleeping near the remains of a fire, leaving Sulema on guard. She listened to the voices of silence and shadow, the hollow echoes of starslight and cold rock, and let grief take her. She wished for her mother, her father, her friend Hannei whole and unbroken. She rubbed the cold and throbbing wound at her shoulder, trying to ignore the painful tingling numbness that radiated out from the center of it, trying harder not to think about what it meant that Yaela and her medicines were beyond her reach now.

If the venom reached her heart, her brain, what would become of her? Would she simply die, or would she become as the reavers, bound to wickedness? Would she turn upon her companions and attack them, like a mindless beast? She did not think Hannei would shy from duty, if it came to that.

I wish I had never left the Zeera, she thought, *or that this was all a terrible dream, and I would wake and tell my sisters all about it over coffee.*

The memory of coffee brought tears to her eyes.

Sulema did not wake Hannei at the appointed hour, but watched through the night, letting the hot wind dry her tears and the mute dirge of the moons lull her heart to a semblance of peace.

They woke well before dawn and shared a mean breakfast of salted fish and precious sweet water. Afterward Keoki sat on his heels, fussing with the strings of a lute, the sounds and sight of which were beautiful—painfully so in that wretched land. Finally having tuned the instrument to his satisfaction, at last the young shadowmancer stood and faced the warriors, though he did not meet their eyes.

"It is time," he told them. "Dawn grows near, and I would be well down the road and into my trance before Akari shows us his true face."

He shed his cloak and trousers as the warriors packed what little they had planned to take with them upon the shadowed road—mostly weapons, water, and dried meat—and Sulema tried not to stare at his exposed flesh. Though she had seen Aasah striding about the fortress in his scraps of red spidersilk, she was not accustomed to men flaunting their bodies so openly, and she was certainly not yet used to skin that was studded in bright and glittering gemstones.

"Did it hurt?" she asked at last, curiosity overcoming both good manners and the dread of what lay ahead of them. Keoki glanced at her, surprised, and then down at his own scarred and bejeweled hide.

"Yes," he told her. "It is *supposed* to hurt. The pain... binds you to the Web of Illindra." He shrugged, sparkling in the growing light of dawn. "I would gladly suffer it again, for my people."

That much she understood. "Why is Yaela's skin not marked, then? Is it because she is still an apprentice?"

Keoki hesitated. When he answered, it was with obvious reluctance.

"No. Yaela—" His mouth worked for a moment, as if he tasted the words before choosing which ones to swallow and which to spit out. "Yaela has suffered in other ways." He stroked his glittering scars. "This I survived. The pain she has had to bear... I am not so certain I could endure that."

If you do not want an answer, Istaza Ani had told her more than once, *do not ask the question.* Sulema nodded and pressed no further. Keoki seemed relieved.

Night was dying, morning not yet born, when the three of them left the Jehannim behind and set foot upon the shadowed road. They did not run, as Keoki could not play while doing so, but jogged along at a pace meant to eat the miles. They would make camp the first night in the ruins of Min Yahtamu, which had once been the heart of commerce for the whole world and was not the final resting place for any foolish or desperate enough to brave the shadowed road. After that they would run. If they did not falter they would make the journey from Min Yahtamu to the Edge of Quarabala—and there find shelter from the killing heat—in three days.

Unless, of course, they died in the attempt. In that case their bones would bake to a fine dust and their spirits become angry shadows, the better to harass and hinder those arrogant enough to tempt a similar fate.

This end of the shadowed road, Keoki told them, was known as the Leavings. He was not sure whether it was because the traveler was leaving the livable world for the Seared Lands, leaving the Seared Lands, or because it was littered with the leavings of unnamed, unsung travelers who had attempted this same desperate journey in order to bring the life-sustaining red salt found only in Quarabala to the rest of the world. There were bits of clothing scattered about, rags of silk and linen and leather. Tools and weapons of various make, necessities that had become unnecessary. The bones of a horse made Sulema fiercely glad she had sent Atemi to Uthrak.

If I die in this place, she silently asked Akari, *let my good mare lead a happy life. Give her stallions and foals to love, and a girl wiser than myself to love her in return.*

Here, it seemed to her, was the story of humankind written in trash. The chronicle of people willing to shed everything in a desperate attempt to flee an inhospitable land in search of new life, and others willing to risk life to travel into the Seared Lands in an equally desperate bid for red salt and wealth. Only refugees and merchants would be foolhardy enough to attempt this crossing.

Refugees, merchants, she amended silently, *and one reckless warrior.* She grimaced as smooth stones rolled underfoot to reveal themselves as a rib, part of a shoulder blade, the head of a femur.

She, Hannei, and Rehaza Entanye bound veils across their faces like the touar of Ja'Sajani, and these were soon caked with the pale gray dust. Sulema's eye burned, her small ruff of hair grew heavy with the stuff, and her skin itched. She prayed to Akari, as he rose in the sky above them, that there were no strong winds in this land akin to the violent dust storms of the Zeera.

Sulema sighed into her veil, already hating the chafe of fabric against her skin and the taste of stale air, and plodded on.

The air grew hotter, drier, and more hateful, the ground harder underfoot, and the eye of Akari more baleful with every step until Sulema could have screamed in frustration—had she been able to catch her breath. They had scarcely left the foothills of Jehannim, and already Sulema felt as if she would burst into flame at any moment.

It burns my lungs, she thought between gasps. *What kind of people would choose to live in a land where the air burns your lungs?*

They did not stop for food or drink, but took mouthfuls of water from skins as they jogged on toward Min Yahtamu. Sulema managed to choke down a bit of salted tarbok and wished she had not, as the salt seemed to immediately leech water from her mouth and throat, leaving them burning worse than before. Neither did she nor her companions speak to one another. The only sounds were the soft *thut-thut-thut* of their feet on the unyielding ground, occasional gasps for air, and the soft music that flowed forth from Keoki's lute.

As Keoki played, shadows boiled up from the road itself, a dark tide of malignant interest which washed over them with each note, each stride, shielding their thin skins from Akari's hungry gaze. The shadows brushed against Sulema as she moved; they played with her short hair and whispered obscene suggestions into her ears, just beyond her hearing. It was all but intolerable, but the Quarabalese paid it no more mind than they paid the heat and the dry air and the silence of a dead land. Sulema supposed they were used to it, just as she had been used to her mother's dreamshifting; in a world of darkness and dangers, some evils were necessary.

Rehaza Entanye led, Hannei had settled into the rear, and Sulema loped along beside Keoki. The shadowmancer moved as if through a dream with his eyes half open and mouth working. It reminded her of her mother's dreamshifting. Sulema assumed he was as vulnerable in his unaware state, so she positioned herself as a vash'ai might have done, eyes darting this way and that, as vigilant as she could be in a land where nothing grew, or moved, or lived.

I will never complain about the tedium of guard duty again, she vowed silently, *or the heat of midsun in the Zeera. I wonder if death is this boring.* An image came to her mind then, of herself as a shade, haunting this very road, of long ages spent doing nothing but waiting for a feckless traveler to pass so that she might hinder and harass them. It seemed to Sulema that this would be the deepest and worst level of Yosh.

Eventually Akari tired of trying to roast them through the veil of shadows and flew on toward tomorrow. Their shadows stretched long behind their weary feet. Sulema's legs burned like meat in the campfire, Rehaza Entanye staggered and nearly fell, even Hannei struggled to keep shuffling along.

Only Keoki, thinnest and weakest of them, seemed to have no difficulty with the pace. His music wound on, over and through their little group, urging them forward to life, to life.

Sulema shot the boy an admiring glance, and only then did she see the streaks of red and black blood smeared across the face of his lute like war paint.

They reached the tumbled rock bones of Min Yahtamu just as Akari dipped his wings and dove beyond the horizon. Though the crumbling walls and collapsed tile roofs afforded no real shelter, Sulema could not help feeling that they had achieved something grand, and let out a dusty yell of victory. Keoki jerked at the sound as if startled from a bad dream; his legs and music faltered to a stop. Tremors wracked his thin frame and he dropped to his knees before the broken gates.

"Water," he whispered. She raised one of her own waterskins, bringing it to his mouth, and held it as he sucked it half empty in one long, greedy, desperate pull—without spilling so much as a drop. His wide, pale eyes rolled up and stared through her, unfocused.

"Thank you," he managed. His hand spasmed across the strings of his lute, striking a discordant note. The shadows which he had ensorcelled dispersed, spitting in disappointed wroth. Sulema meant to take a scant mouthful of water from the skin, but when the liquid touched her tongue, she found herself seized by a violent thirst and emptied the other half.

Rehaza Entanye stumbled to stand beside Sulema. She tore the veils away from her face and breathed in long, ragged gasps as she gazed upon the ruined city.

"Min Yahtamu," she whispered. "The city of lost souls." And she laughed as at a bitter joke. "This was the heart of the world, once; all of the wealth of known civilization flowed through here. Salt and spidersilk, wine and spices, slaves and sweet water. The queen of commerce, they called her. Now the queen is dead, and her sister Min Yaarif is nothing more than an ugly old whore that gives all her customers the pox."

Hannei jogged to a halt beside Sulema and regarded Rehaza Entanye in a long, unreadable stare. She did not hurry to remove her own veils, or partake of meat or water, but touched Keoki's shoulder, startling him again. She gestured at the buildings, the sky, and then back at the road behind them; he nodded and followed her into Min Yahtamu. It seemed to Sulema as if the shadows of Min Yahtamu reached out to greet him.

"Hannei has the right of it; we need to find what shelter we can, and quickly," Rehaza Entanye said. "And build a fire with whatever brush we have left. The nights are likely to be cold, even so close to the Seared Lands—and the smell of blood will bring predators." She followed Hannei and Keoki into the darkening ruins.

Strangely enough, these words gave Sulema new strength. Hunger, thirst, and greater predators—these were dangers she had faced before, honest and straightforward enemies that she knew how to fight.

They found a squat, square building which seemed solid enough, and which was too small to house any unpleasant surprises. It had a narrow doorway, no windows, and a roof that was mostly intact; as good as a palace for travelers in need. Smaller and less grand by far than its wretched neighbors, the building had been used for storage in days gone perhaps, or housing for animals, or some such humble thing. Soot-stained walls and the leavings of fires told them that these stout walls had sheltered travelers in recent days; again Sulema found reassurance in this proof that they were not the only ones mad enough to make this journey, though the sense of comfort was born of her own wishes; she had no way of knowing whether those who had gone on before had made it to their destination in one piece.

Keoki swayed on his feet as if he had drunk more usca than was good for him, mumbled something incoherent under his breath, and then collapsed upon the dirt floor.

Sulema and Rehaza Entanye both rushed to kneel at his side, but he seemed unharmed.

"He is just exhausted," Rehaza Entanye said, and Sulema agreed. They arranged the sleeping sorcerer upon his cloak, covering his exposed skin with another, as Hannei pulled sticks from her pack and built a fire.

Sorcery, treachery, and dragon's magic, Sulema thought as Hannei's fire set the shadows to dancing. *These are things I can neither fight nor control. But thirst, and weariness, and the threat of predators in the darkness? Bring them on, world. Show me yours.*

Foolish child, Istaza Ani would have scolded. *Do not taunt an enemy until you have learned the reach of her sword.*

The women broke the day's fast on dried meat, dried cheese, and cruelly rationed water, and this mean meal was shared in an uncomfortable silence. Sulema did not trust the slave-trainer any further than she could have thrown her after the day's run and had no desire to speak to her. She kept sneaking looks at Hannei, who mostly stared into the fire or into the growing dark.

That one, it seemed, had no desire to communicate with her and likely would not have spoken even if she could. The shadowmancer lay where they had rolled him in his cloak, occasionally letting out a long, low moan in his sleep, like a child suffering from nightmares. Sulema would have welcomed the company of Leviathus, or Ani, or Daru. She wondered where her mother's apprentice might have gotten to, and feared he had met an unkind fate.

This saddened her. The world had never seemed to want the boy around, and he had deserved better from all of them.

A rustling interrupted Sulema's reverie, along with a chittering. The women leapt to their feet, swords drawn, forming a wordless shield between the sleeping sorcerer and the world outside. Sulema understood—they all did—that any of the rest of them were expendable; without one, the others might survive. Without their shadowmancer, however, they would be burned to smoking husks at the first light of day.

The chittering grew loud, louder, and finally its source was revealed. It was an enormous insect like a soldier beetle but longer and flatter, its shiny black carapace marked in red like a splatter of fresh blood. It skittered out of the night and came at them through the narrow doorway, mandibles gaping. Sulema skewered the thing with her shamsi and flung it back out into the darkness, grimacing at the crunching sounds that followed, and wiping yellow ichor from her sword.

Clusters of tiny, glittering eyes appeared in the darkness outside their shelter like stars caught in Illindra's web, and Rehaza Entanye spoke at last.

"It is going to be a long night."

The beetles were no more than the first wave of things that wanted to dine on human flesh, and they were not the worst. The lizards, Sulema thought, were the worst. When killed they smelled of human excrement, and they were the most persistent. The besieged women used an alarming amount of the fuel they had brought with them from Jehannim to build their fire so high and so hot that their little shelter seemed a sweat lodge.

Finally even the lizards abandoned the attack, either daunted by the defenders' fierceness or—more likely—sated by the flesh of their own fallen comrades. The crunching and slurping noises continued almost till dawn, but by then Sulema was too weary to be horrified and drifted off. She fell asleep between one breath and the next straight into a dream of masks and murder—

And it was time to wake, to stand, and to start the whole thing over again.

Keoki woke last and hardest; Rehaza Entanye had to shake the shadowmancer to his senses. He ate a little food and drank a little water as if neither held any interest. When he had finished he ran tattered fingers across the bloody strings of his lute, winced, and began to play. Shadows once again sprang from the ground, weaving themselves into an unwilling protection as they danced to the shadowmancer's tune. The three weary travelers shouldered their packs and steeled their hearts as they made ready to leave the wretched husk of Min Yahtamu and begin the desperate run for the Edge.

"Guts and goatfuckery," Sulema grumbled as she stared out across the shadowed road. "The Jehannim are a blight and last night was a misery. Surely a bit of a run cannot be worse than what we have already endured."

"Ahhhhhh," Rehaza Entanye sighed, "I wish you had not said that."

Hands gripped Sulema's shoulder, digging into the half-healed flesh where she had been bitten and sending waves of agony rippling across her back and arms. She sucked in a breath to scream, but the air burned worse than her wounds, and she managed only a strangled wheeze.

"Sulema." It was Rehaza Entanye. Her words swam up to her like bubbles from the bottom of the river. "Sulema, it is time to stop. Sulema, *stop*."

Sulema forced her legs to cease moving, her lungs to keep sucking air, and willed her heart to keep pumping as someone squirted water between her clenched teeth. Water. *Water*. So cool and wet and good she nearly wept.

She was struck in the face once, twice, three times, so that she reached out and grabbed the hand that was doing so, blinking an angry eyeful of sand away to glare through the deepening gloom into the face of her attacker.

It was Hannei.

Sulema growled at her once sword-sister, and Hannei growled back.

"Stop it, both of you," Rehaza Entanye said sharply. "Get some meat and water into your stupid mouths and get ready to fight. They are coming."

Sulema spat sand and blood upon the seared earth, narrowly missing the collapsed form of the shadowmancer, and stared into the rapidly growing darkness. Already she could see pale eyes staring at them from the deepening gloom, scavengers eager for the taste of her flesh. From somewhere far away, a harsh voice screamed, the sound rising higher and higher till she could not hear it, though she knew it was still there. The eyes winked out as that voice was answered by another, and then a third, much closer now.

"Reavers!" Rehaza Entanye shouted, voice high with panic. "Ware reavers!"

Sulema drew her shamsi, willing it to shop shaking, and spat again.

"Show me yours, you goatfucking sons of... goats."

Hannei drew her own swords, dark blades seeming eager to drink in the night. Her shoulders shook, and a terrible raw laugh came from her open mouth.

Well, Sulema thought, *I suppose it is better than crying...*

There came to Sulema's ears a terrible hissing, as if all the spiders in the world had converged upon the small group and meant to make an end to them. These malevolent voices grew closer, closer, until Sulema could see the creatures to which they belonged.

What might have once been human loped toward them, now and again leaping forward or scuttling sideways like pale two-legged Araids, mouths gaping wide in hungry grins devoid of humor or soul. The sight of them kindled the pain in Sulema's shoulder into a white-hot agony, and she screamed in terror and in fury.

Their faces, the way they moved, the way the rising

moonslight shone upon their chitinous white skin roused Sulema to a visceral wrath. She screamed again, choking on her desire to kill these things, to fall upon them and chop the abominations into pieces so small their own mothers would not recognize them.

Hannei stared at her, surprise upon her face, and then her face broke into the first real smile Sulema had seen since their meeting in Min Yaarif. Their gazes met across drawn blades, and the two of them shared a moment of bloodlust and bravery.

Rehaza Entanye attempted to rouse the shadowmancer, to no avail. She straightened from a crouch, glanced at her companions, then at the advancing line of fellspawn. She drew her own sword and set her feet in a fighter's stance, baring her teeth at their enemies.

One of the pale shadows sprang toward them, and Sulema's world shrank to a pinpoint of pale hides, burning eyes, and clawlike hands grasping at her skin. She ran to meet the foremost of the creatures, so caught up in battle-lust and hatred that all her training, Ani's wise words, and endless battle drills fell away like shed skin. There were only the dark, looming shapes and hated faces to cleave and rend and smash.

Driving the point of her blade through one throat, she dodged a spray of ichor and spun to sweep the legs from beneath a second assailant, cleaving that one's spine between its shoulder blades as it tried to regain its feet. Hannei danced beside her, hewing limb from torso with her dark and dancing blades, mouth open in a terrible silent laugh as the two of them cut a path of destruction through the advancing line of monsters.

For monsters they were, unnatural things born of unclean magic. Though they wore the faces and tattered clothing of the people they once had been, Sulema felt no kinship with these foul beings, no sorrow for what they had suffered in

263

life. She embraced the flames of hatred and revulsion which engulfed her, driving her on even when the remaining reavers hesitated and would have pulled back. Passion sent her into the night in pursuit of the retreating enemy when common sense and years of hard training would have held her back.

She skewered the last of them with her shamsi, turning her blade so that it grated between the thing's ribs, and felt no pity in her heart as a monster with the pale face of a young boy fell in pieces at her feet.

Not human, she told herself as she came to a halt at last, far from the sight of her companions and with nothing left to kill. *These are things. Monsters. Not human.* Chest heaving, muscles in her arms burning, her shoulder a cold inferno of agony, she was so overcome with dark frustrated anger that she threw back her head and howled.

"...Sulema?"

Rehaza Entanye's voice floated through the thick night air, recalling her to her senses. Sulema frowned at the twitching pieces of offal at her feet. She bent to wipe the worst of the gore from her blade and then turned, weary beyond all words, and made her slow way back to her companions.

"That is the last of them," Rehaza Entanye said, wiping her hands on her begrimed tunic and grimacing as she stepped into the ring of firelight. "I hope. I count nearly a score of them; this was a largish swarm, too large to be independent, though I found no sign of any Arachnists. I think this was a feint of some sort, a test of our defenses, and not some random attack." She glanced sideways at Sulema. "It was stupid of you to take off after them like that. Brave, but stupid."

They dragged any foul corpses they could see away from their camp and into the night. The thought of predators feasting in the dark sent them hurrying back to build the fire higher, higher, heedless of their dwindling supply of firewood. As Rehaza Entanye took first watch Sulema closed her eyes, wishing that she could as easily close her ears to the sounds of crunching and snarling.

Lying on the unforgiving ground, she was struck with a longing for the land and the people she had left behind. She missed the small sounds of a warriors' camp—the squabbling, gaming, even snoring and farting of her sword-sisters. The soft singing of the dunes as winds born of poetry and hardship caressed the face of the Zeera. The sounds and smells of horses and churrim, the roars and grumbles and grunts of the vash'ai. She even missed the moons and stars; the night sky looked the same here—was the same, surely—but somehow left her feeling cold and bereft.

I even miss lionsnake jerky, she thought. *I must be sick.*

Hannei shook her from troubled dreams at the stirring of dawn. Sulema leapt to her feet, staggered, and nearly fell as waves of weakness and pain radiated from her bad shoulder. She peered around her, but not so much as a scrap of cloth or bone could be seen in the mean, thin light that presaged Akari's wrath.

Keoki was already awake and beginning in his musical trance, raw fingers dancing across his lute as he played for the shadows, played for the darkness, played for the chance to live one more day in a world that wanted to suck their bones dry. The shadows rose to his bidding, spitting imprecations and promises of treachery even as they rose to protect the travelers from the killing sun.

Sulema reached for her waterskins and found, to her deep dismay, that they had been pierced some time during the battle. There was a scant mouthful left in either of them. Without hesitation, Hannei detached one of the remaining two skins from the belt at her waist and handed it over.

Rehaza Entanye stared at them for a moment, opened her mouth to say something, but closed it again and shook her head.

That woman has never known the embrace of a sword-sister, Sulema thought, and she spared a momentary pang of pity for a life lived in such isolation. Then it was time for a handful of salted meat, time to rub ochre-tinted fat on their exposed skin, and time to run.

TWENTY-NINE

Ssssulemaaaaaa, the bones mourned. *Hhhhhhhannnn-neiiiii...*

Ani's body sat straight-backed in the middle of Askander's tent, but she was not there. Even as her physical form breathed and twitched, her shade crawled among the bones and dead things of the mountain passes, watching over the daughters of her heart.

More than that she was listening. Rumors spread in ripples across the burned and tormented earth. A jikjik had been killed for meat, his bones left to desiccate in the sun. A lionsnake had been routed from her den and slain. A skull had been kicked from its long resting place and now mourned the loss of three teeth. And the reavers...

Not even the bones long dead liked the reavers. These were foul things sucked dry of self, cobbled together of defiled corpses, nameless and songless and dreaded. No predators would come near the thrice-slain and they lay bloated beneath the naked eye of Akari, rotting with a foul stench.

My girls did this, she thought. *They have killed prey, predators, and reavers. They have crossed the Jehannim and fly for their lives.* That had become all the more important, because the scent and savor of human flesh had drawn the attention of those greater predators who lived by feasting upon those who would dare the Bone Road.

This was what the dead called it—the Bone Road—a trail not marked by cobbled stones or cairns, but by the husks of those who fell on this perilous path, never to rise again in this world. Bones long dead and fresh, of humans and beasts of burden, horses and churrim and vash'ai. Most of the bones were content to remain as they were, or where the wind chose to blow them. Some were unquiet, fretting about that which had disturbed them.

There were bones here which had once been sorcerers, dreamshifters, kahanna—or the beloved of such powerful priests of the world—and whose stories had been magically graven into the very core of their being. Ani's bones, she knew, glowed with the faint silvery-blue light of her own power, and could be used by a bonesinger to do great things. Great and terrible things, such as the spell Ani began to work.

If I do not help them, they are dead, she thought as a bintshi cried out, and a wyvern turned its eyes toward the fleeing shapes.

She sang to the bones of the dreaming dead, calling them all by name. *Mutaani* the youth, *Kishahani* the vengeful, *Kulaishkum—all of you*—she called, and they answered. Long bones and short, fingers and claws and ribs, skulls and vertebrae rose from the blasted earth at the bonesinger's bidding and dragged deep furrows in their haste. These she gathered up in her spirit-hands as a child might scoop up handfuls of mud, and she merged them, she molded them, making the bits and detritus of life into a plaything for her folly.

Bonesinger, Inna'hael warned her from far away. *Bonesinger, do not do this. It is abomination.*

You leave the bones of your prey to your cubs for them to play with, she responded, her mind's voice strained and tart. *You let them break their teeth upon the shoulder-blades of tarbok. How is this any different?*

Inna'hael growled.

My cubs cut their teeth upon the thick and empty skulls of your kind, he replied. *Such is the dance between predator and prey, of moons and stars and dragons. This is outside the dance, outside the song, and well you know it.*

She did, and well she knew the cost.

Sulema is my girl, Ani told the vash'ai, *the daughter of my heart. I could not love her more had I birthed her myself. Would you not have broken the old laws, given the chance, if it would have saved your Azra'hael?*

There was a long silence, dark as distant thunder.

I had that chance, Bonesinger. I made my choice, as you have made yours.

Then he was gone.

Ani turned her focus to regard the thing she had cobbled together out of forgotten sorcerers and a bonesinger's whimsy. It had a great skull, formed of many lesser skulls, and the shell of a giant turtle. A knobbed and spiky spine, a long tail, thick limbs. There were ribs and tusks where teeth would be, and even great wings spread wide, with shadows stretched between them like membranes. All it needed was a little...

Far from the construct the bonesinger lifted a child's skull to her mouth, puckered her lips, and blew. Such a small thing, the birth of a wind. A small thing, a tune both forbidden and terrible. It whistled between the missing teeth of a little girl who had kissed her mother one night and never woke in the morning. It sang of sorrow and fear and pain. This wind sang of *mutaani*, and in its wake swam a dark and silent beast that was death.

High it soared, speeding across sunlight and water and sand till it found Ani's plaything and settled upon the bones, filling the void between death and undeath with the silence of Eth.

It was forbidden.

It was done. Far away the bintshi wailed a hunting song, its beautiful voice thick with the anticipation of blooded meat.

In a hidden place at the edge of the Edge of the Seared Lands, a dragon lifted her head. She was a foul thing made of bones and broken promises, of lives and honor lost,

269

of hunger. Crimson flame appeared deep in the shadowed pits that served as eyes. Wings that seemed insufficient knacked and rattled as they beat against the ground once, twice, three times, and then she rose into the sky, hunting and hungering, knowing only that she had to devour everything that might wish Sulema harm. Opening her mouth she shrieked, belching great gouts of pyre flame and ash—

Pain blossomed on Ani's face. A second blow and she cried out, lifting her hands to protect her eyes. A third and she was on her feet, swaying drunkenly, a knife in one hand and the skull in the other, blinking ash and fat from her stinging eyes and snarling at her opponent. Had Inna'hael come to put a stop to her magic and to her? Or perhaps—

"Askander?" she asked as the figure came into focus. He had drawn back his hand for a fourth blow, and now with his arm raised, was staring at her with a look she did not want to understand. "Askander? What—"

"I should be asking *you* 'what' for a change," he answered, eyes and voice hard, lowering his hand halfway. "What in the name of guts and goatfuckery do you think you are doing, girl?"

Ani's mouth dropped open at the sound of her own words falling from Askander's mouth. Never, in all the years she had known him, had she ever heard Askander curse. As she tried to gather her wits, another thought occurred to her, and she frowned.

"How did you know it was me?" In truth, she hardly recognized herself anymore. Bonesinging changed the wielder's face and body with each use, and she had been overly free with her magic of late.

He lowered his arm and now stood with both hands on his hips and snorted a humorless laugh.

"How many girls do you know who would be sitting in this tent, working bonesinger's magic. *Ah-ah*," he held both hands up as she opened her mouth to respond. "Do not tell me what you were doing. Best that I remain ignorant. Better still if you would set aside this folly, but Atu himself could not change your path, once you have decided upon it."

"You did not answer my question." Ani wanted to raise both hands to her head, which ached abominably. She wanted to weep, to put down her knife and skull, and to drink a bottle or three of usca. She did none of these things, but swayed on her feet.

"How did I know it was you?" Askander Ja'Sajani closed the distance between them so quickly that Ani sucked in a breath and would have stepped back, but his hands gripped her shoulders and held her fast. "How do I know the sun? The sky? How do I know my own song? Foolish girl." With those words, he pulled her closer and kissed her.

Ani sighed and relaxed into her lover's heat. After a while, he lifted his face from hers and smiled a small, triumphant smile.

"You dropped your knife."

"Mmmmmmmmhuh," she answered, dazed. "Have you come to sweep me away then, like a hero in the old stories? Are we to run off toward a new tomorrow and leave the cares of the world behind us?" She wished. Oh, how she wished.

"That is, indeed, the fitting end to a hero's story," he told Ani, stroking her cheekbone with one finger. "Alas, we have not come to the end yet."

"Oh?" She reached up and held his hand, stopping him before his touch could distract her further. "What part are we in, then?"

"The shit part," he replied, almost cheerfully. "I have come to take you back to the Zeera, because a new terror is upon us, and someone of your—talents—might be able to stop it."

"A new threat." She sighed all the way to the marrow of her bones, impossibly tired. "What new threat is this?"

"The Lich King has risen," he said. "And he has raised his armies of the dead. They are taking over the world."

"Guts and goatfuckery indeed," she groaned. "I am too old for this shit."

THIRTY

They came for him in the small hours of night, when hatchling birds nestled safe beneath the soft wings of their parents, and not even snakes dared the hunt. Jian did not fight, for his tiny son lay between him and the warm body of Tsali'gei, whose eyes were wide with terror as a blade pressed against her throat. From the next room came the sounds of soft voices, the harsh sound of flesh striking flesh, and an old woman's angry cry of pain.

"Come with me," Mardoni growled close to Jian's ear, "or watch them die." Jian nodded silently.

A sack of coarse cloth was thrust over his head and snugged close about his throat, blocking all light and muffling all sound besides his own harsh breathing. It smelled strongly of some sweetish spice and made his eyes water. Jian sneezed, and someone grabbed him roughly by the shoulder.

"Quiet," an unfamiliar voice growled. "Do nothing to draw attention, or things will not go well for you." Inside the cloth hood, Jian bared his teeth. Had he been alone, he would have taken the form of a sea-bear and ripped that one's throat out. Had he been alone—

His son wailed, a pitiful and helpless sound that was quickly muffled. Jian threw his head back, desperate to see, and jerked half out of his captor's hands. The grip on his shoulder tightened till it dug into his flesh. Jian welcomed the pain.

"If you come quietly," the voice said again, "your family will not be harmed. If you fight…"

"Jian," Tsali'gei whispered, her voice strained with terror. "Jian, please."

He let himself be led, tears of frustration dripping into the hood and fighting with every step not to break free and kill them all. There was no doubt he could do it, but not before one or more of those he loved had been harmed. Which of them might his captors take first? Tsali'gei? His mother? His little son?

Which of them would he be forced to sacrifice?

Though he tried at first to track the route they took, Jian was soon lost in the twists and turns, ascents and descents. Twice he thought they might be in tunnels, for the echo of their footsteps indicated stone underfoot and all around them. Then for a while it seemed as if they were outdoors. The air was cooler on his naked arms, tile and stone and wood gave way to soft earth. Then a heavy door closed behind them, audible through the cloth, and his captors led him down, and down...

And down.

And down.

They were taking him to a dungeon, Jian thought. That had to be true. He had spent years leading his own captives to cells beneath his father's holdings.

I never led any of them out again, though.

It was best not to think on that.

Abruptly they came to a stop. Hands on his shoulders forced Jian down so that his knees barked painfully on an uneven floor. He was bound with thick ropes, trussed as tightly as any beast fresh-caught for a menagerie, and cool air eddied around him. The sounds of footsteps receded, slapping against cold stone. A door clanged shut like the pealing of bells.

Jian knelt, counted his breaths, wriggled his fingers to keep the blood moving through his hands, and wondered when the man who had stayed behind with him would speak.

Even through the sweet-spice smell of the cloth Jian could scent him, sweating and nervous. It was an oddly ungulate smell that brought the sea-bear in Jian's heart too close to the surface.

"Well, my young friend, a fine mess we find ourselves in."

"Mardoni," he said, keeping his voice even and calm, though he swallowed hard at the thought of Mardoni's hot blood in his mouth. He was the son of the Sea King, after all, newly come from the Twilight Lands, and the company to which he had grown accustomed was somewhat—open-minded—in their culinary traditions.

"No use hiding from you." Jian heard the other man's approach and tensed, but Mardoni simply yanked the hood from his head and then retreated a few steps as if unsure what his captive might do. Jian squinted against the mage-lanterns and sat back on his haunches, flaring his nostrils again at the other man's fear scent.

He smells like prey.

"Perhaps I should have said 'my not-so-young friend,'" Mardoni said, also sitting back on his heels and studying Jian's face. He wore splendid white robes embroidered with the images of leaping stags and bulls, and a golden flower sigil at his breast. "How is it that you have been away from us for only a few moons' time, Sen-Baradam, yet seem to have aged years since just this spring? You were barely able to win a training fight with that young bull Naruteo, yet you have managed to become a formidable opponent. How? I would very much like to know."

Without waiting for an answer, he continued. "There are rumors that you somehow managed to slip through the veil and escape to the Twilight Lands, to live among the Dae. Tell me, Tsun-ju Jian *de Allyr*, what is it like to walk beneath the gray skies, in the lands of our fathers?" His eyes were bright.

Too bright.

"Our fathers?" Jian mused, pursing his lips as if deep in thought. "Our... oh! Do you speak of the lands of Allyr, my father, the sho'en? Or do you speak of the lands of *your* father?"

Mardoni rocked back on his heels.

"My father?" he whispered.

"Of course. He is a master archer—I studied under him, for a while—and a watcher in the woods. A fine man, and prideful... no doubt he would feel obligated to seek an early death, were word of your dishonor to make it across the veil. Imagine—a son of Yrnos, licking the emperor's boots."

Mardoni's face went as white as his robes. Jian did not move or let the pounding of his heart show in his expression or manner. He had, after all, spoken truth.

When the blood had returned to Mardoni's cheeks, he shook his head dismissively and stood, though he no longer met Jian's eyes.

"It does not matter," he said. "It has been decided. It is done. It does not matter. You, Tsun-ju Jian de Allyr, Daechen Jian Sen-Baradam, have been sentenced to death."

"For what crimes?"

"For crimes against his Illumination and the peoples of Sindan. Fomenting unrest. Raiding. Murdering his Illumination's troops and property. For daring to think that you, a lowly yellow Daechen, are fit to stand in his shadow. Need I go on?"

"What of my family?" Jian asked softly. "My mother, my wife Tsali'gei? My son?"

"Ah," Mardoni said. "If you agree to come willingly and peacefully to your own death, their lives will be spared. Tsali'gei and the child will be banished to the Twilight Lands—assuming the Dae do not kill them outright, of course—and your delightful elderly mother will be escorted to the borders of Sindan. Let her throw herself on the Dragon King's mercy, if she will."

Jian's mind raced. He did not believe for one moment that his family would be spared his fate.

"What happened to you, Mardoni?" he asked. "Your fine plans to change the empire and lead the daeborn into a brilliant new future. Have you given it all over to lick the emperor's arse, or were those empty words all along?"

"Oh no," Mardoni answered. His words were soft as doeskin, but the light in his eyes was that of a fanatic. "Oh no, de Allyr, not at all. Your death is to be a glorious beginning for us. When your blood mixes with the still-wet ink of the emperor's new treaty—"

"War," Jian's heart sank. It would work, he knew. When his father learned that Jian had been killed, he would tear the veil asunder. He would ravage both worlds with tooth and claw, and to Yosh with the consequences. "You expect that the twilight lords will kill the emperor for you."

"Shhhhh," Mardoni said, a finger to his lips, and he winked. "Such words as those would send other heads rolling besides mine, you know… Your son's would be first, I think. Die quietly and know that by doing so you are freeing us all."

"You are mad," Jian said flatly. "Thousands will die. *Tens* of thousands. And the veil—" Nobody knew for sure what would happen if the veil was destroyed, but most agreed that it would mean death to them all. "You are *insane*. Mardoni—"

"No." Mardoni cut the air between them with the palm of his hand. "Not another word. What is done is past, Sen-Baradam. It has all been decided. There is only the future, and that future lies with the dawn of a new empire."

"And a new emperor, I suppose," Jian replied. "Is there no mercy in your heart for the innocents who will be slaughtered? How can you live with yourself?"

"Well, for one thing," Mardoni answered with a sardonic smile, as he plucked a small golden bell from his sleeve and rang it, "my head is still attached to my shoulders. Come the dawn, you will not be able to say the same. You should have learned your lesson with that peasant girl you did not slay, *Daechen* Jian. Mercy is for the weak."

A trio of soldiers entered the room, and he turned.

"Take this guest to his new quarters," he ordered, "and see to it that he remains unharmed. Give him food, water, and bedding." Mardoni turned back. "This is your last night among the living, Tsun-ju Jian de Allyr. Try and get some rest.

"I hear the Lonely Road is a long one."

THIRTY-ONE

On the seventh day of the rebirth of Kal ne Mur, a handful of the Lich King's faithful used sticks and swords and spears to lever open a tent-sized ball of dung and foul offal which Arushdemma had left behind as a parting gift. Therein they found Sudduth befouled and naked, curled protectively around her little clay pot.

Sudduth uncurled herself and rose, shaking free her glorious waist-length locks and cradling the precious plants close to her breasts as she stepped down from the bonelord's dung-ball as if she were a queen rising with the first blush of dawn. Stepping gracefully, she paid no mind to the jagged shards of bone that poked at the soles of her feet, or the ragged bit of cloak that clung to one heel as she crossed the distance between them. Sudduth looked neither to the left nor the right, but had eyes only for her king.

Ismai groaned inwardly. Wars had been started—and ended—by women less angry than this one.

Shat out by a bonelord, Ismai commiserated. *She is never going to forgive this.*

Shut up, Kal ne Mur snapped, and he breathed through the urge to leap onto Mutaani's back and run for the hills. *You know nothing of women.*

I know enough about women to know when I am in trouble.

You are fortunate she is not vash'ai, Ruh'ayya added. *Or you would be digging through the sand trying to find all the pieces of your face.*

Sudduth took her place at his side. Ismai did not mention the viscous filth that befouled her hair and skin, the loss of her armor and clothing, and he most certainly did not wrinkle his nose at the stench, which was all but overwhelming.

"Sudduth, I am very—"

She held up a hand.

"I am fine," she said in a low and even voice that made all the hairs on both arms stand up.

"But—"

"I am fine," she insisted. "It is *fine.*"

"I found your sword!" Uruk shouted. Still waist-deep in shit, he brandished the weapon and grinned. "And one sandal!"

"Sudduth—" Ismai tried again.

She reached up and patted his cheek, leaving streaks of green and black bonelord shit on his face, which he did not dare wipe. "We will never. Speak of this. Again." Sudduth turned and walked away, pausing only to snatch a cloak shamefacedly offered by Findla, who had been a war-chief of Sundergaard in the long ago. Both women turned and glared at him for a moment, and then Sudduth stalked out of sight.

Ismai let out the breath he had been holding. His face where Sudduth had touched him stung, and it stank, but all in all, he thought, he had gotten off lightly.

"She took that rather well," Naara said as she joined him. She wet a rag with liquid from her own waterskin and reached up to wash his face. Ismai rubbed both arms to rid them of chillflesh.

"I do not remember being so scared in all my life."

"Which life?" She made a face at the rag and tossed it onto the sand.

"Any of them."

"You owe me a boon."

Ismai glanced down at Sudduth. *I thought we were never going to speak of this again*, he thought. But as it would have been inconvenient for him to die this day, he spoke carefully.

"Name it."

"You—the boy Ismai, that is—mentioned that there was a grove of trees tended by the Zeerani Mothers. If this grove still stands, I would like to plant my children there."

"You would go off and leave them?"

"I... perhaps. If the grove, or some part of it, still stands. If I can find a trustworthy person to tend them. Perhaps." She frowned down at the little clay pot, and the vigorous sprouts that seemed determined to outlive them all. "I live a dangerous life. The road is no place for them."

"It is a hard world," Ismai agreed, thinking of the boy Sammai. "No place may be safe for them, but we will go." She stared at him, and he added, "As you wish, we will go. And if it is your desire, I will help you plant them myself, and build a wall around them. If that will make you happy."

She clutched the pot tighter. "Surely we do not have time to spend on such a small thing?"

"We have a few hours to spare for a friend," he answered.

Sudduth looked up at him, eyes wide and shining as a live woman's, and the smile she graced him with was brilliant.

"You know," she told him, "when I was young and hot-blooded—and had a beating heart—and when you were tall and handsome and held the world in your fist, I loved you a little. But I like you more now." Then she dropped back to walk with Uruk.

"If I live and die a thousand times," Ismai said to himself, "I will never begin to understand women." Ibna, who walked within earshot, grinned.

"None of us will. Fortunately for you, you only have to mete out vengeance, subdue a kingdom, and keep a dragon from waking to destroy the world. Simpler things, eh?"

"Simpler," Ismai agreed. "And safer."

❖

A thousand years of deathless slumber had left the world changed not at all. Nothing was ever simple, and nobody was ever truly safe.

The Mah'zula formed a loose ring around the perimeter of Aish Kalumm, but these false warriors and their vash'ai danced aside as the Lich King arrived. Perhaps they had heard of the rout at Urak. None had lived to tell that tale, but rumors flew up and down the Dibris swifter than birds, and bad news swiftest of all.

Kal ne Mur looked upon the ruins and frowned at the grief tearing through him. He had in his lifetimes razed cities far grander than this had been, and never had he felt such anguish.

Cities die, he explained. *People die. Lovers, and children, and mothers. We are all just sand in the wind, after all. A thousand years from now the greatest of us will only be a remnant of song and poorly understood poetry.*

Except for you, Ismai retorted, and Kal ne Mur was surprised at the anger in his tone. *You and your sworn fighters.*

This is true, the Lich King allowed, *unless of course Sajani tires of our human blunderings and rises to destroy us all. I have had a thousand years to think on this, and am almost certain we will be obliterated along with the world.*

And if you are not?

Then we will spend an eternity in the void, envying you who have died.

"Ah!" he said aloud. "The Mother's Grove! So a portion of it survived, after all."

Ahead of him wardens in blue and Mothers in ragged remnants of robes, a sad and shabby reminder of their old finery, toiled among the remaining trees and the broken statues of vash'ai. He rode through jagged, charred stumps and looked upon the shattered statuary.

It was not enough for them to destroy these people's city and their livelihoods, he thought. *They tried to destroy beauty and the memories of love, as well. What heart is so bitter that it cannot abide the joy of another?*

A voice rang out from behind him.

"Hail, Ismai son of Nurati! I see you have returned to me, and this time with a fitting bride gift!"

Ismai closed his dead eyes and reached for control, lest the lich-wrath burning through him escape and destroy what little was left of this place. It was not Kal ne Mur's fury, after all, but his own human heart that had been tied to this place, and which now lay charred and shattered as the grove. When he opened his eyes again, it was the boy Ismai who saw what the Mah'zula had done, he who turned his mount and faced his tormentor.

"Ishtaset," he said.

She grinned at him, the very picture of desert beauty, strength and prowess. Kingdoms had gone to war over women less glorious, and wars had been won by warriors less skilled. She was flanked by two fists of her riders, some of whom had been warriors before the fall of Aish Kalumm.

"Hadda," he called to one of them. "How can you ride with those who murdered your brother?"

The warrior's face reddened, and she averted her eyes.

"Ah now, beloved, have you no care for my heart? You return to me with a worthy gift, but spare words for other women?" Ishtaset laughed as if she had not a care in the world, as if the Lich King and his hordes of undead had not come to put an end to her and her false Mah'zula. "Where are the tender words for your mate? Where is my kiss?"

"I would rather kiss Arushdemma," Ismai replied, and Sudduth burst out laughing.

Ishtaset's smile hardened. "And I had had such high hopes for you, little Ismai. Ah well, I suppose the line of Zula Din is not what it once was. But, oh! I brought you a gift too, and you might as well have it." So saying, she unfastened a largish leather bag from her saddle and slung it underhand at Ismai. He reached out, unthinking, and plucked it from the air.

It was heavy, and it stank. Ismai's gut lurched. He had played aklashi too many times as a youngling not to have an idea what was in that bag.

"Who?" he asked simply.

The dead froze at the sound in his voice, and all eyes turned to Ishtaset.

"That little warden you sent out on your errand. Jasin, was it? He had a mouth full of lies and a head full of ideas too big for one such as he." Ishtaset shrugged and wiped her hands together. "So I relieved him of it."

A howl rose from deep in the Zeera, a sound unlike anything Ismai had ever heard. It was not the soft singing of the hot sands, so like his mother's voice. It was not the wailing cries of vash'ai seeking a kith-bond. It was not even the hopeless wailing of the undead, forever denied the peace and respite of the Lonely Road. This was the sound of trees breaking, of rocks burning, the cracked shriek of a cold and motherless heart.

Ismai's grief and rage welled up, endless, edgeless, bottomless, and found an echo in the song of the Lich King. Even as Ismai opened his hand and let the bag drop, even as his Mutaani reared and screamed defiance, a wave of misery rolled from his mouth like cold black fog across the Zeera. Wind whipped across the shattered landscape of Ismai's youth, the shattered landscape of his heart, and it summoned the Lich King back to his true nature.

The song lifted, it called, it commanded, and the dead answered. The horde screamed as one, heads thrown back, teeth bared, eyes glinting red and wet in the dying light, and as Ismai lost his war with the Lich King so too did they lose what little hold they had on their humanity. Swords and spears and knives drawn they rushed upon the Mah'zula, screaming for blood and bloody vengeance.

It rained in the Zeera that day, a bitter red rain that nourished nothing. Ismai did not see who killed Ishtaset, only that she had been killed, trampled and torn almost beyond recognition. Of the Mah'zula not one remained alive, not even those Ismai had known as warriors and with whom he had played childish games just last year. They had betrayed him, and their people.

False warriors, he thought, and not an echo of sorrow was left to him. *Never again will they betray me.*

He would see to that.

Mutaani danced beneath the Lich King as he raised his arms high and lowered his singing voice to a near whisper. He crooned, he seduced, he cajoled—and he raised them. He raised them all. Bound them to his word, to his will, bound them and bade them stay. Never to rest, never to cease, never to meet up with loved ones along the Lonely Road.

Ishtaset was first to rise, battered and ruined as she was, and stumble to him on broken feet. Ismai reached down to touch her bloodied short warrior's mane, but it was Kal ne Mur who smiled. At his touch, Ishtaset was made whole again, and beautiful, if one could look past the blood and gore and the milk-blind eyes of death.

"My... king..." she ground out in a voice like broken rocks. All around them the newly dead rose in response to the Lich King's song. Most of them, like Ishtaset, were revenants. Those who had been too savaged by their manner of death to be raised whole would, he knew, combine into a new bonelord, and eventually take a name and its place at the rear of his army.

The Mah'zula here had been destroyed, as he would destroy them all, and the people of Aish Kalumm had been set free, if not in the manner any of them might have wished.

Ismai's fist closed in Ishtaset's hair. He leaned down so that his face was inches from hers.

"Now," he said in a voice harsh from singing and thick with grief, "now you are useful to me, and I have had my revenge."

But there was no fear in those eyes, or acknowledgment. There was... nothing.

"How does it taste, Father?" Naara stared at Ishtaset, and then at him, and a faint frown creased her brow. "How does it feel? *Kishah*. Vengeance."

Ismai released Ishtaset's hair and his own hold on life. What was there left for him, after this? Ismai straightened in his saddle and frowned down at himself. He had not so much as a smear of blood on him, and that did not seem right.

"Like nothing," he told her. "Like nothing at all."

The people gathered before him. They came wailing and afraid, stone-faced and angry. They came with fear and sorrow and revenge in their hearts, but as he called them, they came, and that was what really mattered. Those of his followers who yet lived looked upon the horde with horror. They had not been able to lay their dead to rest before they rose again—those who could.

A new bonelord bellowed to the south. *Farrakh Nahol'i'khan*, it called itself, *the black wind that swallows all hope.*

The newly raised dead had sworn no oath to him. They had walked the Lonely Road, if only for a short distance, before being brought back. Had shed their lives, their memories like old clothes, and now, stuffed back into them unwillingly, found the fit not to their liking. These dead wanted no more to do with the land of the living.

Ismai could feel those trapped souls straining and screaming inside their meat cages, could see the grief and horror on the faces of the people as they looked into the eyes of their erstwhile companions, lovers, sons, and saw... nothing. No love, no hate, no recognition at all.

Yes, he thought as he watched the people turn away from him. *I am a monster, but I am* your *monster, so be grateful.*

True to his word, he helped Sudduth plant her small saplings. With his own hands he carried pots of water from the Dibris for them, set a low stone wall around them, and bade the living Mothers to tend them well. Then, not trusting to the goodwill of humans toward things they did not understand, he set Ibna to watch over the grove and see to the rebuilding of Aish Kalumm.

"You wanted to make beautiful things," he told the too-peaceful warrior. "Here is your chance. I charge you with rebuilding Aish Kalumm, the City of Mothers, larger and grander than it was before, with beauty to be found in every corner. Make it a place of peace and respite, for the heart of every mother is like a garden in bloom. Build a city that is well-guarded and easily defended, for the hearts of men are dark and terrible."

"As you will, your Arrogance." Ibna bowed low, his dark face split with a smile that made him look boyish and alive. "It will be done." He sauntered off, nearly skipping, to the grove.

Sudduth stared at the Lich King. "You have done a good thing, your Arrogance."

"A small enough thing," he allowed. "This costs me nothing, will benefit the people, and it will make Ibna happy."

"You have… changed. Your heart is soft."

"A good change, I hope?"

"A good change in a friend, but for a king?" She shifted her eyes to look over his shoulder, north toward the land of the Dragon Kings. "Who can say?"

"You worry that a soft heart is a sign of weakness."

She looked at him again, white teeth flashing in a grin.

"I? I have nothing to worry about." She laughed aloud. "I am already dead."

❖

Ismai led his horde to the river Dibris, and the Atualonian ships that had been dragged upon the sand until such time as the river serpents might subside, allowing them to return to Atualon. But crews had been slaughtered by Ishtaset and her Mah'zula before they could use their vessels to escape.

The great vessels had been dragged from the river and onto the sands where they lay forlorn. Ismai watched as they were now eased back into the water, the striped sails rigged and readied, and strode up the gangplank onto the deck of the bold and beautiful dragon-headed ship.

It seemed large enough to Ismai to carry an entire village up and down the Dibris, but even such a large craft as this would be vulnerable to the great serpents that swam the waters of the river, let alone the sea, and they had none of the red-cloaked sorcerers on board to keep them safe.

Never fear, little prince, Kal ne Mur reassured him. *I created the Baidun Daiel, and there is nothing they can accomplish with their sorceries that I cannot. They amplify my power, it is true, but the magic is my own.*

I am not sure whether I should be relieved by this, Ismai responded, *or frightened.*

Soft-hearted, as Sudduth says. He smiled to himself. He rather liked the boy, and that was just as well, since they shared a body.

The ships were poled groaning and creaking to the river deeps. Striped sails fluttered, settled, filled, and the vessels began to make their graceful way north.

"Do we sail for Atualon, then?" Sudduth asked.

"In time," Ismai answered. "We sail first to Min Yaarif, that I may send messages to the queen in Quarabala. Long have the Kentakuyan owed me fealty, and now is the time for me to call old debts due. Quarabalese assistance will be essential in reclaiming Atualon. Our numbers are great, and with living Quarabalese warriors among us it is certain that we will overwhelm the Atualonians. After all"—and he smiled at her— "my last and most beloved queen, and many of my best fighters, hail from that land."

"Ah, to see my home again…" Sudduth shook her head. "But no, the land of my birth is no doubt as dead as the Zeera I remember. Not to mention the ancient alliance. Friendship is strong if it lasts a season, let alone many lifetimes of men."

"Friendship is fickle, this is true," he allowed, "but hatred runs as deep and cold as this river. The Quarabalese, I understand from young Ismai's memories, have endured many miseries since I… went to my rest. Surely they will be eager to join with me in common enmity. And if they are not eager, well…" he shrugged. "We will burn that road when we come to it."

Far away, river serpents bellowed in alarm. No Baidun Daiel would be necessary to keep the beasts from destroying the ships, after all—the leviathans' natural fear of the Lich King would suffice. It was a silly thing over which to feel regret, but Ismai sighed. It would have been marvelous to see the river serpents and the sea-things, and listen to their songs at sunset.

As the ships picked up speed, a young vash'ai queen wailed from the riverbank.

There is no room for love, Kal ne Mur reminded Ismai. He closed his heart, his mind to Ruh'ayya. *No time for regret. We have a world to conquer, or to destroy.*

Again.

The setting sun streaked the sky with claw-marks and turned the river red as shared blood.

It was glorious.

THIRTY-TWO

Sulema and Hannei flanked the shadowmancer, and Rehaza Entanye brought up the rear. Keoki strummed his lute as they trotted on, humming under his breath even as his companions struggled to breathe the thin, burnt air. So powerful was the sorcerer's eagerness to reach his homeland that the air about them seethed and groaned under the weight of spun darkness. The shadows beneath their feet urged them on.

His shadowshifting protected them from the worst of the heat but Akari soared high, withering the Seared Lands with his hot and angry glare, searching for those who had dared deny him his love, that he might smite them. The world might have forgotten the Quarabalese, their shining cities and poetry, songs and shadow-magic, but Akari Sun Dragon would never forget, never forgive. Those who had traveled this road in days past had left sign of their own desperate struggles as they shed their earthly possessions and fought for their lives.

Here was an ancient waterskin, so desiccated that it turned to dust beneath Hannei's heel. There was a knife, long as a short sword almost, its edge glowing faint blue in the filtered light of Akari's wrath. Infrequently—but not nearly infrequently enough for Sulema's peace of mind—they would pass the desiccated corpse of one who had not, nor would ever, reach her destination.

These last were by far the worst. Some lay curled on their sides, hands tucked beneath their cheeks, as if they had only just fallen asleep and might rise again and join the travelers. Only a bit of exposed bone or a shriveled foot, still in its sandal, gave lie to the dream. Others lay with backs arched, throats torn, mouths and shriveled eyes wide in endless screams of dusty agony as they stared despairingly into the hot maw of death.

At one point they passed the huddled figure of a mother with her arms wrapped about a tiny child. One arm was upraised as if to protect the fragile white skull that she held pressed against her breast. Sulema averted her eyes but knew the sight would stalk her dreams forever.

"Why does nobody care for them?" she asked no one, but knew the answer even so. The small effort it cost her to speak was too much to have spent. To attempt this shadowed road was to make a final, desperate attempt at life. Never so much as a breath or second glance would be left to spare for the dead.

At Sulema's words Hannei cut her eyes sideways, and that look was as heavy as a slap to the face.

You know nothing, she said, as clearly as if she still had a tongue. *You are weak.* Sulema knew it to be true and felt herself shamed.

The shadowmancer stumbled just then, jerking Sulema's attention away, and then his trot turned into a lope, long legs stretching so that the others had to pick up their pace as well, lest they be left behind to become landmarks for future traveling fools.

"What..." Rehaza Entanye began, panting the word, but grunted in surprise even as Sulema herself saw what had caused their sorcerer to pick up the pace. Ahead of them, at the very slice of the horizon, she could see that the ground was rent with deep fissures. They were harsh, these wounds in the earth, dark and sharp as if they had been drawn upon the burnt ground with a quill dipped in ink, and they gaped like thin, angry mouths, ready to swallow the mean flesh of unwary travelers.

They had nearly reached the Edge of the Seared Lands, and it was the most uninviting sight Sulema could have imagined. Part of her wanted to grab the shadowmancer by the nape of his neck and demand they turn back.

"Run," Rehaza Entanye groaned between gritted teeth as she passed Sulema. Her eyes were wide as a spooked horse's.

Sulema glanced over her shoulder and then wished she had not. Through the boiling air behind them she could see what at first appeared to be an advancing storm of some sort, a roiling line of darkness. Through this, as if through the thin veil of a shy lover, she could see a horde of pursuing reavers.

In their midst was a horror.

It was man-sized and roughly man-shaped—if a man might have as many arms as a spider had legs—but the chill that stabbed through her heart and grabbed at her reaver-infected shoulder was born of a terror that no mere human could induce. Eyes red and burning as old coals stabbed at them through the cover of false night, and when the thing raised its many twitching arms, bidding the shadows to its will, Sulema could see the tiny glint of a million stars set into its char-black skin.

It was an Arachnist, she knew, a spider-priest, one who worshipped the Araids as gods. She had never in her worst dreams imagined that a shadowmancer might become such a creature.

"Guts and goatfuckery," she spat, turning back and increasing her pace. Just moments ago she had been weary enough to lie down and die. Now every fiber of her being shrieked at her to run, to live. "What is *that*?" she croaked painfully. "I have never heard of an Arachnist shadowmancer."

Keoki, though still deep in his trance, turned his head and glanced behind them. His dreamful eyes widened, widened, and the shades about them writhed as his music faltered.

"Run," he rasped in unconscious imitation of Rehaza Entanye. "*Run!*"

Sulema sucked in a deep breath of seared, corpse-smelling air, and ran, certain it would not be enough. Her body flooded with the false vigor that came with dreadful fear; she shed fatigue and felt, in that moment, that she could have outrun Atemi. But the cracks ahead of them lingered teasingly at the horizon's edge, while behind them she could hear the rustling, buzzing, and occasional screeching laugh of the swarm of reavers. Chillflesh raised painfully as she imagined them falling upon her from behind, rending her flesh.

Or worse.

Then Sulema felt the call of the sorcerer who pursued her, calling, calling... *He has come for me*, she thought, and knew it for truth. The spider-priest's sorcery pulled at her blood, her bones. It grabbed at her fleeing spirit as a lover might grab at her clothes, stripping away her defenses and leaving the soul naked.

If I was my mother, they would not dare threaten me, she thought. *She would turn his skin into a drum and make him dance to its rhythm. If I was my father, they would run from me in terror—he would call upon Akari and blast them to ashes. But I am just a warrior with a sword, no horse, and no sword-sisters...*

She ran till her lungs seared and legs screamed, till her heart felt as if it would burst from the efforts—and knowing it would never, could never be enough. As the Edge grew near, and her enemies drew nearer, Sulema stretched her legs, pumped her arms—

So close, she thought. *We were so close*. The sun was setting. Just a few minutes more, a few strides more, and they might have made it to safety.

Something brushed her from behind, drawing a line of fire along the skin of her back. Sulema shrieked, ducking her attacker, and then staggered as white agony lanced through her older wound.

One sword, no horse—

It is time, little one, crooned a thin and wicked voice in her mind. Sulema slowed, then turned as if in a dream, filled with dread the color of old blood. There stretched a line of reavers, veiled in shadow, insectoid eyes glittering in their eagerness. They were not as near as Sulema's fear had led her to believe, but entirely too close to lend strength to any hope of escape. The Arachnist-thing rose high in their midst, corpse arms twitching as he raised them toward her. One bloated hand wielded a whip of black fire; Sulema could only surmise that this had been the cause of her pain. The lash flicked out again, and again, hungry for another taste of her.

Come, the Arachnist coaxed, mocking her struggle. *Come to me, to us. Come to Eth, join—*

A hand closed hard on her shoulder and Sulema jumped half out of her soft human skin. Her companions had stopped when she did and stood with her, gasping and desperate.

"*Hhhhaaak*," Hannei growled at her, squeezing again, painfully. Only then did Sulema realize that she had been dragging her feet toward the Arachnist and his promise-threats. She willed her feet to stop moving, and a thin howl went up from the ranks of the reavers. They slowed in their advance.

One sword, no horse... and one sword-sister.

It came to Sulema, in that moment, that a warrior with a sword and one sword-sister needed nothing else in the world. She caught Hannei's gaze with her own. *Sister*, she signed. *Come, sister. We fight together. Mutaani.* Hannei hesitated for a moment and then firmed her mouth and nodded. *Sister*, she agreed. *Mutaani.* She drew the twin blades at her back, and Sulema pulled her shamsi free. Together they would find the beauty in death.

Keoki took a deep breath, bent over his lute, and his fingers attacked the strings in a battle-frenzy. Shadows rallied to his call and the world about them faded to near black. Rehaza Entanye, who had been staring at the girls with an unreadable expression on her face, shrugged and took hold of her war hammer, gripping it with both hands. She rolled her head this way, that way, and spat as if readying herself for yet another battle in the pits.

"It is a good day to die, as you desert sluts are so fond of saying," she grinned. "Might as well get it over with."

Though she was wreathed in shadow and pain, weary and beyond the reach of hope, Sulema felt the world lift from her heart. *I am a warrior, and nothing less.* She tugged her vest open, baring her breasts at the enemy, raised her sword, and laughed a true, deep belly laugh. It was enough that she would die beside her sister, as a warrior should, she realized. It had always been enough.

"Show me yours, you rotten sons of churra shit!" she yelled, mocking the reavers and their foul master. "*Show me yours!*"

The Arachnist hesitated a moment, and then with a high, thin wail of rage brought his many arms down and pointed them toward Sulema and her companions. The black whip snapped over their heads, urging them on.

"Kill them!" he shrieked.

At that moment Akari Sun Dragon folded his wings and dove beyond the horizon. The sky flared bright and hot one last time, and then an indigo veil was pulled across the face of the land. Sulema tipped her head back and took a deep breath, looking up and up and up. By day, the Seared Lands were the stuff of nightmares, but by night they were lovely. And in the end, she had kept her vow.

She wanted to live. Oh, how she wanted to live.

But it was a very good night to die.

The reavers hissed, and laughed, and leapt.

Shy, sweet Keoki, who had been shooting Sulema adoring glances since first they had met, dropped his mantle of impotence and strode toward the swarming attackers. His voice rose in song, a clear, sweet tenor that blended perfectly with the rippling music of his lute—and the shadows along the path rose to do his bidding. Like a sandstorm of lost souls, borne upon the wind of his passion, they crested toward the foul, pale shapes. The reavers halted, and Sulema's heart lifted to see them pull back.

We are so close, she thought, casting a longing glance over her shoulder. She imagined that she could see, deep in the nearest crevice, the faint, encouraging wink of fire. *If we ran—*

A shout rang out from the swarm's midst. The enemy's shadowmancer raised a multitude of writhing, twitching corpse arms as if he would pull down the moons. The shadows around him leapt at his command. Sulema could almost hear them howling, hungry for flesh and the breath of the living. The two darknesses met with a clap as of thunder. Black lightning—that was the only way Sulema could describe it— burned through the air and smote the ground, blasting holes deep enough to swallow a horse, sending chunks of bone and salted earth high into the air.

Every hair on Sulema's body stood on end, and a buzzing filled her head with such pressure it felt as if her eyes would pop. She ignored this, and ignored the stench of the battling shadow-storms, as well—burnt blood and hot metal, an angry red smell. Instead she concentrated on choosing a target.

I cannot kill them all, she realized, *but I can surely take out some of the goatfuckers before they get me. I think... that one, first.*

"You!"

The reaver she had targeted turned its face toward her and hissed, showing rows of inward-pointing teeth embedded in a wide, round maw.

"Yes, *you*, you turd-spawned abomination!" Sulema shouted, pointing her sword. Even though the land about them was cooling, the air was hot enough to burn her lungs. She ignored that pain, too, and laughed in her enemy's face.

"Are you hungry, asshole? Eat my sword!"

Hannei glanced at her, surprised, and then grinned and shook her head. The battling storms howled about them, and the reaver Sulema had singled out crossed the distance between them in a series of deathly quick bounds. Sulema drew herself up into a fighting stance and let all the tension of a lifetime drain away.

I am coming, Azra'hael, she promised the one who had been meant for her. *Soon I will join you on the Lonely Road. And I will bring this one's head with me.*

Then there was no more time for thinking.

Sulema had fought before, with fists and staff and feet, with sword and knife and bow. She had trained with her sword-sisters, fought her enemies, had slain a lionsnake by herself. This, she was certain, would eclipse it all.

The reaver did not move like a natural thing. It flashed this way and that, twitching and jumping, so rain-and-lightning quick it might have outrun its own shadow in broad daylight. It was strides away, and then it was upon her. Sulema twisted away from the monster and brought her shamsi down, expecting resistance as her blade bit deep into its neck. She overbalanced, however, and stumbled forward as she sliced through the night air. Years of training saved her hide as she followed through with a crouch and whirl, taking the reaver full in its chest with the point of her sword.

Bright-sharp as her blade was, it skittered sideways off the thing's body with a scraping sound as of metal on naked rock. Black ichor oozed from a deep wound—not nearly deep enough, not a killing wound—as the thing reached clawed fingers for Sulema's face. It bared venom-fouled fangs at her, insect eyes hungry and mocking as it opened that horrible mouth wide, wider.

A spear stabbed over Sulema's shoulder and pierced the reaver's face. It exploded in a rain of brains, blood, and clotted gore, drenching Sulema with viscous, stinking dead-man-bug guts.

"Pfaugh!" she spat, stomach heaving in protest. "Oh, that is just—"

The spear retracted, leaving the reaver to collapse twitching upon the dead ground. A man brushed past, darker and taller than any Sulema had ever seen. Black as shadows, silent as death as he ghosted past, hardly sparing a glance as he hefted a wicked iron-tipped spear and jogged into the maelstrom. Another passed her, and another, and then a woman, tall and proud and bald as her companions, and as beautiful.

Aasah is of these people, she knew immediately, though their eyes were brown as any Zeerani's and their skin unscarred. *And Yaela*. It occurred to her to wonder—even as she shook free of gore and surprise and made ready to rejoin the battle—to wonder how tiny, lush Yaela could ever have been born of such tall stock.

Three more warriors passed by, all women. Two of them carried spears, the third bore a kind of long spiked hammer and a delicate-looking oblong shield. Their long legs carried them over the ground quickly and gracefully. Sulema had heard that when Akari showed his face over the Seared Lands, any soul unfortunate enough to be caught aboveground would be burned to ash, so the people of Quarabala learned from childhood how to run faster than tarbok, faster than the wind—faster than daybreak. She had never believed those stories growing up. Now, with the stories made flesh, she found it difficult *not* to believe.

Keoki's magic failed him. The song died upon his lute and his half of the shadow-storm faltered and fled. As it did, the Quarabalese warriors poured from the cracked earth at the Edge and ran to their aid. The tides of combat shifted as spear and hammer and bow sang of death and victory and one more sunrise.

The reavers fell back before the onslaught, but it was too late. The swarm was overwhelmed as a warrior with one sword and a single sword-sister and a Quarabalese army found her enemies falling before her like sand in a strong wind. The Arachnist shadowmancer was one of the last to fall. When he did, his magic snuffed out with such force that it made her ears pop.

It is over, Sulema thought wonderingly as she wiped her blade on corpse rags. She grimaced at the ringing pain in her ears and swallowed, trying to clear them. *By Akari, it is over and I am still alive.*

She turned to share this thought with Hannei and stopped mid-swallow. Her sword-sister stood with both swords held loosely in one hand, dripping blood and ichor, though none of it appeared to be hers. Her shoulders were curled forward, and one arm was held protectively across her abdomen. She had a wistful, frightened, faraway look in her eyes, a look that any woman would recognize. Sulema had last seen that look upon a friend's face when Neptara had announced her pregnancy.

"Hannei!" Sulema whispered, shocked. "*Um Hannei?*" Hannei twitched, and for a moment her face was white in the night with terror. Sulema started toward her, but Hannei held up her empty hand in a pleading gesture.

No, she mouthed. *No*. And she turned away.

Just then, someone touched Sulema's wounded shoulder. She jumped, startled and hurt, and turned so abruptly that Keoki released his grip on her and took two hasty steps back. The shadowmancer gathered himself and smiled. His eyes were full of moonslight, his fingers dripped blood onto the angry ground, and his words carried all the tender weariness of the world.

"Sulema an Hafsa Azeina, an Wyvernus ne Atu," he intoned, "Dragon Queen of Atualon, I am humbled to present you to her Highness, the Grand Princess Tamimeha." The woman with the odd hammer stepped forward. One hand curled around the handle of her weapon, which she held casually slung across her shoulders.

"Your Radiance," Tamimeha said, and her smile was solemn in the moonslight. "I thank you for honoring us with

the opportunity to kill our enemies. It is a glorious night."
She held out both her hands.

Pushing the revelation about Hannei to the back of her mind, Sulema clasped them warmly and returned the woman's somber look with the grin that had gotten her into—and out of—trouble, for as long as she could remember.

"*Ehuani*, I am no queen—but it *is* a glorious night," she agreed. "I thank *you*, your Highness, for honoring us with the opportunity not to die."

The Quarabalese went still for a moment, and then burst into uproarious laughter. Tamimeha slung her free arm across Sulema's shoulder and hugged her tight, as a sword-sister might have done.

"Come then, daughter of the dreamshifter, and let us feast and drink to our mutual honor. After," she sniffed the air delicately and winked, "you have bathed. *Aueh*, but you stink!"

THIRTY-THREE

There were no leavings at this end of the shadowed road, nothing to mark the beginnings or endings of desperate journeys, no bones or knives or scraps of life. Sulema wondered at the abandoned hulk of a city she had at first mistaken for a jagged mountain range. As they passed between ruined red-brick buildings, fine as small palaces, she felt the weight of their judgment pressing upon her.

My Atualonian ancestor did this, she thought, remembering the stories Istaza Ani had told her. *That Dragon King—Kal ne Mur, he did this when he loosed atulfah and sundered the world.* The buildings stared down at her with empty eyes, and Sulema felt they loved her not. *This ruined world is the true legacy of the Dragon Kings— and my inheritance.*

The road they traveled became wide and well-worn, and led them through the gaping walls of a city that in its day had been grander even than Atukos. Darkness came upon them as they walked through the giant arched doorway, and Sulema shivered.

"This is the great city of Saodan?" she marveled. "It feels like a tomb."

"This is not Saodan; it is nothing more than a nameless city like any number scattered across the Seared Lands. Nevertheless, you speak of my homeland, and though she is not what she once was—thanks in no small part to your forbears, Sulema—Quarabala is no *tomb*." Keoki frowned. "In ages past she was the center of commerce and culture for all the world. This city was so minor that we do not even remember its name, and yet even this humble place was grander in its time than the palaces of Atualon or Sindan. And Saodan—*Saodan*—was a jewel in this world like no other, so splendid that our dreams are too small now to remember the least of her glory. Atualonian kings and Sindanese emperors alike tried—and failed—to seize our land and claim her riches as their own. Scholars traveled a lifetime to spend a single year in the libraries of Saodan, monks and sorcerers and mystics would have given their thumbs for a glance at our sacred texts. And the music..." His voice trailed off, wistful, and with bloodied fingers he stroked a soft lament upon his lute. "The music. The art. The stories." He sighed. "Saodan was the heart of the mightiest civilization ever to begrace our world, yet it is all but a memory now. Memory and shades of the dead, buried far beneath the flesh of a lost world."

"Not all is memory," Tamimeha chided. "Not all is lost."

"Not all," Keoki agreed, and he silenced his music. "But most."

"It is much the same where I come from," Sulema agreed, thinking of Aish Kalumm, of the empty Madraj waiting for the return of the people.

Keoki frowned. "But Atualon is thriving—so I hear. Thriving and wealthy and prosperous."

"I do not come from Atualon," Sulema explained. "My mother and I escaped from that place when I was small. I was raised in the Zeera. The Zeeranim are my people." Beside her, Hannei grunted agreement.

"Ah, that explains your sword, then. And your, um, your vest."

There was a slight cough, and Sulema glanced at Keoki. He was blushing.

He likes me, she realized. *Just what I need—a sorcerer with a crush.*

Hannei made another disturbing noise, and Sulema realized that her sword-sister was laughing at them.

"When will we reach the city?" she asked for a change in subject. "The new city, I mean—your people did rebuild, did they not?"

"They did," Tamimeha agreed. Her eyes sparkled with pride in the low torchlight, and dimples appeared at the corners of her stern mouth. "The heart of Quarabala is now buried deep beneath the ground, carved into the bones of the world. Even one born as you were in the shining city of Atualon, and raised among the glorious singing sands of the Zeera, would not find our Saodan wanting for beauty and wonder."

"If I can get a bath and something other than pemmican to eat, I will be happy," Sulema said. "Then I am to find a girl, for so I am sworn, and return her to her aunt's care. Maika, her name is. Do you know of her? She is young, not yet come of age, and, ah…" She realized Yaela had never told her what the girl looked like, and scowled. "Most likely she is short for your kind?"

"There are many girls named Maika," Tamimeha answered, and something in her expression was unreadable. "Perhaps we can find yours, but first, we must travel through the Edge of the Seared Lands, where my people await your arrival."

"Await my arrival?" Sulema asked. "I do not understand. There are none in Quarabala who know of my quest." Come to think of it, Tamimeha and her warriors had seemed to be expecting them, which was impossible, unless…

Magic. Sulema made a sour face; even here in the Seared Lands, she could not escape magic or the politics of power. Would she never be free of it?

"You will see. Tomorrow night, you will see. For the rest of this night we will walk, and tomorrow we will rest and tend to our wounds in this old place. Tomorrow night, we make a final run for the Edge."

The Quarabalese warriors shared another enigmatic look, and Sulema rolled her eyes.

"But…"

"You will see," Tamimeha answered in a voice that reminded her of Istaza Ani, one that let Sulema know she would get nothing further from this woman. "Tomorrow night, you will see."

They walked the remainder of that night in silence through the once-splendid halls and passages of the ancient city. As they passed the remains of a garden or statue, or passed through an elaborately carved doorway, Sulema wished she could have seen this place as it once had been. It was not difficult to imagine the ornate fountains filled with water-lotus and fish, or the courtyards with musicians and storytellers, and it ached her heart to think that all of this had been destroyed by men with a lust for war and dominance.

All this beauty lost forever, she thought, trailing her hand along a wall engraved with flowering vines. *And for what? So some man could park his arse on a golden throne and eat stinky cheeses. If I were truly the Dragon Queen—*

The wall beneath her hand trembled and Sulema froze, seized with the irrational certainty that her thoughts had woken Sajani, and that the world was about to end. Dust fell, and then rocks; the walls of the city swayed and danced to the notes of a song even more ancient than itself as the earth tore asunder. The warriors' voices rose in alarm and pain as walls which had stood for millennia swayed, failed, and collapsed, the dust of their destruction rising like the smoke of a funeral pyre.

Mother, Sulema thought, and reached out with her mind—but her mother was dead, gone ahead of her down the Lonely Road, and could not save her. Nor would Wyvernus sing Sajani to sleep this time; they were both gone, leaving the world dim and hopeless, and it was all her fault—

Ja'Akari! snapped the voice of Istaza Ani where it

304

slept deep in her heart. *Stop crying over spilt usca and do something! Are you a milk-mouthed brat, or are you the warrior I raised?*

Under the sun, I am Ja'Akari, daughter of the Zeera, Sulema thought. The storm within her stilled, even as the world around her went to pieces. *I am the daughter of Hafsa Azeina, I am the daughter of Wyvernus.*

I am SULEMA!

She raised her voice in song.

Untrained as she was and without the aid of a dragon mask, weary and wounded and far from the comforts of her home, still she was Sulema, and she was something. She had her shamsi at one side, and her sword-sister at the other, and the song of the Zeera in her heart.

It is enough, she told herself, and let the song that kindled in her heart burst through the dragon's mask, the paper-thin maze of bones in her face that made those of her line unique in all the world. *It will have to be enough.*

And it was, for now.

The infant song of the dragon's daughter rang through the bones of the world. It whispered as a wind through Shehannam; the Huntress paused, lifting her eyes from the game trail, and her hounds raised their bloodied muzzles to howl at the ghost moons. Sulema's song swept across the sands of the Zeera, and roused the golden sands to harmony; it dropped like flowers into the swollen waters of the Naapua, upon the Forbidden City itself, and woke in the heart of a trapped sea-thing a canticle of joy. Born of the innocent hope of a dreamshifter's daughter, the song wove itself into the breath of the world and the dreams of a dragon, who roused, stirred, and drifted back to deep slumber.

Sulema woke and found herself lying next to a small and cheerless fire. The faces of her companions were as grim, and no few were bruised or bloodied. "There was an earthquake?" Rehaza Entanye said. She stared into the fire, and there was a question in her voice.

Sulema did not answer it, but the stares of accusation lay upon her like a cairn of stones. *I am the daughter of the dreamshifter*, she thought, *daughter of the dragon. Death and destruction follow me like shadows.* She said nothing, but sat up and accepted a waterskin from Hannei.

The world had stopped quaking; Sajani, it seemed, had chosen not to wake from her dream just yet. *But soon*, Sulema thought, *soon*. She did not know whether her small song had played any part in this, only that the power she could summon fell desperately short of what would be needed to save the world should the dragon truly fight to wake.

One of the Quarabalese warriors began to moan. At first Sulema supposed he had been among those wounded in the earthquake, but soon learned that it was much worse.

"Niekeke has been bitten," a Quarabalese woman whispered to Tamimeha where she stood near the fire. "He is turning." Tamimeha closed her eyes. When she opened them again, she seemed to have aged ten years.

"At daybreak," she told the other woman, who bowed and faded back into the shadows.

"He was bitten?" Sulema asked.

"By a reaver," one of the Quarabalese said.

"He will die at daybreak," Tamimeha explained in a flat voice that invited no discussion. "Better that than to become one of the forsaken."

"Forsaken?" That needed no explanation, really. "Do your people not have a cure for this... affliction?" She had hoped that the Quarabalese would be able to provide medicines for the reaver venom in her own blood, since Yaela had carried the loremaster's potions with her. Given Tamimeha's unyielding countenance, however, she decided it best to keep that a secret after all.

Tamimeha shook her head. "Such a cure exists, but it requires the venom of a young *nahessa*—what you would call a 'lionsnake.' That, and magic I do not possess and could never afford. Such a thing is more precious than salt." She glanced over her shoulder, and for a moment her eyes went dark with grief. "Worth more than the life of a simple warrior."

"That seems... harsh." *Heartless*, she wanted to say. "How can a thing, even a medicine, be worth more than the life of a person?"

"You think me too hard, daughter of the dragon?" Tamimeha turned her head to glare, never slowing the pace. "What if I were to tell you that Niekeke is the son of my wife's sister, blood of my love? Would you think me heartless, I wonder?" She curled her lip. "We are a harsh people. This is a harsh world. Better you learn that today than tomorrow." She turned away again. "Come now. Too long have we waited for you to wake. Earthquake or no we have far to travel, and daybreak waits for no woman. Not even the daughter of the dragon."

Tamimeha increased their pace to a brisk jog, and there was no further talk of the glorious past or of bright tomorrows.

The group traveled through the night and came to the far side of the ruined city just as the sky came again into view, and was taking on a warning blush. They made camp, and it was a grim affair. Niekeke's groans grew more anguished; the faces of his countrywomen and men grew harder, lined with grief and determination. As shade-cloths were slung over ropes and fires built, Tamimeha called for the youth to be brought to her.

He was young—younger than Sulema, hardly more than a boy. Sweat rolled down his brow, his face was pale ash from

307

the effort it cost him to walk upright, and Sulema could see that he was biting his cheek to keep from crying out in pain.

The front of his shirt was covered in blood.

So young, she thought. *So brave*. Braver than she, who kept her own affliction a secret.

"Niekeke," Tamimeha said, and reached out to touch his face. "Niekeke. You have been bitten by a reaver. You are turning."

"Y-yes, Auntie," the boy said between clenched teeth.

Tamimeha opened her mouth, but he held up a hand and touched her cheek gently, gently.

"It is okay," he told her, and he did his best to smile. "It is okay, Auntie."

Tamimeha's heart broke through her eyes. Fat tears rolled down her face.

"Nie-nie, I am a war leader. I have to—I have to—"

"It is okay," he told her again. He set down the sword he had been carrying, unbuckled the knife-belt at his waist, and let it fall to the ground. "It has been a good run. I am ready."

Tamimeha closed her eyes and firmed her quivering mouth. Then she took a deep breath, opened them again, and enfolded the youth in a long embrace.

"Let us go, then," she said to him. "Sweet boy." She kissed his forehead.

The other Quarabalese averted their eyes as Tamimeha took the boy's hand and led him away, into the darkness.

They broke camp at dusk and set forth along the wide road, which led on and down and steeply down. The cracked, dry walls of the earth rose up to either side as they descended, until the burnt surface of the land was a distant memory far overhead. Tamimeha went before them, her eyes flat and joyless. Hannei and Rehaza Entanye chose to travel among the Quarabalese warriors at the rear, leaving Sulema to walk beside Keoki. She did not mind. Of all her available companions, he was for the moment the least taxing, and she was weary.

"So this is the Edge," she remarked.

"This is the Edge, and welcome to it," he agreed. "Shithole of the world."

Ahead and below them, in the thick gloom, came the occasional rustle and scrape of bodies moving out of the way. "Are those people I hear, or animals?"

"Both," he replied. "Low-caste people with thin blood and no luck. They live here, if it can be said to be living, at the edge of the Edge. They should not bother such a large and well-armed party as ours, though."

"And if they do?" she asked, though the answer was all around her in the hard stares and bright red steel of the Quarabalese warriors.

"I will protect you," he answered, so earnestly that she did not laugh.

They traveled through that night and into the next day as the chasm grew wider and deep enough to shade them from the sun. Here and there the walls cracked open to the sides, revealing tangles of thorny black roots—manna, they were called, and the Quarabalese stopped to tap the roots for clear liquid that looked and tasted almost like water. Occasionally there was the shoddy evidence of human habitation. A pile of moldy blankets, dented cooking pots, the greasy remains of a hastily doused fire. Mean lives, furtive and small, carved out of rock and root and thin air.

Once, Sulema saw—or thought she saw—a small face peeking out at them from a tiny hole high in the wall, no larger than a hare's warren.

"A *girl*," she said, and pointed. "There are children here?" Such a thing was unthinkable to her. In the Zeera, children were precious, and cared for by all. That one might be left in such squalor shocked and disgusted her.

"Not for long." Keoki shrugged, unconcerned, not bothering to look up. "It is a harsh world."

"But... children."

He looked at her then, a pitying expression on his face, and shrugged.

"They are low-caste children, your Radiance. Not such as should trouble the minds of you or me."

There was nothing Sulema could say to that, and the small face—if indeed she had even seen it—disappeared. She resolved to say nothing more.

It is not my concern, she tried to tell herself. *These are not my people, their ways are not my ways. All I have to do is get to the damn city, find Yaela's little niece, get her back to Min Yaarif somehow, and I will have fulfilled my vow.*

The thought tasted like a lie, and she could not spit it out.

They encountered no more of the residents of the Edge— none save a small herd of dhurra, which looked like kin to the Zeerani tarbok. In better days Sulema would have wanted to hunt them. Now she was content to pass them by, and grateful that they were not predators or fighters.

Or little girls.

After three days of marching steadily on and down, the sky was so far above them that sunlight was a distant, dim memory, and the moons just a fever-dream. The Quarabalese climbed the rock cliffs as they traveled at night, searching for manna root to tap or to burn, and for small game animals. The walls grew steeper, the road cobbled with smooth stones and well-tended. Finally their group was hailed by a small and only somewhat shabbily dressed family—a man and four women, one of whom had an infant at her breast.

"*Lokahei,*" Tamimeha called. "*Ka maluhei. O ka anta?*"

"*Lokahei,*" the man replied as the woman clutched her child. "*Eh ta maluhei. Nenu o'Okapai.*"

"*O'Okapai.*" Tamimeha relaxed, and her fellow warriors did the same. "*Hau wen anta mapopi I ka nassa atei annu hoi'I, ta?*"

"*Ta,*" the man agreed, and he turned to one of the women. "*Holo, Ipua.*" The woman bowed to the man, and then to them, and set off down the path at a dead run.

"She will tell them we are coming," Tamimeha said. She did not meet Sulema's eyes, had not since the night she walked off with Niekeke and returned alone.

"His nag is very obedient," one of the Quarabalese warriors murmured approvingly.

"Nag?" Sulema inquired.

"His wives," Rehaza Entanye replied, gesturing at the women.

"Ah," Sulema said, but what she really meant was, *What a load of fresh churra shit.* She had not yet arrived in Quarabala, and already she could not wait to be gone from this place. *Murder and slavery and sunlight that kills,* she thought. *It is no wonder Yaela fled this place. The only question is why she left her niece behind in this forsaken land.*

"Your eyes are full of questions," Keoki remarked. "Perhaps I can give you the answers you seek?"

"I am not seeking answers," she replied, rolling her eyes. "Just one young girl, and then another sorcerer to get us back to Quarabala."

"And maybe a bath," Rehaza Entanye said, laughing. "You stink!"

"A bath," Sulema agreed. She *did* stink. "And then I am away from this place."

"As you say," Keoki replied. "Let me know if you change your mind."

Sulema looked up at the tall columns and smooth walls of yet another nameless abandoned city, the bones of a place which once must have outstripped Atukos for grandeur. "I cannot imagine what Quarabala must have been like, before the Sundering." Then she grimaced, wondering whether she had misspoken. Surely these people did not want to be reminded of their loss, any more than the Zeeranim would wish to be reminded of the empty seats in the Madraj, the empty cradles in Aish Kalumm.

Tamimeha just sighed and shook her head. "None of us can," she agreed. "Nor will we ever see its like again, not in our lifetimes." Then she turned her head as the sound of distant drums reached their ears. "Ah! She is come!"

To a one, the Quarabalese warriors—who had been flanking them as a guard, or as an escort, or possibly both—dropped to their knees, heads bowed in obeisance.

"Down!" Tamimeha growled when she was aware that the uplanders still stood. "On your knees, the queen is come! Not you, your Radiance, but you other two, on your knees."

Rehaza Entanye sank to her knees. Hannei looked from her, to the Quarabalese warriors, to Sulema, and folded her arms across her chest.

"A Zeerani warrior does not kneel to any queen or king," Sulema explained to the tall warrior. "She would rather die."

Swords and spears stirred to life. "Then she dies."

Sulema drew her own shamsi, and Hannei her dark blades. "If you seek to send my sister down the Lonely Road, I will send you there instead, and go with you." Anger welled up that it should come to this at last. To be attacked for not kneeling to an outlander queen! "Who wants to come with us?"

"Come with you where?" a voice called, young and full of laughter. "Are you going on an adventure? Perhaps I should join you. I am weary of this place."

The drums had stopped.

Still scowling, Sulema looked up and saw a young girl with opaline eyes, cat-slit like those of Yaela and Aasah, odd and beautiful. She was surrounded by warriors all clad in red spidersilk and blood-iron mail studded with jewels, brilliant for all that they bore the dust of hard travel. Foremost among these was a stout woman whose braided hair, piled atop her head, was nearly as tall as she herself. The lot of them stopped as the girl came to a halt, and the woman with glorious hair drew herself up to her impressive height and intoned:

"Hail the queen, all hail the queen; long is her shadow and longer still may she reign! The Queen of Quarabala is come to speak with Sulema an Wyvernus ne Atu, Dragon Queen of Atualon. All hail the queen!"

The Quarabalese around Sulema pressed themselves flat upon the ground, so that they were nearly kissing it. Sulema pursed her lips, sheathed her sword, and folded her arms across her chest much as Hannei had done.

"I have told you," she grumbled to Tamimeha, "I am no queen."

"You are," the beautiful child disagreed, "you are the Dragon Queen of Atualon. I have seen you in my dreams, and often. You have been sent by Illindra in our time of need to lead us to the green lands." Those odd pale eyes, cat-slit as Yaela's and Aasah's were, danced with amusement.

Sulema realized she was gaping, and shut her mouth. Time of need? Lead them to the green lands? If this was a joke, it was not funny.

"I, ah, and who are you?" A dreadful suspicion had begun to form in her mind, and with it anger at the manner in which she had been tricked. *Bring back my little niece*, Yaela had said. *Daughter of my dead sister. The only family I have left…*

The girl regarded her with a sober intelligence well beyond her years. "I am spider to your dragon, and queen in these lands. Queen Maika su Palehaleha i ka Kentakuyan, first of my name, to be precise." She bowed her head, and Sulema

313

could see now—in the slump of her narrow shoulders, the shadows under her eyes that spoke of long weariness, and the wary hope that had these people all standing on a knife's edge, that these people had traveled a road as hard as her own. "I welcome you to the Seared Lands."

"You are Maika." Sulema groaned and closed her eyes, conjuring for herself the image of the shadowmancer's apprentice with her wide green eyes, her earnest face, and her solemn mouth dripping with lies. "*You* are Maika. The next time I see Yaela, I am going to *kill* her."

THIRTY-FOUR

The chamber Tamimeha had found for them had only one entrance: a narrow rift in the wall scarcely wide enough to be considered a doorway. The counselors to whom Maika had sent a secret summons had to squeeze themselves through it awkwardly and one at a time, and then seat themselves upon the dirt and bone dust. They shifted for position, eyeing one another and their queen, wondering, she suspected, who knew what and which games were being played.

"These are not people who are used to being ordered about," Akamaia whispered at her side. "They are wearied from the road, and sick with loss. They will not thank you for this."

Let them be angry. Maika lifted two fingers from the arm of her tall manna-wood chair and Akamaia subsided, muttering under her breath. *Let them learn to obey me now. They will thank me once we have reached the cool green lands.* She herself was sweating like a wrestler, and her thin frame was all but crushed by the weight of expectations; those of her people and her ancestors, as well as her own.

Six of these seven were those surviving counselors whom she and Akamaia had deemed most powerful and least likely to betray them. The seventh was invited because he was the most easily manipulated. Once they were settled, she held up both hands for silence.

Lehaila's robes of state, stiff with the slain woman's blood, had been draped across Maika's lap. The counselors to a one avoided glancing at it just as they avoided meeting their queen's changed eyes.

Eyes of Pelang. The eyes of a seer, blessed—or cursed—depending on who was asked. Rare were the children born with such eyes, and to seek the Araids' gift voluntarily was a thing done twice in recorded history. Each of those instances had been leaders seeking power in times of great need.

Each had led to utter disaster.

Let us hope, Maika thought fervently, *that our need is enough to overcome ill fortune.*

"Counselorwomen, counselormen," she said aloud. "Trusted advisors." This last with a nod toward Akamaia, and toward Tamimeha who stood guard at the doorway. "As you know, we have received an—irregular—visitor from Atualon. We find ourselves this night at a crossing of paths, a place at which a decision must be—"

"Decision? What decision?" The nasal tones of Counselorman Tanneu cut across her voice like a claw. "This *Atualonian* girl"—he hissed the word—"if she is who she claims to be, which I doubt, is nothing more than a political refugee come to us for help at a time when we must help ourselves first. What decision do we need to make, aside from the decision of whether to drive her to the surface to die, or leave her behind us for the reavers? A daughter of Akari is not to be trusted.

"It was a Dragon King who broke the magic and sundered the world," he continued. "How can you even contemplate that this supposed daughter of a Dragon King will be our savior? Atualon is the source of all our misery. I say we lock this little *buta* up, her and her pet shadowmancer, as well. This—Keoki—has brought our enemy into our lands and endangered us all. I say his life and hers are forfeit."

Maika firmed her mouth and stared straight over the heads of her counselors. She had anticipated this outburst. It was, in fact, the reason Tanneu's name had been added to the list of invitees. He could be prodded into speaking words of dissent, and so allow Maika the opportunity to quell it. Still maintaining her unreadable expression, she nodded at Tamimeha.

The warrior hefted her spear, strode to the bench where Tanneu was seated, and rapped him smartly on the back of his skull with the ironbound butt of her spear. The counselorman's eyes rolled back in his head and his corpulent form slid from the bench, and boneless as jelly.

"A crossing of paths," Maika continued as Tamimeha resumed her post, "and I have seen that path which will take the people of Quarabala to safety. I have paid the price so that I might see the way—our only way—free from the danger that stalks us. Let there be no further discussion." She stared hard at them, with her eyes of Pelang. She had seen the Web of Illindra, and her vision of truth could not, *must not*, be questioned. If they strayed but a little—

Death for us all. Death, and dishonor, and the cobwebbed embrace of a reaver's grave.

"You tell us that you have the dragon's daughter guiding us to safety, and I cannot doubt you." Counselorwoman Nuha spoke in a low, clear voice. "Please consider this and forgive me—I do not mean to offend, merely to ask—they say that the dragonspawn has powers. How do we know that she has not used her fearful powers to mislead us, Resplendence? Atualonians are well known for being slippery as cave eels. How do we know that she is truly come to save us?"

Maika watched as a trickle of sweat ran down the woman's temple. It grieved her that these people, most of whom had shown her nothing but kindness, had to be made to fear her now.

But a queen could not afford the luxury of a soft heart.

"I appreciate your concern, Counselorwoman, and your bravery." Maika inclined her head fractionally. "But you misunderstand me. The dragon's daughter is not the savior of Quarabala."

She paused, let the soft gasp of their surprise settle like dust, and pinned each of them with her otherworldly stare.

"This daughter of the dragon is not our savior, though she will lead us to the one who is. In this game of spiders and dragons, Sulema an Wyvernus ne Atu, dreamshifter, Zeerani warrior, self-styled queen of Atualon... is little more than a pawn. As are all of you. As am I, truth be told, though I am a stronger pawn than most. Stronger than you knew, before this day. It is time that you learn."

She lifted her hands from the arms of her chair and clasped them together in front of her. When she pulled them apart, a swirling darkness was revealed, a window into an infinite abyss brilliant with the sung bones of dead worlds. Binding them all, naming each world, its song, its doom, the Web of Illindra shimmered with light and life and hope.

Hiding the effort and pain which it caused her, Maika brought her hands together again and the vision winked out with a *pop* and the smell of sulphur.

"There is only one way to save my people, and we *will* take the path I have chosen," she said, her words rich with the energy she had revealed. "What is more, I will kill anyone who seeks to deter us from it." She touched Lehaila's bloodstained robe. "As I have said, there will be no further discussion."

There was shocked silence at her words, her tone. Maika held them all with the power of her eyes—her blessed, cursed, far-seeing eyes of Pelang.

The silence was broken by the sound of a manna-wood staff falling to the floor. Akamaia sank to her knees, and then to all fours, pressing her face to the dusted earth. When at last she lifted her face, her sunken cheeks were wet with tears.

"Oh, my queen," she whispered in a voice hoarse with joy. "Oh, my queen, I swear loyalty to you, obedience to you, upon the song in my bones I swear it."

One by one, the other counselors kneeled before her. Maika noted which of her counselors gazed upon her with adoration, and which of them cut their eyes at their fellows before kneeling, or grimaced, or narrowed their eyes in shrewd thought.

Their obedience was slow, and it was forced. But it would do... for now.

She gestured. One by one they regained their seats, and Maika motioned to Tamimeha. The tall warrior's cheeks were also wet with tears, her eyes lit with a fanatic's joy. Maika knew that the Iponui was hers, heart and soul; they would die for her.

This would do, as well.

"Tamimeha," Maika said, "would you repeat your words to me from this morning, so that our loyal citizens may hear? Reveal to them the latest news from the road behind us... What word from the Iponui?"

"Only this, your Resplendence." Tamimeha gestured, and warriors entered through the narrow doorway dragging a live reaver, bound with spidersilk and sun-iron. To a one the counselors gasped and recoiled. Maika did not, though her heart lurched in her chest. Tamimeha continued, "This reaver was once a woman I knew, a runner from Padua. Of all the runners sent to spy the road behind us, she—*this*— was the only one to return."

One of the counselors moaned, a low, grieving sound that trailed off into muffled sobbing. Maika reached out with sa and ka, and with her sight of Pelang sought to look inside the reaver's chitinous skin. She could feel nothing familiar, nothing which might tell her that this had once been a woman. The voice of Na'eth whispered hungrily in Maika's ear, raising chillflesh along both arms.

Hissssst, hissssst. Give it to me, child.

Maika closed her eyes and let the sticky strands of Na'eth's magic flow through her. The reaver arched its back and hissed, thrashing against her—its—restraints as the spider queen bound it to her web. Power surged through the young queen, making her skin itch, her eyes ache, and filling the audience chamber with iridescence so beautiful it was akin to pain.

The reaver screamed, a high thin wail that trailed off into the distance, and black smoke poured from its fanged mouth as the spirit of Eth was forced to vacate its unwilling host. Finally the monstrous thing collapsed, dead, emptied of the corrupted spirit that had held it in thrall, foul-smelling ichor flowing from its mouth to puddle on the floor.

The counselors were frozen in terror.

Now is the time to bind them to my will, as well, Maika thought.

"Our best and bravest warriors have failed," she said as gently as she could. "Arachnists drive their reavers close on our heels, and as far as we know all of our settlements have been overrun. There will be no respite or rescue from the outer settlements. There will be no return to Saodan, nor to any city of Quarabala, now or ever. Ho'olau is no more. Mawai and Kaha'ai and Auhei—"

"Lehuahei?" Counselorwoman Puani interrupted, clutching her hands before her breasts. Maika, remembering that the woman kept husbands in that beautiful city, met her grieved eyes and shook her head.

"All gone. I am sorry, my friend. They are lost to us, every one. The City of Queens has doubtless been taken by the Arachnists by now, and Araids are close enough to be taking and turning our own scouts against us. The choice is clear. Remain here in the Edge and die—or worse, find ourselves caught in an Arachnist's web and turned to reavers." Silence fell over the chamber thick as grave dust. Again Maika paused for effect, stilling her hands and feet, her face, lest her body betray nervousness. "Or we can fight, fight like the warriors of old, to find a way into the green lands where we might someday, somehow, build a new home for ourselves and our children."

Let them think I am stone, she thought, *for stone is harder to break than flesh, and offers shelter to the besieged.*

Finally Counselorman Moki stood and bowed his head. "Lead us, o queen. The Ho'olau stand with the Kentakuyan, as ever of old. Though I do not believe there is hope, still I will fight with you against this wickedness which pursues us."

"And the Lehuaina," Counselorwoman Puani agreed, her voice shaking but eyes fierce. "For my people. For vengeance." One by one, the counselors stood and renewed their pledges of obedience.

Maika was not finished.

"Even the strongest heart might be swayed with fear," she said. "Lehaila, too, pledged undying loyalty, and she was true—up until the minute of her betrayal. In dark and dangerous times, even the truest of hearts must be made stronger by... other means."

Even as she spoke, warriors poured into the room like sand. Each of them had been painted in an Iponui's glow paints, their braids, the palms of their hands, and the soles of their feet oiled and gilded. Each warrior had a gemstone set into the skin in the center of her forehead. The Eye of Illindra, a soul-binding that marked them as hers to the core of their singing bones. Each of these warriors would die a thousand deaths before allowing the least harm to befall their queen.

As well they would die when this binding was removed, or when their queen died. This was a bond entered into voluntarily, and only in the times of gravest need. Again the counselors fell to their knees in the dirt.

Still Maika was not finished.

She gave a signal and Tamimeha leaned to whisper into the ear of an exceedingly tall, thin warrior. That woman left the room and returned a few heartbeats later leading three prisoners, all robed and hooded in the sky-and-gold spidersilk of the condemned. These hoods were yanked off one by one to reveal the tear-stained and defeated faces of those shadowmancers who had agreed to escape with Lehaila.

A low moan rose from one of the counselors. To violate the person of a shadowmancer was unthinkable.

Let them moan, Maika thought. *Lehaila's plans of escape had to have been known, perhaps by a person or persons in this room, staring at me now with the taste of vows still upon their lips. Let them learn to fear me.*

At the very least, I will teach them to fear the price of betrayal. The shadowmancers dropped to their knees in the sand. Maika firmed her heart as she looked upon their terrified faces.

"I have sentenced you to death," she said.

One woman began to weep. "I have a son! I only meant—"

The warrior holding that woman's collar gave it a brutal yank.

"The dead do not speak," Maika said in a soft voice. A visible shudder ran through counselors and prisoners alike.

They see at last that the child is gone, Maika thought, and she had no time to feel sorrow for their loss. *And that a queen has risen in her place.*

On cue, Akamaia's three young apprentices filed in and took their places beside the prisoners, bearing bowls of manna milk laced with herbs and reaver venom, and bound with spells of Maika's own weaving.

"I have sentenced you to death," Maika continued, "but am willing to commute this." The prisoners stared wide-eyed and mute. "The life you had is over. The one you may yet live will belong to me. There is no betraying this vow. Will you pledge to me, in atonement to the people and the queen you betrayed? When you have come to the end of your path, Illindra may yet look upon you kindly."

"Yes, my queen," one prisoner said.

"I do so swear it."

Maika took a deep breath. A refusal would have weakened her in the eyes of the council. "And you?" she asked the third shadowmancer, an older man from Kaha'ai.

322

"No," he said shortly. "I will not do this. My people are gone, my wives, my husband. I will go to them with no stain upon my—"

Tamimeha's blade ended his speech. The warrior cleaned it on the shadowmancer's robes even as his feet drummed an uneven tattoo on the packed sand floor.

"When it is time to die," she said, "it is best to die bravely, and without unnecessary talk."

Maika bit her lip to keep herself from breaking into wholly inappropriate laughter. *What kind of monster am I,* she wondered, *to laugh at jokes as a man dies at my feet?* And that man's death left her people with one less shadowmancer to shield them on their run from the Edge to the Jehannim.

The kind of monster that wields the power to lead her people to safety, whispered Na'eth in her mind. *Remember what I taught you.*

Maika stood at last, arms outstretched to either side, letting the robes fall back and exposing the flesh of her wrists. Na'eth had shown this to her in visions and dreams: the bloodbound oath. The Sindanese daemons called their bloodsworn troops *dammati*; Maika would call hers *shadowsworn*.

Tamimeha's knife flashed red as it tasted a queen's flesh. Strong brown fingers kneaded her forearm—it hurt—milking bright blood into the bowls as a gatherer might milk manna sap. These bowls were given to the two remaining shadowmancers, who drank the foul brew, and then were led from the chamber.

Best let them work through the pain in private, Na'eth had suggested, *lest the screams of their agony dissuade others from taking similar vows.* Through this magic, Maika meant to eventually bind every Quarabalese shadowmancer and Illindrist to her; through their magic all the people of Quarabala would be bound, as well.

The dead man—or nearly dead, his fingers still twitched occasionally—was picked up and carried out like a hunter's kill, leaving a trail of blood as counterpoint to the warriors' gold-dust footprints.

The medicines Maika had taken that morning began to wear off. Her skin began to tingle, then itch, then burn, quickly. Maika bit back the pain and faced the room.

Be strong, you little idiot, she chided herself. *This is nearly finished. I cannot afford a show of weakness now.* She cleared her throat, and the counselors looked at her, trepidation covering their features. Maika smiled down at them, attempting as she did so to appear as Queen Maika the Benevolent and Completely Unafraid.

I can do this.

I can.

Just imagine that they are all naked…

"Take your seats," she urged, softening her voice so they would know she meant them no harm. "My faithful sisters, my good brothers, listen to what I have to say.

"Long ago, Quarabala was the heart and spirit of this world. Long ago, a Dragon King of Atualon, in his great arrogance, dealt us a crippling blow. He released the fire of Akari, who rained down wrath and caused us to flee to dark places, there to live out our days in hiding. He broke our hearts, our spirit—

"—but he did not break us."

There was a murmur of assent, of anger. *Good*, she thought. It was as Na'eth had suggested—let them direct their disquiet toward a foreign king, and not the queen who they have learned to fear.

"Long, *too* long have our people kept to the dark, hiding our faces from the sun. Like parasites we live in the bones of the world and drink her blood. Long ago, the dragon and his brood forgot about us, their betters, whom they thought vanquished and gone." Maika raised her hands, palms up, and her sleeves fell back. In doing so she displayed the fresh cuts which signified the shadow-bond, and the queen's duty to her people. There, newly emerging from her skin, she revealed glittering gems and strands of the Web of Illindra in all its glory.

"My queen!" Tamimeha gasped, and then thrust her spear into the air, toward the sky beneath which they longed to walk. "My queen!"

The warriors began to pound their spears and chant as the hooded figures of three young girls—Maika's own apprentices, now—bore a gold-chased threefold loom into the chamber. An immense and glorious o'oraid crouched atop this loom, pleased with herself and her creation. She had spun an oracular web, dark and gorgeous, and it shimmered with power.

The o'oraid was called Lailith. She was Maika's, and Maika was hers. In the center of Lailith's web, bound in shadows and magic, hung the Mask of Sajani. It glittered even in this low light and shone with a verdurous light of its own.

"The world has forgotten us, its true masters," Maika said, her words clear and powerful. "It is time now for us to remind them. It is time for us to return to the world above and take what is rightfully ours."

"And what is that, your Magnificence?" a counselorwoman asked in an awed voice.

Maika leaned back fractionally and smiled the brightest, most winsome smile in her arsenal.

"Whatever we wish, of course."

THIRTY-FIVE

Sulema slept through an entire day and woke feeling nearly as tired as she had after attempting to sing Sajani to sleep.

It is this blasted wound, she thought, rubbing her shoulder and shaking her sword arm, trying to shake the feeling back into it. From shoulder to elbow it tingled and ached as if it had been thrust into cold water, and fingers of pain stroked downward toward her spine.

I need to return to Min Yaarif and find Yaela, if she is still alive, or get more medicines from that loremaster somehow. Rothfaust had hinted that a permanent cure was possible, but he was most likely dead. Sulema did not want to think what might happen if the venom's cold fingers took hold of her heart. She did not wish to think of the reavers, their burnt-out bug eyes and shining hard skin. Neither did she wish to think of Yaela, whom she had begun to think of as a friend, and whose lies had led her to this impossible road—likely to her death.

"Is aught wrong, your Radiance?" Tamimeha asked solicitously. She shadowed Sulema's heels, as she had done much of the time since their arrival, and though she was courteous and helpful, Sulema could not help but think she was as much guard as guide. Sulema was weary of being guarded. "You seem angry."

"Tired," she answered. "I am not used to being so far underground. It feels... odd." This was truth, if not the *whole* truth, she told herself. She was tired, very tired of being lied to and used.

"Mmm." Tamimeha gave her a considering look. "Perhaps you would do well to take another sweat bath."

Sulema choked on her own spit. The Quarabalese were, if possible, less shy about bodily functions and bathing than even the Atualonians. The last time she had attempted to clean herself, Keoki had offered to wash her back… and then some.

"I am clean," she insisted. "Bathing too often weakens the constitution."

"Mmm."

They walked along the cobbled path that wove in and out among the crumbling walls of the city and watched the sun set. Before they abandoned this place the ancient Quarabalese engineers had, through a series of shafts and mirrors that Sulema did not fully understand, brought a semblance of the sky down into the deep rifts of the earth so that the people might gaze upon the stars and moons, or even feel sunlight upon their faces. A soft rosy glow warmed the blanched bones of the city and glittered among the gemstones that crusted many of the walls and fallen tiles that littered the road. Sulema, who had never been much for gilt or flowers or shiny stones, found herself charmed.

"Pretty," she murmured. "Even ruined like this, even after so long, it is pretty."

"Would that you had seen Saodan," Tamimeha told her. "It is—it was—glorious."

Sulema glanced sideways at her companion, moved at the grief in her voice. Before she could formulate an answer that did not sound trite a series of horn blasts rang out, their lovely silvery voices reminding Sulema of the Dibris at springtime.

"Ah!" Tamimeha said, stopping so abruptly that Sulema almost trod on her heels. "That is the call to council. We must go."

Sulema followed her guide-guard down and over and through a maze of twisty little passages, all alike. Sulema wondered how her guide knew the way, and whether—as she suspected—this was not Tamimeha's first stay in this place.

Rehaza Entanye and Hannei joined them at one juncture, along with their own guards, and Keoki awaited them at the top of a flight of wide, shallow steps which had once been beautifully tiled in indigo and gold. The shadowmancer's face was grave as he led them into an enormous chamber which had survived not only the years but the recent earthquake intact.

Maika was there, and the stout woman with fantastic hair, and other men and women whose intricately embroidered if travel-stained robes hinted to Sulema that she was—once again—in over her head. The faces that turned as they entered the room were grave.

"Well come and well met, your Radiance." Maika, alone of all those gathered, looked entirely pleased to see her. She inclined her head slightly, and all those assembled fell to their knees. Sulema saw, or thought she saw, a shadow of uncertainty in the young queen's pale eyes and felt a rush of affinity for the girl.

We are both in over our heads, she thought. *Though she hides it well.* Straightening her back she schooled her face into a stern expression such as her mother might have worn. *If this child can pretend such a calm confidence in these uncertain times, by Atu, I can fake it as well.*

"Here, my good people," the young queen said, "is Sulema, daughter of Hafsa Azeina by the Dragon King of Atualon. Seldom have any made the journey from the golden Zeera to Quarabala, and never in such perilous times. Welcome, Sister Queen." She held both hands out, smiling. Sulema could do nothing but go to her, accept the greeting, and take a place at her side. She took a deep breath as she turned to face the assemblage.

It was easier to face the lionsnake. Sulema suppressed the thought that *that* had not turned out so well.

"Perilous times indeed," the stout woman agreed. "Why have you come, Dragon Queen of Atualon? If, indeed, that is who you are."

Sulema opened her mouth to answer, though she had no idea what she might say next. A risk, considering what often came out of her mouth, but Maika jumped in.

"Counselorwoman Puani, you owe the Dragon Queen honor. She has come to save us."

"I have come to bring—" Sulema stopped, registering Maika's words, then turned to gape at the girl. "I... *what?*"

"You have." The stubborn set of the girl's mouth, a flash of defiance in those dark eyes, were strangely familiar. Where had she seen such an expression before?

Oh, yes, she thought wryly. *In the mirror.*

"You *have* come to save us," the girl queen repeated firmly. "Though you did not know it. I have seen it in my dreams, and the oracle agrees—"

"The oracle agrees that it is a *possibility*," a woman's voice said, strong and clear as a bell, "and that is all. Do not put words in my mouth."

Those already in the room rose quickly, preventing Sulema from seeing who it was that had spoken. When at last they were seated, and the speaker was brought forward, she was startled. Such a frail, old woman, to have spoken with such force. She was bent like an ancient tree twisted by powerful winds, and leaned on a staff of dark wood longer than she was tall. Her eyes were wide and pale as Yaela's, a milky blue that was almost white and slit like a cat's. Her robes were a swirl of color, and her hair hung in a multitude of grayed braids nearly down to her knees.

These women have impressive hair, Sulema thought, and resisted the urge to ruffle her own orange fuzz in shame.

The woman walked in a slow shuffle, moving with such deliberation that Sulema guessed she must have been in a great deal of pain. In the next moment two young men emerged from the doorway behind her, bearing between them what at first seemed a great wooden three-paneled loom, but on closer inspection was revealed to support a spider's web like nothing Sulema had ever seen.

The strands of webbing, thick as spun wool, were hung with all manner of jewels and feathers and bits of bone. In the center there hung, head down, the most enormous spider Sulema had ever seen. Easily twice as large as a russet soldier, this paragon of spiders was as resplendent as any human queen and radiated as much pride.

She is magnificent, Sulema thought. *Terrifying, but magnificent.*

"Spiders," Rehaza Entanye groaned behind her.

The stout woman offered her place of honor to the ancient woman, who waved her off impatiently.

"Maika," she scolded, as if the girl were merely a troublesome child and not a queen at all, "you were supposed to wake me."

"You were exhausted. I thought it best to let you sleep."

The old woman's skin had an unhealthy, ashen pallor, and her hands trembled even as she gripped the staff.

She is not long for this world, Sulema thought, and felt a moment's pity for young Maika. The love between these two was as evident as the spider's web, and as beautiful.

"I can sleep when I am dead," the old woman grumbled. "This is important. Now, you..." She pointed her chin at Sulema. "Why are you here?"

Sulema was taken aback. "I made a vow," she began.

"Of course you made a vow. Nobody crosses the Seared Lands for the food."

Tamimeha coughed to cover a laugh.

"What was the nature of this vow?" the oracle persisted. "Have you come to lead us all from this place? To bring us forth into the land of water and sunlight, as our queen believes? Are you a hero? Or have you perhaps come for something... lesser?"

"Lead you all from Quarabala?" Sulema replied, shocked to her core. "No. I vowed to journey to Quarabala and bring one young girl named Maika back to her aunt," *who neglected to tell me that this girl is a dragonforsaken* queen—"and nothing more. What makes you think I could do such a thing?" *Or that I would want to?* "For that matter, I do not understand why your people have left their cities for the Edge. To hear Yaela and Aasah tell it, Saodan is a place of unparalleled beauty, while the Edge is—" she coughed, and felt her face flush as she realized belatedly that her words may cause offense—"um, not."

"Saodan is glorious," Maika agreed, laying a hand on Sulema's arm. That caused her to twitch. "Or it was, at least. But Quarabala is dying. Even as we speak, the Araids move against us. They have been breeding in the deep, dark places, the ancient cities long denied to us, and they are massing armies of Arachnists and reavers. They have already overrun Saodan, forcing us to flee. Some say..." Her voice trailed off, and then strengthened again. "Some say they have turned Illindrists and shadowmancers against us, creating sorcerers that work shadowmancy on the spiders' behalf."

"This is true," Keoki said, pushing to the front of the audience. "One such abomination led the reavers from which we narrowly escaped. A shadowmancer turned Arachnist." An angry murmur sprang up at that, but fell quiet when the young queen took one of Sulema's hands in her own and raised it high.

"In your appearance, my prayers to Illindra have been answered," she said. "There are too few shadowmancers left in all of Quarabala to protect my people from the wrath of Akari, as we attempt to escape this land... unless, as Akamaia tells me, their shadowshifting is enhanced by the song of atulfah which underlies all magic. Only the Dragon King of Atualon can wield this power... and see, his daughter has been led to us in our time of need. She has come to lead us from the Seared Lands and to freedom from the Araids."

"Is this true?" the oracle asked, staring intently at Sulema's face. "Is this why you have come?"

Sulema desperately wanted to agree that yes, this was why she had made the terrible journey to Quarabala—to save them all, like a hero in the old stories, like Zula Din leading her warriors forth in days of old. Desperately wished it was so, that she was the true daughter of a dreamshifter and a Dragon King, gifted with the powers of two lands. But truth is not born of desperation.

I barely made it here alive, she thought, *and that was with help. Is it truly within my power to help these people?*

No, she realized, *it is not. If I try leading these people to Min Yaarif, I am more likely to get them all killed.*

"No," she said, voice heavy with regret. "I made a vow to Yaela that I would retrieve her niece Maika and return with her to Min Yaarif. That is all. She neglected to tell me that Maika is a queen." *And I would like to kick her ass to the Zeera and back for* that *bit of trickery*, she thought.

To her surprise, Maika turned to the stout woman with a triumphant smile. "See?" she said to the oracle. "I told you she would tell the truth. Warriors of the Zeera always tell the truth, is that not so, Sulema?"

"*Ehuani*," she agreed, slowly. "We find that there is beauty in truth. But I do not see how this changes anything. Four of us barely made it here alive. Without Keoki we would have died. He and Yaela have both told me that there are not enough shadowmancers to protect all of your people from the sunlight, should they attempt to leave the Seared Lands in any number. I am sorry, truly I am, but I am just one warrior...

"I do not have the power to help you."

"She speaks truth," the oracle agreed, staring oddly at the spider's web. "She has chosen her path."

"Akamaia?" Maika asked, following it with a command—a queen's command to one she loved. "It is time."

332

The old woman reached out a shaking finger and touched the spider's web. The spider, Sulema was pleased to note, did not stir.

"You are right," she agreed reluctantly. "It is time."

"Time for what?" Sulema could not keep the cross note from her voice. She was tired, sore, well out of her depth—and weary of magic and magic-workers. *They act as if my "no" was a "yes."*

"I cannot wield atulfah," she explained again, trying for patience that she did not feel, "at least not enough to be of use to your people. I am barely trained. Even if I had the Mask of Akari here in my hands, it would not be enough... the sun dragon's mask only resonates to men. I truly am sorry," she continued. "I would help your people if I could, but I did not come here to save you all. I just came for one little girl. Nobody *told* me that she was a queen..."

That sounded plaintive to her own ears, and she stopped.

Maika patted her shoulder. "You *think* you have only come for me, but really you have come for all of us... and for this." She fumbled at a large leather bag that hung at one hip, stained and worn and completely at odds with her raiment. "Ah! I tied this knot too tight." Finally she reached into the bag with both hands, pink tongue sticking out one side of her mouth. "This is yours, you know. We have borne the burden of it for too long."

"Wha—" Sulema began, then stopped mid-word, mid-thought, mid-breath, and the world stopped with her. Maika drew her hands from the bag, and in them she held an exquisitely wrought mask of lapis and tourmaline, agate and amethyst and jade. It caught the stars from the skies far above, caught the light of the fires that raged at the center of the earth, glowed with the illumination of endless dreaming.

Sulema, it sang to her. *Daughter. It is time.*

Sulema reached out, drawn as a moth to flame.

She took up the Mask of Sajani...

and the dragon stirred in her sleep.

Sulema ignored the Quarabalese counselors that vied for her attention, Hannei's nudges and attempts at hunter-signs, paying scant heed to the aches of her own body or anything but the mask which she held cradled in her lap.

The Mask of Sajani. The moment she took it the ground had shaken again. She hoped it was not an omen. Yaela had told her about it, but Sulema had never really believed her and had all but forgotten the second reason behind her quest in the desperate days since. Yet now that she held it Sulema found that she could scarcely take her eyes from its beauty or imagine her life before the mask, and knew that it was precious to her.

Akamaia explained that it was a relic from the First Days, in the long ago of legend when men and women ruled Atualon from a dual throne. Before the Sundering, before the kings of Atualon broke the world into pieces, sa and ka were one. Sun magic and earth magic, dark and light, kith and kin were balanced and there was harmony.

"War came to the lands of men," she finished, "and when the last true queen of Atualon saw in her heart that Kal ne Mur would never be dissuaded from his plan to wield atulfah in battle, she fled to her allies and kinsfolk in Quarabala. Our libraries were great, and we prided ourselves on being peaceful, an illuminated people of learning and lore, elevated above the concerns of more barbaric, warlike folk..." She shook her head and sighed at the folly of her ancestors, and she was not alone.

"Our pride was so bright it blinded us. When the war between nations could not be won with half a magic, Kal ne Mur laid blame at the foot of his queen, and of her people, and he smote our land with the wrath of Akari. Nine out of ten people died in that time of grief. Those few who survived did so by skulking in cellars and storerooms, underground

334

places filled with shadow and spiders and despair. Yet survive they did, and they built our cities again, this time far below the ground. I allow that it is not the land of glory and wonder it was before the Sundering, but until the Arachnists came with their reavers..." Slowly she stroked her fine robe of spidersilk. "We were not so badly off."

"Why leave such a place at all, then?" Rehaza Entanye asked. She stood some distance behind Sulema. "I cannot speak for the Zeeranim, for I have never visited their golden lands, nor for the Atualonians, who live in palaces of dragonglass, but to one who grew up on the streets of Min Yaarif—" Her voice faltered. "To one from Min Yaarif, Saodan is a place of stories and wonders. If I were blessed enough to call such a place home, I would die in her defense rather than let her be taken by monsters."

"And yet the monsters have come, and we could raise no real defense against them," Akamaia answered, biting the words off as a seamstress might bite thread. "Long have the spider queens dwelt in the dark and deep places from the time before the days of old. Seldom have they bothered us directly before now, though those who ventured into their lands rarely returned. Even that uneasy truce is over, I am afraid. Arachnists, those wicked sorcerers who worship Araids as gods, have woken those gods from their neutral slumber and have persuaded them to grow their armies of undead—"

"Reavers," Sulema said, and a cold pain lanced through her wound.

"Reavers," Akamaia agreed.

"They have been attacking our settlements all along the outskirts of Quarabala," Maika added. "We do not know for how long. Just that runners we have sent out do not come back."

"Or worse, they come back transformed, as reavers," Akamaia said. "Our builders have erected walls and barricades, but those have not been sufficient. You have come to Quarabala in our final days. Soon even this forsaken place will be overrun and Arachnists will rule the Seared Lands from the furthest outposts, to Saodan, even to the very Edge." She sighed and leaned heavily on her staff, as if this long speech had taxed the last of her strength.

"The Arachnists are seeking the mask," Maika said.

"Perhaps," the oracle allowed.

"They are," the girl insisted. "I have seen it. Just as I dreamed that a savior would come." She waved a hand at Sulema. "Come to lead us to the green lands." All eyes turned toward Sulema—some hopeful, most as skeptical as the dark whispers in her own heart.

"I am no savior," she said. "*Ehuani*, I am just... just Sulema Ja'Akari. I cannot do this thing. I cannot save you."

Hannei's grunt expressed more clearly than words what she thought of that, and every face in the room echoed the rebuke. Even the mask stared up at her accusingly.

"I cannot," she insisted. "Atulfah broke the world once, in the hands of a Dragon King wearing a mask. It could break the world again." *Especially if I am the one wielding it*, she thought, though shame held her tongue. Akamaia looked as if she had bitten into rotten meat.

"Do not think for one moment, Zeerani, that the Araids will stop at the Edge of the Seared Lands. Once they have annihilated our people, what is to stop them from coming after yours? The only things that have kept you uplanders safe are our walls, our warriors, and the gaze of Akari, which they cannot abide. If it is true that they have turned shadowmancers to their cause, and might travel upon the shadowed roads—" She broke off, shaking her head. "My people, your people are in danger, and you would refuse the only weapon available to us—to you. Why? Because it is the weapon of your enemy?" As the old woman gestured to the mask in Sulema's hands, her voice rose almost to a shout.

"It is not that—"

"I understand."

The room went silent as Maika spoke. Her high and gentle voice took on a strange resonance, and her eyes were unfocused as she laid a hand on Sulema's arm.

"I understand, Sister Queen," she went on. "You are afraid of what will happen if you try to wield atulfah and fail… but you are more afraid of what you might become if you succeed. You are afraid that through you, imperfect as you are and with the heritage of two terrible magics in your blood, the mask would work magic too terrible to imagine."

"Yes," Sulema whispered. Though Sulema had not thought of it in quite that way, her heart froze at the girl's words.

I am the daughter of the dream eater and the dragon. What sort of monster might I become, if I am given power such as this? Her mother's tent had contained the skin and sinew and bones of slain enemies, turned into instruments of dark magic. *Were I queen of Atualon, in truth, I might sit upon a throne of their skulls.*

The idea did not displease her.

That alarmed her even more.

"You say you are only a warrior," Maika said, "and that you want none of the power in this world. But I think you are lying to yourself. I think this mask frightens you because you want it so badly."

Something stirred in Sulema then; an ugly thing, dark and monstrous and lustful. The hunger for might with which to smash her enemies and remake the world in her own image. She met the young queen's gaze, and in those brown eyes she saw an echo of her own desire, the darkest wishes of her heart. She thought of the reavers, the Arachnists, of Pythos and those men who had hurt her. She thought of the Nightmare Man laughing at her over the broken body of Azra'hael.

She thought of her enemies, all of them, lying dead and broken.

Her hands tightened on the Mask of Sajani.

I could defeat them with this, she knew. *If I were to wear the Mask of Sajani, I could truly become Sa Atu, the Dragon Queen of Atualon, with the ability to remake the world—*

Or destroy it.

And which path would you choose, O Queen? Jinchua's voice mocked her from a place deep in the dreaming lands. *Are you a hero, or are you a monster? Do you really want this knowledge, and all that comes with it? The pain? The power?*

"Do you want it?" Maika asked again.

"*Ehuani*," Sulema whispered. "I do want it."

"Then *take* it." And the queen of Quarabala bent her head to the Dragon Queen of Atualon. Sulema hesitated no further. She brought the Mask of Sajani up to her face, and looked upon the world through the eyes of the dragon.

The world was a song. That song was intoxicating.

After the greeting and feasting and endless talking of people who had made a grand plan and were now terrified of facing it, the Quarabalese assigned rooms to the weary travelers that they might rest peacefully before the next round of talk and planning. No sooner was she alone than Sulema retrieved the Mask of Sajani from its bag.

Such an ugly thing, she thought, irritated, *in which to store a wonder.* She held it cradled in her hands, turned it this way and that, admiring the weight of it, the smooth bronze surface where the mask was meant to touch skin, the many faceted jewels that caught the mirrored light and sent rainbows dancing along the pale walls. Gems of grass-green and leaf-green, blue as the Dibris, blue as the sky, mixed with stones the color of coffee and sunrise and amber. The colors and sizes of these gems, the way they had been set into the metal so seamlessly, recalled her father's globe to mind.

Sulema retrieved that, as well, and admired the two treasures as she held them in her lap. She had never had much fascination for jewelry or trinkets, as her friend Neptara had, but she felt in that moment a fierce love of these beautiful things, so finely wrought, so precious.

On a whim, she took up the mask and pressed it once more onto her face. By some magic of its own it clung to her like a second skin, needing no strap or hood to bind it into place, and molded itself to the contours and planes of her features as if it had been made for her and no other.

It is mine, she thought. *Mine.* Though she had not sought this thing for herself, and would not have said she wanted it, now she claimed it for her own as greedily as a child clutching a handful of honey-cakes.

As Sulema looked through the eyes of the dragon it seemed to her that she saw this broken place as it once had been, as it could be again, and this also she coveted. The walls smooth and bright, tiled in vibrant colors. It would have a sand floor, dyed indigo like the sky at midsun, here a gaily painted doorway, there a pile of thick soft mattresses with linens folded and stacked just so. These things spoke to her of a beautiful world, of precious human lives, of songs and stories and art, and she wanted to hold it all and never share, never let go.

Mine.

As she shifted position to look around the room, the globe still in her lap rolled to one side. Sulema caught the heavy orb before it could fall and held it up to her dragon's eyes, and saw—

Oh, she saw—

Everything.

Through the eyes of Sajani, the bauble she held cradled between her hands was more than an artist's depiction of the world, magical or no. It was the living world itself. The sands of the Zeera shifted and sang as she watched and wondered, the seas writhed with serpents, a heavy mist ebbed and undulated along the shoreline of Sindan. She could see a crack of corruption where the restless dead had been interred in Eid Kalmut, and the tiny, glittering splendor of Atualon, the fortress Atukos at its heart.

Mine, she thought, and black anger rose in her heart. *Mine.* She brought the world closer to her face and breathed upon the city of her begetting, which was rightfully hers to rule and which had been stolen from her by Pythos.

That son of worms took my home from me, she thought. *He rules over my people—likely he sleeps in the bed where my mother and father made me.*

As her wrath rose, it seemed to Sulema that the city grew larger in her view, closer, as if she swept down from a great height. There were the fields and farms that lay around her city, little people leading their little lives, the great clean streets, the manses of the parens and craftmistresses. The walls and turrets of Atukos, which let in joyous welcome under her warm regard. It seemed to her that the fortress cried out to be relieved of its occupation, and for her to come home, come home, to oust the usurper.

There he was, the soulless maggot, standing on her father's balcony with his thieved robes and golden crown, arms upraised as he regarded her city as his own. She hissed and drew nearer, wanting to claw and bite, to rend his flesh, to tear him from her rightful place.

Pythos looked up. He must have seen her, then, because his eyes widened and he gave a shout of fright. Sulema cried out in victory, her voice the high, pure ululation of Sajani, and reached out, meaning to strike him down.

Another figure joined Pythos on the balcony. Hooded and robed, dressed it seemed in funereal rags and the armor of forgotten wars. The tall man turned his face to the sky and beheld her. Though he wore a mask of ruin and despair, Sulema through the dragon knew him. She knew those broad shoulders, those narrow hips, she knew the face that lay behind that bleak mask. He raised both hands to her in greeting, in warning, in adoration.

Sajani Earth Dragon seized Sulema in her claws and fled in terror.

THIRTY-SIX

Maika strode with her head high, hiding her horror at the thought of the ashes of women and men who had died on the shadowed road clinging to the soles of her feet.

The Web of Illindra burned inside-out upon her skin, gleaming in the torchlight, and the gems which emerged at every meeting of webs shone brilliant as stars. From her bond with the shadowmancers she experienced the surge of emotion as they worked their magic in her name. Fierce joy alloyed with sorrow as shadows were shifted into snakes, spiders, monsters—even into the great sabre-tusked cats of the Zeera. These they set upon the doomed Edgelanders in order to clear them from the queen's path. Doubtless minstrels would receive ale and lodging for generations to come in exchange for the least retelling of this day. *I wonder*, Maika thought as she walked, stiff-faced and straight-backed beside the beautiful queen of dragons, *if they will sing about how badly my butt itches*. For as the Web of Illindra revealed itself upon her skin, no quarter of her flesh was spared, and *everything* itched. Scratching any part of it only made things worse.

Sulema eyed her sideways, and Maika thought she bit back a smile.

"You know," the Ja'Akari murmured, "when they shaved and oiled our heads"—here she ran a hand along the smooth skin at her temples—"I felt as if I had fallen into a nest of fire ants. It itched for *weeks*."

"Very helpful," Maika replied. Then she added, "How did you deal with it?"

"Oh, I busied myself with thoughts of—" Sulema broke off, and the golden eyes behind the dragon's mask shifted to the mute Zeerani girl at her other side. "Other things. Food and games, mostly. My horse."

Whatever she had intended to say was lost, buried in the pit of sorrow that had been dug between Sulema and Hannei. Maika did not need the eyes of Pelang to see the bonds that time and love and fate had woven between these two formidable youths. They reflected each other endlessly and were made more beautiful for the revelation.

"I have never ridden a horse," she confessed to Sulema. "I have only ever seen pictures, in books... They are very beautiful. Especially your... asil?"

"Well," the fire-haired woman replied, "it is forbidden for outsiders to ride the asil. And even before you rode a lesser horse, you would want to learn how... and you would probably want your ass to heal first." She laughed outright as Maika shot her a foul look, and then resumed the low, beautiful chant which channeled the power of a sleeping dragon into stuff Maika's shadowmancers could use.

Though Maika could see the magic—the bonds and bindings Na'eth had woven over and around the mask, the shimmering of the blue-gold-green dragon magic—she was not sure how it worked. Only that it did, and that with its aid her handful of sorcerers were able to effect the escape of the Quarabalese people.

There would be a price to pay for it all. There always was. In every story from every world in the Web of Illindra was spun an immutable truth: for every action, there would be an equal reaction. For every gift, a price.

For every promise, a betrayal.

None of this, however, made her skin itch less fiercely.

Maika reminded herself that her own physical discomforts were as nothing when compared to the suffering of others. Akamaia, for one, though she was old and frail, and walked

343

with assistance, did so without complaint. A queen could do no less. So she ignored the itching and the burning—just as she ignored the chafing of the threefold loom that she wore strapped to her back and the guilt as the Edgelanders displaced by her shadowmancers' magic fled wailing before them—and walked ever upward, leading her people toward the dawn of a new day.

Today, the scouts had told her, they would leave the scant protection of the Edge to walk upon the very surface of the Seared Lands. Today, for the first time in generations, she and her people would gaze upon the face of Akari.

She was terrified.

"How did you do it?" she asked Sulema, eyeing the tops of the canyon walls with growing trepidation. Here the walls rose scarcely a woman's height above their heads. What if Na'eth was wrong—what if she was lying? What if, despite all their preparations, the alliance of queens and magics, this was just a horde of fools following a stupid girl to their deaths?

Sulema let the song trail off again.

"As I said, thoughts of food and game, and fine wardens—"

"No, not the itch." Maika rolled her eyes. "I mean, how did you do this?" She gestured to the sky above, still dark but heavy with the promise of a killing dawn. "How did you travel from the Jehannim to the Edge, with only one shadowmancer to help?"

"Oh, well..." Sulema laughed a little. "We ran like rabbits, of course, but mostly we were lucky. That Arachnist and his swarm of reavers would have had us for breakfast had it not been for your warriors." She glanced at Tamimeha, and there was naked admiration in her gaze. "*Ehuani*, I am ever in their debt."

"'*Ehuani*'? I have heard you say this word before. What does it mean?"

"It means... beauty in truth," Sulema explained. "That all things a woman might do in her life are better in the open, in the full light of Akari." She frowned and shook her head. "The word does not translate well to common tongue, and I am not good at explaining such things."

"I think you explained it very well," Maika demurred. Despite her best efforts, shame weighed her heart as once again the young Dragon Queen took up her endless singing, spending her own strength, endangering her own life so that people she had never met, and who would never thank her, might live.

All because she had made a vow.

There was no word for *beauty in truth* anywhere in any book in the Seared Lands. Indeed, in a land that survived upon shadows and secrets, such beauty was an unimaginable luxury.

Buoyed by the magic of two queens, the shadowmancers sang and danced the night and the miles into the web of *was*. Keoki led them with his lute. He was now first of all her shadowbound. The ritual had not, however, been entirely voluntary.

"A necessary evil," Akamaia had said as she stood over his senseless and twitching form, and Tamimeha agreed.

Sulema had been puzzled at Keoki's newly muted demeanor. The Dragon Queen had asked about the jewel of Illindra that appeared on his forehead, and was told it was a "mark of high honor." Keoki himself did not dispute this or seem to care one way or another what she thought of it. His eyes were clear and farseeing now, no longer blinded by the flame-haired queen's exotic beauty.

Though the binding of shadowmancers dampened their passions, it had the opposite effect upon their magic. Magic such as they wielded now had not been seen since the time of

Akamaia's mother's grandmother. The shade they wove was thick as fabric, a tent of dusk-dark spidersilk that whispered and sang overhead, shielding them from the terrible heat. Predators and Edgelanders were routed and killed by the nightmare visions made solid.

Even with the advancement of every apprentice old enough to bear the physical strain of shifting, the ranks of the shadowmancers had barely swollen to a score. Nevertheless, the work of these shadowbound—augmented by their queen's blood oath and the song of Sajani—was a display of might and magic grand enough for a bard's tale. It was a thing of beauty.

And of lies. Grand as it was, it would not be enough.

Finally the leading edge of the travelers reached the surface of the Seared Lands, and a palpable tremor of terror and fierce joy shivered through every woman, man, and child of Quarabala. Then the gaze of Akari found and smote them. Before their queen's foot graced the land above, before she could behold her first sunrise, their shadowed veil began to smoke, to steam...

To fail.

"What is happening?" Maika cried, standing on the tips of her toes and straining to see. She tried to push Tamimeha aside, but the frontrunner stood her ground, hammer to the fore as if she expected some threat.

Even the Zeerani girl was taller than she. Sulema squinted her sun-gold eyes against the unaccustomed glare and frowned.

"Smoke," she said, "though I cannot see the source of it. I fear it is the shadowmancers' veil. Some of the people seem to be—"

She did not finish the sentence, as the veil of shadows above them trembled and grew thin. The people ahead of them began to scream. There was a surge as those at the front of the exodus tried to double back, a growing panic as the line of moving bodies became a knot of confusion and fright, and then the great black snake turned back upon itself. Warriors' spears bristled thick and wicked around Maika and Sulema.

Another tremor shimmied through the veil, this one stronger than the last, and a ray of sunlight broke through a fissure in the magic. It struck the ground like a spear of flame not ten strides from where Maika stood surrounded by her warriors. An elder woman, gap-toothed and gaunt, stood bathed in the glorious light. In that moment the woman was beautiful. Surely, she had longed for and prayed for this from the moment her newborn eyes opened to darkness. To lift her face, to feel the sun!

"How glorious it must be, to walk beneath the sun," mothers sang to their babes as they gave birth. *"How we wish we might have seen it,"* sang the crones on their death-beds. From birth to death, every woman and man of Quarabala longed to walk beneath the sun, and this one old woman had achieved her dream.

In the next moment she was gone, vanished with a scream that was half a sigh of delight, leaving a small mound of ashes left to crumble in the light of a sun she had prayed all her life to see.

Maika's hands flew to her mouth. *I have done this*, she thought. *I brought her here—I and no one else.*

Sulema's mute sword-sister—Hannei, her name was—shouldered her way through the bristling spears. Her hands were moving rapidly. To Maika's surprise, she found that this sign language was enough like that of the Iponui that she could make some sense of it.

You must, Hannei waved under Sulema's nose. *You must*—lead or go first, something like that—something-something something *lands*.

"I am not my mother," Sulema responded, golden eyes glowing dangerously behind the dragon's mask. "I cannot simply—"

Hannei made a *very* rude gesture which needed no translation in any language. *You must*, she insisted. Something-something *time*.

"Sulema?" Maika asked. "What is she talking about?"

Sulema's eyes narrowed. "Shehannam," she replied. "My mother would have opened a portal into the Dreaming Lands, and led the people through to—"

"Shehannam?" Akamaia's voice broke through like the ray of sunlight, sharp and deadly. "Heresy. You speak heresy. To set forth upon the Huntress's grounds is—"

"It is the way," Maika said. Her dreams, the o'oraid's web, the whisperings of Na'eth, all came together in that moment to form a complete picture. Maika closed her eyes, the better to see the perfect beauty of this truth.

Ehuani, she realized. *Now I understand that word. Ehuani.*

"Your Magnificence," Akamaia said, "with all respect, I must—"

Without opening her eyes, Maika raised both hands. It seemed to her that the people, the wind, the whole world fell silent and hung suspended upon the web. Then she opened her eyes, and spoke, and their world began to spin again, its fate in this time and this reality having been decided by a girl still fresh with the flush of her first moons-blood.

"I have seen it," she said, and even to herself her voice sounded... different. "Our savior, come to lead us to the green lands, to peace and prosperity and safety. I have seen it." She smiled upon Sulema, willing the foreign woman to agree. "You will save us," she insisted.

Sulema took a deep breath and nodded, jeweled mask flashing.

"I have come to know the magic of your people," she agreed. "If you say you have seen me leading your people through Shehannam, then I must try." Her eyes crinkled as if she smiled. "I will succeed, of course. Ja'Akari never merely try, *ehuani*."

Maika bit her lower lip and stared at the fire-haired woman.

"*Ehuani*," she breathed. "Beauty in truth. I have seen it, now. I understand." She thought fiercely, *I have seen beauty in truth, indeed. A pity I must lie to get it.* Aloud she asked, "What can I do to help?"

"Guard my body," Sulema replied. She sat upon the ground, laying her fox-head staff across her knees, and her folded hands upon the pale wood. "I will seem to be asleep, or dead, but I am neither. Guard my body while I am gone. Keoki should play his lute near me, if he will. Music will give me a way back, and then I will be able to gather my strength and open a doorway to Shehannam. I think."

"You think?"

Sulema shrugged. "I have never done this thing, but I will succeed, or I will die trying. You are the one who dreamt this; you tell me." She chuckled and closed her eyes.

Nothing happened.

Maika sent a runner to fetch Keoki. He stood beside the Dragon Queen and with scarred fingers played his lute. Maika could see the magic, the Web of Illindra spun thick as wishes to wrap Sulema tight and call her to sleep, to sleep, to sleep...

Nothing happened.

"Ugh," Sulema said, and she groaned, scrunching her eyes closed behind the mask. "I cannot relax. I—"

Hannei touched her shoulder, and then folded her legs to sit on the ground next to Sulema. She tugged the fire-haired girl into a gentle embrace, pulling Sulema's head down into her lap and playing with the other woman's short red wizard locks as she hummed a gnarled, tuneless lullaby. It was neither beautiful, as Keoki's lute was beautiful, or soft as the

349

whispering of spiders was soft. But it was a thing so pure, so right, that tears sprang up into Maika's eyes and flowed freely down her cheeks.

I thought I understood ehuani. *I thought I knew love. I thought I saw beauty in the truth of my chosen path, but I understood nothing. I was blind.*

And she was shamed.

Still, a dragon was a dragon, and a spider was a spider, and a queen was a queen. She would do what needed to be done, beauty or no. Shame or no.

Even as Hannei hummed Sulema into a trance state, Maika drew Akamaia to one side.

"Help me work this thing," she said, unstrapping the threefold loom she carried upon her back. As always, she breathed a sigh of relief to find Lailith alive and well. The o'oraid crawled nimbly into her hand, bobbing in anticipation. "It is time."

"Time for what?" The Illindrist looked at her askance. Maika did not know whether her old friend was angered at her decisions, or afraid. It saddened her, but in the end it did not matter.

"Help me call our savior," she said, "the one who will lead us to safety."

Akamaia frowned. "But…" She gestured to Sulema.

Maika shook her head. "That one is not our savior. In truth she is the Dragon Queen—and our dearest enemy."

The oracle stared at Maika as if seeing her, truly seeing her, for the first time. Finally she bowed, a simple gesture filled with worlds of conflicting emotion.

"Your will," she said. "My queen."

The threefold loom beckoned to Maika with its promises of was, is, and will be. The girl who had spent most of her waking days searching for secrets and lost treasures in the Queens' Library found the treasure of secrets now in the brilliance of a spider's web, the elegance of simple design, and the comfort of knowing that whatever she did here, no matter how badly she might muck things up, the worlds would spin on. The dragons would sing their mating songs, Illindra would bind them all in her great web, and love her forever.

Maika hardly flinched when Lailith sank envenomed fangs into the meaty palm of her hand, hardly made a sound as she sank down, down, down to float among the stars.

Forever she had drifted, formless, nameless, in blissful ignorance, content to bathe in darkness and gaze upon the brilliance of Illindra's web. Each world, every spark of life that dared shimmer across its surface was perfect in its imperfection.

One world in particular attracted her attention and she allowed herself to drift closer, to fix her attention upon a tiny bright point of brilliance flaring defiance in the face of the void. She swam down through the dark, the too-thick air overstuffed with ambitions and desires and life, and as she drew closer to this particularly interesting spark a ripple of surprise breathed across her soul, rousing the entity within.

On the ground beneath her were a scattering of lives, and in the middle of it lay prone the body of a young girl, nearly a woman. Her pale eyes were open, and Maika was nearly jolted out of her ensorcellment by the shock of recognition.

It is me, she thought.

"Beautiful, is she not?" The voice came from behind her. Maika would have cried out, but she had no voice here. Would have turned, but for her lack of feet. She panicked like a bug caught in a web, and her struggles threatened to tear the whole of it apart.

"*Sssss*, little one, I did not mean to frighten you. Hush now, stop now, you will tear yourself loose, and you really do not want to do that. Here, let me help you."

As if someone had laid a hand on her shoulder, she was turned so that she was facing the source of the voice. A blinding figure stood before her in robes the color of fresh bone. He wore rings upon his fingers, worlds on a chain about his neck, and his smile was sweet enough to break her heart. He held a delicate instrument made of bone and secrets, and Maika would have screamed with excitement.

It is he!

Am I? he laughed in her mind. Then he opened his mouth and spoke. "No need to shout, little one. Imagine yourself whole—yes, just so."

Maika found herself standing on...

Nothing...

"Best not think of that," he told her, still smiling. "And best not to look down."

Maika kept her gaze fixed upon the stranger's laughing dark eyes. "It *is* you," she insisted. "I have seen you in my dreams."

"Have you?" He sounded so much like Akamaia that Maika could not help herself. She rolled her eyes in exasperation.

"Yes," she told him. "In dreams and visions. Illindra has sent you to help us. You are meant to lead my people to safety."

"Am I indeed?" His smile faded, and he stared into Maika's eyes as if reading all the secrets she kept there. "How can you be so sure, little one? Prophets are false. Visions lie. The dreaming eye finds no beauty in truth."

"I have seen it," she insisted, frustration threatening to overwhelm her. "You are meant to lead us out of the Seared Lands."

"Yes, but then what? How do you know that I am meant to lead you to safety, and not to some worse fate? Prophets lie. Visions are false. Your own heart will lie to you, if you let it."

"Anywhere you choose to lead us is better than where we are," she cried. "You cannot lead us into a worse fate than the one we are suffering. See for yourself." She turned, looked down upon her own prone body.

He had been right. To look down nearly made her sick.

Still she looked at the tiny figures surrounding her. Beloved Akamaia, and Tamimeha, her tiny warriors like ants determined to sacrifice all for their queen. The shadowmancers, falling beneath the strain of Akari's assault. The Dragon Queen, brilliant and doomed, and her mute friend—

"Oh." The figure behind her breathed out a long, low sigh. "Oh. I did not know. I will come."

"Praise Illindra," she breathed, turning to face him again. "We are saved."

"Perhaps," he replied, eyes dark and unreadable. He lifted the bird-skull flute to his lips...

"Perhaps not."

...and *pip-pip peeeee, pip-pip peeeee-oh* he played a tune that sent Maika dancing away, away...

THIRTY-SEVEN

She looks like a candle that has been blown out.

Even as she held Sulema's head in her lap and brushed the short wizard locks back from her face, Hannei was certain they had failed. Her onetime sister's face, more familiar to her than her own, was wan beneath the dirt and freckles and the gem-crusted Mask of Sajani. Her cheeks were pale and her long, muscular limbs shook as if the Nightmare Man of stories had seized her and would not let go.

Though Sulema gripped her fox-head staff till her knuckles went white, the air about them shimmered and swirled as the Dreaming Lands resisted her attempts to open a doorway and usher them to safety.

A hot wind blew down from on high as Akari tried to claw his way down, and the earth beneath them trembled as Sajani sought to wake. Hannei ignored them, as she ignored the frightened mutterings of the crowd and the whispers of that girl queen and her advisors—that they were up to something was painfully obvious. She ignored the pain in her tailbone and back and neck as she bent over Sulema and hummed, though the sound that came from her brought shame. It was a silly song, one known only to herself and the youth who had been her sister. They had made it up on the night they snuck into the stallion herds of Uthrak and braided breeding-rights beads into the manes of Zeitan Fleet-Foot and Ruhho the brave-hearted black.

Moons ago, years ago, lifetimes ago.

In those days she had been whole and hopeful. Neither of them had wanted anything more than their horses, their bows and swords, and the approval of the pride. Sareta had praised them, Ani had watched over them, Nurati had baked honey-cakes for them with her own hands. To steal a kiss from Tammas Ja'Sajani had been the greatest quest they could imagine, and being denied a place among the warriors of their pride the greatest fear. They played at aklashi, not this game of dragons and dreams and spiders...

Sudden realization took Hannei and stopped her song short.

Sulema never wanted this, she realized, *no more than I did. She would have shunned the staff she clings to now, would have shunned the mask and the dragon's legacy that goes with it. She wanted neither of those worlds, and now lies trapped between them, caught like a fly in two spiders' webs.*

For a moment she felt pity for Sulema, fear for the delicate bones beneath the thin freckled skin, sorrow for the warrior's locks shorn away even as hers had been. They had wanted so little, asked so little from the world, and now found themselves crushed like millet between hard stones. Beneath the heavy dragon's mask Sulema pressed her eyes shut, and her body shook with effort as she tried to force her will upon a magic she hated.

She would kill herself trying to save people she does not know, Hannei thought with a surge of fierce pride. *Some of whom would see her dead. She is trying so hard...*

Too hard. Hannei had watched Hafsa Azeina, more than once, as that dreamshifter had sloughed off her mortal cloak and slipped into the world of dreams and nightmares. *She needs to relax and let it happen, lest it break her.*

That thought was enough to make her laugh, almost. Sulema was fire and rocks and hasty arrows. She never simply relaxed and let things happen. The only time she could ever fully concentrate was when she was fighting.

Oh.

Of course!

Hannei eased herself out from beneath Sulema's stiff and shaking form. Golden eyes flew open behind the jeweled mask, startled and bloodshot and desperate.

"What are you doing?" Sulema whispered hoarsely.

Hannei grunted and drew one of her swords. She pointed it first at Sulema, and then up at Akari, unfathomably high above them but still there. Then she used the point of her sword to draw a wide and careful circle in the dust. She wiped the blade clean and sheathed it, then clapped her hands together once, twice, three times before her heart, never once taking her eyes from her onetime sister.

"Ahhhh," Sulema breathed. She removed the mask and set it aside, laid the staff beside it as well. Sitting up slowly she then stood, shrugging off the touch of those who would have helped her to her feet. She stepped slowly, deliberately, into the hoti which Hannei had drawn, drew back her arm, and slapped Hannei hard across the face once, twice, three times. Then she threw back her head and *laughed*.

The people of Quarabala stared at them.

"Challenge accepted, sister!" Sulema said. "Show me yours!" She laughed again as if there was not a care in the world, the very picture of *saghaani*, beauty in youth.

Hannei spat blood at Sulema's feet, and grinned. Let the kings and queens and sorcerers play their games. Let the spiders weave their webs. She and Sulema had been warriors—*were* warriors, no matter what the world thrust upon them or stripped away. Hannei looked into Sulema's eyes, hoping that her own bloody smile might convey the words that were in her heart.

If I die today, she thought, *though I die in exile far from the singing sands, let me die as a warrior, shedding blood that the people may live. Let me die Ja'Akari, under the sun.*

THIRTY-EIGHT

If I die at dawn, Jian implored silently, *though I die far from the Twilight Lands, let me die as the son of Tsun-ju Tiungpei, facing the sword with such grace and honor as she has always shown.*

Let me die as the son of Allyr, shedding no coward's tears. Let the blood I shed spare the blood of my most beloved.

The men shoved Jian through a narrow doorway and into an ink-black room so that he stumbled and nearly fell. A heavy door slammed shut, sealing him off from the world, sealing his fate. His own breathing sounded harsh in his ears, a discordant final note in the song that had been his life. He stank of anger and despair. There came to his mind an image of three dead girls, bound to their thrones of prophecy by the same blackthorn vines which bound Sajani to her blood-soaked bed. He heard their rotting voices murmuring, as if they had lain in wait in the chambers of his heart.

"He thinks he knows fear," the first sister had said, "but he has not yet heard the drums of war. He will."

"He thinks he knows pain," the second sister had answered, "but he has not yet seen the face of despair. He will. He will."

"Aaaaaah," the third sister rattled then and now. "Aaah aaah aaaahhhh."

They were right, he thought. *I knew nothing of fear or pain. The torments and terrors I had suffered then were mine alone.* To fear for one's own life, he realized, was as nothing compared to Tsali'gei's. *My mother. My son. My little son.*

A cry of pain escaped his lips, as it had not then, waking echoes of mocking laughter from the shadows.

"Jian?"

The voice was weak, so weak it was almost lost in the shadows. Jian's heart tripped and he fell to his knees in the darkness.

"Mother!" he cried, for surely it had been her voice. He shuffled forward in the darkness, widening his eyes as if by doing so he might drink in light by which to see. He found her soon enough by feel and by smell. The scent which had enveloped him in comfort and love now danced with a smell Jian knew only too well: the sharp tang of imminent death. "Mother," he said again, softly this time as he bent to gather her to his chest. She hissed through her teeth a little as he pulled her close, as good as a scream of pain from any lesser woman.

"My boy," she murmured against his shoulder as he sat on the cold stone floor, rocking her as once she had rocked him. "My sweet, handsome boy."

"You will be okay, Mama," he told her in a voice that cracked and wept.

"Do not lie to me," she scolded, her voice faint as a shadow's sigh. "Jian, listen to me. Listen…"

"Yes?" he asked, when she paused for breath.

And paused…

and paused…

for breath…

Long into the night Jian held Tiungpei close, cradling her body in his arms as her flesh cooled and stiffened, as the smell of death rose about them like the perfume of wicked flowers. He sang to her—songs he had learned from her in his childhood, songs he had learned from the other yellow Daechen, songs he had heard in the Twilight Lands. He sang with the voice of the sea, of the wind, he sang with the voice of a boy who was lost in the woods and trying to find his way home.

When his breath failed, he hummed to her.

When his heart failed he wept against her thin shoulder.

At last, at long last and far too soon, Jian removed his own outer robe and wrapped her body, doing so by feel, then laid her out as best he could with her hands folded over her chest. He wished for a silken shroud covered all in seed pearls. He wished for a red-robed priest with a shaven head, one who could pray to the sky for his mother's peaceful journey to the Lonely Road and beyond. He wished to hear her voice just one... just one last time.

As he knelt beside his mother's still body, Jian could hear a rushing as of distant thunder, feel the floor tremble beneath his fingertips as grief and fury rose up in a dark tide. Caught unawares he threw his head back, gasping for air as the storm found him, found its heart, and tore him all asunder. That part of him which had been human was ripped loose and flung screaming into the void. That greater portion of his soul—daeborn, fellborn—rose up and he rose with it, snarling his defiance.

The living rock screamed as he raked his claws across it, and the night's face went pale with fear beneath the gaze of his daemon-spawn eyes. Jian had seen his father shift his shape many times, but had never been able to achieve the change himself.

Now I am truly an Issuq, he thought, *and now I am truly alone.* For surely they had killed Tsali'gei as well, and murdered their unborn babe.

"Motherrrr," he cried, an animal's howl, and gnashed his teeth with impatience. In allowing harm to befall Tiungpei, the emperor had broken their treaty, and unleashed the Sea King's child.

Dawn broke over the land as it always would, dead mothers or no.

When they came for him, he was ready.

THIRTY-NINE

Dawn broke over the land like a new-forged sword. Sulema sat cross-legged across the hoti from Hannei Ja'Akari and allowed herself to be prepared for battle. Keoki the shadowmancer stood as her second. Rehaza Entanye stood for Hannei. As a horde of long-limbed and giggling children took turns beating the travel dust and sweat from her clothing, she sat still as a vash'ai at hunt and he sponged the stink from her body with perfumed manna water. He painted her face as best he could with colored dust and kohl so that her visage would resemble a cat's snarl, kneaded her muscles until they were loose.

Neither she nor her opponent had a proper warrior's braids, having been shorn of their pride by wicked outlanders. Keoki smiled slyly and insisted that he knew what to do with the orange hair that had now grown to a finger's length along her scalp. Oils and combs were proffered up by Nanevi and the two of them had tugged and muttered at her head until she sported a short mane of wizard locks, not as crazed and untidy as her mother's had been, but neat and fierce, adorned with precious beads of red salt clay.

Gazing into a polished brass mirror, Sulema thought it suited her better somehow than had the braids of a Ja'Akari. She made a face, and the warrior in the mirror snarled back at her. It would suffice.

The seconds pulled back, allowing the warriors time to meditate. Akamaia raised her voice to Illindra, beseeching guidance and deliverance for their people, and strength for their chosen savior. A handful of the refugees brought beaten metal hand drums and played them with intricate, repetitive tones that were soothing and arousing at the same time. Focusing on the way her heart beat in time to the drums, Sulema closed her waking eyes.

Focusing on her breathing, she matched it to the flow of the song as Aasah had taught her, letting sa and ka flow freely through her body and out into the world. Blood and bone, breath and heart, earth and sky, water and wind, she was one.

It was all, and it was enough.

Sulema opened her dreaming eyes, and beheld Shehannam. The Dreaming Lands, which before had seemed dim and strange, now felt cool and comforting and overfull of life. She did not miss the hard stare of Akari, but welcomed its absence, and sucked in a great lungful of misted air, grateful for this brief respite. Birds trilled from the otherworldly trees all around her and small animals scurried through the underbrush, unconcerned with her presence. She may have been the Dragon Queen of Atualon, but in this place she was nothing more than another two-legged interloper.

It was oddly reassuring.

In front of her, cutting through the dense woods, lay two distinct paths. Sulema took another deep breath and stilled her mind. Her mother had warned her about such tests.

One path was made of soft, golden sand and seemed to shine even in this drear land. At the beginning of it lay an elaborate headdress of lionsnake plumes, and a golden shamsi had been thrust into the loam. Sulema could see herself donning the headdress and drawing the shamsi, choosing the way of the warrior. It felt natural to her, and right. For the space of a breath she could not imagine choosing any other course.

Am I not Ja'Akari? she asked herself. *A daughter of the dreamshifter, riding free under the sun?* Ehuani, *this is who I am.* She took a step forward, but something fluttered and caught her eye.

The second path was straight and neat, cobbled with smooth dragonstone which glowed a warm welcome. The blue and gold robes of Sa Atu hung from a blackthorn bush, and the golden crown of a queen winked at her from among the midnight blooms. Sulema could feel herself slipping into the linen and cloth-of-gold and taking her rightful place on the golden throne of Atualon. This was her path, her legacy and birthright. For the space of a breath she could not imagine ever having considered any other course.

Am I not Sa Atu? she reasoned. *Daughter of the dragon, champion of my people? Ehuani, this is who I am.* And she took a step toward the second path...

Then stopped, shaking her head.

"There is more beauty in truth," she said aloud, "than in the lies of the most beautiful dream." Because the truth—and she knew it—was that the way of the warrior was no longer hers to take, any more than the robes of Sa Atu were hers to wear. "I am not a warrior of the Zeera, daughter of Hafsa Azeina," she said again, addressing Shehannam itself. "Neither am I the Dragon Queen of Atualon, daughter of Wyvernus. I am myself, and nothing more.

"I am Sulema."

A hunting horn sounded once, twice, three times through the darkling sky, and the paths to the left and right of her disappeared as a figure emerged from the woods. A magnificent beast of a woman clad in skins and furs, antlered and doe-eyed, with skin pale as sand and a wild tangle of hair that hung past her knees. Her smile was as sharp and predatory as those of the dark hounds that rose up from the shadows to surround her, and when she clapped her hands together the birds stopped singing.

"*Maith-na thau,*" she growled at Sulema, and the hounds growled with her. "*Issa tir aulen.*"

Thus saying, she drew her hands apart, and a third path sprang open through the trees, midway between where the other two had been. Before Sulema could blink, or say a word of thanks, the woman and her hounds disappeared.

A single, shaggy-haired white beast remained behind, a great hound with a bloody muzzle and one torn ear. It gazed upon her for a moment with sorrowful golden eyes before it, too, faded away.

"The Huntress," Sulema breathed. Her mother had warned her away from the guardian of Shehannam, who did not suffer intruders to live. And yet, she had offered no harm.

Or had she?

Sulema walked forward, slowly, until she had reached the beginning of this new path. The fox-head staff of a dreamshifter lay upon the ground at her feet, and the Mask of Sajani nestled against it, winking up at her from a bed of soft grass.

"Neither Zeerani nor Atualonian, then," she said, her voice a soft song in that hallowed place, "but both." She took up the staff of a dreamshifter and it felt true, fitting her callused hand better than a warrior's shamsi. She took up the Mask of Sajani and placed it against her face. It felt natural, settling more comfortably against her skin than a queen's golden crown. A breeze sprang up, ruffling her fiery locks.

She raised her staff high, toward the woods from which she thought the Huntress was still watching. Recalling her mother's words, she did not thank the forest guardian. Instead, she tugged a bead of red salt clay from her locked hair and let it fall to the ground.

"For you," she called. "In payment of your… hospitality."

She heard, or imagined that she did, peals of laughter from deep in the wood's wild heart. All around her, louder and more lustily than they had before, the birds began to sing. She lifted a foot, set it firmly on the path before her—

—and stepped into the hoti.

❖

Sulema looked down at herself. She was dressed as a warrior, and yet she was not. Her vest and leggings were white as river sand and embroidered all over with dragons of blue and gold. She wore a heavy headdress, and without looking knew it would be fashioned of gold, with the red and blue and ice-white plumes of a lionsnake matriarch.

In one hand she cradled the orb of the ne Atu. In the other she bore the fox-headed staff which proclaimed her a dreamshifter of the Zeerani prides. Upon her face, as before, she wore the Mask of Sajani.

As she peered through the eyes of the dragon, it seemed to Sulema that the opponent facing her across the ring was no longer Hannei. This was Kishah in truth, the blades of bloody vengeance. The shadows of death coursed eagerly about her feet as the hounds had followed the Huntress. Hannei Two-Blades was cloaked in death, muted and masked by it as well, her face a grim ruin of the laughing youth she once had been. There was no love for a sister in her eyes, no mirth, no forgiveness.

Sulema firmed her grip on the staff in her hands and took a warrior's stance. Hannei drew her swords, crouched, and nodded at the Quarabalese oracle who stood just outside the circle. Akamaia thumped her staff down on the hard-packed earth once, twice, three times, as silence seized the Seared Lands.

"Begin."

The drummers stroked and struck their metal drums, and the *bong-pong-tangggg* drew an echo from Sulema's heart. From every heart among those gathered, she imagined, especially those whom an unkind fate had forced into opposition with a beloved. *Bong-pong tangggg*. The dance was joined.

Sulema moved first, stepping cat-stance toward the woman who had been her sister, staff spinning before her in a blur of wood and feathers. A threat. *Give ground before me*, it warned, *make way lest your skull be the first set into my throne.*

Hannei's blades answered in kind. *Ware*, they sang, *lest your blood rain upon the ground at my feet, and you become nothing more than the latest of my enemies to die. Beware.*

They were upon each other in a twirl, a whirl, a clash of souls, wood and steel, blood and bone. One of Hannei's blades licked a shallow wound down Sulema's left arm. Sulema's staff connected with the back of Hannei's knee, sending her staggering, face a mute snarl of pain and fury. Back and forth they stalked and spun, struck and countered, and all the while the drums sang, *bong-bong-tanggggg, pong-pong tanggggg, bum-bum.*

Then Sulema leapt back to avoid a vicious downswing from one of Hannei's swords, and her opponent's face wavered oddly before hers in the deadly heat until it seemed not to be the face of her former friend, not a Zeerani face at all, but the ruined mask and wrecked flesh of the Nightmare Man.

"Sulema," he whispered to her as shadows sprang up all around them, hiding the combatants from view. "My daughter. My sister. My love… why do you fight me so?"

Sulema stopped, panting hard, hands gripping her staff so tightly the knuckles showed white.

"I know you," she began.

"Yes," he replied, waving her words away. "Why do you fight me so? There is no need for you to struggle, to die here on the shadowed road. These are not your people. Lay down your staff—give me the mask you wear, the burden you bear—and I swear to you, on Akari's eyes I swear to you, I will allow you to return home to your people and live out your life as a Ja'Akari. A warrior riding free, under the sun. Is this not what you want, beloved? To be Ja'Akari once more?

"Is this not the darkest wish of your heart?"

He knew her well. Too well.

"It is," she agreed. She would not lie, even to the Nightmare Man.

"Then give me the mask—"

"It is my wish," she went on before he could finish, "but it is not my fate. I am no Ja'Akari."

"Then you are nothing," he snarled, raising his massive hammer high.

"I am not nothing," she replied, and to her surprise she laughed in his face. "I am Sulema!"

Her words rang with a truth more powerful than any Sulema had ever known, and as the clarity of them sliced through her Sulema could feel bonds and bindings being sheared away. She laughed as a weight she had not known she carried was lifted from her, and she was filled, filled to bursting, with the knowledge of who and what she had always been.

"I am Sulema!"

With that she kicked a spray of sand and salt and bone into his face—the same dirty trick Hannei had used on her, back in the fighting pits of Min Yaarif—and before he could blink it away, she was upon him. Her staff arched high, swung round for a killing blow—

And stopped short, Jinchua's laughing face carved atop her staff just touching his hideous mask.

"Begone," she told him, and she blew into his face through the mouth of Sajani's mask. "You have no power here."

With a clap as of thunder the Nightmare Man disappeared, taking his shadows with him.

As the illusion faded Hannei swayed, stunned, and dropped her swords upon the ground. All around them people leapt to their feet, pointing and shouting. The air itself split, revealing a passage out of the Seared Lands, and into Shehannam.

It was a way out, but—

"I do not know the way," Sulema whispered. She knew they had precious little time, but still Sulema hesitated.

Though she had opened a doorway into the Dreaming Lands, she knew no more of that place than any child might. The realization struck her with the power of a physical blow. She clenched her teeth, air hissing out from behind the dragon's mask as fresh pain stabbed through her shoulder. "Atu forgive me, I am no true dreamshifter. *I do not know the way.*"

The rent in the air shuddered and tore at her grasp as if she held a live lionsnake. As Sulema froze, caught between the fear of doing something and the terror of doing nothing, the ground began to heave beneath her feet. She cried out in alarm as she lost her footing, and then again in rising panic as the passage into Shehannam flickered, wavered—

And held. The light of Shehannam flared bright, silhouetting that dark figure that appeared now before her, cloaked and hooded in robes as silver as moonlight. Slender brown hands reached up to push the hood back, and a handsome young man grinned down at her as he stepped into the hoti, using a booted foot to break the circle.

He knows Zeerani ways, she thought, shocked. "Who are you?" she asked. Though he had about him the look of the Zeera, this stranger was dressed in clothes unlike any she had ever seen.

"Aaaaaah!" Hannei said, staring. "Aaaah!" and then in her broken voice whispered, "*Aaaaru.*"

The handsome man laughed, and an enormous glowing mantid peeked out from his mantle.

"*Pip-pip peeee*," it fluted at her. "*Pip-pip-peeee-oh!*"

"Daru," he agreed. "That was my name... I am Daru! I have come back at last." He reached out both hands not to Sulema, but to Hannei. "I have come back to show you the way home."

FORTY

The world was not as he remembered it.

For so long he had carried memory in his pocket like a talisman, and this felt like a small betrayal. The faces he thought should be familiar were sharper and more real than memory had painted them; uglier, meaner, more flawed. Colors were darker, duller. And Sulema—that was Sulema behind the Mask of Sajani, was it not?—was both less and greater than he remembered. Her hair was knotted in the short locks of a dreamshifter, and her golden eyes burned as hot as her mother's. Everyone was shorter than they should have been. That made sense, he supposed with some amusement, as he had been much smaller the last time he had seen any of them.

And it stinks. He had become accustomed to living among people who bathed daily, to perfumes and lotions and unguents meant to mask the natural smells of human beings. *This*, he thought, *will take some getting used to.* He breathed through his mouth and tried not to be too obvious about it.

Among the faces that stared at him with varying degrees of suspicion, one was most changed and most familiar at once. Hannei. Had a thousand years separated them, instead of just a dozen, his heart would have known her anywhere. Hannei had been badly hurt, badly damaged, but their souls still sang the same sweet song. Their eyes met, and Daru smiled as gently as he was able, with dreams of murder clouding the edges of his vision a dark red.

I will find those who hurt you, he promised silently, *every one of them, and I will lay their heads at your feet*. Her eyes warmed as if she could hear his thought, and the corners of her mouth deepened just a little.

It was enough.

"Daru," Sulema breathed, echoing her sword-sister's whisper. Or were they sword-sisters still? Daru frowned at the hoti he had broken. Then he shrugged. It did not matter, and he had no time for riddles.

Time, he thought with fleeting amusement. A way-master who had run out of time. Doubtless Rothfaust would make a limerick of it, if the ways allowed their paths to cross again.

"Come," he told them, "and hurry! You must hurry. I cannot hold this open forever, and—" He broke off. Best not tell them what was following, or how close it was, lest in a panic the people trample each other to death and bring his mission to a ruinous end.

Again.

"Just hurry," he urged.

An ancient woman whose face was a mass of wrinkles peered most suspiciously up at him. Daru could not help but stare back. It had been so long since he had seen someone who had let their face age naturally that he had forgotten what it looked like.

Like parchment, he thought, *with all the wisdom of a world written on it, then crumpled till the words are hidden. And so small!*

"Who are you, young man," she said sharply, "to tell your betters to hurry? Or think that we would follow you without—"

She stopped as a harsh wind picked up; a hot wind and dry. It smelled of sour musk and sweet rot and carried within it, faint but to those ears which have been trained to listen, the whispering voices of a thousand Araids. "*Pip-pip PEEEEE!*" Pakka shrieked, making him wince.

"If you do not come now," Daru told the old woman in a voice meant to carry no farther than her ears, "you will all die, down to the last child." He held the way open, held his breath, and prayed to Illindra that *this time* they would listen to him. He prayed to Ganuth and Chavelle and Beha'a, as well. They were not of this world, but they were gods, and as Rothfaust was fond of saying, it never hurt to hedge one's bets.

The old woman opened her mouth to argue, but Hannei held up a hand for silence. The wind whispered again, and her eyes widened.

She hears it, Daru thought. *She knows.*

The Ja'Akari struck together the two dark swords she carried, drawing sparks, and pointed to the open door, scowling in such a way as to need no translation and brook no argument. Sulema glanced at her through the eyes of the dragon's mask, hesitated for a moment, and then brought the butt end of a fox-head staff down on the ground, gently, as if she feared that in doing so she might cause the earth to shake again.

Oh, but you have, Daru thought, his heart heavy with grief for her pain. *Oh, but you will.*

"We will go now," Sulema agreed. "Children and the elderly first, warriors and walkers bringing up the rear."

"I will lead the way," Daru insisted. "I can get you to Min Yaarif, but for the sake of all gods we must *make haste.*"

"I will go with you," Sulema agreed, "and you will tell me everything."

"Everything, Dreamshifter?" Daru could not help it; despite his growing sense of urgency, he laughed. "Perhaps not. But I will tell you what you need to know, if you can get these people you have found to move their blasted feet." He laughed again. *Tell you everything, indeed; how many lifetimes do you think we have?* He was still chuckling as he entered the Way, leading them all from certain death and into deadly danger. Laughter was better than anger, after all, and they had no way of knowing how many times he had died for them already.

The Ways of Shehannam were more familiar to him now than the world which had birthed and nurtured and killed him a thousand times over. Lush and green, unnaturally so, filled with the songs of birds and the songs of things that pretended to be birds, and thick with webs of dreaming. A fennec fox white as starlight flitted just at the edge of his vision, allowing Daru to catch a glimpse of her but no more. It was Sulema's kima'a, judging by the staff and furtive sideways glance the girl kept shooting him.

She does not know how foxlike she is becoming, he thought, *or how like her mother*. Daru did not need to ask after Hafsa Azeina, since the Web of Illindra had sung a dirge at her passing. Long ago Daru had mourned the loss of his mentor and almost-mother. The sight of her peering out from behind her daughter's eyes brought him little more than a slight wistful pang.

"This way," he said, taking the left-hand path just before a dying glade. He averted his eyes from the sight of old char, wrinkled his nose at the memory of death. His mission had failed here at least half a dozen times before he had learned the correct turning. "Keep to the path."

"I have to pee," an older woman muttered.

"Pee on the path, then," Daru told her. "Or hold it. Or die. Your choice."

She muttered darkly, but kept going.

"Are you going to tell me, or do I have to guess?" Sulema asked finally. "You disappeared moons ago, not years. Yet now you step out of Shehannam like Zula Din in the stories, all grown up and acting as powerful as my mother."

"Not as powerful as Dreamshifter," he objected, old loyalties taking him by surprise. "Not in the same—"

"Daru," she interrupted. "Guts and goatfuckery, stop prancing around like an oula-dancer and answer the damned question."

Daru grinned. "You look like your mother and you sound like Istaza Ani. All of your worst nightmares have come true."

Sulema's face went white at that, so that her freckles stood out. Her eyes flashed and her mouth flattened in a hard line.

"Yes," she said in a voice like flint and tinder, "my nightmares." Hannei, who walked a little way behind them, made a soft and sorrowful sound.

Daru thought of all the times he had watched them die—and the few times he had killed either or both in an attempt to change the end of their story—then shook his head to dispel the images. "I am sorry," he said at last. *For everything*, he added silently. *I am so, so sorry*.

"*Pip pip*," Pakka chirruped, light flickering in sympathy.

"I was lost beneath Atukos, deep in the twisting little passageways," he said. He could not tell them everything. To do so would doom this world. Still, he owed them what explanation he could give. "Khurra'an chased me into a hole as if I were a mouse, and I could not find my way out again."

"Khurra'an?" Sulema asked, softly. "But why? He is gone," she added, voice breaking on that last word. "Gone down the Lonely Road with my mother."

"I am not sure why he chased me," Daru answered. "At the time I thought he wanted me dead because I was weak. That is what he told me, but the ways of the vash'ai are stranger than we ever knew. They are an ancient race, much older than our own, with minds and magic I do not think we can ever understand."

Hannei grunted at that.

"They have their own sorcerers," Sulema said, nodding. "Kahanna. One of them has befriended Ani, though she claims they are not bonded."

"Ani," he breathed, but shook his head. "That is another path for another time." He gathered himself and continued.

"I was lost for quite a long time. Days, I think, though I have no way of knowing. I found water here and there, and Pakka brought me rats." He petted his little friend, who preened at the attention. "And bugs, which taste nasty no matter where you are. I found dungeons, and catacombs full of dead Baidun Daiel."

"They were not dead," Sulema said. "They—" but she shuddered and would say no more.

"Catacombs filled with sleeping Baidun Daiel, then, thousands of them. I hate to think what trouble they could be, if they might be roused, but I suppose we will have to deal with that later."

"I suppose we will." Sulema's voice was dry.

"I was lost, and hurt, and probably would have died, but Loremaster Rothfaust found me. He took me... far away. For a long time."

Hannei made a rude noise, and Sulema rolled her eyes at him. "'He took me far away for a long time,'" she mocked gently. "Daru, that is not an explanation, nor even the sad shadow of one, and you know it."

"I cannot tell you much," he said, keeping his voice steady. "It is a long story, and I am... constrained." Even now, the medallion at his chest burned in warning. "I can tell you that I have been, ah, an apprentice of sorts."

"You are an apprentice? So Loremaster Rothfaust is... a dreamshifter?"

Daru kicked a rock from the path. It bounced into the underbrush, and he wished he had not done so. It was dangerous to change anything at all in the Ways. Even something so small and trivial as moving a stone from your path might prove the undoing of a thousand carefully laid plans.

"Not a dreamshifter," he said, choosing his words carefully. "And I have not been an apprentice for a long time." Many lifetimes, in fact.

"What are you, then? Are you a dreamshifter? You have no staff."

"Not a dreamshifter. Yet I am stronger than you know." He smiled at the daughter of his mentor and felt his heart break for her pain over and over again. He had spent three lifetimes of men trying to find a way back to her, to Hannei, to this moment, only to have their lives slip through his fingers time and again. Perhaps this time, this Way, he might succeed where so many times he had failed them. But she would understand none of this, even if he was allowed to tell her—and explaining the Ways to the inhabitants of a dragon-infested world was strictly forbidden. Not even Daru, who was somewhat infamous among the students of the Academ for rule-breaking, dared flout that law. So he said only, "I am a waymaster."

And I hope I do not have to kill you again.

"I have no idea what that means."

"No," he agreed. "So you will just have to trust me for now. Ah!" They had come to another clearing, wider and more wholesome than the last. Birds sang there—real birds, not nightmares pretending to be birds—and the trees nearby were laden with sweet-smelling fruit. "Here—we should rest here."

"Is it safe?" Sulema asked.

Daru shook his head. "You know better," he chided as gently as he could. "Nowhen is safe for you, Sulema, or for those who love you. You bring trouble wherever you go."

"It is only trouble if you get caught," she insisted, and stuck out her tongue.

You have no idea, he thought wryly.

Then Hannei laughed, a terrible tortured sound, and Daru surprised himself by laughing with them. Just like that, though they were in a place and time that had never existed, could never exist, and though he had already come this way a handful of times, leading them all to a horrible end, Daru felt as if he had finally come home.

FORTY-ONE

The best thing about being a queen, even a queen without a throne, was that no one expected her to take a turn on guard duty. The worst thing about being a queen with a sense of honor was that she expected it of herself.

Long into the hours that felt most like night—for there was no true night in the Dreaming Lands—Sulema sat with her back against a tree with strange, soft bark and gazed over the huddled forms of sleeping people. Occasionally someone would cough, or sigh, or a baby would cry. At one point a man farted so loudly that the people about him muttered in disgust and moved away, leaving him laughing in a small space of his own. Sulema sniggered. Even in times of fear and war, she realized, farts were funny.

This vigil was no different from any she had maintained back home in the Zeera. Were it not for the strange trees, the alien birdcalls, the occasional howl of a hound at the hunt, it might have been... boring. Sulema leaned back, closed her eyes, and imagined herself back home. Warriors would be playing stones and bones, and the sands would be singing...

I thought you would never fall asleep.

Sulema sat upright with a start. She reached for her sword but found only her staff.

You have forsaken the way of the warrior, the laughing voice reminded her. *Though you might have chosen a less warlike time in which to do so. You humans are a curious lot.*

Sulema looked down and saw a tiny, pale fox with enormous ears sitting primly near her knee, one paw on an ugly obsidian knife that looked suspiciously like the one her mother had borne. Sulema inched away from it, and from the fox. She was a spirit beast and a trickster. She was also the embodiment of Sulema's soul, and her tie to Jehannim.

"Jinchua." Sulema took a deep breath and tried to slow the racing of her heart. "You startled me! What are you doing here?"

What am I doing here? The fox looked around them with exaggerated puzzlement. *I am of this place, Dreamshifter. What are you doing here? In the flesh, and with what appears to be the entire populace of Quarabala? The Huntress will not be pleased. At the best of times, she does not like visitors, and these are not the best of times.*

"I am... Daru is leading us all to safety outside the Seared Lands. I went there to get one small girl, and she turned out to be their *queen*. And I had to agree to rescue all the people of Quarabala... what?" She frowned at the fennec's response. "Stop laughing at me, it is not funny." She felt her own mouth quirk, though, as she thought back on the ridiculous nature of her quest and the way she had been duped. "It is an odd tale, I suppose. And I have not decided whether or not to kill Yaela for lying to me. Retrieve her niece, indeed."

Remind me never to send you to fetch a lizard, the fox teased. *Likely you would return with a dragon. Ah, Sulema! I have missed you, and I will miss you even more when you have been killed.*

"When I have... what?"

Pythos knows where you are, now. Since you spied upon him with that mask—you may as well have tweaked his nose and told him. And he is working with the Nightmare Man—how do you think he was able to regain his throne? Your throne, my apologies, your Radiance. Jinchua bowed, foxlike. *This enemy is beyond your abilities to fight, little warrior. Mask or no mask, it is likely this is the last time you and I will meet.*

Unless...

"Unless?"

Do you know how your mother gained her powers, young queen? The fennec curled her bush-tail about her tiny feet and tipped her head to one side, enormous ears twitching. *She was more than a simple dreamshifter, you know.*

"She was a dream eater."

Do you know what that means?

Sulema considered the question. "No," she admitted at last. "Though I know it is something... wicked."

"Wicked" is not quite the word, Jinchua said. *"Unfortunate" is more like it. A dream eater is a dreamshifter who has sacrificed everything in pursuit of great power, usually out of a desperate need. Occasionally there will be one who desires power as an end, and not as a means to an end—that is wicked.*

"I do not see the difference," Sulema protested.

No. The fox smiled. *You do not. Therefore I hold hope for you.*

"You are speaking in riddles again."

I am a fox. It is my nature to speak in riddles. Jinchua laughed again, showing bright white teeth. *A dream eater is a dreamshifter who has killed her own soul, eaten her own dreams.*

"But... I do not understand. I thought my mother killed her enemies?"

Oh, child. Oh, sweet child. Your mother killed your enemies—and in order to do that, in order to become the monster she needed to be to keep you safe, she first had to kill herself. In a manner of speaking.

Dreamshifting is in nature a gentler, weaker magic than that used to wield atulfah. Had she not become Annu, she would never have possessed the strength to snatch the two of you out of the dragon's maw and into the safety of the Zeera. She killed Basta—her kima'a—and ate her heart. In so doing she became the Dream Eater Annubasta.

377

Sulema's heart went cold. *My mother did this... for me.* Annoying as she found the fox, she could not imagine life without her soul-self, now that they had found each other. She looked at the staff. Then at the wicked obsidian blade—there was no doubt that it was the daemon-possessed instrument her mother had wielded. She looked last at Jinchua, who sat gazing up at her.

"You are saying I could—"

Kill me, the fox agreed calmly. *Eat my heart. Become one of the Annu—Annujinchua, a being of two worlds with power you cannot imagine. With the magic of a dream eater, and the Mask of Sajani through which you might wield atulfah, you would become the most powerful being your world has ever known.*

"None could stand before me," Sulema said wonderingly. Such power was unthinkable. For her to wield it—

None could, Jinchua agreed. *Not the usurper Pythos, the Nightmare Man—not even the armies of the Daeshen emperor could withstand a dream eater with the song of atulfah upon her tongue. With such power, you could move mountains...*

What are you doing? Jinchua demanded. *This is serious. Pay attention!*

Sulema could not take it anymore.

She burst into laughter.

"Me, a dream eater! With the power to move mountains!" She clutched her ribs and rolled to one side, bent double in her mirth. "Sulema Firehair the Freckled, first of her name! Who smites her enemies with brimstone and churra shit! Oh! Who—who—" by now she was laughing so hard she could hardly speak. "Who incites men to such lust that their kilts melt! Their touar ignite with passion!" She howled as the fennec looked on. "All shall love me and... and... disrobe!"

This is hardly a laughing matter, kima'a.

"Oh, but it is. Oh, my gut hurts." Sulema's hilarity subsided and she was able to push herself upright, though every now and again she would erupt in a fit of giggles and snorts. "Me, queen of the world, with the armies of mankind kneeling at my sandaled toes. You are funny, kima'a. Blind, but funny."

Blind? How?

"My heart desires none of these things." As Sulema said the words, she could feel the truth in them, and relaxed. *I have passed the test.* She continued aloud. "Not power, not armies, not a golden crown on my head or a golden throne under my arse."

What, then, does your heart desire, O Humble One?

"A fine horse. A good blade. My sword-sisters beside me, sunlight upon my face—and a good man to warm those parts of me the sun cannot reach. These are the treasures I covet, this is wealth without measure." She smiled—at last she knew her own true self, though she had hidden from this knowledge her whole life. Now that she had stopped running from her truth and turned to face it, she knew what she must do. "I wish to be Sulema, nothing more. And certainly nothing less."

The world does not need another warrior, Jinchua argued. *The world needs another Zula Din. You know what you must do. You must save the world from the Nightmare Man. You must convince the dragon not to wake. No simple warrior can hope to do these things.*

You know this.

"Yes," Sulema agreed. She did know. "There is only one way to save the world." She reached out and took up the blade—Belzaleel, her mother had called it, and warned her never to touch the foul thing. Jinchua closed her eyes and turned her head away, baring her pale throat.

Do what you must, kima'a. It has been an honor to love you.

Sulema could feel the demon stirring deep within the blade. *Use me,* it called to her from some unfathomable world. *Wake me. Feed me.* She held the blade in front of her with both hands, as if it had the weight of the world. She brought it up high over her head.

"Forgive me, Jinchua," she said. "I have to do this."

Yes, Jinchua agreed, trembling like a leaf in the wind.

Belzaleel screamed in victory.

The blade screeched again, this time in fury and pain, as she brought the obsidian knife down hard upon a rock.

"I abhor you," she told the daemon, smashing it down a second time, grinding the words out between her gritted teeth. "I repudiate you." Belzaleel's shriek of fury rose to an ear-splitting, world-splitting screech as she raised it one final time and brought it down with all her might. "I refuse you," she finished. "Begone! Fuck off, daemon! You stole my mother's soul away, but you will not have mine!"

The blade shattered in a thunderclap. Sharp fragments buzzed like hornets in all directions, stinging Sulema's face and arms. She held up both hands before her eyes to protect them, but as the wicked chips of rock cut her skin, drawing blood, a curious thing happened. They also cut away the last of her bonds, chains and cords and strangling vines she had not known existed. Bonds of magic, bonds of love and of enmity, of friendship and honor and duty, all fell away like a warrior's vest, baring her soul to the world.

Belzaleel's scream rose to a wail, thin and impotent. It was caught up in a playful breeze and carried away.

Jinchua opened one eye. *It is done, then.* Sulema could not decide whether she sounded relieved or sorrowful. Perhaps a bit of both.

"It is done." Sulema stood and rolled her shoulders. She felt lighter, freer than she could ever remember feeling.

You will never become Annujinchua, Jinchua said. *Never wield the power that is your birthright.*

"I will be Sulema," she replied, running her fingers through her short wizard locks. She took up her fox-head staff and smiled as the dream faded from her vision. "And it will be enough."

FORTY-TWO

Min Yaarif was a city with two souls, neither pure. Legend held that the First People had stopped here and, finding the waters of the Dibris sweet to drink, had built homes in which to abide. Houses of red salt for themselves, houses of mud for their slaves.

So it was still; those few upon whom fortune had smiled lived in splendor beyond belief, while the greater masses of people lived in squalor, trying to scrape the life-giving red salt from the mean dirt. Min Yaarif was a magnificent city of salt and steel, but it was also an ugly place of mud and blood and death.

As a boy Ismai had never been to any place more populous than the Zeerani city of Aish Kalumm. The bustle and otherness of Min Yaarif threatened to overwhelm his senses, and the Lich King stared through his eyes with surprise and amusement.

How small your world has been, Kal ne Mur thought.

No smaller than yours, the youngling replied, *centered as it has been on yourself. Who loves you? Whom do you love in return? Sudduth and the others follow you because they are bound by magic, not by love. Your own daughter uses you for her own ends, and she is mad with the lust for vengeance. You could count your true friends on one hand and have fingers left over.*

I have friends, Kal ne Mur responded, surprisingly stung. Then the absurdity of the situation hit him—he was standing on a rough-cobbled road at the edge of a backwater nothing of a town, arguing with the ghost of a boy who had needed to die before he could live.

"I am the Dragon King," he said aloud, shoving the boy and his troublesome thoughts aside. "A dragon has no need for the love of sheep."

"Are you arguing with yourself again, Father?" Naara asked. "I had thought that you and the boy would be at peace with each other by now. Certainly you need to be of a single mind if we—if *you*—are to retake Atualon."

You see... Ismai began.

"I am hungry for mutton," Sudduth grumbled. "When will you feed us real food, your Arrogance? I tire of the Zeerani pemmican. We should not eat food that tastes like shit just because we are dead."

"Enough, all of you!" Ismai snapped. "Do I have to destroy the entire world to get a moment of peace?"

I come, Kithren, Ruh'ayya sang. *I have swum the river for you.*

"Atu take you all," Ismai growled under his breath. He kicked a rock, which ricocheted off a nearby cart and struck him painfully on the shin. Sudduth chuckled, but when he turned on her she made her face carefully blank.

Sometimes, he thought, *being a king is a pain in the ass.*

It was not as difficult as he might have imagined to find lodging, or food for the ungrateful undead, all of whom seemed to have developed a desire for sheep's meat. The largest inn in Min Yaarif was wholly abandoned at his approach.

The people of the town must have discovered that the horde would remain outside the city proper as long as they were fed, for it fairly rained mutton and mead on the banks of the Dibris.

Ismai claimed a suite of lavishly appointed rooms, partly because they smelled of cinnamon and honey and sandalwood, but mostly because an entire wall of one room was laden with shelf upon shelf of books. He and his young host shared a love of reading, and the thought of a warm bath followed by a long read by firelight was more tempting to both of them than all the crowns of all the kingdoms.

He bathed, and supped—on leg of lamb, though he would not admit it to Sudduth—and was well into a book of stories about dragons, spiders, princesses, and the unexpected luck of widows' sons—when a knock came at the door.

"Enter," he snapped. Yosh take them all, could he not even read a book in peace?

The door opened. Sudduth, who had been guarding it, stuck her head into the room. She had a strange expression on her face, a mixture of consternation and hunger.

"Someone to see you, your Arrogance. He claims to be…" She seemed at a loss for words. "He has many claims," she finished lamely. "Each more outlandish than the last."

"And each of them more truthful than the next," a man added as the door widened and he stepped into the room. He was tall, and broad-shouldered, and wore an elaborate half-mask like a serpent's face. "My name is Mattu ap Serpentus ne Atu, brother of the Dragon King—my apologies, the *current* Dragon King—teller of lies, wearer of masks, beloved of… well, my sister still loves me."

Ismai frowned, marking his page carefully and setting the book aside.

"Do *I* know you?" Ismai frowned, searching both his minds but coming up blank. "And do you know whom you are addressing?" Few people, his memories told him, would dare approach the Lich King in so flippant a manner if they knew his true nature.

"I have no idea whether you know me, or know of me," the newcomer admitted. "I am rather a small player in a vast game, to be honest. I remember seeing you, during my short stay in the Zeera. Only your face was not… well, you know…" he gestured to his own masked face, "and my brother Pythos was still believed to be dead. I was the flippant ward of the Dragon King, you were a young man named Ismai, and the world—flawed as it was—still made sense. Does anyone know anyone anymore? It seems to me that someone has shuffled our cards in the middle of the game and mucked up the lot of us."

"Mattu... *Halfmask*," Ismai said, as he dragged up a vague memory. "Of course. The dreamshifter Hafsa Azeina knows you."

"Knew me," Mattu corrected gently. "We have much to discuss, I fear, you and I."

"You have admitted to being a liar and the brother of my enemy. Why should I discuss anything with you?" Ismai felt Kal ne Mur quaking with rage, but he was curious. Why *had* the man come?

"Because," Mattu answered, taking a seat much too close for Ismai's liking, and leaning close as if they were friends, "we love the same woman, and she needs our help."

Sulema.

The name, as whispered by Ismai, was warm as the golden sands, rich and sweet as mead poured from a pitcher of gold. No woman had ever been as beautiful, the Lich King thought, could ever possibly be as beautiful as the girl he beheld with memory's promise. She was as firmly rooted in Ismai's heart as the Lich King's soul was rooted in the boy's body, and there was no escape.

The girl is echovete, his treacherous heart whispered, *and ne Atu. She could wear the Mask of Sajani, and I the Mask of Akari. Together—*

Even as a longing for the life and love he had left behind stirred in Ismai's heart, desire welled up that part of him that was the Lich King—the desire for power. This new development was... invigorating. Ismai picked up a horn of mead and stared into the golden liquid. Sulema was mead and honey-bread, he thought, laughter and life. She was all things good and beautiful—

And she was Sa Atu, the Heart of Atualon.

Together we could take Atualon, he thought. *Together we could weave sa and ka in equal measure and send the restless Sajani back into her deep and dreamless slumber.*

Or together, the dark shadows of his soul whispered, that part which had slept through ages and should never have been roused. *Together we could* wake *the dragon, and watch the world end. It would be something new, after a thousand years. Something… interesting. It would be glorious.*

Ismai raised the horn to his lips, and drank.

FORTY-THREE

The Lich King was a man with two souls, neither pure. Legend held that Kal ne Mur, the greatest Dragon King ever to rule from Atualon, was descended from both the First People and from the Dae. The old stories held that he was more than a man, more than human, and the very fact that he had risen from the dead was, Ani thought dryly, proof of that.

While Ismai...

Ismai, she thought, and her heart was wretched with grief. *Sweet boy, what have they done to you? What have you done to yourself?* She could feel pain in his bones that went beyond charred skin and ruined eyes. He was all wrong on the inside, desecrated by misuse and betrayal, strayed so far from his soul's intended path that Ani could not see how she might ever light his way home. To attempt it, she was certain, was to risk becoming lost herself.

And the Lich King...

Ani shivered. Nothing in her life—not being sold away from her family when she was a child, not her first battle, not even her own wicked magic terrified her as deeply and utterly as did Kal ne Mur. His face, to her magicked eyes, was a column of black flame and a pit of a mouth endlessly screaming. To others he no doubt appeared charming, handsome even, with the face of a fine youth overlaying that of a king. To her he was the epitome of horror.

She could not simply drive the Lich King from Ismai's body, as if he were a song that needed to be unsung. That tenebrous soul had permeated the boy's body as the smoke of battle might cling to a warrior. More deeply still. Even the foulest ash might be steamed from the face and skin, whereas Ismai's bones were steeped in the stench of undeath until not even she could tell where one left off and the other began. If she attempted to separate the two, certainly Ismai would perish. And if she did nothing, this war they waged for Ismai's body would leave them dead sooner rather than later. Dead, or worse.

What of the undead legions, Bonesinger? Inna'hael asked, his voice a soft snarl. *What of the monstrosities your kind have called into existence? If the Lich King is killed, will their unhappy shades be banished in his wake, or will they be loosed upon the world to wreak what vengeance they might? I rather think it is the latter.*

Ani rather thought so, too, but kept it to herself. She could feel the struggle within Inna'hael, whom she knew was powerful among the vash'ai—how powerful, she could not guess, though she had her suspicions—and whom she feared might yet side with those of the greater predators who wished to simply wipe out humans and their incessant abuse of the world's magics. Faced with the horror that was the Lich King, and for which humans were wholly responsible, Ani could not entirely disagree.

Ani could not cure Ismai from the Lich King's taint, but she could not simply let the two of them remain as they were, locked into a single body and with a war raging between them. Neither would the danger be mitigated—even had she the heart to do it, which she did not—by slaying Ismai's body, corrupted as it was. Ani could see only one way through this goat-shit-laden path, and that was to use a bonesinger's deepest and most strictly forbidden power: she would have to fuse the two souls into one, erasing both songs from the music of the world and creating a new one.

Any other bonesinger would have been obliged to kill her for entertaining such a thought.

Fortunately for me, she thought as she readied herself to the task, *I am the last of my kind.*

She breathed deeply, taking in and letting go, taking in and letting go. Let the scents of the inn imbue her senses, acknowledged that her stomach was empty and her bladder full, that the smells and sounds of riverboats and their captains vied for her attention with an itch at the tip of her nose, and then just... let it all go. She sank deep as if into a lover's kiss, or a pleasant dream, or a warm bath, or a well-deserved and honorable death.

There!

Listening to the songs of the bones of the world, she beheld them both, the Lich King and the youth, like the flames of two candles lit too close together. The fires burned too hot, too close, but there might be a way, if she was as foolish and reckless as she had always accused her girls of being. With a great deal of unearned luck, if she just...

Istaza Ani sang, low in her throat and her rib cage she sang of raindrops joining to become a river, of rivers joining and flowing together, together into the ocean. She sang of lovers twined, of flowers and bees and sweet spreading warmth. She sang of letting go, and letting be, of drops of ink taken into paper to become a mother's book. Of letters joined into words, into poetry, into song.

Ah, she thought.

Almost...

Almost...

There! I have them.

The twin flames began to ebb and swell in time to her music, her song, to flicker and flare and dance as one.

As one, she thought, making it so. She imagined reaching out to two candles and pressing, pressing them together into a single column of flame. High it burned, and white-hot, a flash of heat furious enough to sear all the lands of men to dust and bones.

Ani withdrew her dreamhands, withdrew her song slowly, slowly, and with some trepidation surveyed her handiwork. Where there had been two flames, two candles in her imagining, there was now one. A single column, imperfect and twisted but whole, and from it burned a clear, clean flame.

It is finished, she thought, *for better or for worse. I have killed their songs and written a new one.* It was a small thought, scarcely more than a whisper against the great maelstrom that was Kal ne Mur, but he heard her. The flame twisted and turned, and in it now she saw a face—a man's face, strong and severe and bearing upon its brow an antlered crown.

Bonesingerrrr, he growled, and the flame crackled. She felt the searing heat. *What do you do here?*

Ani longed to flee, but her bones were deep as the mountains, a legacy passed down to her through a line of powerful women, her flesh strengthened by a lifetime of true living. Had she not called Hafsa Azeina friend? Had she not, in turn, raised a girl who would become queen? She stiffened her knees and spine, and stared death in his fiery face.

I am helping you, you goatfucking idiot, she replied.

A flickering.

Istaza Ani, is that you? Ismai's face peered out from the flame.

Yes, she replied, wishing that she could draw him whole and unharmed from the heart of the fire. Wishing that she had enough truth left in her bones to apologize for killing him. *As much of me as is left, I guess.*

You called... the Lich King... a goatfucking idiot. His astonished laughter was lost in the next swirl of flames but would burn forever in her heart.

This magic... is forbidden. The Lich King roared, threatening to engulf her.

But Ismai held it back. His song rang true still, cool and sweet, and it kept the world from burning in the wrath of Kal ne Mur.

The Lich King looked surprised, and then thoughtful.

So… you have joined us together, he said. His voice was odd, swinging back and forth from youth to man and back again as the two halves merged into a frightening new whole. *You have made me… less… than I was.*

That remains to be seen, she answered. *It was the only way to save both of you. As it was, sooner or later your struggles for dominance would have torn the heart you share until it stopped beating, and you would have both died—or become something worse. This world cannot risk such a sundered soul, not at this time.*

Did you do this to save us, then, or to save yourself from us? Ismai's bitter laughter rippled forth.

Both, she answered, stung by the truth in his words. *And the world, maybe. I do not care for the whole world to become as the Seared Lands—or for the living to become meat for the dead. What I have done here, I have done for love.*

Perhaps. Ismai frowned. *And it is possible that you have done us a great service, on this day. Yet such magic is* forbidden. *It has* always *been forbidden. To tear a song from the web of the world is worse than murder, as it erases a soul from the fabric of life. You have done this not to one soul, now, but two. Even among bonesingers, this would be seen as anathema. You have broken the ancient laws and must pay the price.*

No! Ismai wailed, but his voice deepened, even as that of the Lich King grew smoother in timbre. Soon where there had been two faces, two thoughts, two souls, there would be only one—and that one would want her dead.

Not dead, the voice said, gentler than she had expected. *Not dead but gone. Banished from the lands we claim— Dzirana Ani, last daughter of the deep magic, Keeper of the Song of Souls, you are hereby banished from every land we have claimed or will claim. In no city of mine may you show any of your faces, from Quarabala in the west to Eid Kalmut in the east you are hereby banished upon pain of death. In consideration of this service which you have rendered us, and at risk of your life, I give you four moons' time for your preparations and farewells. After such a span of days—and not one day more—you must absent yourself from my lands.*

It is done.

The Lich King pursed his fiery lips and blew.

Ani's world went dark.

"Ani, Ani! Oh, sweet girl, do not go, do not leave me here alone…"

Ani's heart broke to hear Askander's voice thick with weeping, and so she decided to open her eyes and live. She drew a great breath as she imagined a fish must when thrown back into the river, and it burned.

"I am not dead," she rasped, and was seized by a fit of coughing fit to crack her ribs. "*Ow!* Help me up. I—" Another fit of coughing, worse than the first, and for the next little while she could do nothing but fight to keep her lungs on the inside where they belonged. All the while Askander held her as if she was precious, as if she was fragile, as if she was the last good thing in the world and only he could keep her safe.

Finally the terrible coughs subsided. Askander offered her a waterskin, which she drained in one long pull.

"That helps," she said, and she relaxed back into his familiar embrace. "Ugh, I feel half dead."

"You smell half dead," Askander said into her hair, muffling a sob and a laugh at once. "You smell like… smoke. Like a funeral pyre. What happened?"

"Well, I either helped to save the world, or to doom it," she said. "At this point, I may be too tired to care. I need a bath, and a meal, and a good night's sleep, and then I need to get my girls out of one last mess before I leave these lands forever. I have been banished from all the cities of men between here and Eid... Eid Kalmut." The enormity of this hit her at once, and her voice broke. Was she never again to set foot in Aish Kalumm, to rest beneath the trees? To ride with the warriors of the Zeera, to see Akari Sun Dragon spread his wings across the desert sky?

Was she never to see Sulema again, to hold the daughter of her heart? It was too much, too much. Tears flowed like the river in springtime, washing away all traces of hope.

"Ah well," Askander said slowly, as his arms tightened around her, "I never much liked cities anyway." Her heart leapt, but Ani tried to shake her head, to pull free.

"You do not have to come with me."

"Of course I do." His arms were a tight band, strong and unyielding. Ani knew then that he would not let her go, not willingly, ever again. "Silly girl. You are not alone. You have never been alone—do you hear me?"

"I do," she said, and she meant it. In that moment, tired as she was, in pain, and sorrowing, Ani smiled through her tears, finally seeing for herself the beauty in truth. She would never be beautiful as Nurati had been beautiful, or wield such power as Hafsa Azeina. But she was Ani.

That was, and always had been, enough.

FORTY-FOUR

The young man walked at first ahead of her, then behind, shadows dancing at his feet and his lovely mantid trilling a harmony as he played the bird-skull flute. Waymaster, he called himself now, and smiled a silent refusal whenever she asked what he meant by that.

Sulema had often found herself resenting the attention paid to her mother's frail apprentice, scant as that had been. He had not been so much like a brother to her as a shadow and an unwanted one at that; his disappearance from Atualon had scarce raised any more fuss than had his birth, and grieved her less than it should.

Daru had vanished from the world moons ago, *pop!* like Mad Perian in the old stories, and *pop!* here he was again, full-grown and with eyes full of secrets. He wore strange, soft clothes of shimmering fabrics and walked with strength in his step. Daru played his flute as he led them through Shehannam, and shadows fled. Dreams begged for attention like children at his feet.

Sulema was made happier than she would have guessed by his odd and wonderful reappearance into her life, and not simply because he had come back from the moons—or wherever he had been—to lead them through the Dreaming Lands.

Shehannam was not a place, she had come to understand, that one wanted to wander through in the flesh without a guide. She had traveled to Shehannam in her dreams, but walking these woods in her waking flesh was not the same thing at all.

Even more than she had resented Daru's presence in her life, Sulema had begrudged the time her mother spent

393

wandering the mysteries of Shehannam; she had imagined it a place of beauty and deep mysteries. And it was; beautiful as a sandstorm, mysterious as the Lonely Road. But it was a perilous beauty, a terrible mystery, and if it was a dream it was the kind of dream you might wake from and be glad of the light. There were voices in this place that belonged to no body, winds that blew with no sound, and birds that were no more than clusters of eyes and wings.

The worst were the trees. They moved, she was sure of it. Sulema's eyes ached just from watching the trees, waiting for one of them to drop a branch on her head or try some other wicked trick. Daru had warned them not to pluck so much as a flower or leaf from the trees in Shehannam, or to even gather dead sticks for a fire, but they had scarce needed to be warned: nobody wanted to touch a tree that growled, the bark of which felt like human skin.

I love Daru more than I had expected, Sulema mused, *and Shehannam rather less.*

Sulema did not know how long they had been walking through the Dreaming Lands. More than an hour, she thought, less than a day. But it could have been a day and a half for all she could tell, or they might only have come a mile. The sky overhead—if such a thing could be called a sky—was cottony-gray and drear, giving no indication of the hour. The only shadows in this place were the ones they had brought with them, and Daru did not let them stop to eat, or drink, or answer any call of nature.

"Stray from the path but a little," he had warned, "and you will be lost."

None of them, not even the children, needed to be told a second time. The trees crowded oppressively close to the path, while the odd eye-birds careened through the air above them.

From somewhere deep in the woods there came a wail that was half-howl, half-scream; Sulema was altogether certain that she did not want to meet whatever foul thing made that noise.

A horn sounded, two short blasts and one long, and a chorus of dream-rending howls sprang up behind them and to either side.

"We are being hunted," Tamimeha remarked. She spoke the words in a matter-of-fact tone, but her eyes shone white round the edges.

Hannei slapped the back of one hand sharply into the palm of the other, and jerked her chin at the long line of people moving in a slow huddle like frightened sheep along the wild road. *Hurry*, she signed. *Hurry*. Though it was hardly necessary—the blood-chilling howls had encouraged even the most wretched and road-weary of them to greater haste. Daru's music leapt into a livelier tune: *pip-pip peeeeeeee, pip-pip peeee-ohhhh!*

Daru did not need to sleep while dreamshifting as her mother had; he simply half-closed his eyes and played the little bird-skull flute as he danced along, choosing this path or that seemingly at random. As he played now the trees seemed to press in on either side, moving closer together on some paths and clearing the way for others. Daru invariably took the closer, darker, more difficult paths.

"Who made these roads?" Sulema had asked him earlier. "Do humans live in the Dreaming Lands? My mother spoke so little of Shehannam."

"There are people who keep dwellings here—but they are certainly not humans," Daru had said. "And these are not roads."

"Not roads? What are they, then?"

"Game trails," he had answered.

Game trails and traps, she thought now. The trees were trying to herd them as hunters might herd tarbok into a ravine for easy slaughter.

"Hurry!" Sulema bellowed toward the end of the line, and heard the cry taken up by the Iponui. *Hurry, hurry, hurry*.

A branch crashed to the ground so close that had Sulema not jumped back, she would have been crushed.

Somewhere in the glooming woods, *something* laughed.

"It smells like a trap."

Sulema looked up into the brilliantly painted face of Tamimeha. The older woman stared straight ahead, grim-mouthed, but glanced at Sulema out of the corner of her eye.

"It probably is a trap," she allowed. "The trees—"

"Not the trees. Not just the trees, *ta*?" She nodded at Daru. "That one. You are certain this man is the same boy you lost?" It was not the first time she had asked.

"Yes," Sulema told her, and it was true. She was not sure that the trees in this place were really trees, or that the birds in this place were really birds, but Daru was Daru, sweet and true of heart, and always had been. "I am certain. He was my mother's apprentice. I trust him with my life."

The tall woman snorted. "You trust him with all our lives. Too easily, I think. At your word we have followed this stranger through a strange land, following blind as cave rats. What if he is leading us into a trap, as I suspect? Or... what if he leads us back to our own world, but we emerge into our world years older, as you say he has done?"

"Well," Sulema told her as the chorus of screaming howls sprang up behind them with renewed vigor, "I suppose you could try to retrace our steps and somehow make your way to the Seared Lands to be eaten by reavers. For my part, I am going to follow Daru to Min Yaarif. The food is better there, for one thing."

Tamimeha's lush mouth quirked and she almost smiled. "Beg your dragon you are right, greenlander. Because if you are not—"

The howls grew closer.

"—*we* are food. I believe we are being hunted."

"We *are* being hunted," Daru agreed, "and the hounds are quite close. We should hurry. But we are nearly there, if the place has not moved."

"Nearly where?"

"Nearly to a place where a door opens into the foothills of the Jehannim, not far from Min Yaarif. I have used this way before, many times—" He sighed wearily. "*If* the place has not moved this time. When we are close I will open the way, and you must gather the people and send them through quickly. Very quickly—we will not have much time. When the last of them has left Shehannam I will see to it that the way is shut, so that nothing might escape."

"Escape?" Sulema asked. That did not sound promising.

"What do you mean, 'this time'?" Tamimeha asked, frown deepening.

But Daru did not answer their questions. He simply raised the flute back to his lips and played on as he led them through the hostile forest toward an uncertain future.

The clearing to which Daru led them seemed small at first glance—too small to accommodate the throng of weary and frightened people—but either the trees made way, expanding in an ever-widening circle, or things were not as they appeared to her eyes.

Either way, Sulema would be glad to leave Shehannam as quickly as possible. It had not been so terrible a place to visit in her dreams, when Jinchua was there to guide her, but she could live the rest of her life without stepping upon these strange and shifting roads, and never feel a moment of regret.

Yet when they emerged once more into the waking world, what then? It had been a simple plan—somehow she would travel to and then escort a girl through the Seared Lands, retrieve the Mask of Sajani, and—again, somehow—use it to overthrow Pythos, retake the Dragon Throne, then figure out how to wield atulfah so that she could soothe the dragon's waking dreams and save the world.

"*I wanted an easier path for you,*" Hafsa Azeina had said.

Sulema touched the pouch at her waist, which held the mask, and tightened her grip on the fox-head staff.

I would have liked an easier path for me, too.

She missed her mother.

Her mother's apprentice—a man full-grown now, powerful and strange—played his bird-skull flute. As he did so the air rippled like water, shuddering and pulsing to the tune of his music, at last parting like the lids of a blind eye. This doorway—for so it seemed to Sulema—grew wide enough that several people might walk through it at once. When Daru stopped and tucked the flute back into its ornate pouch, it seemed to Sulema that the music played on, tangled in the air like beads braided into a stallion's mane.

The way steadied and held, as real as a tent-flap or doorframe in the waking lands. Daru opened his eyes, saw her and smiled, but it was a distracted expression, as if his mind had already flown beyond this small matter of walking between worlds.

As he has outgrown his clothing, Sulema thought, *so has he outgrown us.*

"Is it done?" Maika's high voice broke through her reverie.

"It is done," Daru answered, "and will hold until I close it again. Gather the people and send them through."

"Yes, let us be finished with this place," Maika said as she moved toward the door.

"I will go ahead of you," Tamimeha said, stepping before her queen, "and the Dragon Queen with me. You may trust this sorcery, Sulema an Wyvernus ne Atu, but I have my doubts."

"As you wish." Sulema schooled her face to politeness. "But we should—"

A long, low wail rose into the wind, a cry of such loneliness and despair that tears prickled at Sulema's eyes. The sound stirred her heart to pity, and to fear; her mother had told her stories, warned her of the dangers she might find if ever she was to enter Shehannam.

Of this peril, she had warned most vehemently.

"The Hounds are here," Sulema breathed. Another cry joined the first. This one sounded... hungry. "We need to leave *now*." She had not realized how unquiet the Dreaming Lands were. Between the wail and woe of the Quarabalese, the sound of the hounds, the wind in trees, the song of Shehannam was a paean of pain—

Until it stopped, and the silence came.

The wind stopped whistling on the heath. The weary travelers held their breaths. The hounds stopped howling among the trees.

The Dreaming Lands went quiet as death. All went still; the woods became nothing more than a gathering of trees bearing dumb, blind witness.

The silence settled upon them like fog. It stole the air from their lungs, stifling the sense of urgency that had brought them all from the deep heart of Saodan through the Edge of the Seared Lands and across the bone-strewn smoking length of the shadowed roads—

the silence had a name, it was sleepless, it hunted them

—to die.

The silence was broken by a fennec's bark—*Fly, foolish girl!*—but it was too late to run.

Three figures emerged from the mute woods. The first was a man, or man-seeming; broad-shouldered and tall with a ragged blue touar sagging round his face. He stopped an arrow's flight from Sulema; even at such a distance she could see the pale and shining skin of a reaver.

The second was a boy, perhaps, just shy of manhood. He was dressed in rags that had once been the robes of an apprentice dreamshifter, and stood with his head canted horribly to one side, one arm dangling loose and long as if it had been partly severed. The third figure...

Sulema stifled a yell. The third was a man she recognized. Had been a man she recognized; dreamshifters from the other prides would often come to consult with her mother, and Hamran of the Nisfim had been no exception. His robes billowed, though the wind had died. Then in the next moment he moved, raising his dreamshifter's staff as if to greet them, and she saw that the dreamshifter had corpse arms sewn down his sides and back. These twitched and flailed and flopped about so that her stomach heaved at the sight.

Hamran—the thing that had been Hamran—leveled its staff at her.

"You sssshall not—"

The sun rose over Shehannam, warming Sulema's back. She spared a startled glance over her shoulder and froze in shocked wonder. Maika, the child-queen of Quarabala, had thrown off her robes and blazed with the lights of a thousand worlds. She was the night sky and the stars, eyes round and bright as hunting moons, and her voice when she spoke sent tremors through the land.

"You dare," Maika thundered. "Foul thing of Eth, you dare turn that face to me?" The stars on her skin shone so brightly that Sulema could not bear to look upon her any longer. She looked back toward the dark figures who, faced with the splendor that was Maika, seemed to shrink back upon themselves.

Then the tormented thing which had been a dreamshifter raised his staff, and his many arms, and hissed. Shadows boiled from the trees and dropped like spiders to fall burning among the massed people.

Hannei brushed past Sulema and rushed at the corrupted dreamshifter, dark blades drawn, her face a mask of beauty and courage. Daru ran after her, seeming to grow larger with each step, his face hard and fearsome as any warden's. Maika's voice raised in a shout—"*A'olek hanolo o'aino o' ainakane au!*"—heat seared Sulema's back, and a burst of incandescent light lit the Dreaming Lands, leaving her half-blinded.

Sulema shifted her own dreamshifter's staff to her off hand and reached for the hilt of her shamsi, but froze as a sweet voice whispered in her ear. *Little sister*, it sang to her. *Let me see.*

Sulema had put the mask away when they had come into Shehannam—through the eyes of Sajani the place looked even stranger than it had with her own, and it spoke to her here too sweetly, too convincingly for comfort. As if in a dream she drew the precious thing forth now and pressed it upon her face. It felt warm, as always, and fit better than her own skin.

A jewel of time lay frozen in her sight, sparkling and pretty and precious. The dreaming shadows of this place had been raised and came against them as an army; Daru stood between these and Hannei, bird-skull flute raised to his lips. Hannei was poised like a dancer on the balls of her feet as she prepared to charge toward the reft Zeeranim, dark blades naked in the half-light. Tamimeha and her warriors were herding their people through the opening Daru had made between worlds, placing their bodies between their countrymen and danger.

All this she saw in one moment, and this she knew as well: they would die, all of them, their quests and lives come to naught as they fell into shadow. For it had been a trap deftly woven by the Nightmare Man, baited by the loves of her life, and it held her fast. Sulema could, if she so chose, run through the portal and into the waking world, saving herself.

No, she refused, countering the mask's unspoken suggestion. *No.*

Very well, replied the mask.

The next moment in time took a breath, setting the world to motion.

The big reaver, who had once been a warden, rushed sideways and leapt toward Hannei. His insectoid eyes shone with delight—

—but so did hers.

Hannei was beauty in youth and beauty in death as those blades danced to meet the reavers. She moved with all the deadly grace and speed of a wild vash'ai; Sulema knew in that instant that their match in the fighting-pit had been nothing, a child's game. Hannei Two-Blades, vengeance made flesh, was not playing now; her blades whistled through the air, calling for the reaver's second and final demise.

The smaller reaver, who had once been a boy even as Daru had been a boy, stretched his mouth impossibly wide and crouched, burnt eyes fixed on Sulema, hissing a death-rattle at her. But before he could leap Maika stepped into Sulema's line of sight, and she had been transformed by the moons-and-stars of an Illindrist's magic. The young queen's arms were raised as if in supplication, and she held the oracular spider cupped in her small hands. A seething mass of shadow boiled in the air before her. Tendrils of the stuff tore loose, whipping toward the boy reaver. He squealed, leaping back and away.

There was no time for wonder. The Arachnist-dreamshifter's many arms twitched, reaching for Sulema, and he screeched. Tangled webs of twisted weaving poured forth from the dark forest. This conjuration rose high, higher than the trees, obliterating the wool-gray sky. A plague of shadows rained down to land between the people and the wide doorway; they flew on wings of fear and crawled on legs of wrath and they were legion, they were endless, they were the death of all hope.

Even now you can save yourself, crooned the Mask of Sajani in Sulema's mind. *You have only to leave your companions behind, and they are going to die anyway. Their flesh will slow the advance of our enemies, their blood will slake the shadows' thirst for yours. You have only to run through the doorway and you will be safe, you will be free.*

Sulema drew her sword and laughed. "You do not know me," she said aloud. "I am a churra-headed brat, rash and foolish, and my faults are many. But I would never, *never*, abandon those I love."

Nor, it seemed, would those who had loved Sulema abandon her.

From the deeps of the dreaming forest came a ringing call, golden and pure as the reavers were foul. A bright light rose from behind the shadowed trees; it came with cleansing fire as no dawn ever could in the Dreaming Lands, driving out the unclean shadows before it. Hounds poured into the clearing, red-eyed and terrible, their slavering jaws flecked with bloodfoam and joy in their bass bayings as they fell upon the befouled shadows.

The reft warden had fallen to Hannei's blades, and the reft boy had been smothered beneath the weight of Maika's weavings. The Arachnist-dreamshifter raised his arms, raised his staff, and the putrid pulse of his power trembled through the thick air as he raised nightmares to life in the Dreaming Lands—

You have passed the test, little one, the Mask of Sajani sang. Her voice was a light in the dark places of Sulema's heart. She raised her own voice in song, like her father's yet unlike, green and cool and full of life where his had been hot and wrathful. Green things sprang up at the feet of the corrupted dreamshifter; vines wove about his feet, up his legs, winding round and round his many arms, trapping them against his side. The wide fanged mouth and burning eyes were lost to sight as a profusion of foliage smothered the nightmare thing, circling it as a forest might creep round an abandoned tower in a thousand years' time. Sulema sang, and Sajani laughed, as a green mound rose up to stand where the reft shadowmancer had been. It burst into bloom, a riot of colors for which Sulema had no names. As the dreamshifter came to this final verdant end his shadows burst into black dust which disappeared before it hit the ground.

The horn sounded again, a single clear note of victory, and the hounds faded back into the woods whence they had come. One of them, a massive pale beast with golden eyes, paused to regard Sulema for a long moment with eyes that held a mother's measure of suffering and love. Sulema took a step toward the beast, hand outstretched, as a terrible certainty rose in her heart.

A wail of terror rose up from the people of Quarabala. Daru touched her shoulder. His face was streaked with blood and soot, and his eyes were bright with grief.

"Sulema," he said. "We need to go. We need to get these people out of here; these lands belong to the Huntress. She suffers our presence for now, but if we linger—"

"My mother," she protested, turning to him. "Daru, that hound is—"

"Shhhhh," he said. "To speak of this is khutlani."

"You knew...?"

"Khutlani," he said again, and there was iron in his voice. "We need to leave now, Sulema. I cannot hold this Way open indefinitely, and if any are still here when it closes—"

Child, Jinchua urged, and her voice was not laughing. *Sweet child. You must do as the waymaster says; there is nothing more you can do for your mother. She knew the price, and paid it willingly.*

"We will go," Sulema said. Her voice cracked on that last word, and she hardened her heart. In this, she was her mother's daughter. "Tamimeha!" she called, seeing that the woman had survived and was walking toward her. "The way is open—we need to get these people out of here as quickly as possible."

Tamimeha gave a quick, short nod and raised a shout; the people of Quarabala began to pour out of the Dreaming Lands and into whatever future lay before them.

"This is not over," she said to Daru. "If my mother is being held here in some form—"

"Beware of promises made in the Dreaming Lands, Dreamshifter," he warned. "There are forces here beyond your understanding."

Sulema snorted a laugh. "There are many things beyond my understanding, Daru," she told him. "But you should know this—if my mother is a prisoner here, I will return, and I will free her. I swear it."

"Sulema—"

"I swear it," she insisted, and brought her staff down hard upon the ground once, twice, three times. "By my blood I do."

Somewhere deep in Shehannam the Huntress raised a golden shofar to her lips, and blew once, twice, three times.

It is done.

Those who had survived the exodus from the Seared Lands emerged wounded and weary into the waking world not far from Min Yaarif beside the twisted pillars of stone so like the Bones of Eth. The russet earth was hot as yesterday's embers, the sky a thin and angry blue, and Sulema could smell the city's shit-pits even from a distance. She was so glad to be once again in the waking world, and away from the Seared Lands, that she could have wept.

Rehaza Entanye took a deep breath of the foul air.

"Ahhh," she sighed, "thank Atu, I am home."

"*Uh!*" Maika twisted her tear-streaked face. "It stinks!"

Rehaza Entanye spat. "You think this stinks, you should smell the slave pits, *eh*—"

Abruptly Hannei reached for her swords.

"Ware!" Daru cried in a voice like that of a hunting eagle. He pointed at the twisted stone pillars, from between which a hooded figure emerged.

405

Nightmare Man, was Sulema's first thought. She had half expected him to be waiting for her, him and Pythos, to snatch her up before she could lay claim to the wretched throne. At second glance, however, she saw that the figure was female, slight of build and bold in manner. She had a warrior's swagger, though she wore no vest and bore no sword. Her dark arms were mottled from bonding, though there was no vash'ai at her side. She led a chestnut stallion, older but fine enough to—

Sulema jerked, and Hannei's jaw dropped open.

"Thief!" Sulema shouted and started toward the woman, staff upraised as fury and grief bloomed in her heart. It was too much; after the golden-eyed hound, it was too much. The old chestnut stallion could be none other than Ani's Talieso, and there was no way short of murder that any stranger might claim him. Behind her she heard Hannei's blades whisper free of their sheaths, eager for blood. "Step away from that horse. Do it now." She raised the fox-head staff and felt atulfah stir in the ground beneath, the sky above, the air in her lungs. "I *said*—"

"I heard you the first time." The woman stopped. Brown hands reached up and pushed the hood back, revealing the laughing face of a young woman. She was deeply striped and spotted, marked more strongly Zeeravashani than any warrior Sulema had ever seen, and her grin was pure mischief. "I may be old, but I am not deaf."

That voice!

Sulema froze in place, even as her sword-sister brushed past her at a dead sprint. Hannei dropped both swords as she ran, laughing and crying horribly, and swept the woman up into a crushing embrace. Talieso snorted and tossed his head, dancing to one side, pretending to be spooked. Sulema stared from the stallion, to her sword-sister and this... *stranger*... and back again.

"Istaza Ani?" she asked finally, as Hannei set the woman back on her feet, patting her and grinning from ear to ear, tears streaming down her face. "Istaza Ani? Is that you? But how..."

"It is just Ani now, brat," the woman said. "I am too young to be youthmistress now, I think."

"But... but..." Daru had grown old, and their youthmistress had grown young. *Next thing we know*, she thought sourly, *the moons will rise in the daytime, and Akari will fly at night. Men will be warriors and women will wear veils*. "I do not understand," she wailed at last, feeling every minute of five years old again.

"That has not changed, at least," the not-so-strange stranger laughed. "Though I see that you are a dreamshifter now, and you—" She broke off, looking at Hannei, and her face darkened with anger. "Ah, my Hannei, *you* have not been well treated at all. I would like a word with whoever has done this to you. You have both changed."

"*We* have changed?" Sulema squeaked. "You—you—I thought you were a stranger, leading Talieso. I might have killed you!" she finished lamely, though in the next moment she realized this woman would not be easy to kill.

"Ah well, it is a beautiful day to die." Ani laughed, arms outflung, her snarling cat's face turned up to the sky as if she would drink it. "But it is a better day to live. Come! We have much to discuss. I have food ready for you, and usca!"

"Usca?" Sulema exclaimed. Her eyes met Hannei's. They shared a grin, and for a moment—a moment only—all was right in the world.

They made camp there, under the shadow of the Bones of Illindra. So Sulema named them, having no better idea for what to call the stones and mindful of the stories she had heard of the spider-goddess who gave birth to all worlds and hung them all in her great web.

The people of Quarabala broke off in small groups to tend their hurts, to tend their young, to tend their hungry bellies with meager dried meat and gulps of water. For so many people to descend upon Min Yaarif at once would have been seen as an act of aggression. It would be best, Ani suggested, that they send a small contingent to the city to negotiate passage through and onto other lands.

Which other lands, she did not say, and Sulema hoped someone had an idea. Her father, she knew, had promised lands to Aasah in return for the Illindrist's service, but that was as far as her knowledge stretched.

Yaela might know, she thought, and sent up a fervent wish that the shadowmancer's apprentice had survived Jehannim and would meet them, perhaps as early as tomorrow. *And perhaps*, she thought wistfully, *my brother will be with her.* Perhaps one or the other of them might have a plan to resettle the people of Quarabala—for certainly the citizens of Min Yaarif would not be willing to accept so many refugees into their midst, and the proud warriors were unlikely to accept a life of slavery. Sulema also wanted to have a word or three with the green-eyed bitch for not mentioning that her little niece was also queen of Quarabala.

Her arm was a hot mess of fiery pain, and she had been having odd dreams of spiders and dark places filled with the restless dead. She needed the reaver anti-venom, and she needed it yesterday.

She stood beneath a carved spider's leg of twisted stone, rubbing her shoulder absently, when she heard footsteps approaching from behind. She turned and was surprised to see Ani, carrying something cradled in her arms. The youthmistress had always moved in silence.

Either my hearing is getting better, she thought to herself, *or Ani is getting old, no matter how she appears.*

"Where have your scars gone?" she asked. The youthmistress had been as proud of her battle-scarred hide as Askander had been of his.

Ani shrugged. "Gone," she said. "When I sing my bones

into another shape, and then back again, there can be… changes. I am never quite the person I started out to be."

"Sing your bones into another shape. So it is true—you are a bonesinger."

"I am." She stared at Sulema over the dark bundle. "Does it matter?"

"You knew my mother was a dream eater."

"I did."

"Do you know what that means?"

Ani regarded her for a long and solemn moment.

"I do."

"Friends do not judge one another for practicing forbidden magics."

"No." Ani smiled at her, and Sulema saw the shadow of a much younger Ani, one whom she would have liked to call "sister." "Friends help friends bury the bodies. Here, help me with this, would you, daughter of my old friend?"

"Certainly I will," Sulema said, taking the bundle. For all its bulk, it was lighter than she had expected, and sent a strange cold tingle up both her arms. "Mother of my heart." For so Ani was, and so she had always been. It was past time Sulema acknowledged all this woman meant to her.

Ani stared at her, and tears filled her eyes. "Daughter of my heart," she said slowly. "Let us camp here tonight in this dark place, shall we? Beneath the shadows of the stars. Let us eat, and drink usca—you and I, and Hannei, as well—and let tomorrow bring what it may." She reached out, took a corner of the bundle, and tugged.

"Nothing would please me more… oh. *Oh!*" Sulema gasped as the cloth she had been holding billowed out into the windless night. It filled the night sky, writhing and rippling like the sides of some tormented creature. Scales gleamed, teeth flashed, claws grasped, and eyes—dozens of them—stared out at her from the sides of her mother's tent.

"What? How did you… what?"

"Best not ask," Ani replied easily. She grabbed a corner of the unruly shelter and used a bone peg to set it firmly into the ground. "I will get this set, while you fetch Hannei. I want drink, and sleep, and my man Askander, but two of the three will do for this night, I suppose."

Sulema turned on her heels and trotted off in search of Hannei. She wondered whether her sword-sister would agree to join them, and how Ani had come by her mother's dreamshifting tent, and whether there was usca enough for all of them. In the end, she was gifted with answers to two of her three questions, and counted herself well satisfied.

She lay that night beneath the moons, beneath the humbled stars, beneath the eyes of her mother's vanquished enemies, and let herself be spun into darkness.

Upon waking the next morning, Sulema realized three things, and in quick succession.

Usca still gave her the worst hangovers.

Hannei snored worse now that she had lost her tongue.

Ani had slipped away some time during the night.

The first realization—the dull throb of her head and the hare's-ass taste in her mouth—was so all-encompassing that it took Sulema a moment to fully realize the import of Ani's absence. When at last it sank in, she shook Hannei awake, dodging fists and feet. Apparently usca was no kinder to her sword-sister than it had been to her. Then she struggled free from her tangled vest, which was sorely in need of a good wash, and ducked out the tent flap into the thin light of a new day—

There she found the whole world waiting to greet her.

Ani stood at the fore. Sulema's heart leapt in the presence of her erstwhile youthmistress, and she pushed away any notion of treachery. Forbidden magic or no, the song in Ani's bones was a true one and loyal. A vash'ai stood at the bonesinger's side, nearly as big as Khurra'an, pale as the dawn before a storm. He was a broken-tusked wild king of the desert, and the sight of him filled her with an equally fierce pride.

We are Zeeravashani, she thought. *My people and his. Wild or no, bonded or no, we are one.* The great sire looked at her, into her, and grunted his approval.

"Instead of bringing you to Min Yaarif," Ani said with a grin, "I brought Min Yaarif to you."

Sulema's eyes widened with surprise. Leviathus was there, resplendent in the striped trousers of a river pirate and the white vest of an Atualonian princeling.

I knew it would take more than a mymyc to bite through his stubborn hide, she thought with pride for her brother. Even so, a wave of relief surged through her. A crown of sea-bears' claws graced his brow, and a pair of long, thin blades were sheathed at either hip.

Then the smile dropped from her face. At his side, swathed in spidersilk the color of new leaves, eyes wide with dancing delight, stood Yaela.

Yaela may have freed me from Pythos's dungeons, but her manipulations and half-truths nearly got us all killed, Sulema thought. *She has much to answer for. If she gives me the cure I was promised, and the world for which we bargained, still I am not sure I will forgive her. She sent me on a quest into the Seared Lands to bring back a girl, and instead I have walked into a nightmare and returned with her people.*

And Sulema was not the only one with a mind to vengeance.

From the corner of her eye she saw Hannei start forward, swords drawn, a snarl contorting her beautiful face. Her eyes were fixed on Sharmutai, who in turn was staring at Sulema with an expression of naked hostility. Rehaza Entanye stepped toward Hannei, hands upraised, as the whoremistress turned to a swarthy woman behind her and that woman hefted an iron-tipped staff, ready to fight.

"Guts and goatfuckery," Ani spat, "put your weapons aside, all of you. No bloodshed before breakfast." When it became clear that her words were not being obeyed she repeated, "*Put your weapons down.*" There was a power in her voice, old as the roots of hills, of a kind that Sulema had never felt before. Weapons were sheathed and hate-filled eyes averted... for the moment.

"Wise choice," the bonesinger noted dryly. "I will set the lot of you to shoveling churra shit—do not think I would not. Now! Let us break our fast together as we decide the fate of the world."

"We are missing a player," Leviathus noted. "The Dragon Queen is among us," he nodded to Sulema, "the queen of Quarabala—and the pirate king as well, or so I am told—but where is the Lich King?"

"Lich King?" Sulema stared. "What, or who, is the Lich King?" He did not sound like someone she would care to meet.

"A horror from the old stories." Maika's voice rang out as she took her place beside Sulema. She had dressed in Quarabalese finery, orange and red, black and yellow— hastily, it seemed, as her braids wanted straightening and her robes were wrinkled. A jeweled filigree like the Web of Illindra bound up her braided hair, and a crown of pale jewels graced her smooth dark brow. "Do you claim now that those stories are real?" There was an edge of fear in her voice.

"All stories are real," Ani smiled. "You of all people should know that, queen of a lost people. Welcome, young Maika. I am delighted to see that you and your people have made it to safety."

"There is no safety in this world," Akamaia said. She had taken her place beside Maika. "You of all people should know *that*, Bonesinger. And you will address Queen Kentakuyan a'o Maika i Kaka'ahuana li'i as 'your Magnificence.'"

"There is no safety in this world," Ani acknowledged with a slow nod, "but the Dziranim, like our Zeerani cousins, give no honorific to queen or king. Still, empty bellies make for hard heads. Let us fill ours, that our minds may be open and our words soft, shall we?" Her eyes were bright and her smile wide, but Sulema knew the threat behind her words. Tension built beneath the twisted rocks like thunderclouds in the spring. Silence fell upon them.

Hannei's stomach snarled like a vash'ai.

Snickers broke out among those close enough to hear, and the tension was broken.

"It is settled, then," Ani said. "Let us eat!"

The servants and slaves of Sharmutai laid out pillows and cushions, dining-cloths and bowls of sweet water, and the assemblage settled down to break their fast. Sulema chose a particularly beautiful purple cushion for her own, and leaned close to Hannei, who reclined nearby.

"You did that on purpose," she accused. That had been one of her friend's oldest tricks, swallowing air so that she could make her stomach rumble loudly at inopportune times, to the delight of her pride-mates and the disgust of their elders.

Hannei stared at her, the very picture of youthful innocence.

"*Ehuani*," Sulema whispered to her friend, and touched her arm. "You were right all along." There was more beauty to be found in facing the truth than in dreams and wishes.

Saghaani, mouthed Hannei, touching her heart and pointing. *You. Right. Also.*

Then Sulema knew that all was well between them. As voices rose and rumbled all about them, as introductions and alliances were made, two warriors of the Zeera exchanged mugs of sweet water and a solemn, silent vow.

Sisters.

Forever.

413

All that remained were crumbs, and a third mug of coffee had just convinced Sulema that she might, indeed, be able to conquer the world, when the Lich King joined their party.

Her first warning was a low rumble, nearly inaudible. Ani leapt to her feet, Inna'hael following. Only then did Sulema realize that the pale sire had been growling. The party's attention was turned from the thin niceties of people who were politely—but with growing impatience—avoiding a necessary and ugly discussion. Sulema raised a hand to shield her eyes from the bright midmorning sun and gasped.

A man moved toward them across the hot sands. The way he strode spoke of a warrior-king—of that there could be no doubt—conquering and claiming all around him with every step. Broad of shoulder, loose and narrow of hip, he wore an antlered helm and gold-chased armor, and the sword at his side was long and broad.

A fell light was in his eye, and his mouth was hard; grim was his face and grim his companions too, and these could be none but the armies of dead roused somehow from their ages-long sleep in Eid Kalmut. At the king's left side walked a young girl, dark and darkly lovely and no less formidable than the antlered man. At his right hand, wearing half a mask and all the confidence of youth, walked the last man Sulema might have expected—or wished—to see.

All thoughts of fear or wonder were driven from her mind as fury bloomed hot and dry in her breast.

"Mattu Halfmask," she hissed, making as if to rise to her feet. *He said he loved me*, she thought. *That he could not live without me. Then he left me to die in his brother's dungeons.* "That half-faced, half-witted, half-dicked son of a diseased goat, he—"

A hand clamped hard on her wounded shoulder, drawing a surprised yelp of pain. Sulema shook free of the grip and rounded on her attacker but froze at the look on Hannei's face. Her sword-sister had gone pale with shock and was pointing toward the Lich King, mouthing something that Sulema could not quite catch.

"What?" She looked at the king, then back at her friend. "Yes, Ani—Bonesinger Ani—seems to know him. So what is it that—"

She stopped, struck dumb with her mouth hanging open.

"What!" she shouted. "*Is that...! Is that...!*"

It was Ismai, as Hannei had been trying to warn her. The younger son of Nurati was also—somehow, impossibly—the Lich King of Eid Kalmut. Sulema moaned and bowed her aching head, cradling it in both hands.

"If I am dreaming," she said to Hannei, "please wake me. If I am not—ow. *Ow!*"

Hannei punched her again, *hard*, in her wounded shoulder. She glared at Sulema, hands flowing into the quick, harsh hand-language of hunters.

Sleep. No. Wake. Everything—here she gestured around them, at the entire assemblage, the land and river and sky above—*everything. Gone. Shit.*

Then all eyes were on the two Zeerani warriors, as disapproving scowls appeared on every face, and they offended allies and enemies alike.

By bursting into uncontrollable laughter.

The world had indeed, as Hannei had said, gone to shit. The dead walked again, and Ismai—Tammas's sweet little brother—was their king. The Lich King! Pythos ruled from Atukos, and the Nightmare Man was working to wake Sajani through him. She had helped to lead an entire people onto the very doorstep of Min Yaarif, and she had no idea where they might go from here. Hannei was a cold-hearted killer, Ani was a mistress of dark forbidden arts, and Sulema—

415

Sulema would have torn her way back into Shehannam and run all the way back to the Seared Lands if it would get her away from the endless talking. The sun set, food was brought—three meals in all, plenty of food if not of the best quality—and still the planning rolled on and on.

She supposed it was necessary, but Sulema was a warrior, not a general. The rush of their final battle had worn off, and Sulema mostly just wished for sleep.

Now and again the ground would rumble and that would cause a momentary lull in their discussions; the reminder that if they failed here, if their desperate plans to topple Pythos and put Sulema on the Dragon Throne were unsuccessful, the whole world would pay the price.

Finally, the edges of the sky went to red, and an agreement was reached. Though it seemed at times like madness, they would combine their forces, meeting on the banks of the Dibris in a two-moons' time, and set forth for Atualon. Together they would wage war upon Pythos, upon the Nightmare Man, and any who dared oppose them.

They would place the Dragon Queen on her throne.

Sulema had agreed to alliances and concessions which she only half understood, looking to Ani, to her brother, and to Yaela for guidance. She promised lands which may never be hers to give to the Quarabalese and to the river pirates; her brother and the sorcerer's apprentice dreamed, it seemed, of building a splendid city at the mouth of the Dibris. She even conceded lands and riches to Sharmutai the whoremistress, though in Sulema's estimation that woman deserved no more land than would be needed to build a funeral pyre. Much as it galled, Sulema had to admit that Yaela had not precisely lied to her about her niece, and that the whoremistress had access to fighters and weapons that they sorely needed. She had to temper her anger and focus in ways her training had never prepared her to endure.

The fate of the world depended on it.

By the time they were done, though, round and round in her head like sand-dae, there swirled the words of a poem—or the end of one at least. Ani had forced her to recite it when she was young and the world was full of hope.

> *When the Dragon wakes at last,*
> *Who will rise and who will fall?*
> *Shaman, sorcerer, lover, liar,*
> *Who will rise and rule them all?*

Sourly she thought, *If I had ever suspected that the poet might be talking about me, I would have run away, far away, and never looked back. The only thing that could possibly be worse would be if the dragon were to truly wake.*

The earth rumbled again, mocking her and all her grand plans. If the dragon woke, all the planning in the world would not save them.

FORTY-FIVE

Jian could not have said for how long he stood in the tiny cell he shared with his dead mother, his Issuq eyes cutting through the gloom. He could feel the passage of time, the ebb and flow of it, moons rolling overhead like waves over a coral reef. Several times the world around them had been gripped in a violent shaking, as if it, too, shared his grief.

The dragon is waking, he thought. *Only let me avenge my mother, my Tsali'gei—and my son, my murdered son— before Sajani destroys the world, and I will be at peace.*

The sharp stink of death burned in his nostrils as the indignity of Tiungpei's unwashed, untended body burned in his heart. These things were to him as the flames of a funeral pyre, cleansing his spirit for the fight ahead.

His ears twitched. There were footsteps in the hallway, furtive and soft. Not the iron-nailed bootsteps of imperial soldiers, but the hurry-scurry-shush of sandaled feet. So it was to be a secret assassination after all, and not a public execution. He growled low in his throat, skin prickling.

Cowards.

He bared his teeth but breathed softly, gently stifling a snarl. If this was to be the end of him, let him make such an end that poets could only speak of it in hushed tones, and scribes would write his name in blood ink. Let him die not as his mother had, a bright flame pinched out without so much as a wisp of smoke to protest the dying of her light, but as Sajani herself, whose waking would consume them all.

Metal scraped against stone and there was a faint snick as a key was turned in a lock. The door cracked open, so carefully as to be silent to all but an Issuq's ears.

Come for me, then, he bade them silently. *I am ready.* The door swung wider and he sprang—then twisted midair, giving a soft yelp of surprise at the pale face which stared up at him, dark eyes wide. Giella stepped quickly to one side, and Jian landed in a crouch at her feet, bristling and trembling all over.

"Hush," she said in a voice softer than a flower's death. "Hush now. Come with—" She took a deep breath, and let it out again in a long *hissssss*. Her eyes widened, flashing crimson in the netherlight.

"Oh, Jian," she whispered. "Oh, Jian, I am so sorry."

She reached out a tentative hand to touch his shoulder, but he flinched back. Turning instead to the still and shrouded form of Tiungpei, he stooped to gather her into his arms. Giella said no word—not to hurry him along, or to suggest that he leave his mother's body behind in their haste to be gone from that place. She waited for him to do what he must, as if they had all the time in the world.

For this act of kindness, Jian would be forever grateful.

There was a faint light in the hallway, effective as the midmorning sun to Jian's preternatural eyes. He stopped short, clutching his precious bundle, when he realized that Giella had not come alone. A girl was with her, dressed in raptor-hide armor, young but hard-eyed. She flashed a quick smile, and Jian saw that her teeth had been filed to sharp points. She made hand-signs to him and the White Nightingale, signs with which Jian was not familiar but which clearly said, *Come. Follow me. This way.*

He glanced toward Giella, but she had already fallen into step with the girl, moving at a fast lope down the hallway. What choice had he, after all? Hugging his mother's body close to his chest, his heart, Tsun-ju Jian de Allyr followed.

❖

They did not travel upward, in reverse to the direction Jian's handlers had brought him, and from which they would soon come to drag him to his death. They moved down into a maze of twisting, narrow passages, all of which seemed alike.

Deeper they went as the passage became narrower, the roof steeper till Jian had to jog bent nearly double, the robe that was his mother's shroud dragging on the ground between his feet. On they ran till it seemed to him that they must have been swallowed by Sajani Earth Dragon from the old stories. Perhaps he was sleeping and caught in a nightmare—or perhaps he had already been executed, and this was one of the levels of Yosh, in which he would run forever carrying his mother's dead body.

Holding onto his Issuq-form as they ran began to exhaust his energy, so he let it slip. Once he had shifted, however, it felt to him as if he could do so again with far less effort than before. It was there, part of him, swimming beneath the surface of his flesh as the creatures swam in the sea.

Padding near-silently along the stone floor, passing hallways on this side or that, they were joined by people the likes of whom Jian had never seen. They came singly or in pairs or even small groups. Most, but not all of them were young, grim-faced, no few of them scarred, all of them dressed and armed for battle. If they glanced at him at all it was with the kind of look used by one hunter to acknowledge another, without indicating deference or challenge. One older man grimaced when he saw what Jian carried, and made a hand-sign near his heart that might have indicated sorrow. Aside from that brief gesture, Jian might as well not have been there at all.

Eventually the path ended in a wall. The girl with the raptor armor held up a hand, indicating that they should stop—though with no passages to either side, there was not much else they could have done. Then she held her hands up to her mouth. Jian noticed with some surprise that she was missing the middle finger on either hand, and that these wounds appeared to be recently inflicted. Her cheeks puffed out and she blew gently, so that a high warbling trill almost like a bird's call rose up and danced around them.

A crack appeared in the wall and widened. Cool air curled in to meet them, as a cleverly hidden door swung wide. What looked like a small round room lay beyond. When they had all gathered together in that space, the door shut again. The air eddied around them and up, drawing Jian's eyes toward the pearl-gray sky of first dawn high above their heads. They were at the bottom of a pit, or—

"A well," Giella whispered, her words quiet and dark. "A witching well, long covered and forgotten." She reached out and grasped the end of a long, thick rope and gave it a tug.

"Witching well," Jian said, and he shivered. "Wicked."

"Yes," Giella agreed. She waited for Jian's nod of assent before beginning to wind the rope about his waist, securing Tiungpei's body to his as she did so, and then giving the cord a series of sharp tugs. Jian fought the urge to struggle against them as they tightened and then began to draw him slightly upward. "Very wicked. Let us go now and grant the darkest wishes of our hearts, shall we?"

Jian bowed his head so that he pressed a kiss to Tiungpei's cold, enshrouded forehead, and allowed himself to be raised up into the dawn.

> *Heart of Illindra, Soul of Eth,*
> *Blood of the innocent condemned to death.*
> *Under the moons, combine the three,*
> *Coin enough to set you free.*

As it turned out, the witching well had been bricked up, buried, and lost beneath the garden path of one of the emperor's most exclusive comfort houses. Ancient and fell-hearted, Jian could hear it talking to him, wicked whispers that tickled the back of his mind, but he was Issuq, not human. Such things held no sway over him unless he wished to let them. Still, Jian was aware of what the thing was, what it could do to him.

What it could do *for* him.

"Vengeance," he murmured as he reached the mouth. He sat on the edge and the rope was removed. Hands reached to take his mother's body and he let them, the fabric of her shroud slipping wetly through his hands, anointing his palms with her blood.

Blood of the innocent, he thought. There was not a child in Sindan who did not know that rhyme. He grasped the object that he wore threaded on a thong about his neck, a trinket gifted to him upon his arrival in the Twilight Lands. It was a red disc a bit smaller than his palm, taken from the carcass of a shongwei. It was a powerful talisman worth more than the combined wealth of three or four villages the size of Bizhan. Enough that it would have bought his freedom from the emperor, were he still a slave. Such a thing was called *daes-olouru*, in his father's tongue. In the lands of men, it had a different name.

Blood penny.

Jian held the blood penny up to the light of the full moons. They were fading with the dawn's first light, but his need was great, and he called to them with all the power of his sea-born soul. He paused, ignoring the hands that still tugged at him, the voices imploring him to *hurry, hurry*. Closed his eyes and flung his challenge.

"Vengeance best served hot," he growled. The blood penny burned in his hand with a hungry, eager heat.

"Vengeance best served cold," he continued, louder now, and his voice broke as he thought of the cold, still body of Tiungpei. *My mother.* The blood penny shifted in his hand like a live thing, and then burned his flesh again, this time with a searing chill.

"No!" Giella cried, as if from a great distance. She grabbed at him, but he was stronger than she, and determined to do this thing no matter the cost to himself.

"Serve it up with meat and wine," he finished, opening his eyes and staring into the horror-stricken face of the White Nightingale. "One day old." For that was how long it had been since they murdered her.

One day old, the well crooned. *One day cold.*

One day dead.

Jian held his fist over the well's hungry mouth and forced his fingers to uncurl. Even in the dying moonlight the blood penny shone bright and eager with malicious intent, a thing of terrible beauty. It pulsed for a moment and then burst into light like blood made fire, a living flame that seared his heart but not his flesh. The witching well burst into song, a dirge, a canticle of bone and ash.

Then Jian smiled at Giella, a smile that tasted as bitter and sweet and full of promise as the last dawn of Khanbul. Bitter as his mother's blood, smeared on his lips with which he had kissed her. Sweet as the innocent child she had raised, and who had died with her in the emperor's dungeons.

Giella let go of his arm and nodded.

"I see you," she whispered.

"Yes," he said. The moonlight and the bloodlight of a new day floated across the surface of the blood penny as he turned his hand over and let it fall down... down... down into the blackness, carrying with it the darkest wishes of his heart.

"Let them burn," he said, thinking of his mother, of Perri, even of Naruteo, who had only been what they had made of him. "Let them all *burn*."

Though such things were generally expected of the Daechen, Jian had never been inside a comfort house. His mother had been wealthy by village standards, but he had had no experience with things such as magical colored lanterns of spidersilk and wormsilk, of fine robes and golden harps, of sandalwood floors soft as a woman's skin.

All these things and more he would have traded for one stern look from Tiungpei, and in that moment none of them was worth a handful of goat shit to Jian. For *she* stood there, bathed in light, surrounded by beautiful girls and boys like a lotus among lesser flowers, and she was holding their son in her arms.

"Tsali'gei!" he cried aloud, not caring who heard, not caring about anything but that she was alive, alive, she and their son both. He crossed the floor in half a dozen strides, swept her up in his bloody arms, buried his face in her neck, and burst into great gulping sobs fit to tear the heart from his chest. His son, displeased at being dislodged, burst into howls of outrage.

"Tsali'gei," Jian said again, this time a harsh whisper. "Tsali'gei, oh my love, oh my heart, you are alive." It had not occurred to him that this might be so. He had buried all thought of her fate and that of their son deep in the bitter soil of his heart.

"I am here," she answered. "We are here... but you are squishing the baby."

Jian pulled back a little. Not much.

"The baby," he said, and frowned at a distressing thought. His son might have died without so much as a name. How could they have found one another along the Lonely Road, if his son had had no name? It was a ridiculous notion, perhaps, which once lodged in his mind would not let go. He reached up and stroked the infant's fat little cheek, grimacing at the smear of blood he left behind on the innocent skin. His son met him stare for stare, bared his gums in defiance, and wailed all the louder.

Tsali'gei laughed a little, despite their circumstances.

"He howls like a storm out to sea," she remarked. "He is your son, blood and bone."

"My son. My little son. The delight of my heart." That he could even feel joy at such a time was a wonder. It felt like treachery.

"And of your mother's, as well. Jian…" she began.

"I know," he said. His eyes met hers, storm and sea, and the world around them disappeared. He was there, she was there, and their tiny son, who had remembered he had a thumb and was sucking it noisily. "She died in my… in my arms." His last word broke on a sob and he was weeping again, hot tears dripping down his face and soaking the thin undershirt. He thought of the yellow silk robe she had made him so long ago—*just this past spring, in the world of men.* The realization that even that was lost to him now was more than his heart could bear.

"I have nothing left of her," he said. "Not even a pearl."

"You have *you*, and you were her greatest treasure," Tsali'gei said, gently as morning in the Twilight Lands. "And him," she continued, bouncing the child on her hip. "And those two damned goats, still back at her house." She was trying to tease a smile from him, Jian knew, but her big eyes were red and deep with grief.

They clung to one another like humans who had been lost at sea, with no shore in sight. Finally he pulled back a little further and held his arms out for the child, who came to him willingly.

"My son," Jian said again. The words still felt strange to him. He had been but sixteen when the child was conceived, and though he had spent five years fighting his father's wars in the Twilight Lands, still he felt much too young to be a father. How much worse it must be for Tsali'gei, he realized, who bore and cared for him all alone?

"I was not there," he began.

"You are here now," she said firmly, putting one hand on his shoulder and the other on their son's. "You are not alone. We are your family." Her eyes held every treasure Jian had ever wanted.

"We will not forget Tiungpei," Tsali'gei went on. "I loved her, too."

Jian looked from her to their child, and back again. "Maybe..." he began but then stopped, unsure how to go on. His heart was heavy.

Tsali'gei looked at him and said nothing, waiting for him to continue.

"Maybe," he said at last. "I was thinking... thinking we could name him Tiungren," he finished all in a rush. "I know it is too early for a name, but—"

"Tsun-ju Tiungren," Tsali'gei said, gazing thoughtfully upon their son. "First of his name." She looked up at Jian, and there was fire in her eyes. "It suits him."

"First of his name?" Jian stared at her. His Issuq-self growled approvingly at the fierce look she gave him. "You make him sound like an emperor."

"Do I?" she asked. "Perhaps I do." She turned to look over her shoulder and clucked her tongue at one of the painted girls, who hurried over and took little Tiungren up in her eager young arms. "Do you mind watching him for me?" she asked unnecessarily as the courtesan was cooing and gurgling in an attempt to charm a smile from the baby.

"Where are you going?" the girl asked, never looking up from her charge's face. He had Issuq eyes, like those of both his parents, and she was obviously smitten. "Will you be long? Shall I heat some goat's milk?"

"Yes," Tsali'gei told her, "and take him to the estate, the one in Bizhan. Wait for us there. Take as many guards as you like, and protect him well."

"I will guard him with my life," the girl proclaimed solemnly, glancing up. Jian saw that her eyes were golden-green, much as a cat's, and that her face had a faintly feline cast to it. She was Daezhu, then, not human. This notion was borne out when she smiled a predator's smile. "If anyone but me touches him, I will *eat* them."

"You do that," Tsali'gei said approvingly. "We will meet you at the estate when we can. There are servants there, and guards... You and Tiungren will have everything you need until we can join you."

"Tiungren?" the girl's voice rose with delight. "He has a name, then? So soon!"

"Yes. He is named for Tiungpei, his *ah-ma*."

"Tiungren." The girl's voice softened to a contented purr, and she cast a quick look at Jian. "Hai-bao Tiungren de Jian. A warrior's name. It is good."

Tsali'gei nodded solemnly, and Jian grunted his approval. The girl had given Tsali'gei's family name, as was proper, and she was right. It was good. It was, perhaps, the only good thing about this night. And then the words Tsali'gei had been speaking all came together, and Jian peered at her.

"You are not going with them?" he asked.

"Of course not," Tsali'gei said. Her voice was calm and sure, but all the pain in the world was in her eyes as she bent to kiss her infant son goodbye. "We are going to war."

As the sun rose in the sky, the comfort house became a staging ground. This was to be war, not some skirmish led by a handful of malcontents ill prepared and quickly crushed beneath the emperor's heel.

The White Nightingale, it seemed, had been singing a song for discontent for some years, and enough people had listened to her tune that a formidable force was ready to come dancing to her tune. Blacksmiths she had, women and men who worked by day to make swords for the emperor and by night to forge swords which might be used to bring

427

an emperor down. Stockpiles of weapons and armor had been building, waiting for a day that might never come, a day when the citizen-slaves of Sindan and those of the Daechen who longed to break free might unite under one banner and throw off the shackles of tyranny.

Or die trying, Jian thought, which seemed a much likelier outcome. He had seen the emperor's forces, and his luminists, and truth be told he did not believe with all his heart that they could do this mad thing. *Certainly, it is a thing worth fighting for, worth dying for. But Tsali'gei—*

"Stop," she growled at him as one of the serving-girls helped lace up her lacquered armor. "For the third time, stop thinking that I should run to safety with Tiungren. If you so much as hint at it again, I will bite your ear off."

Jian risked his ear. "I am thinking it," he grumbled. "And where did you get that armor, anyway?" It fit her as perfectly as any lady's gown.

"Your mother made it for me."

Jian gaped. "She did not."

"She did. It was my bride-gift." Then she huffed. "Are you going to stand there and say Tiungpei did not know what she was doing?"

"But—"

"Jian," she said, placing her hand against his cheek, "let us not fight, today of all days. My place is here, with you, fighting this fight. Let us not take the risk that our last words to each other will be said in anger." Jian's heart squeezed painfully in his chest, but he bowed his head to her.

"As you wish."

"That is better." She laughed a little, patted his cheek, and pulled a helmet on over her hair. "Just remember to end all of our arguments with those words, Tsun-ju Jian, and you may yet survive to a ripe old age."

Jian smiled as the maidservants giggled, wishing he could preserve this moment like an insect in amber, safe from the marches of time. He glanced up and caught Giella's eye. She was staring at him, at him and Tsali'gei, with a look on her face that said *this is all I've ever wanted*.

Do not envy us, Jian wished at her silently. *Not until the sun has set on this day, at any rate*. It might seem to the White Nightingale that Jian and Tsali'gei had found great good fortune in their love for each other—and they had—but it felt to Jian that they had far too much to lose.

FORTY-SIX

Genzhou Field had been many things over the course of its history. Orchards and crops had been planted and harvested here, according to the whim of the day's rulers. Peach trees had spread their arms wide to the summer sky, fields of grain had covered the ground, and for a while there had been a mill with a wheel-house and a colorfully painted wheel which combined all the magics of earth and air, fire and water so that priests could bake rice-cakes for the emperor's feasts.

Had they known the place's deeper secrets, its darker magics, men might not have been so eager to eat the fruits which grew in this rich soil. Great battles had been fought here, in the days of the first empire. The bodies of the dead, too numerous to bury, had been left to find their own way back to the earth. Those farmers who tilled too deep, who spent too much time looking at the round stones and long bones unearthed by their labors, knew well that the sweet fruit of their harvest held a dark and bitter truth.

That the best things in Sindan grew from the remains of the fallen.

It was in this place that Jian met his army. Not his entire army, but a select few of those who had pledged to fight and die for him. There were bands of wild daeborn whose parents or villages had hidden them from the emperor's clutches, or who had escaped on their own. These were represented by the girl Awitsu and her strange dark-skinned, moon-haired companion Kanati.

Others came from the sea tribes and forest peoples, the plains folk and even members of the raptor clans, strange mountain folk who so rarely came down from their jagged peaks. These had elected as their champion another girl who seemed too young to be a warrior of any kind, but whose eyes were filled with ancient pain. This was the eight-fingered girl with the raptor hide armor who had come with Giella to bring Jian up from the emperor's dungeons. Jian had seen her before—he was certain of it—but could not for the life of him remember when, or how, they had met. The confusion must have been written upon his face for, when presented to him, she burst out laughing, startling the chinmong at her side so that it raised its crest and hissed menacingly.

"I am Holuikhan," she said, staring into his eyes. "You do not remember me."

An image came to him then of a young one, face streaked with dirt and tears...

"The girl in the field!" he exclaimed. "The one who saw the yellow Daechen training—I remember you, now."

"Yes," she said, "the girl you did not kill." She brought both fists to her chest, mountain-style, bowed low from the waist and held it, indicating deep respect. The raptor at her side, however, drew the scaled lips back from its sharp teeth and issued a series of whistles.

"Jijao!" the girl hissed. She straightened, and Jian could see that her face had gone as red as sunrise. "Do not be *rude*!"

Jian laughed, causing the raptor to cock her head and give him a skeptical side-eyed look.

"Fortunately, I do not speak raptor-tongue," he said, "but no doubt she is right in her assessment of me."

Near the end of the line stood a man, young and proud in stance, wearing armor unlike any Jian had previously seen. Boiled leather lacquered in blue and studded with white steel, it shone like silver and sapphires. The hairs at the nape of Jian's neck prickled as the man came near, and the scent of bullhide filled his nostrils. The bull was sacred to Emperor

Tiachu, the use of its hide an offense punishable by death. To fashion armor from the hide of a bull was to declare war not upon Sindan, but upon the emperor himself.

When the crowd between them parted, and Jian got his first full look at the armor, the full impact of what they were doing hit him like a massive wave, destroying the villages and cities of the world in his heart. Upon his chest, this man wore the image of a blue sea-bear, Jian's own sigil.

I have declared war upon the emperor, he realized. It was a thing he had known, of course, but seeing his own blue bear made it real, somehow. The young man strode up to the little knoll where Jian stood and gave a shallow, stiff bow as from one general to another.

"Daechen Jian."

Jian gasped when he recognized the voice which echoed from behind the lacquered helm.

"Chei!"

"Your Illumination." The boy who had once befriended Jian, and once tried to kill him, held his bow a moment longer than was necessary. "The blue Daechen have come. We stand ready." A rumble, then a low roar rose from the assembled crowd. Human and Dae alike, fierce-eyed and proud, raised fists to the sky as this Daechen prince spoke aloud those words which had grown up in all their hearts like the fruits of a bitter harvest.

"We stand ready."

As first Tsali'gei and then Giella climbed the hill to stand beside him, Jian turned in a slow circle, trying to see every face, every banner. If he was to send these people to war, if they were all going to die for him—the likeliest outcome of this morning's events, no matter which way he looked at it—Jian owed them this much, at least. That he had looked upon their faces.

He had studied the words of the great generals, had read the stirring accounts of heroes as they rose up from the dust of old parchments. Many times he had sat in his father's study, bent over scrolls and books and stacks of loose paper, dreaming of the day he would wage war upon Khanbul. Of the fine words with which he would stir his troops' hearts to bloodlust and victory. Looking at these people before him, Jian found that his dreams, his words, were too small to have captured this moment.

Nothing he could say now, or do, would ever repay the blood debt he was about to incur. He closed his eyes and bowed deeply to them all, letting the tears fall from his eyes, to better express his gratitude.

Giella, the White Nightingale, unfurled a banner which she carried in her arms, and raised it high for them all to see. It swam upon the wind like an Issuq in stormy waters—the blue bear on a field of pearl, calling them home. Jian held up one hand for silence, only then knowing the words he would say.

Ehuani, he thought, savoring the desert word in his mind. It suited the moment. *I give them the truth*.

"We ride to Khanbul," he said so that his voice would carry. "We ride to war. It is likely, my friends, that we ride to our deaths." He thought of his mother, windblown and ruddy-cheeked, in love with the sea. Of his own son, who would grow up an orphan, if fate allowed him to grow up at all. And he thought of Perri, his friend, who like so many Daechen before him had been killed for no reason at all.

"Whether we live today or we die," he told them, and realized that he had at last found the heart of the matter. "Whether the emperor and his palace fall to our swords, or whether he rises tomorrow morning as if none of this had ever happened, we are planting a seed here today. A seed which, soon or late, will grow to a tree whose roots will tear down the walls of those who live in the Forbidden City. Let our blood sweeten the soil of this planting, that the tree of new life may rise from our bones and spread to give shade to our children.

"Yesterday the Daechen emperor in his palace of flowers sat upon his powdered arse, content in the knowledge that he could do with our lives as he wished, forever. Today is the day we break him free of that dream, my friends. Today we take the first steps along the long road to our peoples' freedom. Today we ride to Khanbul, and to war!"

"To war!" Chei bellowed, and he went to his knees before Jian. The movement spread like ripples upon a pond as those assembled also fell to their knees and raised their voices as one.

"*To Khanbul!*" they shouted. "*To freedom! To war!*"

To death, Jian thought, raising his hands to the sky.

He smiled.

Three times Jian had come to the shining wall that surrounded the Forbidden City. Once as a prince, once as an ambassador.

Now he came to conquer the shining Wall of Swords, or to die upon it.

The army had swelled in size as they moved toward the city. Peasants and soldiers, raptor hunters and wild daeborn, they came singly, or by the tens, or hundreds. Teams of ghella lowed as they pulled carts laden with the engines of war. Soon the ground trembled at the news of their coming.

A pair of figures broke from the trees and dashed toward them. Jian, recognizing them as Holuikhan and her chinmong, held up a hand. Shouts of "Halt, halt!" rang up and down the line, and slowly the great machine of war ground to a stop. The ground, however, did not stop trembling. Rather, it grew in power and volume, louder and louder. Wind howled through the trees with the sound of a thousand trumpets of war, and through it all Jian heard, or thought he heard, the laughing whisper of the witching well.

> *Vengeance best served hot,*
> *Vengeance best served cold.*

Serve it up with meat and wine,
One day old.

"Your Illumination!" the raptor hunter gasped. "Forgive me, but—the Dae—" Face red with the effort it had taken her to run to him she bent double, hands on her knees.

"The Dae?" Giella said, voice sharp and hard. "What about the Dae?"

"They have set foot upon the shores of Sindan, my—my lady! The veil is no more! The twilight lords have come to the world of man!"

A cry went up from those near enough to hear.

"The Dae! The Dae! The Dae are come!"

"Is this true?" Jian demanded. Surely with his father beside him, victory was assured.

"It is true!" the girl cried. "I have seen this with my own eyes."

Several among them cried out in fear. If Jian did not do something, and quickly, he might lose his army to panic. He held up a hand for silence.

"My father has come to our aid!" he roared. "The Sea King rides to war!" A murmur ran through the crowd nearest him; not acceptance or jubilation, but a permutation of panic into something watchful, waitful.

It would do.

Giella leaned in, her mouth close to Jian's ear. "The darkest wish of your heart might yet come true, Tsun-ju Jian de Allyr," she whispered. "I hope you wished that some of us might survive this day."

Jian's heart went cold. Had he? What had he wished for… exactly?

Deep in the back of his mind, the witching well laughed.

❖

The land around the Forbidden City was empty and dead as if the war had already been fought there, and every living thing slain. Not so much as a rat or stray dog scurried across the red-stone road. The merchants' stalls were closed or gone, and the sound of marching feet rang like the brass bells of priests in a funeral procession.

The sounds and smells of industry rang out as Jian's followers built a siege camp bigger than the village in which he had grown up. Towers and ballistas were assembled, tents struck, fires lit, units organized. Jian nodded at a lean raptor handler running with her clutch of chinmong, and sighed to himself as she passed him by, glancing wide-eyed over her shoulder. *Was I ever so young?* he wondered. And in the next moment, *I hope she survives this day.*

He and a chosen few of his generals walked a short distance from the organized confusion toward the city proper and stood close enough that they might see and be seen, not so close that a lucky arrow might find their flesh. Still the ground groaned and shook as if it wished to shake them off.

The shining walls of Khanbul seemed higher, wider, and more ominous even than he remembered from just days before. And the stone giants—the hairs on Jian's arms stood stiff. It felt as if the hair on his head did, too.

"Do you see that?" Tsali'gei asked, voice echoing oddly from the warrior's helm that covered most of her face. "Jian, look! The giants... they have moved!"

It was true. The red giant had gained his feet and stood facing the golden giant, hands balled into defiant fists. The smile on the golden giant's face was gone, replaced with a grimace of anger. Or was it fear?

"How can this be?" he asked Giella.

"Old magic," she told him, eyes huge and bright in the light of an early day. "Stone magic. Magic as old and deep as mountains."

"Dae magic," the girl Awitsu said, appearing out of nowhere. "Dark magic and deep. Can you hear it, Kanati?" She turned to her dark-skinned, moon-haired companion. "A well. A witching well. Can you hear it?"

"Yes," he said. Silvery eyes glittered oddly as he regarded Jian. "Someone has made a wish, I think." His teeth, when he smiled, were fox-sharp and impossibly white.

"The giants!" someone cried nearby, breaking the tension that had sprung up between Jian and this daeborn boy. "The giants have moved!"

As Jian stared at them, he realized that both the red and golden giants were staring not at each other, but at him. Though he did not detect a shadow of movement, if he so much as glanced away or blinked it seemed as if they had moved lightning-quick, in a heartbeat's time. Was it enmity he saw in those stone faces? When he drew abreast of them, would those enormous stone fists smash down upon him?

The trembling in the earth grew louder, nearer, as if an invisible army would trample them at any moment. Skulls shook loose from the red stone road and rolled away, mouths gaping in silent laughter. Swords tumbled like rain into the waters of the emperor's moat which boiled like an angry sea. As Jian stared, trapped like an insect in amber, the rumble grew to a crashing shriek, as if Sajani had succeeded in waking from her long slumber to tear the world asunder.

Behold, the witching well whispered. *Behold, son of the eastern winds, child of the shimmering seas. I grant you the darkest wish of your heart.* Then it laughed deep in his bones, a sound that made the ground shake and his soul tremble.

A few paces from them the ground buckled and split. Deep fissures shot toward Khanbul, growing in number and in depth, laughing in crackling stone voices as they raced one another to the city walls. The ground sank, and rose, and sank again, and a sulfurous stench rose to engulf them.

There was a series of deafening explosions, and a wall of dust rose to obscure their view. When it settled, Tsali'gei gasped and pointed.

"Jian!"

He looked where she was pointing and cried out in amazement. Both giants were kneeling, heads bowed—to him.

Where the gates of Khanbul had been there was only a low mountain of rubble. Beyond that, rising from the dust like rocks rising from the ocean mist, the emperor's army could be seen picking itself up off the ground. Banners whipped about like sapling trees in a storm. There was the black three-headed serpent of Saimonju, the silver dogfish of Hoen, the red and orange sabre-tusked tiger of Shimendo. Over them all rose the shimmering white bull of Daeshen Tiachu.

Where is the white stag? Jian wondered, squinting to peer through the dust. *Where is Mardoni?* He did not want to hesitate and lose this advantage, but neither did he wish to launch headlong into a trap.

"If you must bring war to your enemy in his own fortress," the great poet and general Zhao Quan wrote, *"do so in a time or place of upheaval, when you are not expected. The key to victory against great odds is to use a surprise attack."*

"Seize the dream," he whispered to himself, and hardened his heart. The disarray of the imperial soldiers was no sham. His own troops stood but a few paces behind, white-faced with shock but already armed and armored for war.

"Gather your troops," he shouted, though there was little need; no general would be so foolish as to waste such an opportunity as this. "To arms! To arms! To war!"

Jian held up his war fan. It flashed blue and white, and his force went to point like the Huntress's hounds scenting blood. Then he brought it down sharply, pointing straight at the imperial troops and the emperor beyond.

"To the palace!" he cried, and was lifted up, carried along on the tides of war, a child's toy in a maelstrom.

❖

They poured into the once-immaculate streets of the Forbidden City as a muddy river pours into the sea, and were met by rank upon rank of the emperor's soldiers—daeborn princes who had survived the great wheel, every one, ready beneath the banner of the white bull.

Arrows hissed down upon Jian's forces like a rain of vipers, and pikes lowered as they were met with a high, thick wall of shields and iron that would seem to the untrained eye as impenetrable as the scaled hide of a dragon. But Jian's eyes and heart were not untrained. He had trained with, then led, his father's armies during his long years in the Twilight Lands. Every moment of that time had been spent in preparation for this moment.

Lifting his fan, he turned it to the south three times— and sent the raptors forward. Each of the chinmong, those creatures with which the mountain tribes lived and hunted, was half the height of a tall man and nearly twice as long. Lithe and quick, they did not slow at the sight of the shield wall and bristling lances. Obeying their handlers' whistles they rushed at the imperial troops with great leaping bounds, quicker than the human eye could track, then set upon any exposed flesh they could reach with tooth and claw.

Men who were used to facing human enemies—or at least half-human enemies—were not trained for the alien ferocity of such a maneuver. Precious minutes passed before the shield wall began to show gaps as men fell, screaming, and the raptors tore into them. The tortoise-shell formation—so effective against arrows and light infantry—was no defense.

Human soldiers rushed in and the battle unfolded in the streets of Khanbul as a flower opening to the first light of spring, no less beautiful for being expected.

"The outcome of a battle," Allyr had told his son, *"is decided in the first ten heartbeats of the fight. One side will*

have an advantage over the other, be it the high ground, strength in numbers, quality of force, or the element of surprise. An effective general will exploit this advantage without hesitation and smash the enemy before they have time to work out an effective counter-strategy.

"*This does not mean,*" Jian's father had warned, "*that a general should presume the outcome of any battle, no matter how predictable it may seem. For every trick you have up your sleeve, assume that your enemy has ten, and you will never be disappointed.*"

Directing the course of a battle was much like captaining a massive sea vessel through the heart of a storm. It was necessary to separate the heart from the mind. Necessary also to control as best one could the larger course of events without losing sight of the many smaller incidents playing themselves out within the larger drama. A slip, a misstep, a moment of inattention on the part of the field general might spell disaster for them all.

Jian felt suspended in time as he called the chinmong back, ordered the archers to hold, and the ghella handlers to loose their heavily armored, long-trunked beasts among the hapless defenders. He could not afford to listen to or care about the screams of his own men as the emperor's arrows found their targets, nor those of the imperial swordsmen as they were trampled and gored. Nor could he rejoice as a massive force of crudely armed human peasantry came to join the rebel army.

Giella and her country bards had long worked to shape his years-long campaign against the emperor's troops, transforming it into a hero's story, framing him as a champion to the common people. Quickly the emperor's troops lost ground. Fear bloomed in their hearts. It appeared in the whites of their eyes and sang in the pitch of their screams. Defeat showed in the way they stood, the uncertain fashion with which they held sword and spear and bow, in the way they clung to their tiny, meaningless lives rather than throwing themselves wholly into the fight.

The battle, Jian knew, was already won.

Then a light rose up from the Palace of Flowers and moved toward them like the dawn of a dying day. Bright it was, lovely, and terrible. Jian had seen the likes of it before, many times.

"Luminists!" he bellowed. "Ware luminists!" and across the field of battle a cry went up from all sides.

"*Luminists!*"

The emperor's light-sorcerers spared none when they came with their killing light, and they cared not. Yet Jian's forces were prepared for this, having faced the threat before. Most of them wore helms with silken gauze affixed over or under the eye-slits. Those who were helmless made haste to tie strips of spidersilk over their eyes and the eyes of their beasts. Others, who were less prepared—mostly the common folk—drew clothing up over their heads in a frantic effort to spare their sight, or ran for cover.

The light came striding down the emperor's path, fanning out like a plague of fire, naked women and men soulbound to the emperor, sworn to the heartless flame. Too brilliant to look upon, too terrible to imagine. All those pieces of them which had been woman or man, Dae or human, had been stripped away—they were scooped hollow as an old skull and filled instead with a killing flame that revealed and destroyed all truth.

The sorcerers spread out, raising their arms and chanting with voices like the crackling of wildfire, the strike of lightning from a clear sky. Screams rose from those who were nearest to them—imperial troops and rebels alike—as the clothing beneath armor began to smolder and smoke, flesh began to char, and hair to singe.

Jian raised his fan, flicked it this way and that. His archers had overtaken the ramparts inside the shining walls, and their arrows arced overhead, a shroud of death which caught fire midflight and fell like smoking rain. Raptors, maddened by the searing light, turned shrieking upon friend, foe, even their own handlers. The heavy armored ghella also broke free and ran trumpeting, bellowing in agony and fear, leaving trails of broken soldiers in their wake.

Those hapless fighters too slow or unprepared to withstand the terrible faces of the emperor's wrath screamed in burbling agony as their bodies turned to ash, their voices to smoke, their dreams to naught and they dropped dead at the feet of their fellows, no more now than heaps of cooked flesh. Jian's stomach growled and then turned at the smell of roasted meat.

But he was long used to this, as he was to disregarding the softer corners of his own heart. There would be time to mourn the dead later, if later ever came. Now there was only war, and an enemy to kill. He closed his heart, and his eyes, raised his own arms in mocking mimicry of the luminists' stance, and called upon his own magic—deep magic, dark and cool, magic sung deep into his bones by the voices of his ancestors. It was knowledge and fear of this magic which had led Daeshen Tiachu to purge the Daechen of those whose blood sang with the song of the sea. It had led Xienpei, Jian's trainer, in her ambition to spare his life.

Come, he called to the sea, to the river, to the rain. *Hear me. See me. Feel my need and come to me, for I am your son.* He opened his heart, his soul, bared the very essence of his nature to the water that slept deep and dreamed of dragons. The water heard, it woke—and answered his call.

The air thickened as if preceding a rain, dimming the baleful eye of Akari and depriving the luminists of some of that power. The sound of his own heart thundered in his ears even as scores of his enemies reeled and fainted, the water in their blood and bones answering his call, as well. The ground trembled and stirred, softening under the feet of the sorcerers so that they became mired in mud.

Furious, the luminist at their center—a woman whose face Jian vaguely remembered—turned her deadly gaze upon him and began to chant. Feeling the air around him begin to heat, Jian matched her chant with one of his own, a thing he had learned from his father.

> "Auri auri thunrenothel beno beno falrevoi!
> Sharra sharra Danuroshev vel a rassa soloroi!
> Vel a rassa soloroi!
> Soloroi! Soloroi!
> Danu rassa soloroi!"

So he sang to the heart of the sea, that which exists in the soul of all things that live or have ever lived. The water in the emperor's moat broke loose with a roar so loud it seemed as if Sajani must surely be roused from her sleep. The waves rose high, higher, till they cast a shadow upon the wall. A black mass rose up within the face of the water—the zhilla, poor captive that it was, writhing silhouetted against the sun's dimmed rays, singing a watery song as its tentacles burst forth. Several of the emperor's pikemen were snatched up like sweetmeats and carried, screaming and flailing, to a watery grave.

The luminists redoubled their efforts, all of them staring now at Jian, pointing as if to single him out for scorn. Their leader blazed so white-hot in her wrath that scores of men writhed weeping upon the ground, clawing at their eyes. A voice rang out from the center of this inferno.

> "Three words thrice shall stay the prince,
> Three names twice shall slay him.
> Three drops once shall bind his heart
> *Lest that heart betray him.*"

"Dammah!" the high luminist cried, as if calling for blood to be spilled. "Dammah, dammah!"

443

Jian's breath caught in his throat, and his song faltered. Three words—the weakness bound to his bones at his inseeing, chains woven around his soul by the emperor himself. He had thought only the oracle knew these words, and his yendaeshi Xienpei, dead these many years.

"Tummohai!" another luminist cried, as if in longing for the ocean. "Tummohai, Tummohai!"

"Issuqan," a third cried, as if naming Jian a sea-thing child beneath the eye of Akari. "Issuqan, Issuqan!"

No, Jian cried deep in his heart. *They cannot know these things. No… no no no…* But surely, *surely* they did not know the names. Names of those he had killed, or of those who had died for him—it was not possible that the luminists would know those names.

"Perri!" one of the luminists cried. "Naruteo!" another cried.

"Tsun-ju Tiungpei!" their leader howled, and Jian's heart faltered, the song cracking between his teeth like a pearl.

"Perri!" the luminists cried in unison. "Naruteo! Tsun-ju Tiun—"

"No!" Jian screamed, outraged that such small mouths would ever dare to speak his mother's name. The darkness in his heart rose up like a wish, like a dark tide, like a curse upon all the land beyond wrath or reason. Water in the air, in the land, in the bodies around him rose up in a mist, licking at the feet and legs and bodies of those who would dare defy the son of a Sea King.

The zhilla raised her sweet voice and danced as the mist thickened into a cold black fog, swirling and rising, rising like a black veil drawn over the face of the sun.

The veil parted, and the armies of the Sea King poured forth, star-eyed and monstrous. With the spilling of Tiungpei's blood, the stilling of her heart, the treaties between the Sindanese emperor and daekind had been broken, and the horde was let loose upon the land. At the front of this nightmare army rode the Sea King Allyr, at the back rode the Huntress with her mad-eyed hounds, and between them the imperial army was crushed like pearls beneath the booted feet of soldiers. The emperor's luminists were devoured as candle flames in the wind, for between the Huntress and the sea rode Death, and Hunger, and Wrath—but never Mercy. On this day of days, it seemed, Mercy had stayed home to tend her gardens, and she was not to be found anywhere in the Forbidden City.

Not on this day, this day of blood and water.

And Sea Kings.

FORTY-SEVEN

Sulema was surprised to learn that she had a love of the
sea.

In two moons' time an army had been raised. It
was a patched-cloak army of Zeeranim and Quarabalese,
citizens and slaves of Min Yaarif, pirates and mercenaries
and the walking dead. Her brother's ships carried them up
the Dibris and into the tourmaline waters of the vast inland
sea Nar Bedayyan.

They sailed up the eastern coast, past the roiling tributary
of the Kalish river and parallel to the Great Salt Road.
Tarbok bounded along the white cliffs to one side, dolphins
leapt from the deeps on the other. On three occasions great
shadows lingered beneath their boats, forms so monstrously
large Sulema's mind could not imagine what might have cast
them, but each time those Baidun Daiel who had chosen to
join them chanted and sang, and the guardians of the deep
let them pass.

After one such incident Sulema stood shoulder-to-
shoulder with her sword-sister at the prow of her brother's
greatest ship, which he shared with her and Yaela, with
Ismai-who-was-not, and Mattu Halfmask, to whom she still
refused to speak. Her brother and a handful of his crew had
stripped down to loincloths and dove into the waters where
the serpents—greater predators of the sea—lay in wait.

Rather than eating the sailors, the serpents crested the
surface and bore them upon their backs like water-steeds.
The women and men of Leviathus's group whooped with
delight, standing upon—and often falling from—the broad
scaled backs of the sea-beasts, who seemed to enjoy this

odd sport every bit as much as their tiny companions.

"I wonder if they could learn to play aklashi," Sulema said aloud. It looked like great fun, and she wanted to join in, but she was no more allowed to ride one of the serpents than Leviathus would have been allowed to touch an asil. The kings of the deep had an accord with the pirates, but any other human would become a tasty morsel.

Besides which, Sulema had never really learned to swim. If she were not eaten, it was likely that she would drown, and then this entire venture would have been for naught. Too much had been invested in this budding war for her to get herself killed doing something foolish.

"It is not worth the risk."

At the sound of Ismai's voice, Hannei stiffened and strode away without looking at either of them. Sulema watched her go, heart heavy, wishing she might mend the chasm that lay between her two old friends.

But some wounds, she knew, ran too deep to ever truly mend. She turned to face Ismai.

"You used to be a lot more fun," she complained. "What happened to you?"

"What happened to me," Ismai said. He stepped closer—when had he grown so tall?—stared down at her with his ruined face, his burned and blinded eyes which somehow saw her, and frowned. "The same as happened to you, Sulema an Wyvernus ne Atu. The same as happened to turn Hannei into *Kishah*. The world turned, and the world burned. We burn with it."

"No," she said. "That is not you speaking, not our Ismai." Sulema stepped closer. Ismai shifted almost imperceptibly to a fighting stance, as his undead followers shifted behind him, muttering. Most of the Lich King's soldiers were on another ship or belowdecks, utterly still as only corpses could be.

Ismai had been Sulema's friend, had tried to hide a crush on her since childhood in fact, so she ignored her misgivings and took another step toward him.

"What happened to you, Ismai?"

Ismai—really Ismai, this time—closed his opaline eyes, and a shudder ran through his lean frame.

"Ishtaset, rajjha of the Mah'zula, happened," he answered at last. "They came upon us in the night and burned Aish Kalumm to the ground. They killed mothers. They killed children. They killed—they killed little Sammai." His ruined face contorted with grief. Sulema had heard parts of this story already, but not from Ismai himself.

Aish Kalumm, gone? The city, the trees, all of it, gone? She had not wanted to believe any of it. Those few vash'ai who had not left their kithren, she had heard, had turned as vicious and unpredictable as their wild brothers and sisters. She wanted to scream, or to throw up, but instead she laid a hand on Ismai's arm, soothing him as she might a half-wild colt.

"Ishtaset and her riders claimed the right of rule over all the Zeera," Ismai went on, opening those eyes again. He looked out across the river but did not pull away from her touch. "She claimed rights over me. Because of my blood." He touched his chest, frowning. "Mastersmith Hadid, he—he—he sacrificed himself, so that I could get away, but not before her snake-priestess of Thoth did this." He brought his hand up to his face, stroking the shining, twisted scars.

"I am sorry, Ismai. I wish I had been there."

"You were busy being held in your brother's dungeons, I guess." A hint of the old Ismai leaked through the cracks in his mask, and he smiled. A little smile, a start. "It all worked out in the end. Char saved me—she is Naara now, my daughter. The Lich King's daughter, anyway. And Ishtaset is dead."

"Dead-dead or walking dead?" Sulema could not help glancing at her friend's dead-but-walking soldiers. "I am sorry," she added lamely to the beautiful Quarabalese corpse that shadowed Ismai's every step. "I do not mean to give offense."

"None taken," the woman answered solemnly. This one, as far as Sulema had seen, never smiled. "Ishtaset is dead-dead. I ate her myself."

"Oh. Ah, thank you?"

The woman nodded acknowledgment and turned away. It was, Sulema thought, the strangest conversation she had ever had.

"Ishtaset wanted to return to the old ways," Ismai told her. "I returned the old ways to her, but not as she might have hoped." There was a dark, sweet satisfaction in the words, as if he spoke around a mouthful of mad honey.

"I used to dream of meeting my father," Sulema said slowly, "and to be free of my mother's influence. Be careful what you wish for, I suppose. Sometimes it is the darkest wishes of our heart which come true."

"Yes," Ismai agreed. "But, Sulema—"

Here he turned to face her. He placed both hands on her shoulders and peered into her face. As if he could not get enough. As if she were the last beautiful thing in the world.

"I used to dream of you. I still dream of you," he told her. "Sometimes it seems that thoughts of you are all that connect me to this world. And I will never be sorry for that. I believe that we have come to the end of our world. That nothing we may do or say, no wars we may win or lose, will be enough now to stop Sajani from waking. It is too late for us to save the world."

She could hardly breathe. "Why follow me, then, if this is what you truly believe? Why try at all?"

"Why not?" He shrugged, and for a moment Ismai, her Ismai, stood before her. "I would rather die by your side than anywhere else. It is not a bad thing, to die chasing a dream." He reached up and touched her cheek, the barest caress. "And love is a dream worth chasing."

With those words, Ismai—who was still Ismai, Lich King or no—turned and walked away from Sulema, leaving her with a heart as troubled and clouded as the angry sea.

449

"He does love you, you know. And who can blame him?"

Sulema spun to face her once and only lover, voicing a snarl which would have made Khurra'an proud.

"Halfmask!"

"Guilty as charged. Oh, wait, there is no need to get—" Her fist struck his sternum. "*Oof!* For the love of—" Another grazed his jaw. "Oh, Sulema, sweet Sulema, light in my heart, please do not cry."

"I am not crying," she snarled again, shaking the pain from her bruised knuckles. "These are tears of anger. I should kill you here and now and feed your worthless carcass to the serpents. I should—"

"You should kiss me," he urged gently. "Because the night is short, and tomorrow is for war." He reached up a hand to brush away her tears, and his mismatched eyes shone like the sea. "Because the dragon is waking—Ismai is right in this, as well—and tomorrow may be a fool's dream, though I have ever been a fool for you."

"You left me!" she cried, then bit her lip. How was it that her voice sounded so cursed weak when she spoke to him? She *did* want to kiss him, damn him, and that made her angrier still.

"As a matter of fact," he replied, smiling that crooked smile which had gotten her into such trouble in the first place, "I came looking for you, and was captured by my brother Pythos's men. They threw my ass into the darkest hole they could find and left me to rot."

"So how did you—"

"Matteira, of course. My twin sister and I used to play in the dungeons when we were small and it was safer for us not to be seen about court. There are ways in and out of that place, and we know them all. She and two of her fools dressed as ragtag men came to collect the day's bodies from the dungeons, and somehow one of the bodies and I swapped places. He was recently deceased, and a reasonable likeness to me, after certain—adjustments—were made to the face." He grimaced. "The unfortunate man and I swapped clothes, I was rolled out of the dungeons and dumped out with the rags and offal, and here I am, begging for a kiss." He batted his eyes at her, and Sulema snorted a laugh in spite of herself.

"Are you not worried that Matteira's role in your escape might be discovered?"

"I am not escaped, I am dead. And do not trouble yourself with worry over my sister—she is more dangerous than you know. It would not surprise me to find her on the Dragon Throne one day, with all of us sitting at her feet wondering what in Yosh just happened."

"So you came to the dungeons looking for me?" she asked. "If you know them so well, how did you not find me?"

"How could I hope to find you, when you were within me all along?" he said. His hand lingered on her cheek as if he could not bear to stand so close and not touch her. "My whole life, you have been here." He touched his chest with his other hand. "You are my heart and my soul, Sulema. I could not find you before I found myself."

"And did you?" she asked, swaying closer to the heat of him, even as she cursed herself for a fool. "Did you find yourself, Halfmask?"

By way of answer, Mattu reached up and took hold of the white fennec mask he had been wearing and pulled it up over his head. This he tossed into the sea as casually as a boy might throw flower petals into the wind on the first day of spring. Sulema watched the mask spin through the air and then disappear beneath the waves with a soft splash and a little spray of sea foam.

"Your *mask*," she protested. She had never thought his scars hideous, but she was a barbarian, after all. "Though I suppose you have more of them…"

"I do not," he told her, and smiled. His smile was beautiful. "I do not need to hide behind a mask any longer, sweet girl, now that I know who I am."

"And who is that?"

Mattu stepped close, so close that only the whisper of wind lay between them, carrying the heat of their bodies back and forth like messages. He reached up to cradle Sulema's face in both his hands—

—he was taller than she remembered, his eyes more piercing—

—and bent his mouth to hers.

"I am yours," he whispered against her mouth, stealing her breath away, "my queen." Then the Queen took the Thief to her own tiny cabin and let him steal her heart. For liars make the best lovers, she decided, when they tell the truth, and warriors know that trouble is especially sweet if you get caught on the eve of war.

FORTY-EIGHT

Leviathus listened to the talk of war, of kings and queens and sorceries, with one ear and half a heart. The rest of him, the better half, soared the deeps as a hawk commanded the air, king of a vast domain. The wind danced upon the waves, crafting castles and stories on the wave crests as it went, never regretting the loss as they faded away to naught. It was a lesson, a warning, an omen of the doom of men.

A gust of wind tugged at his windlocked hair, bringing him back to here and now, to dry air in his lungs and two feet planted securely on the hot sharp boards of a ship. Cruelly it reminded him that he shared the world's fate, whether or not he had a hand in shaping it.

As if in concert with the mourning wind the voices of war-horns wailed out across the water, deep and fluting like the bellowing of wounded beasts, and were in turn answered by the joyful calls of leviathans. Huge triangular heads thrust from beneath the waves, mirror-scaled and sleek, jewel-crested and more beautiful in his eyes than any creature had a right to be. The sea between his boats roiled with the great forms as the sea prince and his court gave escort to the frail vessels floating upon the water bearing tiny, precious lives.

The sailors brought down the striped sails and lowered masts, while oars thrust from the sides like slender fins. The ships' eyes and carven faces stared toward the approaching shoreline, as snarling and eager as their human crews who even now readied siege engines and horses, donning armor and preparing weapons.

Azhorus Ssurus az Lluriensos himself breached the sea's skin, jewel eyes gleaming in mirth as he beheld the tiny two-leggeds preparing for war. His head, nearly as big as the ship upon which Leviathus sailed, briefly blotted out the sun and threw dark shadows upon them.

Little human, he sang in Leviathus's mind, *you are nearly arrived. I have brought you safely to the shores of your kind, that you may seize this territory and breed with the queens therein.* Enormous self-satisfaction rolled from him like water drops. *You may thank me now.*

Thank you, Leviathus replied, shading his eyes against the sun's angry glare as he looked up and up and up, a fond and foolish smile on his face. Never had he loved a thing in this world as he loved this incredible, silly, terrifying prince of the dark waters. *We never would have made it this far without your kind assistance.*

This is true, the sea prince allowed. *Were we not bonded, you and I, my people would have taken great delight in crushing these tiny vessels and dining upon sweet manflesh.*

Truly you are gracious. Leviathus bowed, not at all ironically. Azhorus dipped his head in acknowledgment and slipped beneath the waves with hardly a splash.

The war horns cried out again—or perhaps it was the serpents. When Leviathus was in his smitten state, sometimes he could not tell the difference. Oars flashed down toward the water as the drums began to boom—*thrum-thrum-thrum, thrum-thrum-thra-rumble*—like the beating of a thousand great hearts beneath the waves.

"Magnificent," Daru breathed, standing at his shoulder. "Simply marvelous, and none of the books I have ever read so much as mentioned the serpents as anything other than beasts. I wonder what else we do not know about our own planet?"

Leviathus looked at the boy and frowned. "No more than I have heard of a child becoming lost in the catacombs beneath Atukos and reappearing half a world away as a grown man." He could not help mistrusting this grown version of the boy he had once known, any more than he could help liking him. Daru—if indeed his impossible tale was true, and this was Daru—was every bit as sharp-eyed and quick-witted and kind of heart as Hafsa Azeina's young apprentice had been.

Most likely this is an impostor living a ridiculous lie, a spy in the employ of Pythos, he thought. Certainly, it was likelier than Daru's strange cut-short explanation of a life lived among the stars.

"The Web of Illindra is woven of wonders," Daru replied, undisturbed by Leviathus's naked distrust, "too great for you or me to comprehend."

"That much is true," Leviathus agreed as the ships sped toward Atualon, crammed stem-to-stern with undead soldiers and painted warriors from the Seared Lands, escorted by serpents, and bearing the would-be Dragon Queen to claim her throne. "Divines know we live in a strange world, and in strange times."

"*Ehuani*, and well said." Daru smiled, and in that moment Leviathus knew that the youth's story was, indeed, true. However impossible it might seem, this powerful young sorcerer was Hafsa Azeina's frail apprentice, returned to them as a hale young man who had walked roads they could not imagine.

The excitement aboard the ships was a palpable thing as they drew nearer to the shores. None of the soldiers or warriors or sorcerers, and few even of his river pirates, had been especially happy about journeying over the deep blue waters, fearing that the serpents' friendliness was feigned, and that a watery death awaited those who dared the open sea. Such had been the fate of any such venture for time immemorial.

Yet here they were, scant heartbeats away from Atualon and the fight of their lives. The last fight of many lives, to be sure, and the greatest of all. These events would be dutifully recorded in history books and passed down through the ages. All that remained was to determine how that history would be written, and by whom.

"Victors or vanquished?" Daru asked, correctly guessing his mind. "I guess we will know soon enough."

"*Ehuani*," Leviathus agreed, then he fell silent. There was a time for talk, and a time for action. As far as he was concerned, the time for words had passed.

Three days hence, Sulema summoned the captains of water and of war to a council aboard their father's ship as the fleet lazed upon still waters. The great dragon-headed vessel had carried Leviathus to Aish Kalumm in search of his long-lost sister, setting in motion the chain of events which had brought them all here, and he agreed that it was fitting. Leviathans ferried them from vessel to vessel at Azhorus's request and the sea filled with their bubbling laughter at the humans' excited fear. Leviathus, aided and advised by Mahmouta, assigned places in battle to each ship and complement of fighters according to their strengths.

A thrill ran through him—fear or excitement, he could not tell which. Probably a bit of both, truth be told, and he made no apologies for either. Half his life and more had been spent in preparation for this moment, reading about war, writing about war, training first as a soldier and then as a commander, all in anticipation of one day leading his father's armies in their defense of Atualon. Therefore, he was in a unique position to know all of her weaknesses, and to appreciate her defenses.

"If we attack from the bay," Leviathus warned, "the tide will run red with our blood. It is true that the Dragon King has only a token navy—and his best river ships are returning from their voyage into the Zeera with an unwelcome surprise. It is true also that the leviathans are no friends to Pythos, and keen to hinder any effort he makes to attack us—"

Here he was interrupted by the high, fluting laughter of serpents.

"Still, my father and Aasah laid layer upon layer of traps, both magical and physical, against the unlikely event of a Sindanese attack from the sea." He grimaced. "Mostly at my urging."

Therefore little effort had been spent on stealth. The usurper Pythos had no sea fleet to speak of, and Atualon's own river ships were manned by the undead and sailed now against him. Two hundred and thirty ships Leviathus commanded in total, ten times perhaps the size of the Dragon King's navy, and the alliance of the leviathans besides. Unless Pythos had by some trick of foresight girded the northern shores against them, the motley armies were likely to face little real opposition until they set foot upon the white beaches. Perhaps not until they had begun their march on Atualon.

Still, Leviathus was uneasy.

"*Never count upon luck in war,*" the great Sindanese poet and general Zhao Quan had warned, "*unless it is to count upon bad luck, in which case you will never be disappointed.*" Their alliance with the leviathans had made their sea passage too easy. He could not allow himself to slip into complacency and expect their good fortune to continue unabated.

Already the first line of ships—eleven in total—had peeled away from the main group to weigh anchor before the harbor's mouth. Well beyond the reach of those tricks and traps about which Leviathus had warned them, still they would be close enough to act should Atualon issue forth a surprise navy or magic of some sort. Leviathus had no doubt that the usurper Pythos had gained control of the Baidun Daiel, nor that he commanded the shadowmancer and the Salarians as well.

The bulk of the fleet would disgorge fighters and siege engines upon the northern shore, under cover of archers, and from there they would launch an attack upon the city. The slower fat-bellied merchants' ships in the rear would deliver a second wave of troops even farther to the north to act as a vanguard on the off-chance that Pythos or Aasah had hidden forces in the trees or foothills.

It was a fine plan, on paper.

Leviathus had read too many papers concerning war to believe in his heart that it would proceed so smoothly.

As they drew nearer the shoreline, the cloud-crowned peak of Atukos loomed above in their eyes and their minds, and Leviathus beheld the great fortress of his childhood, set upon the mountain's face like a massive dark jewel. Set also in darkness it seemed, refusing to reflect the bright light of day, choosing rather to drink it in and vomit forth shade and shadow, as if it brooded still over the loss of Wyvernus.

Even as the thought swam across Leviathus's mind he watched as Sulema, standing warlike and golden upon the deck of the nearest ship, shoulder-to-shoulder with the Lich King and her sword-sister Hannei, raised up the glittering Mask of Sajani. It settled upon her face and flashed in the sunlight like a blue-green jewel with the heart of a star, blinding in its brilliance and cold as winter snow. Sulema lifted the fox-head staff of a dreamshifter and brought it down once, twice, three times upon the ship's deck.

The leviathans went silent—until that moment, Leviathus had not realized they were singing in his head— and a wave of atulfah, discernible even to the magic-deaf son of a Dragon King, burst forth as his sister raised her voice in song, causing ripples like small waves to shudder out from the ship until the wave lapped at the foot of Atukos. Sulema sang as surely Aasah or their father had taught her, wielding atulfah.

Atukos sang back.

The fortress blazed in response, a golden inferno captured in black diamond, and the dragonglass walls roared to life. The mountain shuddered and groaned, a low sound at first almost impossible to discern, and then louder, stronger, till the timbre and pitch was a deep throbbing in his bones. The ground trembled and shook, trees dancing upon the shore as if caught in a tempest, and the waves of the sea grew dark and fell, tossing their ships like a child's toy boats.

The leviathans grew wild and frenzied, throwing themselves full length from the sea's embrace as if trying to fly, till it seemed the fleet was in danger of being swamped before they could make landfall. A final mighty blast seized Atukos, and the mountain's top was lost in a plume of thick gray ash and smoke that boiled upward to the sky, rent with flashes of silver and gold and green.

The ship lurched beneath Leviathus's feet and he flung his arms out to steady himself. One flailing elbow struck something soft and solid, and a small hard fist punched him back. Leviathus turned to see Yaela, locked hair streaming about her in the rising wind, wide-eyed and laughing in wild delight. Leviathus grinned back. Despite everything, it occurred to him that he would not be anywhere else in the world, at that moment, given a choice.

"Yaela, my dear," he shouted to her, even as she snugged herself under his upraised arm and he pulled her tight to his side, "we are home."

FORTY-NINE

Beyond the white-capped waves of Nar Bedayyan, Hannei could see the black face of Atukos looking down on them from on high, quiet and brooding in the high hot sun. Lines of tall dark trees flowed down from the mountain's sides like a mother's skirts.

Those ships that had been sent to the north had landed first and disgorged their forces in preparation for the main landing party. Flags and banners which had been sewn in haste were raised and glittered like cloth-of-gold—bright Akari and lovely Sajani twined in a lover's knot around the black form of a rearing horse. That was Sulema's standard.

Hannei's mouth twisted at the thought of it, and she spat into the stinking sea. The bloodlines of Tammas had stretched back to the first light of the first dawn, and her own were nearly as remarkable. Did the blood of the ne Atu run thicker than that of Zula Din? Sword-sister or no, Sulema had done little more to earn these accolades than be born of the sweat of man and woman, same as any other babe.

Still, she reasoned, *someone must sit on high in that black tower and sing the cursed dragon to sleep, and I have neither the will nor the tongue to do so.*

Horns sounded from among those already massed on the shore, low and mournful calls like the shofarot of Aish Kalumm, and these were answered by the low *hooooo-hoooo-arooooo* of the serpents who roiled in the water all around their ships. Dragonkin, they were, nearer to dragons even than bintshi or wyverns, and the smallest of them was thrice the length of Sulema's own dragon-headed ship.

460

That Sulema's brother could talk to the dragonkin was shocking enough—one of them had bonded him, as vash'ai to warrior! Even more astonishing, from time to time the pirates would lower themselves from the great boats and stand upon the broad scaled backs, laughing and fearless as if they rode horses across the golden sands.

Such merriment was short-lived, however. Pirates and warriors, sorcerers and walking corpses all shared the grim look of those who like as not had eaten their last meal and said their final farewells to sun and sea and sword-sister. The drums beat *tha-rumm tha-rummm tha-rummmble* like her heart, urging the rowers to dip their oars faster, harder, shepherding them that much more quickly to their doom.

Hannei had faced death and far worse for longer than she cared to remember. Since the night Tammas had died she had not much cared for life. Yet excitement akin to fear surged through her, hot as blood. It sharpened her senses so that she could smell the serpents, feel the vibration of their shrieks, taste the war to come.

We live today, or we die today, she thought, *and either way the world will never again be the same as it is now*. It was the ending of an age, she knew, and not at all untimely.

Then the ship thrust itself shuddering into the soft flesh of Atualon's shoreline. Hannei staggered and nearly fell as Rehaza Entanye, ever at her side, grabbed her shoulder and only just saved her from plunging headfirst into the serpent-boiled waters.

"Easy now, girl," Rehaza Entanye said, laughing. "You do not want to die now and miss the war, do you?"

Planks were steadied and lowered, and those on board the ship made ready to disgorge. Shouts and the ring of sword on sword sounded from the tree line. Hannei drew her own blades as she took her place among those others eager to kill and to die. Akari Sun Dragon kissed her face, and Hannei found herself grinning up at him.

If I die today, she decided, *I will die facing my enemy. There is beauty in this, at least.*

Ehuani, whispered a voice across the sands of her heart. *Ehuani, little warrior.*

From the woods and the mountain above them came those bearing the Dragon King's banner—a serpent biting its own tail, coiled about the sleeping form of Sajani, with Atukos soaring above. Hannei had been stung in her heart when first she beheld it.

The serpent king has no right to Akari, she thought then. *We warriors of the Zeera are his children.* She was not truly Zeerani anymore, but as the opposing forces pounded into each other there on the beach, she ceased to care one way or the other. Surrounded by tightly packed bodies, with the sound of steel upon steel ringing just ahead, Hannei only had time to launch herself toward the enemy. Here there would be pain, and death, a never-ending feast.

Those who had come to seat Sulema upon the Dragon Throne crashed upon the defenders like the waves upon the shore. Archers had been hidden in the tree line, and these loosed volley upon volley of arrows which fell among them like a rain of hissing black snakes. Many in the first wave fell, so that when the second wave of attackers ran they stumbled up the shoreline over the fallen bodies of those who had gone before. Even so, they hardly slowed at the sight of the mangled carcasses of women and men with whom they had broken fast just that morning.

No few of those corpses rose to fight, then fell, and rose again. The Lich King's armies paid no more mind to dying than Hannei might have paid a stubbed toe. The enemy pulled back in horror from the sight of armies of the risen dead, only to be whipped forward again by lash and spear and force of magic.

The two sides were well-matched, as those who rode for Sulema found themselves facing a wall of white-cloaked Salarians with their bright silvered steel. Her warriors matched swords with Draiksguard and Atualonian soldiers. A knot of shadowmancers faced off against a knot of Baidun Daiel, each side wielding such magic that the sky flashed light and dark, light and dark, as if the battle took place in the heart of a storm.

Swinging her blade right and left, sending up sprays of blood and viscera, Hannei fought and killed women and men whose names were forever hidden from her. She could not help but think back on her time in the fighting pits of Min Yaarif. There she had faced and slain strangers and beasts, but she had also fought—and killed—pit slaves such as herself, some of whom she might have thought of as friends in other circumstances.

But the world was not as fair and true as her mother's stories, or Akari as just. There was irony, however, in the fact that she fought shoulder-to-shoulder with Rehaza Entanye, the woman who had saved her from and fed her to the slave pits, and whose fortune depended upon delivering her back into slavery.

Life is dark and inexplicable, she thought in a rare moment of calm as she wiped blood from her eyes with the back of a hand. She tripped over something soft, looked down, and saw the bloodied face of Mahmouta's son, who had snuck aboard the ships and was not supposed to have come ashore. He was not meant to have died this day. Hannei stooped to close the youngster's staring eyes, and to jerk free the shell necklace he wore, so that she might return it to his mother.

Life is odd, and it is short, and less beautiful than we are told.

Light, dark, and light again. There were screams in the tree line and a blossoming of fire, and then the defenders broke and fled for the fortress. Those around Hannei roared and surged forward, a many-faced beast with a thousand voices and no heart, eager for blood.

Ahead of her Hannei could see Sulema's banner and that of the Lich King streaming in the wind as their bearers made for Atukos. Rehaza Entanye snatched at Hannei's torn tunic and pointed after them.

"Follow," she panted. Hannei nodded.

Mutaani, she thought, even as she ran, bloodied swords drawn and eager. *If I cannot find beauty in life, I will find it in death*.

The beautiful gates had been torn down before Hannei reached them, shattered by the machines of war, by the near-constant shaking of the earth, or by treachery, she knew not which. The battle flowed up the slopes of Atukos, into the narrow alleys and even the houses of her citizenry. They fought and killed and died till the golden streets were as slick as stones in a foul red river.

Again arrows hissed from wall and battlement, interspersed with crashing stones or the plummeting bodies of defenders, of attackers, alike in death. The Atualonians fought well and bravely, but the sheer numbers of Sulema's forces and the horror of the army of undead pressed them up and back till finally the line broke, and the Dragon King's armies were scattered or slaughtered.

They shrank in fear too from the sight of Hannei as she danced among them, gluttonous blades drinking deep but never sated. Had she truly wished to die, just that morning? She could not remember. Her only wish now was to kill—perhaps, after all, that was all she had ever wanted. Forward and on she pressed, hacking face and throat and limb as she climbed the steep and narrow ways of the city, eyes fixed on Sulema's flag as if it were the only whole thing left in her life.

Rehaza Entanye fought at her side, but she hardly noticed. Neither did she heed the ache in her arms, the hollowness in her breast as every life she claimed stole a mouthful of what was left of hers. She could no longer have said why she followed the banner at all, only that she had to do so.

There was a brief glimpse of fiery locks and golden shamsi as the Dragon Queen's guard and Ismai the Lich King disappeared through a hole that had been blown in an inner wall. The dead followed, as did a knot of pirates whose bright silks were rent and bloodied. Hannei followed as well, swift and silent as a vash'ai engaged in the hunt. Up they went, at times running, then fighting back-to-back with Rehaza Entanye or a pirate or a corpse that had forgotten to lie still and be dead. Ever on and ever up, through winding narrow roads cobbled with stone and bone and littered with the shattered glass of a thousand broken windows.

At last they came to Atukos, the fortress of the Dragon King.

Or the Dragon Queen, Hannei thought, awed by the sharp black stone. The brooding black towers leapt to incandescent life as just ahead Sulema passed through them. Indeed, the gates swung inward almost of their own volition and the dragonglass walls shone blinding bright in welcome, leaving none to doubt with whom the loyalties of the fortress lay.

The inner courtyard was thick with white cloaks, and golden and red. These last—the Baidun Daiel—moved as if of one mind and faced Sulema's banner. It was such a strange, inhuman ripple of movement, so unnaturally coordinated, that the chillflesh on Hannei's arms stood up even through the blood and gore and myriad tiny wounds of the day's battle. Golden masks flashed bright and expressionless in the sunlight, and then the blood-cloaked sorcerers sheathed their black swords and stepped back from the battle to stand aside, still as statues.

Good fortune, Hannei thought, even as a white-clad Salarian soldier ran screaming at her. She slapped away his spear almost contemptuously and hacked into the meat at either side of his neck with a quick wet *thuckk-thuckk*, then spun to the side to avoid the spray of bright lifesblood as he collapsed at her feet. How many times had she practiced that very move? How many times drained a life with it? More than she cared to count.

Good fortune for me, and good riddance to him.

Hannei did not fear death, but she did not care to die blasted to bits by fell magics that she could neither understand nor fight. She heard Rehaza Entanye grunt and curse, and nearly fell as the woman slammed heavily into her and then fell away. Hannei did not spare a glance backward as she followed Sulema through the wide doors into Atukos.

Good riddance to you too, she thought.

It was odd, odd and horrible, to fight within the confines of the fortress. The narrow halls and doorways reminded her too much of the Mothers' rooms and kitchens, too much of comfort and laughter. Women and men sprang bellowing from doorways or down staircases and were hurled screaming to their deaths, torn by spear and club, rent by Hannei's blood-glutted blades, or—twice—thrown from a high window to fall wailing to the streets below.

Such a place should smell of cinnamon bread and sweet rushes, it seemed to her, not of blood and shit and death. But blood and shit and death were all the gifts she had brought, and she doled them out with a generous hand. The dead swept before her, fighting even as she fought, and the dead lay behind her torn and bubbling. A river of death, a sea of blood; it was all she could do to swim.

They burst from the hall into a wide room so abruptly that Hannei crashed into the undead called Sudduth and they both nearly went sprawling. Rehaza Entanye fell through the doorway behind her, blood streaming from a crushed nose and eyes wild but not nearly as dead as Hannei had hoped.

Sulema had come to a stop at the heart of the chamber and stood with her back to them. She was panting with exertion, gripping her staff in one hand and a golden shamsi in the other. Her sunset locks were drenched in blood, her skin streaked with gore, and she had long since lost her warrior's vest.

Her back straight, she faced the man who sat on her father's throne, one leg thrown over the arm in an indolent and insolent pose. The Illindrist Aasah of whom Hannei had heard tell stood behind him, arms folded over his massive chest, jeweled skin aglitter like a scattering of stars. He twitched when he saw the Lich King, and his pale blue eyes narrowed, but he did not move or speak.

The golden Mask of Akari glittered bright on the seated man's face, and waves of heat pulsed from it fit to sear the flesh from their bones as he stared at those who had come to kill him, if they could.

"We have visitors," he said, his voice resonant with dragon's magic. "Aasah, why did you not tell me? I would have had wine brought. Or a headsman, at least."

Sulema lifted her fox-head staff and brought it down once, twice, three times on the dragonglass floor. The walls about them, the floor beneath her feet, the arched ceiling flared blinding-bright with joy as Atukos welcomed her home. Sulema, daughter of Hafsa Azeina and Wyvernus.

Truly she is the Heart of Atualon, Hannei thought. Though she had grown up with Sulema, though she had bested the girl in combat more times than they had fingers, this woman before her was a stranger. Never had she seemed more like her mother, more like a warrior from the old stories.

More like a queen.

The room about them went silent. Even the sounds outside seemed very far away. It seemed to Hannei, in those moments between the death of one dragon and the birth of another, that the world held its breath. Into that silence a voice hissed close to her ear.

"Kill her."

Hannei turned her head fractionally and met the eyes of Rehaza Entanye. That woman's face was hard as stone. The pale cast of her skin and smashed, bloodied nose made her look more like one of the Lich King's horde than the living woman with whom Hannei had trained these past moons.

As she turned her head, a wound near her shoulder pulled and stung, and a hot wash of blood spilled down her side. When had she been cut? She could not remember. Her muscles trembled with exertion, now that she stood still, and breath came in shallow gasps.

"Kill her," the pitmistress repeated, voice low as a shadow's breath so that it carried to no ears but hers. "Kill the red-haired bitch and be free. This is Sharmutai's command, and her revenge. This is the price of your freedom and the hour of your vengeance. *Kill her*."

Indeed, as luck would have it, nothing but a couple of short strides lay between Hannei's drawn blades and Sulema's naked back. Her eyes, the eyes of Ismai the Lich King, indeed every eye but hers and Rehaza Entanye's were fixed on the glittering mask of the Dragon King, waiting for his next words. In two strides, three, Hannei would have her revenge for the death of Tammas and all that had been taken from her. She would buy her freedom from Sharmutai, and that of her child. It was equally possible that she would perish in the deed, but would that also not be just?

Was she not Kishah, whose blades sang of vengeance?

No, she thought, and *no*, she mouthed. Whether Sulema was her friend or her enemy, and even if her blood was the only coin with which Hannei could buy back her life, she would not do this thing.

No, she mouthed again, and this time Rehaza Entanye saw it. Her features darkened with rage. The older woman moved quick as a striking lionsnake, and Hannei felt the point of a blade press against her skin.

"Then you die."

Before the world could draw its next breath, Hannei closed her eyes, and let go of life.

Better I should die with an enemy's sword in my belly, she thought, *than I should live with my sword in a friend's back.*

The point of the pit-trainer's sword sliced a burning gash down the front of Hannei's stomach, shallow but painful, and the hot blood welled free. Then came a clatter as the sword fell away, and a soft gasp. Hannei opened her eyes and her breath caught in her throat.

Daru stood behind Rehaza Entanye, a knife pressed to the woman's throat. His eyes were dark and beautiful as he met Hannei's shocked gaze, and he smiled.

"You will not hurt her," he murmured into the woman's ear. "She is stronger than you know." Then in a single powerful stroke he jerked the sharp blade. Hot salty blood sprayed into Hannei's face, her eyes, her mouth. It washed down her front and filled her nostrils with the sweet stink of death and freedom.

Daru let Rehaza Entanye slide, lifeless and limp, to lie twitching at their feet. He grimaced at his knife, cleaned it somewhat on his tunic, and slipped it back into his sheath before meeting Hannei's eyes with a saucy wink that reminded her of the boy he had been.

"Now," he told her, "we are even, you and I."

A voice soft and dark as midnight caressed Hannei's mind, there and gone again.

It is good.

The world expelled its held breath in the form of the Dragon Queen's voice. It carried across the room, rich with the tones and power of Sajani Earth Dragon who slept fitfully far beneath their feet.

"It is over, Pythos," Sulema said to the man on the throne, as the undead horde and her borrowed armies filed into the chamber behind them.

"Surrender."

FIFTY

"It is over, Pythos," she said. "Surrender."

Sulema could smell sweat and blood, hear the grunts and heavy breathing of weary women and men as the room behind her filled with fighters live and undead who had brought her to this moment. She burned with fatigue and the small voices of a thousand wounds, and blood rushed in her ears like a rain-flooded river singing, singing.

No, she realized, and the breath caught in her throat. It occurred to her that this new voice, a low sweet sound at once new as green leaves and familiar as a mother's breath, was not the singing of her own heartbeat. Neither was it the song of the sea, the sands, the harsh whisper of hot winds across golden sands.

This was the song of a dragon.

Sajani slept fitfully in the belly of the earth, far below their feet, and as she slept, as she dreamt, she sang. She sang of rivers and seas and life-giving mud, of trees and moss and small, precious lives. She sang of the first steps of making, the first words, the first songs.

The first wars.

She sang of mothers and daughters, fathers and kings. She sang of lovers and sisters and hard, jagged rocks. Of fire in the moonslight and cool sweet water. She sang of life, and the stories humans told one another in the long dark.

She sang of love, and of loneliness.

She sang of a flame-haired warrior riding across the sands with her sword, her good horse, her sister. Sulema reached for that song, yearned for it. This was her heart's desire, her life's purpose, the one thing she must have or die, and she stretched, gasping, like a child reaching for a fruit that was tantalizingly out of reach. Like fingertips her sa and ka brushed it, the slightest touch, and then—

"Surrender?" Pythos laughed, a harsh sound that wrenched her back into the present moment and all its ugliness. "What is this? You would have me give this throne and these people into the hands of an usurper's half-tamed and half-trained daughter. Who, then, would stand between Atualon and the fell armies of Sindan? Who would shield my people from the priests of Eth, the river pirates of Min Yaarif, the undead hordes? Most importantly, who would sing Sajani to sleep, when even now she rouses and threatens the existence of our world? Surrender? I think not... unless, of course, you wish to surrender to me." He laughed again, swinging his leg as if none of the dangers he had just named might threaten him, and certainly not as if death faced him with a thousand swords.

The Mask of Akari glinted hard and gold.

"Sa Atu offers you mercy." Ismai spoke in a voice rich with wrath. "You should take it. Mercy is more than I will offer you, I and my soulsworn, you stinking dung-maggot." The dead pressed forward as he spoke. Little now did they look like living women and men. The skin had drawn tight on their faces as they bared yellow teeth like feral things, eyes glowing red in the tired light, and a fell air hung about them.

"It is not I who stinks of the grave," Pythos answered, eyes gone hard behind the mask. He straightened, booted feet striking the ground and hands tightening on the arms of the golden chair. "It is not I who stinks of betrayal."

"Who have I betrayed?" Sulema demanded.

"I am not speaking to you," Pythos sneered. "You know of what I speak, do you not, Kal ne Mur? Or perhaps you need a reminder?"

Ismai growled in reply. Sulema glanced at him in surprise, and saw that his stare was fastened straight ahead, his face a mask of fury. She followed his line of sight and gasped aloud before she could catch herself.

Arachnists!

Arachnists… or something worse.

From the low doors behind the throne, Atukos disgorged a host equal to Ismai's in size, and perhaps in number, as well. Women and men in all shapes and sizes, from elderly grandmothers to youths scarce out of childhood they came. They were many-limbed and walked with a horrible sideways shuffle, as the Arachnists did, but wore the black leathers, crimson cloaks, and faceless gold masks of the Baidun Daiel. In their midst walked a tall man, narrow-waisted and arrogant. Power and command radiated from him as if he were Akari made flesh. Sulema knew him at once, by his layers of shadowy robes, his massive hammer, his ruined mask—

—and by her response to him. Something grabbed her arm, and she looked down to see Yaela's hand gripping her so hard the knuckles were pale. She met the girl's jade eyes.

"No," Yaela whispered. "Stay." Only then did Sulema realize that she had been trying to move forward, and she could not have said whether she meant to kill him or kiss him.

Perhaps both.

She shook off Yaela's restraining hand, and cried out in a voice made strong and clear by years training as a warrior in the Zeera:

"I know you!" she drew a deep breath. "Nightmare Man."

"Indeed you do," the tall figure agreed as he took his place beside the golden throne. "Perhaps you would care to know us better?" And he winked at her.

"Perhaps," she allowed, "I will use your guts to string a lyre and you can sing me to sleep at night."

"Oh, my dear," he laughed. "I think not. Your mother might have threatened me so, once. You might have, had you grown to be half the woman she was."

"But she has not, beloved."

Sulema started. Though his mouth yet moved and his eyes never left hers, the Nightmare Man spoke now with another voice, soft and cringing. The voice went on.

"She has neither her mother's heart nor her father's song," it said. "She has nothing. She *is nothing*."

"Perhaps not nothing, sweet one." His voice was smooth and low again. "We shall see." It sounded oddly as if he was arguing with himself, or as if more than one person inhabited his body.

Like Ismai, Sulema thought.

"In any case," he continued, "whatever you are, whatever you have, you are *mine*." Thus saying, he drew a knife and held it point-down before his face, smiling. It was a golden thing, heavy and ornate. A silvery spider crouched atop the pommel, its body a shadow-jewel the size of a plover's egg.

Sulema staggered and would have fallen if not for the fox-head staff. The knife in his hands grew closer in her mind, brighter. It slashed across her throat and she was choking—

No, not I, she thought, even as she fought for breath. *Not I. Azra'hael. He killed my kithren. My Azra'hael.*

The spider moved, a living thing. It waved its forelegs in the air, and Sulema knew that it sought her. She could not tear her eyes from it, or move, or speak.

"You are weak, and you are mine," the Nightmare Man said in a voice dark and sweet as mad honey. "Your parents would be *so* disappointed. Join with me, little queen... or die now."

Even as the ruined man spoke, however, there was movement behind him. Shadows curled around the foot of the throne like dark waves, or thick smoke, lapping at the gold and the king's robes. Dark tendrils like writhing snakes tasted, tested the air in the room. These twisted and twined back upon themselves and rose up, a great dark angry funnel of nothing that engulfed Aasah until it seemed as if he wore robes of shadow and sorrow, stitched together with bursts of black lightning. His pale eyes glittered with fury and he spoke, biting off each word as he might bite through an enemy's throat.

"You ally yourself with Arachnists, those foul priests of the Cult of Eth," he spat. "You *dare*."

Pythos drew himself up at that, frowning, brows drawing together in the beginning of an angry scowl.

"You forget yoursel—"

"You. Are working. With the *Cult. Of. ETH!*" Such was his fury that Aasah shook, his voice shook, and shadows flew about the room like wicked birds. It almost seemed to Sulema that she could hear them shrieking with delight.

"You should not have done that," Yaela added in a voice that was as smooth and still as her master's was enraged. From the corner of her eye, Sulema watched as the shadowmancer's apprentice raised herself up on the balls of her feet and began to dance. As she did so Aasah burst into song like thunder, like a fell prayer. Shadows rose about them in a black tide and rushed at the throne.

Pythos drew his booted feet up away from the shadows, and his eyes flashed snake-green behind the mask. His own voice rose, filled with the bright power of Akari Sun Dragon. The corrupted Baidun Daiel took a step forward, and another, corpse arms flapping and writhing, pitiable moans escaping from behind the smooth golden masks.

Behind her Sulema could hear moans and cries of pain from those of the Baidun Daiel who had chosen to ally themselves with her. Yaela and Aasah fell to their knees, then to all fours, and the shadows fled in terror from the bright face of Akari. But Sulema had seen what Pythos was doing and heard the command in his song. It seemed to her much like those exercises Aasah had forced upon her, when she was his student.

I can do this, she thought. *Command the Baidun Daiel*. She drew a breath as the shadowmancer had taught her, imagining that the power of Sajani flowed emerald-green and river-blue from the heart of the earth up into her lungs and from there—

Pain exploded in her shoulder, then her head, and Sulema's song was broken. Her arm went icy, and then numb. She dropped the fox-head staff and reeled, nearly fainting. The shadow-jewel spider on the golden knife weaved and bobbed, dancing her into its fell web, binding her to the Nightmare Man's will.

He smiled to see her pain.

"Sulema," he crooned, "Sulema. Sweet little princess, dear little queen. Why fight your destiny?"

Ismai raised his sword high and prepared to charge, but the Nightmare Man pointed the hilt of his blade at Sulema and she fell to her knees, crying out as fire boiled through her veins, licked the back of her eyes, gnawed on her mind.

"One more move," he said in a voice as cold as the void, "and she will *beg* me for death."

Gold flashed across the Mask of Akari and the Baidun Daiel stood rigid as statues, or corpses. The shadows winked out and both shadowmancers collapsed senseless upon the dragonglass floor.

"Excellent," Pythos intoned, voice resonant with dragonsong. "Sulema, there is no need for this... strife. We are not so different, you and I, nor do our goals have to be at odds. Join me as my queen consort—no, as my *queen*—and we will rule together from Atukos. Together, we will sing Sajani to sleep for all time, and the world will know peace. Peace, instead of this pointless war! Our people—all our people—will rest easy at night, knowing their leaders are there to protect them. Is that not what you want? Is this not the legacy you fight for?"

With every bit of strength she could scrape up, everything she had ever learned, every bit of stubbornness honed through a childhood at the feet of a powerful and indifferent mother, Sulema reached for and grasped the fox-head staff.

Jinchua, help me, she thought.

Mother, help me, if you can.

Father, help me.

She used the staff to push herself to her feet and stood tall and proud, a warrior staring death straight in the face.

Sulema spat.

"Your words are pretty," she forced out, voice thick and slow as if she had a belly full of usca. "But they stink of lies. I am Sa Atu. This is my place, not yours. You know it, I know it... Atukos knows it." *Ehuani*, the walls and floors shone with a green-gold light which pulsed in time to her own heart.

Pythos's face darkened with rage. "You!" He pointed at the Nightmare Man, stabbing as if his finger was a knife. "Bring her to me! If the little *puta* will not sit by my side, she will rot in my dungeons—but I will have her, either way!"

The Nightmare Man laughed.

"You think you command *me*?" He laughed again, harder, a great deep belly laugh of genuine amusement. "Little king. Little man. You do not control so much as the dust at my feet. You think I am here to help you sing Sajani to sleep? I have been awake for a *thousand years*, caught up in the fate of that seven-times-cursed daemon Kal ne Mur. I cannot rest, I cannot die, not till the last days of this world... and I am *weary*. Weary beyond imagining. It is time for me to end this. It is time for me to sleep. If the only way I can get a bit of peace and quiet is to destroy the world, that is what I will do."

As the Nightmare Man spoke, tendrils of shining darkness flowed from the air about him to wrap like spiders' webs about the usurper king. He gestured with his knife, the webs went taut, and they—yanked—some bright and shining thing from the man on the golden throne. Pythos screamed, a thin and weak sound of utter terror. Then his eyes rolled back in his head till only the whites showed; he sat stiffly upright, and began to sing.

This was no sweet song meant to soothe Sajani's dreams and keep her still. This was a harsh discordance, filled with the clang and clamor of war. A breaking song, a waking song, a call to death and fire.

The world shuddered and bucked as Sajani stirred.

The Nightmare Man laughed again, more softly now, as he pointed the pommel of his knife at Sulema. The spider leapt, flew shining through the air, trailing a shining gossamer strand behind it, and landed light as dreams upon her shoulder.

"No!" she shouted, but it was too late. Needle fangs plunged deep into her flesh, pumping venom beneath her skin, filling her with blackness and poison and death. Sulema drew a long, shuddering, agonized breath for one last scream, but felt her body go stiff all over. She was frozen as stone, unable to so much as blink under her own will.

"Now, sweet Sulema," the Nightmare Man whispered, "sing for me."

Sulema raised her voice and began to sing, to sing Sajani awake.

FIFTY-ONE

Daru stood shoulder-to-shoulder with Hannei, the corpse of a slain enemy still warm at his feet, and watched as—once again—Sulema began to wake the dragon Sajani from her eons-long slumber.

He could feel it in his bones. They itched, worse than his arm had itched those many years ago after he had broken it in a bad fall. His skin crawled exactly as if thousands of tiny spiders were crawling over him, and his vision had that strange flat-and-double quality that could mean only one thing.

They had come to a crossway.

He had known as much already, of course. There was that sense of having been here before, of knowing what was going to happen next, a vague dread and anticipation. Pakka was glowing that weird rose-gold hue that she only got when they had come to one of those perilous bubbles in time and place where the events of a world might be altered with ever so slight, ever so careful a push.

If one was a waymaster. He was, and Daru had long since proven himself incapable of following rules with which he did not agree. He touched the medallion he wore about his neck, took a deep breath, and opened his aetheron eyes.

"There you are," he whispered, "nasty thing."

The spiderling that had fastened itself to Sulema's flesh was no spider at all, but a renderer, meant to separate soul and song and free will just as a flensing knife might separate meat and sinew and bone. If Daru's actions here were unsanctioned, the actions of he who had created such a thing were utter anathema, a violation of all the laws of nature and punishable by termination with prejudice.

Daru reached out in the aetherlands and touched the thick ropes of unlight that wove like fell spiderwebs between the creature and her master.

Nightmare Man, Daru thought, *that is what he is called here*. It hurt his soul to touch the strands, much like the sound of metal scraping against slate or the smell of rotting flesh pained the body's senses. Such utter wrongness, such discord, the antithesis of beauty and life that was a dragon's song.

So very, very unnecessary.

Daru drew one of the knives from the harness he wore across his chest. Its blade glowed a perfect blue-green in his aethersight, the color of emeralds and amethysts in the light of a young sun, the color of elves' song. With it he hewed through the burning, sticky stuff. Several strands of it snapped free and rebounded, striking the Nightmare Man full in the chest, causing him to cry out in pain and turn his maddened eyes.

Ah, he thought, *that got your attention*. He smiled to show that he was unafraid—a silent lie—and sketched the sigil of Illindra in the air between them. The ruined man's eyes widened behind the ruined mask, and lips pulled back in a feral snarl. He gestured, and the spiderling returned to its resting place on the pommel of his knife. This he raised before his face and, holding Daru's stare, answered the challenge with a spell of his own.

He traced the sigil of Eth in the air. It hovered for a moment, spitting and hissing, burning an open wound across the soft skin of time itself. A smell of sulphur and burnt things filled the chamber.

Sulema cried out in pain, then resumed singing.

The world flickered, and Daru beheld with his dreaming eyes a clearing in Shehannam, quiet and untroubled by the worries of the world of men. In this clearing lay a fennec fox, her fur stained red with blood, eyes half-closed, panting in pain as dark bonds wrapped tightly around her delicate body. Fewer than they had been before Hafsa Azeina, Ani, even Sulema herself had hewn them, still they threatened to tear flesh from spirit and send Sulema hurtling down the Lonely Road.

Back in the waking world, the city of Atukos shuddered in the first throes of death. A crack ran lengthwise across the chamber floor between Sulema and those who would support her, and black grit fell from the ceiling like corpse dust. Smaller cracks branched out from the first as the schism grew wide and deep, and the chamber's floor began to fall away into the void. The walls of Atukos trembled and heaved, groaning in extremity, as veins of red and green and gold snaked up through the living walls to pulse violently before his eyes.

Daru saw both worlds at once now, juxtaposed upon one another. In one, Sulema stared at the Nightmare Man through the Mask of Sajani and sang, sang the dragon awake, compelled by his foul magics. In Shehannam the fennec lay bound and dying. Bright eyes closed and she whimpered, a pitiable thing abandoned to death.

In both worlds the Nightmare Man smiled, seeing at last the fruition of the darkest dreams of his heart. Jinchua would die alone in this dark place, and Sulema; thus Sajani would wake, the world would end, and he would be free. Free to sleep, to die.

Oh, but you are wrong, Daru thought. *You are a foul and friendless creature, and you cannot hope to understand. Jinchua is not alone, because Sulema is* never *alone. She is loved.* He turned his head and caught Hannei's eye. She nodded. Despite everything, her face softened and she smiled at him. *We are loved*, he amended, *and none of us will ever truly be alone.* That thought helped him to breathe more deeply and fully.

None but you, Nightmare Man.

Daru hardened his heart against knowledge and pity. He knew the histories of their enemy, his sufferings, the paths he had trodden to bring him to this place and time. Some of the choices had been his own, but many had not.

There but for the roll of the dice go I, Daru thought. Still, he would do what needs must. He slipped his free hand into the pouch at his belt and drew forth his old bird-skull flute, long concealed from his teachers at the Academ, worn smooth and delicate with a young boy's tears. As the Nightmare Man's eyes widened in panicked understanding Daru brought the flute to his lips, and he played.

He played a child's tune, a lover's song, a lullaby. He played flowers in the springtime and a mother's sacrifice, he played dry wind and sweet water, and stolen kisses beneath the stars. He played friendship and love, and the laughter of children, and a grandmother's dying smiles. He drew a breath into his strong young lungs, and he played.

It was a song of love, a song for all times and all places. As the music wound round and round the room, seducing them all, Sulema's breath hitched and her own song faltered as she hearkened to Daru playing. Horses in the sunlight, and aklashi, and a belly full of mead. Hannei's hand rose to touch Daru's shoulder as he played lovemaking in the morning hours, a young boy's first crush, a warrior's laugh for no reason at all.

He played for them singly, for everyone in the room, for the world. He played for the children, most of all, the children in each of them and those who had been stolen away. As he played, and as those assembled mid-death stared rapt, the Exceptional Children were called forth from passageways long forgotten. They danced. Most of them were shades, unquiet souls fell and deadly with eyes like dark stars, but some were living children, thin and feral-eyed but still breathing, still real.

A very young girl of perhaps six summers, clad in a filthy

gown of indeterminate color, half-stumbled, half-skipped to Daru and stood, looking up at him with hollow, hungry eyes.

"Play," she commanded, then she looked around at the other exceptional children, and at the adults who had failed them. Her voice rose high and piping as Daru's flute. "Play!" she said again, smiling a fox smile, sharp white teeth and a taste for blood, then she ran laughing to touch a bigger boy on the arm.

"Play!" he shouted, and then the room was full of children skipping, running, dodging between pillars and over dead bodies in a frenzied game of not-it. They howled, voices rising like the Wild Hunt, and one by one the adults began to join in.

Watching them over his wicked flute, Daru saw the dead Sudduth and a white-cloaked Salarian sit cross-legged, facing each other to begin a game of bone-dice. Two Zeerani warriors drew a hoti and began to spar, while others watched and cheered. Yaela threw back her head, ululating, and threw her body into a dance that sent all the shades in the room to spinning with delight. As his own magic, world-born and star-trained, began to take hold, every soul living and dead joined in the game of life.

Screaming they ran, they danced, they gamed and sang, compelled to show their love of and to the world. Only the Nightmare Man stood apart, the only one among them who was truly and forever alone and unloved.

Ah, Daru thought, *how his eyes burn!* He played on, and on, even as his heart wept at the man's wretchedness.

The Nightmare Man lifted his knife again, hand shaking, and pointed it at Daru. A long tendril of darkness broke away from its binding of Sulema and her fennec, and swayed like a venomous snake seeking a rat. Finally, it scented Daru and struck, quick as thought, quick as death.

Pakka was faster. She launched herself with a shriek at the dark thing, and her furious light flared blinding bright, burning the tendril away to smoke and ash.

"PIP-PIP-PEEEE OH!" she screeched, triumphant.

Again and again the Nightmare Man struck, trying to silence Daru's song, the gorgeous, terrible reminder that of all things everywhere he was least loved. Again and again Pakka trilled and flew, striking the shadow-webs with her serrated forearms, snapping them in half with her powerful mandibles, blinding them with her butt-light. *Little queen*, Daru thought, *how I love thee.* How far they had traveled together, and through such perils. The Nightmare Man could never comprehend such a love as theirs, and so he could never hope to combat it.

At long last, the assault accomplished what Daru had hoped. The Nightmare Man's strength and attention had been diverted enough that Sulema's little fennec slipped her dark bonds and darted away into the green forests of Shehannam. This in turn enabled Sulema to break free. She stopped singing to the dragon Sajani and turned to face the Nightmare Man, and her golden eyes behind the jeweled mask burned hot with an inhuman wrath.

"YOU," she said, and her voice sent shimmering tremors through the fabric of the world. "*YOU!*" She raised her golden sword, and it shone like the heart of the sun.

"Ahhh," the Nightmare Man said. The knife fell from his trembling hand, but before Sulema could move he reached up to grasp the medallion he wore at his throat.

Daru started, and his music skipped a beat. *No*, he thought, *no. It cannot be.* Then the Nightmare Man turned his terrible tortured gaze upon him. When he held up the medallion in anguished defiance, Daru knew that yes, it was so.

"*Akhouti,*" ground the nightmare voice. "*Salhach a akhoutek. Anneh akhoutek! Salhach a hei!*"

Never in all his endless years of hunting had Daru heard a more heartfelt plea. Tears stung his eyes, but he shook his head. "It is too late for forgiveness. I am sorry, *akhouti*," he said. *Brother.* "I am so, so sorry." He reached for his knives.

"*Eh na mutaahna kulkem!*" the Nightmare Man spat. He made an obscene gesture with his free hand—a fist opened and shut, a flick of the wrist—and the greater part of those humans who had moments before been fighting, playing, or dying fell motionless as old bones to lie upon the rubble of the floor.

The Nightmare Man had lived long, long beyond the reckoning of men, of vash'ai and even waymasters, though not perhaps in the reckoning of dragons. He had been fighting, and he had been running to fight another day and another, since the days of Zula Din, of Ishmalak and Devranae and Kal ne Mur. He ran now, tearing open a door between worlds as casually as a warrior might flick open the flap of a friend's tent. The Nightmare Man stepped through, and it began to close with a flash of dark light.

But Daru, who was much, much older than he seemed, had hunted prey nearly this dangerous and desperate, and was not easily taken by surprise. Grasping his own amulet he reached out in three worlds, holding the way open. Sweat sprang up on his brow and he trembled, though to untrained eyes it would appear as if he simply stood in the middle of a broken chamber with one hand held upraised. A dark shimmer of air like a small cloud hovered just beyond his fingertips.

Shadows began to pour into and out of the dark place. In the belly of Atukos, buried and forgotten to the world of men, he could hear—or perhaps feel—the thousands upon thousands of not-dead Baidun Daiel as they began to moan and stir.

Sulema had not fallen, nor Ismai, nor—strangely—had Sulema's half-masked lover. "Sulema," Daru called to her in a strained voice. The medallion clenched in his fist began to hum, then grow hot, and finally to crack. "Sulema—GO! Follow him!"

Sulema turned her face to hiss at him, and in that moment, she seemed more dragon than woman. Then she turned toward that doorway through which her enemy had stepped, and which Daru held open only through great strength of will. She nodded to herself and seized her fox-head staff. With his dreamshifting eyes Daru watched her spirit self, her intikallah, step out of her earthly body and into the portal through which the Nightmare Man had escaped.

The dark doorway wrenched itself free from Daru's grasp and slammed shut.

Sulema's body slumped to the ground, pale and lifeless.

The stones and bones of Atukos one by one began to tear loose and fall to the ground, threatening to crush the humans within. In the catacombs far below the Baidun Daiel—those once exceptional children who, like the Nightmare Man, had been betrayed, buried, and forgotten by the Dragon Kings of Atualon—began to scream.

FIFTY-TWO

"**S**ulema!"

The sight of her dropping lifeless to the cold floor was more than Ismai could bear. Crying out, he fought the invisible web of the Nightmare Man's weaving, straining forward till he could feel the cords in his neck standing out. It felt as if he would tear muscle from bone.

The pain was exquisite—worse than dying, worse even than living—and he halted to catch his breath, blinking bloodied tears from his dead eyes and shuddering in agony. Just then Pythos, released from the Nightmare Man's spell, cut his magical song short and shook his head as if waking from a dream.

Then the Dragon King smiled to find his bondage lifted, the Nightmare Man gone, and his enemies unable to move. When his eyes lit upon the still form of Sulema he laughed aloud, staggering to his feet and reaching for the sword scabbarded at his waist. This he drew and started down the steps to where she lay helpless, one arm folded unnaturally beneath her, hair a tangle of sunset wizard locks, and her face—

I love that face, Ismai thought. *I love her. I have always loved her.*

As do I, Kal ne Mur agreed. *She is... everything... to me. To us.*

Even as sand and wind combined become a storm, Ismai and Kal ne Mur roared with fury and with one last great effort burst through the bonds of magic that held them fast. Moving slowly as if in a dream he hefted his own sword and pushed forward to meet the usurper king. When Pythos brought his sword down for a killing blow, it was met and blocked by Ismai's shamsi—the very blade his mother had given him, marking him out as the favored son of her heart. The ring of steel on steel was as a bell tolling.

The shock of that blow traveled up Ismai's arms to his shoulder, to the very core of his being. Shaking him, waking him, making him whole. Filled with a sudden fire that was half joy, half rage, he threw his head back and laughed at the surprise on the Dragon King's face, and then used the blade's momentum to wheel round, pivoting on the ball of his foot as he had seen the warriors do a thousand times. As he had done himself as Kal ne Mur. He brought his blade round again to slash across Pythos's sword arm just below the shoulder.

Blood sprayed in his face hot and salty and good. Pythos ap Serpentus ne Atu, first of his name, dropped his sword and yelled in pain. He did not have time to recover, or run away, or even turn from the next attack. So swiftly did Ismai's shamsi turn about, hissing through the air and whispering of death, that Pythos still had a look of surprise and the beginnings of anger on his face when his head toppled free of his shoulders to roll and bounce across the floor of his throne room.

His headless body, spraying blood in all directions, jerked in a death-jig before folding at the knee and waist to flop indecorously close to Sulema.

Ismai flicked his blade, sending thin ribbons of blood to fly across the chamber, then drew it across his tunic and sheathed it as if he had all the time in the world. Crossing the room he bent over the bleeding head of his foe and seized the Mask of Akari. It was surprisingly light in his hands and regarded him with sober intent.

Deep within him, Kal ne Mur shuddered in pleasure and dread.

It begins again.

So it does, Ismai answered, and gently—gently—he placed the dragon's mask upon his face.

It burned. *Ah*, it burned. In his mind's eye Ismai saw again the snake-priestess of Thoth as she sprayed venom into his face, his eyes. This, however, was a fresh torment, hot and new, searing the skin and bones, stabbing into his eyes like knives heated in a smith's forge. Ismai clenched them shut, which availed him little, and ground his teeth together against the agony, allowing only the smallest, softest hiss to escape. It was worth it. Sulema was worth it—if by this he could gain some small hope of saving her, he would pay this price a thousand times over.

There was a flash bright as the birth of a new sun. Ismai staggered but did not fall. As the light faded slowly, slowly, it took with it the searing pain. The mask grew cool against his skin, comforting. It accepted him as a rider chooses a new mount and worked to train him to its will.

Kal ne Mur, still and forever part of Ismai's song, was no stranger to the dragon's magic and pushed back against it, setting boundaries so that he would not be suborned.

Thank you, Ismai whispered deep within his soul. He opened his eyes carefully, braced against the pain, expecting to see only those things the dead king might show him.

He stared about the room with surprise.

His living eyes had been restored to him.

No, he thought. *Not restored. Akari has taken my eyes from me and replaced them with his own.*

Never had he seen the world like this. Colors for which he had no name leapt out at him, heartbreaking in their loveliness. So keen was his sight, so sharply defined, that it almost seemed as if he could see *through* things into the heart of them, the essence.

A sound disturbed his fascination. A soft sound filled with anguish, it pierced the dragon's spell and brought him back to the world of men. He glanced down and beheld his love, his Sulema. Mattu Halfmask had gathered her limp form into his arms and was bent over her, weeping.

Ah, Ismai thought. *Ah*. Sympathy for the man filled both his hearts, but it was the pity of a rich man for the poor, for someone who never had and never would claim his own golden fortune. Mattu was the second son of a forgotten king, and he was a man who loved a dragon. For these sorrows Ismai would forgive this trespass. Lowering himself, Ismai crouched beside Sulema and her grieving lover and pulled her into his arms. Mattu was loath to let her go but Ismai's strength would not be denied.

"Give her to me," he said as gently as he was able. "I can do what you cannot. I can help her." Reluctantly, Mattu surrendered Sulema's limp and still-warm body into Ismai's care.

"If I thought you meant her harm," he said in a choked voice, "I would kill you."

Ismai smiled, then stood, clutching Sulema to his breast. Precious she was to him, beyond salt or breath or all the beauty of the world. Life radiated from her, hot and wild, belying the stillness of her face and pale cast to her skin. It seemed in that moment that he held everything in his arms that was right and good, every true thing that made life's next breath worth fighting for.

Chaos still reigned in that chamber. Paying no heed to the blood at the steps of the throne, to the dead and the undead and the unwholesome things which had once been Baidun Daiel, to whom he owed a soul-debt, Ismai strode out through the broken door. He shone with the light of Akari, and so dreadful was his masked face that none could bear the sight of him.

The secret ways of Atukos were known to him, above and below. Kal ne Mur had caused many of these same hallways and passages to be carved from the living stone, shaped as the sleeping dragon herself would have them. Down and around and up he hurried, moving faster as he went, unhindered by battle fatigue or the dear weight in his arms, till at last he reached the mountain steps. Steep and slick, treacherous to those feet not meant to climb them. To Ismai they were welcoming as a garden path, and he ran up them two and three at a time.

Finally he reached the lake of dragons' dreams and kings' songs, and only then did he stop. His chest heaved and he trembled, not from exhaustion, but from some nameless excitement. The lake smoked and boiled with Sajani's disquiet and Akari's wrath. Walking slowly to the very edge, he saw clearly that this was not water but the fine, clear stuff of magic. Any stone thrown into this lake would dissolve and be lost forever.

Sulema was not breathing. Though the Mask of Sajani glittered with the lively light of a thousand green stars, her eyes behind the mask were half-closed and dull, and her flesh was cooling.

She is lost already, he thought, *and I am lost without her.*

"Sulema," he whispered, and bent his face to her. The masks met, and a single clear note pierced the cool morning air like a bell.

Ismai gathered his courage, the audacity of hope, and stepped into the lake.

FIFTY-THREE

"Sulema..."

His call was a chain, a thorned vine, a binding web, trying to trap her in place and in time. She flitted aside gossamer-light, death-quick, content to forget and unbecome and simply be.

Sulema rose up on the wind, spreading herself out thin as a dragon's wings, and let the skinned man's dreams of agony bear her up, up, pressing like a kiss against the blissful dark. She burst into candescent song, and lost herself in the wonder of her own creation. She was light, she was love, she was song and story and color, she was—

"Sulema!"

His voice trapped her; her name wrapped her within the limits of a human skin. The song shattered into words, harsh and atonal. The words became flesh, and the flesh became pain, and she remembered who she was.

"I am," she whispered, and she wept at the sound of her own voice, at the human mouth too small to speak of big things. "Sulema."

The infinite became finite. *Nothing* thickened, quickened, creating a Sulema-shaped void which she filled with tears and blood and pain until she had arms, legs, and hair, and a beating heart. Sulema opened her eyes and saw far above her a thin and wavering light.

Sun, she thought. *Sky.*

Air.

She moved her arms, her legs, sluggishly at first but with purpose as she became reacquainted with flesh and bone, thought and need. Her lungs remembered that she needed air, her legs remembered how to kick, and her heart remembered everything else. Ismai, she remembered. Daru, and Ani. Mattu Halfmask.

Hannei.

Kishah—*vengeance.*

Love for her sword-sister smote her, pierced her, made her whole again. In the end it was not vengeance, but love, which drove her to kick and thrash her way back to the surface, breaking through the Dibris with a gasp and a wail as the air burned her lungs, as the pale moonlight burned her eyes, even through the mask…

She brought her hands to her face, wondering. Indeed, she wore the Mask of Sajani, comfortable as her own skin, cool as starlight. Her fingers remembered its ridges and facets, and her soul remembered what it had been like to *be* a dragon, outside of time and space and the confines of human life.

I am so small, she thought, dismayed.

So limited. So… human.

The thought slipped away with the current, washing over her, bouncing away down the river like debris after a cleansing storm. With a grunt of effort she struck out for the shore, wishing—not for the first time—that she had paid better attention when her mother had tried to teach her to swim. Not that there had been much use for it in the desert.

Her bare feet found purchase at last, and Sulema pushed herself up through the strong waters onto the river's edge, shivering a little with cold and exertion. She wished for clothing, and a weapon, and for a horse—

A soft whicker made her jump halfway out of her sodden skin. Further up the river's edge stood a horse. Not just any horse, but Hafsa Azeina's snarky little gray mare, who had thrown Sulema more times than she could count, and who had died during the attack on her mother in Eid Kalish.

"Keila," she said, "what are you doing here?" She walked warily to the mare, who stood with one leg cocked, placid as any gelding and real as Sulema herself. Beside her, neatly folded as if laid out by Atualonian servants, lay a warrior's garb—trousers and vest blue as a warden's touar, embroidered all over in gold, and a headdress of lionsnake plumes grander even than Sareta's had been.

Thrust into the soft sand, laughing at her—Sulema was sure of this—was the fox-head staff.

"Jinchua," she said, shaking her head. "I might have known. Am I dreaming, then, or is this real?"

Yes, her kima'a laughed, deep in the forests of Shehannam. *Also, yes. Life is a dream, and human life is a nightmare. Have you learned nothing at all, then, in all your travels?*

"Neither so much as I should have, nor as little as you might think," Sulema answered, donning the warrior's garb. It was light and comfortable, and fit perfectly—of course it did—and Sulema ran a hand over the thread-of-gold. Despite the odd circumstances, she wished for a hand-mirror. Snugging the headdress firmly into place atop her wizard locks, she took up her staff with a sigh of long suffering, then eyed Keila askance.

"You are not going to throw me this time, are you?"

The little mare huffed as if she had been insulted, but made no protest when Sulema leapt easily onto her back, nor gave one of those sideways hops for which she had been so famous.

"Okay then," Sulema said, still mightily suspicious. Dream-clothing and a dream-staff were all well and good, but she was not going to trust the illusion of a placid dream-Keila.

"Let us be gone."

Do you know where you are going? Jinchua asked. Sulema could see the little fennec in her mind's eye, pink tongue lolling, laughing at the world. She smiled at the image.

She really is my kima'a, she thought. *Churra-headed brat.*

"Back to the beginning, of course," Sulema replied. "*Het het!*" She put her heels to Keila's sides and the gray leapt to life, sweet as a song, swift as the wind. Sulema gave an exultant "*Ai-la-la-la-la!*" brandishing her staff and leaning forward into the whipping mane.

It will be a beautiful day, she thought as the first pale fingers of dawn parted the sky above them. *A beautiful day to die.*

He was waiting for her in the Madraj, as she knew he would be.

Standing upon the hallowed grounds, long the living- and loving- and dying-place of the Zeeranim, defiling their memories with his foul presence. The late light of the moons, the early light of dawn kindled on his dull and ruined mask, setting it aflame. There in the arena he leaned on a hammer, mocking her with his stance, his eyes, his very presence, as he watched her dismount and approach. Sulema's heart clenched and her stomach churned as she saw the ring he had laid around himself—a ring of burned-out skulls. Some of them had been children, she saw, and others still had the remnants of charred braids clinging to them, leaving no doubt as to their identity.

He draws a hoti of death, she thought, *with the faces of my people*. She stopped mid-stride to glare at him, and he smiled a beautiful smile at her reaction.

"Welcome, Sulema an Wyvernus ne Atu," he said, holding his arms wide, hefting the great war hammer as if it weighed less than his conscience. "I have been waiting for you."

"Nightmare Man." She spat upon the ground. "I have come to kick your ass."

His eyes lit on the staff she bore, on the mask she wore, on everything she was. His lip curled in a sneer of *such* contempt.

"So." He nodded. "You have become your mother's daughter after all. And your father's. You have become that which you hate."

"Not at all," she replied. There was no anger in her voice, none in her heart. "I have become that which I am."

"And what is that, Sulema?"

She laughed at the Nightmare Man, then again at the flash of fury in his eyes.

"*Khutlani*," she told him. "Do not say my name. Your mouth is too small to speak such big things." With that, she stepped over the small, sad skull of a child, and into the fighter's ring.

There was no play, none of the feints or posturing that would have marked a match between two warriors. The hammer whistled through the air with a thousand-voiced howl. Sulema crouched and drove up into the blow, snarling like a vash'ai behind the dragon's mask as she spun the staff from hand to hand. Their weapons met, slid, rebounded, whirled and met again.

Sulema was strong.

He was stronger.

The hammer shaft thrust at her belly, the head smashed through the air and Sulema leapt, legs churning, staff singing a song of sand and fire as the hammer failed, again and again, to find its target. But only just. Sulema was fast.

The Nightmare Man was faster.

She landed solid blows on his wrist, his upper arm, his ribs, and one on the back of his knee, but to no avail. The Nightmare Man stalked her around the hoti, hammer shrieking its bloodlust as it missed her face, then her leg by the breadth of a bad dream, a shadow's kiss. His smile told her this was a game to him, and the obsidian chips of his eyes said that it was only a matter of time before his blows landed.

Akari Sun Dragon spread his wings across the desert sky, kindling the Zeera to light and life, the sands to song. A blow Sulema did not see coming took her in the gut and she stumbled back, gasping, hunched about the pain and trying to keep her guard up. A low moan of fear rose up from the ring of skulls as her heel brushed the edge of the hoti.

"Leave, and you die," the Nightmare Man told her. He held his hammer easily and turned his face to the morning, closing his eyes as if nothing she might say or do could possibly matter. Sulema straightened as best she was able and brought the staff back up.

"I am going nowhere," she said. Her voice was a low growl that echoed in the empty eyes of the Madraj. "You will die this day."

"I will not die this day, daughter of the dragon," he replied. "I cannot die, nor sleep, nor escape the dream of this mortal horror, not till the end of this world." He turned his face and looked upon her with eyes that were ancient and terrible with grief.

"The nightmare is your own," she murmured.

"It is—and do you feel a moment's pity for me, beautiful child? Would you put down your staff if you could, and heal my pain?" He took a step toward her, and Sulema's breath caught in her throat as his gaze caught hers and held.

All the stars in the sky are in his eyes, she thought. *All the worlds in Illindra's web.*

The Nightmare Man lifted a gloved hand and gestured her nearer. Sulema's feet dragged against the sand as she took a step toward him. Another… and another. A low growl rose in her throat, again to echo among the empty seats of the Madraj. Then she glanced over the Nightmare Man's shoulder, beyond the hoti, and saw the eyes.

Gold eyes and green, yellow eyes and amber, they stared. The vash'ai had come, wild sires and queens with tusks ungilded, spirits untamed, untrammeled, free and deadly as the Zeera herself. The great cats sat and lounged and prowled among the seats and arches, peering at the combatants and singing a low, growling, monotone song unlike anything Sulema had ever heard.

Her steps dragged her ever nearer to the Nightmare Man, so close she could feel the cold heat of his body, hear his breaths. He smiled, reached out and took her fox-head staff, dropping it upon the ground. Next, he tore the Mask of Sajani from her face and tossed it aside as one might a trinket.

"Sulema," he purred, cupping her cheek in one hand. He raised his hammer high with the other, and it laughed at her in the cold morning light. She could not tear her gaze from his, not even to witness her own impending death. The Nightmare Man gave off waves of grave-cold, bone-cold, drowned-in-the-river cold. She shivered, and he smiled to see it.

"You," he said, drawing her closer, the hammer higher. "You have caused me such trouble."

The song of the vash'ai rose about them, and Sulema smiled between chattering teeth.

"You f-forget one thing."

He hesitated, eyes flashing. "And what is that?"

"It is only t-t-trouble if you get c-caught."

Quick as cat's claws she struck, reaching over the Nightmare Man's shoulders with both hands, taking hold of his cloak, and yanking it up over his head so that he became entangled in it, just as Hannei had done to her in the fighting pits. Dishonorable, she had said then, and dishonorable it was.

But it worked.

She twisted the cloth so that the Nightmare Man's face and arms were well and truly tangled, and then wrested the hammer from his hands. She dropped her grip on his cloak and took a step back, swinging from the leg, from the hip, with all the strength in her wounded shoulder and all the *kishah* in her heart, and when that blow landed the sun—

Just for a moment—

498

Winked out.

The Nightmare Man's skull crumbled like a fistful of eggs. His hideous mask flew end over end to land outside the hoti and the hammer shattered with a high, metallic shriek. He fell to his knees, and then to his face in the sand, and the ground beneath Sulema's feet opened to receive him.

She stumbled backward, away from the widening crack, snatching up the Mask of Sajani and her fox-head staff lest the gaping maw swallow them both. As she and the vash'ai stared in silence, the limp dark form fell from sight, one arm sliding and flopping in a grim parody of a farewell wave as he disappeared.

"*Jai tu wai*," she called, and then wished she had not. Dead or no, she had no wish to see that face ever again, not in the least of her dreams.

The sunlight flashed again, or perhaps it was her. Sulema remembered, now that it was too late, that she had used her mother's tricks to get to the Madraj. She was in this place in spirit only, and could feel the connection to her body growing thin and weak. Too late she realized that although her mother had taught her how to leave the corporeal form, she had never learned how to get back again.

Perhaps if I dove into the river? But even as the thought surfaced it swam away again, leaving not so much as a trickle of bubbles to show her the way home. A wave of dizziness overtook her. Sulema raised a hand to her face and realized that she could see through herself. She was fading, blowing away on the wind, lost like a bad dream in the light of a new day.

Perhaps it is best, she thought. *Perhaps it is best that I die.* Ani herself said that none should hold the powers of dreamshifting and atulfah in the same body. *It is too much power for one person to wield.* I *am too much.*

A glint of sunlight on twisted metal caught her attention and she thought she smiled.

At least he died first. I accomplished that much, at least—and the Zeera is singing, she is singing me to sleep.

Then she realized it was not the Zeera.

The vash'ai stirred from their perches and lounging spots in the sunlight, left off their circling and posturing, and came to her. Young cats dark as soot, old queens with yellowed eyes and hanging bellies, and greatest of all, the pale broken-tusked form of the kahanna who walked with Ani but claimed her not.

"Inna'hael," she said, recalling his name, and smiled as the sunlight flowed through her to stain the dirt. "I am glad you are here. I would not want to die alone."

Nor shall you, he replied in her heart and mind. His voice was stern and deep and all things good, and Sulema wept with joy to have heard the words of a vash'ai before she died. *He sounds like Azra'hael*, she thought. *My Azra'hael. My everything.*

Azra'hael was my son and heir. Inna'hael drifted closer, until his face eclipsed the sun in her eyes. *He was one of our greatest warriors. I forbade his leaving the prides, I forbade his bonding you. I did not think a human worthy of one such as he.*

Spirit though she was, and dying, Sulema's heart cracked and bled.

I am sorry. And she was. Had he remained in his place and not come seeking her, Azra'hael would not have died.

I am not, he replied, purr-soft. *My son was right: you are worthy. I was wrong.* A flash of broken tusk, a cat's laugh. *It will not happen again.*

She is worthy. Another voice, deep but lighter than that of Inna'hael, and a bright light that hurt her weary eyes. A young vash'ai, thick-maned and powerful, stepped up to stand beside Inna'hael. *I will have her. She smells of blood and fire, and I am hungry.*

And I, a third voice said, light as a spring breeze and full of laughter. This male was dark and heavily scarred, with a torn ear and laughing blue eyes. *She smells of mischief, and I am bored.*

There you are, Inna'hael said, displaying his tusks in a cat's grin. *Long you wished to be Zeeravashani, little one— you should have been more careful of your wishes. These sons of mine are trouble enough to make even one such as you have second thoughts.*

They are beautiful, Sulema protested, reaching out her fading hands toward the vash'ai. *They are perfect.*

So be it, the broken-tusked sire said. He opened his mouth wide and breathed upon her face. The hot carrion stink of his breath enfolded her. He opened his mouth wider, and roared, propelling her away, away, away.

FIFTY-FOUR

Sulema swam again, but this time she was not alone. Two beings of light supported her as she rose through Illindra's web, the worlds glistening and tickling her skin like bubbles as she drifted out of time and mind until at last she was caught up in the swirl of song, a riff, a chord of the discordant, beautiful, gorgeously messy life that was her own world, her own time and place and bonds of honor.

Newly born, the Song of Sajani swept her up in a rising tide, swirling and rolling around her, dragging her over reef and wreck and casting her at long last on the sands of the same beach and into the same life, the same body from which she had wandered.

So the Song of Akari called her, as well, called her home whole and alive. Sunlight warmed the mask she wore, falling once again upon her face. It warmed her throat, her skin, her hair, her eyelids. Strong arms held her in the here and now, and a voice—a man's voice—chanted her name like a prayer.

"Sulema. Sulema," it said. "Oh, Sulema, oh my love..."

Stirring, she opened her eyes and looked into the other half of her soul. She reached up to touch his face, knowing at last that his wounds were a prayer of love and that she was the answer.

"Ismai," she whispered. "Ismai, I am here."

"I see you," he whispered. His arms tightened about her, and hot tears washed her face. "I see you."

The Mask of Akari gazed down upon the Mask of Sajani, and Sulema could feel them, could hear them—dragons beyond all thought of here and now, beings of such magnificence that life itself was just a dream to them, this world a passing fancy.

Akari sang to his mate, calling her to wake, to live, to come to him, to love.

Sulema was swept away in the beauty of their joy as Sajani, roused from her dream of ages, answered. The ground beneath her trembled, then shook. Ismai released her from his embrace, stood, grasped her hands and pulled her to her feet.

"Come," he said in a voice that was not wholly his own. "It is time."

"No, *you* come," she corrected him, none too gently, in a voice that was deeper and richer than hers had ever been. "This is my world." She led him down the mountain path and into the forest as the lake began to boil, the fog to rise, the ground to ripen, to tremble and swell as if it would burst open.

She sang as she walked, as powerfully and as naturally as a human babe taking in its first breath, and he sang with her. Their voices rose in prayer, in exultation, in the mating-song of dragons, the dirge of a dying world come to its rightful end. Their path took them down into Atukos, her dragonstone walls lit in a boreal display of scintillating greens and blues and golds blazing in ecstatic welcome at the return of the queen.

Sulema-Sajani trailed her hands along the walls as she took him down into the heart of Atukos and then into the great hall. She ran up the steps to her throne. There was blood there as she claimed her rightful seat, and Ismai-Akari took his place beside and behind her.

"It is time," she told him.

"Yes," he agreed, bowing his head. "It is time."

The dragonstone walls of Atukos began to coruscate with flames of gold-green and sea foam, the floors to buckle. A fine mist rose about her feet, thickened to fog. A storm of magic rose in answer to the dancing of her heart. The dragon would wake, as dragons must, and this world, this finite pearl, would be strung in the web of her memories, to live on only in the infinite heart of a dragon.

Ismai went to his knees and lifted his arms high. His mask glowed as brightly as the desires of her heart and he sang, of life and love and poetry, of strife and betrayal and war, of all the doings of kith and kin he had witnessed unfolding on this tiny, bright world beneath his wings as his love slept on.

Something dragonish appeared in Sulema's heart, then—the fierce and jealous love of life. She wished to wake, to sing to the infinite her adoration of humans, of sisters and lovers and vengeance. She opened her mouth to sing, to wake Sajani fully, to break the bonds of slumber and set her free.

A single note caught at the edge of her soul and tugged.

She paused, mid-breath, to listen.

It was a delicate sound, dark and lovely, thin as birdsong and strong as a young girl's determination to live. It rose into a trill like a sweet-throated exultation and fell with a clash like the breaking of swords. This was a new music, limited and imperfect, but for all its imperfection it had a rough, wild beauty.

The world was a song—an exciting song, born of the loves and stories and tears of countless tiny lives. Old as rock it was, and yet—and yet, there was a new voice on the wind, a refrain she had never yet heard. Sajani stopped mid-stretch to listen to this new sound, this delightful cacophony, and thus her soul was trapped. A web was woven around her not of balance and purity and perfection but of strife, and pain, of the fool's song of courage to press on when all hope has failed. The laughter of a sword-sister with no voice; the lament of a mother over a lover she has killed with her own hands; the wails of a sea-thing child caught between wave and wind.

The bonesinger sang to the dream eater sang to the waymaster and they all sang to her, called to her, called her to hearth and home and sleep, sleep, *sleep*...

The bonds of life and love steeled over her, the most delightful of traps, the sweetest of prisons. Sajani, content to have been caught once more, settled her heart and her claws, closed her tourmaline eyes, tucked her nose beneath her wings, and drifted back to dream once more of warriors and wardens, of lovers and liars.

After all, she reasoned, the story was not over… and she wanted to know how it ended.

Sulema.

Sulema.

SULEMA!

Let me sleep, she snarled. Let me be. Sulema rolled over, scowling in annoyance. She had been enjoying her dreams and did not wish to be reminded that she had a body, at least not just yet. *I am tired. Let me dream!*

This is not your dream, Kithren. You do not belong here. Wake, Kithren. Wake now.

But the dream…

Are we always to rescue you? The voice was teasing, gentle, but there were teeth to it as well. These fastened upon her soul, lifting her from the dragon's dream like a sire carrying his precious cub. They carried her home.

Sulema woke.

The first thing she noticed was that her shoulder did not hurt.

The second was that her mouth tasted of week-old corpse.

The third thing she noticed, as she came fully into herself, was that she was bare-ass naked and twined about an equally naked, very male body. She jumped, rubbing sand and salt and blood from her eyes and trying to push away.

Strong arms held her fast.

"It is okay," a deep voice said, familiar and yet... not. "Shhhh. You are safe. You are safe."

"*You* are not!" she growled, breaking free and sitting up. She shook her head to free it of cobwebs, and looked down upon the lean, dark body of Ismai. "Where are we? *What happened?*"

"We are—I am not sure where we are," he said, sitting up and drawing his knees up to his chest. He sounded young and unsure of himself, but not nearly as young as he had been just a few moons before. His voice had changed, and his face—

"Ismai!" she gasped. "Your eyes!"

Ismai reached up to touch his face. Though he still bore the hideous scars of burning, his eyes were clear as a summer sky—and as golden as her own. They regarded her with wary amusement.

"Your skin!" he replied.

Sulema looked down at her naked body. Her skin, though still as freckled as ever, was so deeply mottled that she thought she looked half vash'ai. She craned her neck and gazed around with a growing sense of wonder and confusion. Somehow, they had managed to wake up naked as babes on a white sand beach within sight of Atukos. Thick plumes of clean white smoke billowed up from the fortress, and she could smell the odd tang of burnt magic. They were alone, unharmed.

Completely bewildered.

Memories surfaced, faint and sweet.

"I was—I was caught in the dragon's dream," she said. Faint sounds of music were there in her heart.

"So was I," Ismai answered. Then he bolted upright.

Snarling forms, golden and glorious and fierce, burst from the sedge grass a short distance from the dreamers. Sulema shrieked with surprise, and Ismai tried to scramble to his feet before falling hard on his butt, legs splayed and eyes as round as moons. Three young vash'ai—two sparse-maned sires and a dusky queen—leapt to the beach, tumbling round their humans like overgrown kittens, tusks gleaming in the bright light of day.

Got you, Mai'hael the laughing exulted. Sulema knew him instantly; knew his name, his heart, the color of his bright soul. He was hers, and she his. *Got you, Kithren.*

Little cub, Ga'hael the serious chided, padding toward her like the fires of dawn and ignoring the rambunctious play of his brother and Ismai's Ruh'ayya. *You need to be more aware of your surroundings, lest you become meat. Were you a tarbok, my teeth would be in your belly!*

I love you. That was all Sulema could manage before her kithren bowled her over with their paws and their adoration, even as Ruh'ayya wrapped her forelegs around Ismai, bearing him to the ground and licking his face half off.

Drunk on new love and the surprise of finding themselves still alive, the five of them rolled and played and laughed on the beach as the day grew long and old. Loath to seek out their companions, even to find out how much of their world was left standing, they found themselves content to chase the waves and each other and let the great gray waters wash away blood and ashes and the taste of memories. Awareness woke slowly in Sulema's heart—that they had nearly destroyed the world, that they may have saved it. That neither they nor their lives could possibly ever be the same. Soon enough the world would come looking and it would find her, shackle her once more with the bonds of friendship and honor, pin her down with the weight of a dragon's legacy.

For these few moments, however, she was content to simply *be.*

More than content. She was complete. She was—

"Sulema!" Ani's voice sounded, recalling them to here and now. "Ismai!"

"Dreamshifter!" A deep voice she knew was Daru's, clear and strong as the call of a golden shofar. Then a sharp whistle sounded once, twice, three times. It was Hannei's hunting signal. They had been found.

"We are in trouble now," Ismai whispered. He grinned, winked one golden eye, and Sulema knew him in that instant as a man and a king and a lover. She walked to him, and he enfolded her in his arms.

Let come what may, she thought. *I am ready.*

"It is only trouble if you get caught," she reminded him.

"Then we are in trouble, sweet warrior queen," he said, "for surely I am caught."

Ismai bent his face to hers, and they kissed.

Far below them, in the dark and deep...

The dragon smiled in her sleep.

FIFTY-FIVE

He found her in the healer's rooms, seated cross-legged beside the body of Aasah. His late father's shadowmancer lay still, the bier around him piled high with white flowers, hands crossed over his chest in the manner of their people. The stars set into his skin glittered even in the dim light of a single oil lamp. For a mercy the sorcerer's eyes were closed, his face peaceful in death as it had not been in life.

"Yaela."

Her face when she turned it to him was tear-streaked, wild and dreadful in her grief and impossibly beautiful.

"I loved him," she said without prompting, "and I hated him. He was my friend, my master, my brother. He brought me forth from the Edge and made me who I am, and then he broke me. He was everything I had in the world, and he betrayed me." She bent her head over the dead man, hair falling like a shroud. "He gave his life for me. How can I still hate him?"

"Yaela." Leviathus crossed the floor to stand by her, heedless of the jagged stones, the still-rumbling mountain, the bitter-sharp smell of death. "Yaela, come away. We will see him buried, or burned if that is your wish. Come away." He reached a hand to her and she took it, let him pull her to her feet.

"Are you hurt?"

"No," she answered. "Are you?"

"I will have a few new scars," he admitted, "but none worth writing a book about." She looked at him in surprise at that, and laughed, startling both of them with the sound.

Together they walked from the sad room, leaving the empty shell of Aasah behind them.

Free of the Draiksguard, whose services Leviathus had politely but firmly refused, and unhindered by the imperators, whose confusion he could not help but pity, he wandered with Yaela through the halls and rooms of his childhood home, marveling that a place could feel familiar and alien at the same time.

Then again, he reasoned, *I myself am changed.*

I have made some improvements, Azhorus noted in the back of his mind. *Though you are a work in progress, to be sure.*

At last they came into his suite of old rooms and stood upon the balcony, looking out over Atualon and the sea beyond. A red day was dawning, sharp with hope and foreboding. Yaela laid a hand upon the balustrade and Leviathus covered it with his own. She did not pull away but sighed deeply. Leviathus thought that he had never in his life seen a woman so lovely, or so sad.

"What is wrong?" he asked, for it seemed to him that they had grown close enough that she might answer, where before her heart and mind had been closed to him.

"The people of Quarabala, such as would flee their homes, have been saved," she said at last. "Their future is yet uncertain, and the danger they face now is no less than before, only different. Aasah had treated first with Wyvernus, and then I suppose with Pythos, to aid the Dragon King in return for lands where my people may abide, and wherein they may build homes and cities.

"But Aasah is dead. Who now rules in Atukos? And with the thoughts of Atualon turned inward, who now might speak for the Quarabalese, now that Quarabala is lost to us and Aasah fallen into shadow? What future have I given my sister's daughter—a homeless people to lead in rags, as beggars with no homeland and no hope?" She sighed again.

"My sister rules in Atualon, or will once she is elevated to the throne," Leviathus told her. "Sulema is fair-minded and soft-hearted, for all that she was raised by barbarians. More so for having been raised by barbarians, perhaps. A childhood spent in Atualon might have simply molded her into one more golden-tongued liar. Sulema has spent time and shed blood with the warriors and leaders of Quarabala; surely she will grant them a boon of land."

"Grant them a boon." Yaela made a face. "The women of Quarabala do not accept charity, king's son. Should the Dragon Queen offer land in return for nothing, Maika will refuse it. To accept another queen's charity would be to lose face before the people, and then she would be no queen at all."

"Ah. Well." Leviathus hesitated. Her hand beneath his was so warm, so precious, and her face so grave and strong, that his tongue clove to the roof of his mouth, making speech difficult. He drew a deep breath and went on, though he was in that moment more daunted by the prospect of her rejection than he had been by the likelihood of death in battle. "Well. I have a proposal for you, if I may."

She looked at him, and it seemed to him a strange light was in her eyes. Strange, but not unfriendly. "Go on."

"Well, ah. The river pirates and I, some of us at least, are of a mind to found a city of our own. Land was promised to us by the Dragon Queen, fertile land near the mouth of the Dibris, land which has never been settled because the leviathans claim those beaches and have never suffered the presence of men. But Azhorus has been speaking with his people on my behalf. Many of them are of a mind to parlay with us, as there are things we two-leggeds can offer them. They have a taste for land-meat, and a love of pearls and jewels, and—what?" he broke off at the look on Yaela's face. Her eyes were bright with mirth, and dimples appeared deep in her soft cheeks.

"You have maps drawn up already, I would wager on it," she told him.

"Well... yes," he admitted, and felt his face flush warm. "Maps help me envision things, you know. There will be a place for a great library, greater than the world has ever seen. We can lead expeditions into Quarabala some time hence and retrieve the books and scrolls of your people. It will be wonderful," he finished. *If only I could make her see*, he thought. *Perhaps if I showed her my maps...*

"A place for my people. A place for my Maika to grow into her power. A place for our books," she said, and the dimples deepened, by some magic making Leviathus's knees go weak.

"Yes," he said. "For all those things."

"And what of me?" she asked, pulling away and placing both hands on her hips. "Shall I have no part to play in this new world of yours?"

His tongue clove fast to the roof of his mouth again. "What? I, uh, of course, you—"

"I suppose," she went on as if he had not attempted to speak, "I should have to make a place for myself."

Then Yaela the shadowmancer stepped close, twined her arms about his neck, brought his face down to hers, and kissed him as if no woman before her had ever kissed a man.

Thus was Leviathus ap Wyvernus ne Atu—son of a king, brother of a queen—conquered.

FIFTY-SIX

Before the sun had fallen far from the moon, a great ringing voice rose out of the east, powerful as the dawn, sweet as birdsong. The White Nightingale raised up a canticle of joy for all the people of Sindan to hear:

> *"Sing now, O people of the Forbidden City,*
> *for the days of your slavery are ended for ever,*
> *and the Shining Walls are thrown down.*
>
> *Sing and rejoice, ye people of the Sundered Lands,*
> *for your deepest wish has been answered,*
> *and the veil is torn,*
> *your emperor has come through the Twilight Lands,*
> *and he is victorious."*

Jian stood alone upon a balcony of the Palace of Flowers. He could see below him, spread out like an embroidered cloak, the cities and towns and farms of Sindan, and beyond them the Kaapua, sweet River of Flowers. Beyond that, away to the west...

"What are you doing?"

The soft voice of Tsali'gei broke through Jian's reverie. He turned slightly and smiled, gesturing so that she might come stand by his side and look out upon the land. He held out his hands for his son—the small one was sleeping, for a change. Holding him close, he kissed the impossibly soft and sweetly fuzzed little head.

"What are you doing?" his wife asked again, regarding him with wide and too-knowing eyes.

"Look," he said, pointing with his chin. "The wall is nearly down. Soon all the people of Sindan will be able to come to Khanbul without fear of punishment. They are free—free to go as they will, to love whom they will, and to dream of a better tomorrow. We have done this."

"I hope the people remember it when there is little but dreams in their bowls," she remarked somewhat dryly. The war had, indeed, made a mess of things. The harvests would not be robust this year, maybe not for many years to come. "And you never answered my question."

Nor did he now, but Jian put his arm around her waist and drew her close, and she let it be. Though his sword had been washed clean of an emperor's blood, nevertheless his eyes were drawn inexorably to the west, and it seemed to him that the peace in his heart was no more than the stillness between one breath and the next.

The Dragon Queen of Atualon, he thought, *holds the chains that bind Sajani in one hand, and atulfah in the other. Until those chains have been broken, none of us can be truly free. Tiachu's crown will not be the last to fall at my feet.*

For the moment, however, Tsali'gei was there, and their little son Tiungren, and the sunset was beautiful. Let tomorrow come tomorrow; for now, he would have peace. He stood with his arm around his wife in the rose-gold light of a dying day as the White Nightingale sang on.

> *"Sing and be glad, O ye children of the East,*
> *for your Daeshen emperor has come to you*
> > *from across the veil,*
> *and he shall dwell among you.*
> *Caring for you as a son*
> *as a brother*
> *as a father*
> *all the days of his life.*

The lands that were sundered shall be renewed,
and the deep magic returned to the world of men,
and Sindan shall be blessed
above all others
in the dreams
of Sajani.
Sing all ye people!"

In his mind's eye the people of Sindan lifted their long-bowed heads and looked to Khanbul. When they saw that the shining wall of swords was being torn down, that the Forbidden City would be forbidden to them no more, and that the chains of slavery had been lifted from their shoulders, they sang.

He heard the song rising up from below. With all their hearts, they sang.

FIFTY-SEVEN

All things had been made new and ready in Atukos, the queen's fortress at the heart of Atualon. Kentakuyan a'o Maika i Kaka'ahuana li'i's own Iponui had run themselves to exhaustion in order to spread glad tidings to all corners of the known world, from Min Yaarif in the west to the Sindanese empire in the east.

The new emperor of Sindan had sent emissaries and gifts of goodwill to the new Dragon Queen and her consort Ismai ne Mur. From every land known to humankind and Dae the people came, women and men, soldiers and scribes, to stare in wonderment at the sparkling city and her now-legendary queen. The flame-haired warrior from the Zeera—she who had inherited the gift of dreamshifting from her mother and the gift of dragonsong from her father, she who had raised armies of the dead and sang the dragon Sajani back into eternal slumber, and in so doing had saved them all. She had become a hero from the old stories, her shadow grown longer with each minstrel's retelling.

Of the Quarabalese queen, made a refugee along with those of her people who had escaped the Seared Lands, there were a few mentions, a few wondering glances, but these Maika brushed aside with a humble smile. "Let the night be eclipsed by the bright new dawn," she told her aunt Yaela, "as it always was, as it should be—for the best stories, the best plans, are woven in secret and told in whispers."

Now the imperators in their splendid armor led their host toward the shining fortress, and every eye of Atualon shone with tears of wonder as they advanced, line upon line, their ranks swollen with the braided and antlered and horned heads of those who had been Zeerani warriors, Salarians, and pirates of river and land. Dragon helms of gold and lapis glowed in the sunlight, sword and spear flashed bright with pride as the Dragon Queen flexed her claws for all the world to see.

Such an impressive display of force had not been witnessed for ages, not since before the dark days of the Sundering. They came to the Sunrise Gate and halted in front of the walls. There stood women and men in the new blue-and-green spidersilk robes of the Divasguard, armored with snarling helms of Sajani and armed with newly made shamsi, single-edged swords of rare red iron, a gift from the queen of Quarabala as a gesture of goodwill and gratitude.

Maika smiled when she saw them and smiled again at the many Iponui woven in among the imperators, the shadowsworn standing shoulder-to-shoulder with Sulema's newly bonded Baidun Daiel.

In front of the gates stood an assemblage of persons most of the celebrants at best knew by name. Bretan il Mer, who had been named king of Salar Merraj now that his mother and the wicked Bashaba were among those whose bodies decorated the outer ramparts. He was accompanied by his brother Soutan Mer, and a score of Salarian troops all wearing the blue-and-green badge of those sworn to Sa Atu.

Gaia, daughter of Davidian, had been raised to the position of imperator general in honor of her father's sacrifice. In her blue mail she had the bearing of a hero of old, and stood beside Umm Nuara First Mother, Askander First Warden—and the bonesinger Ani, whose magics were no longer forbidden under Atualonian law and who appeared now younger in age than her former students.

The parens of Atualon, emissaries from Min Yaarif and even from the distant city of Sindan, all vied with one another for positions of importance. Leviathus ap Wyvernus ne Atu—the pirate king—stood near his lovely new bride. Yaela herself was the center of a great deal of gossip and speculation as the erstwhile apprentice of Aasah, aunt to the refugee queen, and newly named Illindrist in her own right.

Yaela caught Maika's glance and smiled. Those jade eyes, which had been watching over Maika from the moment of her birth, shone with fierce pride and determination.

Kentakuyan a'o Maika i Kaka'ahuana li'i stood amid the personages of Atualon, unremarkable in borrowed finery, accompanied only by Tamimeha and Akamaia. Wide-eyed and waifish she appeared, and knew it—she had perfected the look well.

She met Yaela's look with one of her own and inclined her head slowly.

A hush fell upon the crowd as from the host the Divasguard appeared in their green dragon's helms, red shamsi raised in salute. Beneath these strode the Dragon Queen, stern-faced and splendid, looking neither to the left nor the right. At her side walked Ismai ne Mur, the Lich King and king consort, fearsome and glorious. Each bore a dragon mask—hers of blue and green gems, his of gold—and were robed in white-and-gold. If ever a pair of lovers were fit to inspire hearts to song and to deeds of glory, Maika thought, it would be these two.

Bretan il Mer strode forth from the assemblage and met them. He bent his knee and his bare, horned head in obeisance, took the thin golden circlet from his brow, and held it up to them.

"The king of Salar Merraj begs your forgiveness, your Radiance, your Arrogance," he said to them, "and mercy for his people, if not for his person."

Sulema took the golden circlet from Bretan and placed it back on his head. Then she raised him to his feet and kissed either cheek before slapping him so hard that the big man's head snapped back with an audible crack.

"Mercy is granted, where it was not asked," she replied, "and you shall be our steward in the east, to keep our roads safe, and the hearts of our people true." The king of Salar Merraj bowed again, and the crowd erupted in roars of approval, understanding that a civil war had been averted ere it had begun, and that an empire had been born, both in the same day. Then Bretan faced the crowd and spoke in a clear voice.

"Peoples of Atualon, of the Zeera, of Salar Merraj," he said. "Peoples of the west and east, listen to my words and rejoice! For the queen has come among you, the Dragon Queen of Atualon. Raised in the harsh Zeera by her mother, the formidable dreamshifter Hafsa Azeina, trained by her father Wyvernus Ka Atu, forged as a blade upon the anvil of Quarabala, in the deadly Seared Lands.

"Before you stands Sulema an Wyvernus ne Atu, warder of the long sleep of Sajani, guardian of the Dreaming Lands, keeper of the Song of Dragons. Sulema Firehair, first of her name." He paused, then added, "Long may she reign! Shall she be known to you as your queen and dwell among you, above you, keeping watch and faith from Atukos on high?"

Before the crowd could react to his words, Atukos itself answered for them all. The dragonglass walls erupted in green flame and blue, a scintillating display so profound that for a moment the brilliance of the queen's fortress eclipsed the sun itself, and it seemed as if Akari Sun Dragon cried out a welcome to his daughter.

As quickly as they had burst forth the flames subsided, but where the walls of Atukos had been dark and forbidding, they became bright with the promise of abundance.

It would be seen as a blessing from Sajani, Maika knew, and that was just as well. The land that had been sundered was made whole, and the world that had been broken was made good by the coupling of the Dragon Queen and her consort, the twining of the songs of Sajani and Akari, as should have never been torn asunder.

"Yes!" someone shouted, then more joined in, until the host cried out with one voice, then fell to their knees, overwhelmed by the tableau before them.

Hannei, first warrior of the Zeeranim, stepped forward and set a golden casket by her feet. She drew forth a headdress of lionsnake plumes the likes of which Maika had never seen. The plumes were of purest white chased with gold, blue, and green. These were set in a crown of red gold crusted with diamonds and precious jewels. She held this above Sulema's bowed head, and grinned, and spoke to her queen in handspeak. They both laughed, and it pained Maika to hear the sound that came from the first warrior's throat.

Tamimeha grunted. "They are using Zeerani runner signs," she whispered. "The silent one says to her sister, 'I have killed this little thing for you.'" She looked impressed. "That must have been the grandmother of all lionsnakes, to boast such plumes. I have never heard of such a feat."

Maika looked long at Hannei, who wore two swords upon her back, the beaded vest of a Zeerani warrior, and a medallion around her neck that looked more than a little like stars hung in the Web of Illindra.

That one merits watching, she thought. *Perhaps even eliminating.* But she said nothing, not even to Tamimeha whom she trusted, for a spider's secrets were best kept to herself. Her own web was yet unfinished.

Sulema knelt, and her sword-sister placed the crown upon her brow. Then Hannei raised a circlet of white gold and yellow and placed it upon the bowed head of Ismai ne Mur, at which point the crowd again erupted in a deafening roar. Horns were blown, flowers thrown, and babes raised high in the air by parents who wished their small new souls to be lifted and blessed by this grand moment.

And when will our *moment come?* Maika thought. *When will we set foot upon the lands we were promised, and raise our own flags, and our own babes to be blessed*

520

in peace under the sun? When will our sundered lands be made whole again, and good, when will the tears from the Night of Sorrows be dried? When? She looked upon the face of joy, and bit back tears of despair, of anger.

Lost in the tumult, Yaela—swathed in spidersilk of gold, weighed down in precious gems as befit a high princess of Saodan and beloved of the pirate king—appeared at Maika's elbow, leaned close, and whispered in her ear,

"Long live the queen."

Maika turned, stared into her aunt's cursed, all-seeing eyes, the eyes of Pelang—so like her own.

She smiled.

"Long live the queen."

FIFTY-EIGHT

Akari Sun Dragon had long since flown beyond the horizon crying for his lost love, and the night unfurled silken-soft. Those warriors and wardens, mothers and craftmistresses—indeed, every member of the prides who could walk or ride, had left their homes before daybreak and traveled to the Madraj. Only a handful had been left to guard their borders.

Dreamshifters were there, most of them newly raised too soon from apprentice or journeyman. Their youthful faces were hard and determined, nonetheless. Moonslight and starslight shone upon the faces of the Zeeranim, a remnant of a remnant, little more, but they yet breathed. *"Where there is life,"* old Theotara would have said, *"there is yet hope."*

In the days of their glory, hordes of mounted Ja'Akari had rolled across the Zeera like thunder and the songs of the Mothers had fallen like gentle rain. Hannei had looked upon the census books, upon the thousands and thousands of names of the ancestors, stretching back in a proud line back to the dawn of days and the first ride of Zula Din. Time, and war, and the Dragon Kings of Atualon had worked their fell magics upon the people. Had almost driven the Zeeranim to extinction.

Almost, but not quite.

The voices of their ancestors echoed in the halls beneath the seats of the Madraj. They called for *kishah*, for vengeance. They called for her. Hannei, alone in the deep heart of the Madraj, looked up at her people and allowed herself a small, hard smile.

They have not killed us yet, she thought. *We are stronger than they know.*

The sword-sister of her childhood had argued that the people might someday regain their former glory, that the young riders and young vash'ai might again form bonds of kinship and blood, that they might once again breed great herds of asil, take up bow and shamsi, and work their will upon the world.

"*Saghaani*," Sulema had argued, years ago, "*there is beauty in youth.*" They were young, they were strong and unconstrained by the failures of their elders. They would find a way to secure a future for the people. If there was no way to be found, they would make one.

"*Ehuani*," young Hannei had countered. "*There is beauty in truth.*" She had seen neither beauty nor wisdom in an attempt to deny the inevitable. The time of the Zeeranim was over and done, and the world would move on without them.

They had both been right, if only through ignorance. There was beauty in all things. In truth, in youth, in death...

In vengeance.

The clouds to the east glowed an angry orange-red, seared with torch and bonfire, and the night was rent with sound. Hard sounds, angry sounds, hammer and anvil, whip and shout. The Zeeranim, who had never in their history traded in human flesh, had refused honorable deaths to Ishtaset's people, the Mah'zula, choosing rather to enslave them and bend their backs to labor. From the ashes of Aish Kalumm a new city was rising, one with walls and towers for archers, with narrow stairs and deep dungeons, with armories and forges and stables for war-horses.

Aish Kalumm itself was no more, nor ever would be again. Aish Kishah, this city would be called, the City of Vengeance.

She stood upon the very ground where Tammas had once danced with Azouq and Dairuz, beneath the moons, in those lost days when the world had seemed a good place in which to live. The sky grew dark as a bruise, dark as old blood.

Dark as a scream with no tongue to give it voice. The moons Didi and Delpha raised themselves in the sky thin and sharp as pale shamsi, and they were pointed toward Atualon. It was an omen of death if ever Hannei had seen one.

Khutlani, she admonished herself. *Your mind is too small to hold such big thoughts.*

Hannei could hear the breath of the people of the prides, hot with long-suppressed anger. She could feel their heartbeats shivering through the air like the drums of war, could feel the silent horn-blasts of their impatience. The wind shifted and she could smell the cat musk, stronger than ever. Eyes flashed in the deepening dark, first by the dozens, then by the hundreds. Low growls and soft snarls punctuated the silence, and a warm presence curled heavy in the back of her mind. They were there, in the night, watching and waiting.

For too long have we watched from the shadows, a voice snarled in her head. *Too long have we waited. It is time to hunt.*

A great fire roared to life, shattering the night. Hannei's heart leapt in her breast like the flames, hot and hungry. A gasp rippled across the assembly like wind through sand, and somewhere a baby cried. Even this far from the people Hannei could feel the tension of held breaths, of bellies hungry for what crumbs the Dragon Kings and Queens in Atualon had left for them.

The prides' most powerful dreamshifter stood before her, above her, wreathed in flame. Once a sickly boy, weak and shy, he had been claimed by the moons as their own child, had walked among the stars and through time.

"*I have seen the future*," he had told her, touching her face, "*and it is us.*" Now he stood hale and whole and powerful, naked skin gleaming gold in the firelight, eyes dark and deep as the furious stars.

Daru held in one hand a horse-head staff of some strange metal, and a pale stone globe in the other. As he raised the staff above his head, Inna'hael—first kahanna of the vash'ai—bled out from the shadows to stand beside Daru. He threw back his head and roared, and the desert sang in answer to his call. No vash'ai had ever seemed so magnificent, no dreamshifter so formidable, as they.

Nothing in Hannei's short, brutal life had prepared her for a moment that felt so right. As she stared up at them, man and vash'ai, dreamshifter and kahanna, the tears streamed down her face hot as blood.

The child chose that moment to announce herself with her very first kick. Hannei laid a hand over her belly and stared unblinking into the fire, into the future.

Remember this night, little warrior.

Hannei felt her sa, the breath of her spirit, quiver like a star trapped in Illindra's web. She refused the fear that would have risen in her soul, consigned it to fire and smoke and the memories of childhood.

This is our world now, she thought, *mine and my child's. And his.*

As the newmade slaves hurried to light torches all around the Madraj, Hannei felt hope—wild, fierce, and terrible—rise from the ashes and curl itself around her heart. This was the night she had dreamed of, fought for, lived for. No longer would the Zeeranim be as children seated before a stranger's fire, fed on crumbs and pity and denied their birthright. No longer would their children be hunted, their warriors dismissed, their voices go unheard. They were born of the desert, bred of the blood of Zula Din, beloved of Akari.

We are not alone.

Never alone, the soft and deadly voice agreed. *Never again.*

The wind picked up, and the Zeera sang, and Hannei's heart sang with it.

Three Zeeranim stepped into the light. One was Ja'Akari, tall and proud, and in her hands she bore the Book of Blood.

The second was Ja'Sajani, straight and true, and in his hands he bore the Book of Asil. The third was a mother, gravid with child. In one hand she bore a stylus of bone, in the other a bowl made from the fresh white skull of a woman. Hannei looked upon this, noted the broken nose, and smiled.

Rehaza Entanye, she thought. *I would recognize that face anywhere.*

The three were naked, even as she was naked, for under the moons and stars all women, all men are equal. Their faces were painted to honor the vash'ai, their skin deeply dappled as well, for each of them had long been Zeeravashani, and their kithren had not abandoned them even during the recent troubles.

Their heads were bare, new-shorn, and what little hair had grown back had been rubbed with ash and fat so that it sprang up from their scalps like pale manes, in the old fashion. These three were among the first to have been made *Aulenui,* the First People come again, a new and stronger pride born from the ashes of the weak.

The Ja'Akari and Ja'Sajani opened their books, each to the first blank page. Hannei held her arms out from her sides, like the wings of a bird, and stared without flinching into Daru's eyes as the young mother jabbed the stylus into the flesh of Hannei's inner arms and let the blood drain drip, drip, drip into the broken-nosed bowl. When enough of Hannei's life had been drained away the mother dipped the stylus into the skull of her slain enemy and wrote in the Book of Blood with a tidy, deft hand.

"Nazmah Din," she intoned, "born Hannei of the Shahadrim, daughter of Deaara and of Mazuk Ja'Sajani of the line of Zula Din. Also, Hannei Ja'Akari, champion of the Zeeranim under Sareta Ja'Akari Akibra, also—" She glanced up, and with Hannei's nod of approval she finished. "Also known as the slave Kishah, renowned among the pit fighters of Min Yaarif." She went on for some time, naming skirmishes in which Hannei had fought, and the battle in Atualon, and those people whom Hannei had killed and whose names she could remember. Her dalliance with Tammas son of Nurati was noted, and his bloodlines, and that he had died, and that she had loved him and of that love had conceived a child.

When the mother had exhausted the story of Hannei's short life she used the blood, now cooling and congealing, to write in the Book of Asil. In this book she named those horses which Hannei owned—her mares Mekkia and Lalia among them, as well as Zeitan Fleet-Foot and Ruhho the brave-hearted black, and Azouq, and others whose owners had gifted them to her as tokens of goodwill. Last named was Atemi True-Heart, who had once belonged to a sword-sister. That sword-sister had passed into Atualon, never to return, and so care of the fine golden mare had been passed to her.

Hannei pushed aside the pain in her heart. Though Sulema an Wyvernus ne Atu yet lived and ruled from Atukos, Sulema Ja'Akari was gone from the world. Atemi belonged to the people, and with them she would remain.

By the time they were finished, Hannei had stilled her pain and stifled regret. The books were carried away with reverence—of all the treasures in Aish Kalumm, these alone had been spared by Ishtaset and her riders, and they were precious—and Hannei walked, alone, up to the roaring fire and to Daru.

Dark eyes old and wise peered out at her from a stranger's face, a stranger who smiled with Daru's smile and spoke from Daru's heart. They burned like stars, as though they would sear away the layers of her names and find her worthy. The words, when they came, were deep and resonant, and the shadows leaned in close to hear them.

"Hannei Shahadri."

"Nnnnh," she refuted, shaking her head. *There are no Shahadrim here, only the people, now and always.*

"Hannei Ja'Akari."

"Nnnnh." Again she shook her head, more vehemently this time. *The truth of the world has broken my heart. I am a warrior no more.*

"Kishah of Min Yaarif."

"Nnnnnnh!" *There are slaves here, but I am a slave no more.*

"Umm Hannei."

She laid a hand over her belly again, and for a moment said nothing. The singing sands fell silent. And then, reluctantly, Hannei shook her head and said softly,

"Nnnh."

A mother must have love in her heart and healing in her hands, she knew with bitter regret, *and I have neither.* This child would be raised by the Mothers, as was good and proper.

Daru's eyes flickered in acknowledgment of her pain and sacrifice, or for some other reason, Hannei was not sure. Inna'hael growled softly as Daru raised his horse-head staff and touched Hannei's forehead, softly, just between her eyes.

It felt, oddly enough, like a kiss.

"Who stands before me?" he asked, and then, for her ears only, he added, "Who stands beside me?"

Hannei brought her hands up and replied in hunter-speak.

It is I.

"Nazmah Din I name you before the people, of the line of Zula Din, first of your name. I see you. The heart within you, the sa and ka burning bright." As he spoke, more of the Zeeranim gathered around them. "*Ehuani* I name you. *Mutaani* I name you. *Saghaani* I name you. *Kishahani* I name you. Nazmah Din you shall be to us now, in our hearts and on our tongues." He took a deep breath and held it, and then in a voice that roared like the wind he went on.

"I name you Nazmah Din, first of your name, first among sisters, first queen of the Zeeranim." He brought the staff down once, twice, three times on the ground between their feet.

Even as his words rang across the Zeera, even as those who stood around them responded with a chorus that rolled and swelled and sang like the very desert from which they had come in the long ago, Paraja padded from the fallen night to stand at her side. Beauty she was, and death. She butted her head against Hannei's—Nazmah Din's—chest, looking well pleased with her new-bonded kithren.

The stupid humans take a queen at last, she purred. *There may be hope for you yet.*

Inna'hael threw back his head and roared, a sound that made her feet tingle where they met the earth, and hundreds—perhaps thousands—of vash'ai added their voices to his, a sound which had not been heard in the Madraj for long lives of men. Paraja did not deign to answer. She was a queen, herself, and answered to none, but she dug black claws into the soft sand and purred.

Nazmah Din had been found worthy. Her heart burned fierce in her breast, hot with love for her people and the night and the sweet singing sands of home. She met Daru's eyes. He smiled and bowed low.

"Long live the queen."

JEHANNIM

His name was Ba'esh, son of Perthor son of Iftallen the Damned. "Nightmare Man," they called him, and "Shadow King." For a thousand years he had existed—he would not have called it living—without song, or sleep, or hope of death. These things had been stolen from him, as punishment for another man's crime.

The tattered cloak swirled around his ankles as he bent forward and climbed the steep path into the Jehannim. Though the day was as harsh and unforgiving as any other, he did not feel it. The searing gaze of Akari avoided him, just as the Lonely Road was closed to him. He was, of all things that had ever been, singularly alone.

A harsh cry, and a fall of rocks. He glanced up, peering through the ruined mask that hid his ruined face, and caught the flicker-flicker of harsh shadows as a herd of mymyc fled before him. He was a man with no song in his bones, no dreams, and no hope for tomorrow.

He was the Nightmare Man, and the world was his nightmare. All he wanted—all he had ever wanted—was to sleep.

Ba'esh lifted his face into the wind, opened his eyes wide to the dawning of yet another day that should not have been—

—and screamed.

APPENDICES

THE LANDS
OF THE PEOPLE

From the Notes of Loremaster Rothfaust

ATUALON

The mightiest kingdom in the Near West, Atualon is the seat of Ka Atu, the Dragon King. Fabled to be built on the back of a sleeping dragon, Atualon is the wellspring of a deep and ancient magic.

This magic is known as atulfah, and is comprised of sa and ka, female and male, heart and spirit, the Song of Life. Only those born echovete—able to hear the magical song of creation—have the potential to manipulate this magic, and only an echovete child born and raised to the throne may be trained to wield it.

SINDAN

The Sindanese empire stretches from the pearl-choked waters of Nar Kabdaan in the Middle East, over the ice-tombed peaks of Mutai Gon-yu, to Nar Intihaan in the Far East: End of the Bitter Lands, End of the Great Salt Road, End of the Known World. The story of Sindan stretches far beyond written memory and into the misted memories of the First Men, before the thickening of the veil. The Daemon Emperor of Sindan rules absolutely from his throne in Khanbul, the Forbidden City, though his thoughts turn ever westward. He is covetous of atulfah, for its power is the only thing greater than his own.

QUARABALA

Once a place of beauty and art, high learning and gentle culture, the Quarabala was scorched clean of life and hope during the Sundering. Few now survive in these Seared Lands west of the Dibris. Occasionally a story will turn up in the slave-trading town of Min Yaarif, rumors of the wonders of Saodan buried deep in the world's heart, stories of wicked beasts and wickeder men driven to desperate acts as they struggle to survive on the Edge of the Quarabala. Even more rarely a shadowmancer, a shadowshifting Illindrist, will emerge from the smoking ruins, night-skinned and demon-eyed, leading traders with packs full of the precious red salt and eyes full of waking nightmares.

THE ZEERA

A land of silk and honey, great warriors and greater predators, the Zeera is a vast golden desert and home to the desert prides. Once a proud and prosperous nation, the Zeeranim are now a remnant of their former glory. The Mothers live in mostly empty cities along the banks of the Dibris, the Ja'Sajani take census and record the final days of a dying people, and the Ja'Akari guard the people against enemies within and without the prides. Too few are born, too few survive, and too few are chosen to become Zeeravashani, bonded to the great sabre-tusked cats with whom they are allied. The wardens write, the warriors fight, and the Mothers sing lullabies against the coming darkness, but their struggles are like the notes of a flute, lost and forgotten in the coming storm.

THE PEOPLE

From the Notes of Loremaster Rothfaust

Aadl (Istaz Aadl): Zeerani youthmaster

Aaraf (Loreman Aaraf): Zeerani storyteller and bard

Aasah (Aasah sud Layl): priest of Illindra, shadowmancer and advisor to Ka Atu

Adalia: warrior of the Mah'zula

Akamaia: Illindrist and oracle of Saodan

Amalua: Quarabalese Iponui

Ani (Istaza Ani): Zeerani youthmistress; also the last known Dzirani

Annila (Annila Ja'Akari): young Zeerani warrior, peer to Sulema and Hannei

Annubasta (*see* Hafsa Azeina)

Ashta: journeyman mantist studying under Loremaster Rothfaust

Askander (Askander Ja'Akarinu'i): First Warden of the Zeeranim

Ba'esh: also known as Nightmare Man

Bardu: Daechen prince

Bashaba: former concubine of Ka Atu; mother to Pythos, Mattu, and Matteira

Basta (cat): kima'a to Hafsa Azeina

Bellanca (Matreon Bellanca): Matreon of Atualon

Belzaleel the Liar: an ancient, wicked spirit, currently trapped in a dragonglass blade

Boraz (Boraz Ja'Sajani): Zeerani warden

Breama: the Huntress

Bretan Mer (Bretan Mer ne Ninianne il Mer): salt merchant and liaison from Salar Merraj to Atualon; son of Ninianne il Mer

Brygus: member of the Draiksguard

Char (Charon): Guardian of Eid Kalmut; also Naara, daughter of Kal ne Mur

Daeshen Baichen Pao: the first Daemon Emperor, ruler of Sindan

Daeshen Tiachu: the current Daemon Emperor, ruler of Sindan

Daru: young apprentice to Hafsa Azeina

Davidian: Imperator General of Atualon

Davvus: a legendary king of Men

Dennet: a daughter of Nurati

Devranae: legendary daughter of Zula Din; abducted by Davvus, king of Men

Deyenna: a young woman who seeks to escape Atualon

Douwa: bathhouse attendant in Atualon

Duadl (Duadl Ja'Sajani): Zeerani warden and churra-master

Eleni: attendant at the Grinning Mymyc in Bayyid Eidtein

Etana: Iponui and First Runner of Saodan

Ezio: Atualonian Master of Coin

Fairussa (Fairussa Ja'Akari): warrior of the Zeeranim

Gai Khan: Daechen prince

Gavria (Gavria Ja'Akari): Zeerani warrior

Ginna: Atualonian maidservant

Hadid (Mastersmith Hadid): Zeerani mastersmith

Hafsa Azeina: dreamshifter of the prides and queen consort of Atualon. Rarely: Annubasta

Hannei (Hannei Ja'Akari): Sulema's peer and good friend; also Kishah Two-Blades of Min Yaarif, and Nazmah Din of the Zeera

Haoki: Counselorwoman of Saodan

Hapuata (Istaza Hapuata): Zeerani mentor to Theotara Ja'Akari

Hekates: Draiksguard of Atualon

Hyang: village boy from Bizhan

Ippos: stablemaster of Atualon

Isara (Isara Ja'Akari): Zeerani warrior

Ishtaset: Mah'zula warrior

Ismai: Zeerani youth; son of Nurati

Istaza Ani: (*see* Ani)

Jamandae: (deceased) youngest concubine of Serpentus, deposed Dragon King of Atualon

Jasin (Ja'Atanili'i Jasin): Zeerani youth and would-be warden

Jian (Daechen Jian, Tsun-ju Jian): young Daechen prince

Jinchua (fennec): kima'a to Sulema

Jorah: Zeerani craftsman

Kabila (Kabila Ja'Akari): Zeerani warrior

Kalani: Zeerani maiden

Karkash Dhwani: powerful Daechen prince, advisor to the emperor

Kekeo: Counselorman of Saodan

Kishah: (*see* Hannei)

Lavanya: Zeerani warrior and peer of Sulema

Lehaila: Counselorwoman of Saodan

Leviathus (Leviathus ap Wyvernus ne Atu): Sulema's half-brother, son of Ka Atu, Leviathus is surdus—a princeling without magic

Maika: Kentakuyan a'o Maika i Kaka'ahuana li'l, queen of Quarabala

Makil: Zeerani warden

Mardoni: Daechen prince

Marisa: maidservant in Atualon

Mariza: Renegade Ja'Akari. Once banished and declared Kha'Akari, she now rides with the Mah'zula

Matteira: daughter of Bashaba, a former concubine of Ka Atu. Twin sister to Mattu, and sister to Pythos

Mattu (Mattu Halfmask): son of Bashaba, a former concubine of Ka Atu. Twin brother to Matteira, and brother to Pythos

Naara: (*see* Char)

Naruteo (Daechen Naruteo): Sindanese youth. Daeborn and yearmate to Jian

Neptara (Umm Neptara): daughter of Nurati

Nightmare Man: Ba'esh

Ninianne il Mer: Lady of the Lake, matriarch of the clans of Salar Merraj, city of the salt merchants; mother of Bretan Mer, Soutan Mer

Nurati (Umm Nurati): First Mother of the Zeeranim; mother of Tammas, Neptara, Ismai, Dennet, Rudya, and an as-yet unnamed infant daughter

Paleha: Quarabalese Illindrist

Perri: Sindanese youth; daeborn and yearmate to Jian

Puani: Counselorwoman of Saodan

Pythos: (long thought to be deceased) son of Serpentus, deposed Dragon King of Atualon

Rama (Rama Ja'Sajani): Zeerani warden and horsemaster from Aish Arak

Rehaza Entanye: pitmistress of Min Yaarif

Rheodus: young Atualonian man, member of Leviathus's

Draiksguard

Rothfaust (Loremaster Rothfaust): loremaster of Atualon, keeper of tomes and tales

Rudya: daughter of Nurati

Sammai: Zeerani child

Santorus (Master Healer Santorus): Atualonian patreon and master healer

Sareta (Sareta Ja'Akarinu'i): ranking warrior of the Zeeranim

Saskia (Saskia Ja'Akari): Zeerani warrior and peer of Sulema

Serpentus: Dragon King of Atualon deposed by Wyvernus

Soutan Mer (Soutan Mer ne Ninianne il Mer): son of Ninianne il Mer

Sulema (Sulema Ja'Akari): Zeerani warrior, daughter of Hafsa Azeina and Wyvernus

Sunzi: Daechen prince

Tadeah: (deceased) daughter of Bashaba and Ka Atu

Talilla (Ja'Akari): Zeerani warrior

Talleh: young Zeerani boy

Tamimeha: Grand Princess of Quarabala, chief among the Iponui

Tammas (Tammas Ja'Sajani): Zeerani warden, eldest son of Nurati

Teppei: Daechen prince

Theotara (Theotara Ja'Akari): honored Ja'Akari

Tiungpei (Tsun-ju Tiungpei): a Sindanese pearl diver who took a lover from among the Issuq; mother of Jian

Tsali'gei: Daezhu woman

Tsa-len: yendaeshi to Naruteo

Umm Nurati (*see* Nurati)

Valri: warrior of the Mah'zula

Wyvernus: Ka Atu, the Dragon King of Atualon

Xienpei: yendaeshi to Jian

Yaela: apprentice to Aasah
Yeshu: Atualonian weaver

Zula Din: trickster/warrior of legend, daughter of the First
People

TERMS, PHRASES AND PLACES OF INTEREST

From the Notes of Loremaster Rothfaust

Aish Kalumm (the City of Mothers): Zeerani river fortress

Akari (Akari Sun Dragon): according to legend, Akari is a draik (a male dragon) who flies across the sky bringing life and light to the world as he seeks to rouse his sleeping mate, Sajani the Earth Dragon

aklashi: a game played while on horseback. It involves a sheep's head and quite a lot of noise

Arachnist: a human mage, who worships and does the bidding of the Araids

Araid: massive, intelligent spiders that live deep in the abandoned cities of Quarabala

Atualon: a western kingdom founded upon the shores of Nar Bedayyan; home to the Dragon Kings

Atukos (City of Dreams, City of the Sleeping Dragon): dragonglass fortress of the Dragon King, named for the living mountain into which it is built

atulfah: sa and ka combined to create the song of creation

Ayyam Binat: a period of time in the spring during which young Zeerani women vie with one another for the sexual favors of men

Baidun Daiel (also known as the Sleepless, or Voiceless): warrior mages who serve Ka Atu

Baizhu: a religious order of Sindanese monks

Bayyid Eidtein: trading town near the mouth of the Dibris, a

known den of miscreants and rogues. The southernmost
trading post along Atualonian-maintained roads

Beit Usqut: the Youths' Quarter in Aish Kalumm

bintshi: a winged greater predator with the ability to
immobilize and lure prey using psionic song

Bohica: patroness divine of soldiers

bonelord: one of the greater predators, bonelords are massive
carnivorous creatures that rely on camouflage, speed, and
mind-magic to capture prey

bonesinger: Dzirani sorcerer

Bones of Eth: an ill-reputed ruin or monument in the Zeera,
formed of a rough circle of tall, twisted pillars of red and
black stone

churra (pl. churrim): a hardy desert omnivore prized by the
Zeerani as a pack animal, and seen as a suitable mount for
outlanders

craftmistress/master: Zeerani women and men who have
been trained in and work at their particular craft—
blacksmithing, painting, building, weaving, etc.

Dae: a race of magically gifted people who reside in the
Twilight Lands

daeborn: of Dae descent

Daechen: half-Dae, half-human Sindanese warrior caste (male)

daemon: commonly used to describe any wicked thing (also
daespawn)

Daeshen: half-Dae, half-human member of the Sindanese
imperial family

Daezhu: half-Dae, half-human Sindanese ruling class (female)

Delpha (Big Sister): one of two moons; has a twenty-eight-day
cycle

Dibris: a river that runs through the Zeera, supporting a wide
range of life

Didi (Little Sister): one of two moons; has a fourteen-day cycle

Dragon King: Ka Atu, the monarch of Atualon (currently Wyvernus)

Draiksguard: elite military unit assigned to guard members of the Atualonian royal family

Dreaming Lands: *see* Shehannam

dreamshifter: Zeerani shaman who can move through and manipulate Shehannam

Dzirani: clan of wandering storytellers, healers, and merchants

Dziranim: members of the Dzirani clan, known for their forbidden magic of bonesinging

echovete: one who can hear atulfah

Edge, the: the geographical and socioeconomic fringes of Quarabala

ehuani: Zeerani word meaning "beauty in truth"

Eid Kalish: trading town, a stop on the Great Salt Road, known for its thriving black market and slave trade

Eth: Quarabalese destruction deity, he whose breath creates the darkness between stars

Great Salt Road: trade route that stretches from the edge of the Quarabala in the west to the easternmost cities of Sindan

Hajra-Khai: Zeerani spring festival

hayatani: a Zeerani girl's first consort

hayyanah: Zeerani couples who are pledged to one another and remain more or less monogamous

herdmistress/master: responsible for the health and well-being of a pride's horses and churrim

Illindra: Quarabalese creation deity, an enormous female spider who hangs the stars in her web of life

Iponui: Quarabalese runners, messengers, and warriors

Issuq: twilight lords and ladies who have a clan affinity for the sea and can shapeshift into sea-bears

istaza/istaz: youthmistress/master of the Zeerani prides

Ja'Akari: Zeerani warrior, responsible for keeping all the pridelands safe from outside threats

Ja Akari: Zeerani phrase meaning "under the sun"; loosely translates to being completely open and honest, hiding nothing

Ja'Sajani: Zeerani warden, responsible for maintaining order and security within his local territory

Ja Sajani: Zeerani phrase meaning "upon the earth"; loosely translates to being present in the moment

Jehannim: a mythical hellish place of fire and brimstone; also the name of a mountain range west of the river Dibris and east of Quarabala

jiinberry: a water-loving berry that grows along the banks of the Dibris during the flooding season

ka: that half of atulfah which is known as the breath of spirit. It manifests to most as an expanded awareness of one's surroundings

Ka Atu: the Dragon King of Atualon

Kaapua: a river in Sindan

kahanna: vash'ai sorcerer

Kha'Akari: Zeerani warrior who has been exiled from the sight of Akari

Khanbul (the Forbidden City): home of the Sindanese emperor

khutlani: Zeerani word meaning "forbidden"

kima'a: avatar spirit-beast in Shehannam

kin: intelligent creatures descended from the first races and considered relatives of dragons—vash'ai, wyverns, and mymyc are numbered among the kin

kith: term used to describe creatures that are more intelligent than beasts, but lack the awareness of kin or humans

kithren: Zeerani person bound to a vash'ai, and vice versa

ladies/lords of twilight: Dae lords

lashai: modified half-human servants that wait upon the
  Daechen and yendaeshi

lionsnake: an enormous, venomous, two-legged plumed serpent
  that lives in the Zeera

the Lonely Road: in Zeerani mythology, the road traveled by
  the dead

Madraj: an arena and gathering place of the Zeeranim

Mah'zula: a society of Zeeranim who live a purely nomadic
  life and abide by the ancient ways of the desert, seeking to
  return to the glory days of the First Women

Min Yaarif: trading and slavers' port on the western bank of
  the Dibris

Min Yahtamu: ancient trading post west of the Jehannim

mutaani: Zeerani term meaning "there is beauty in death"

Mutai Gon-yu (The Mountains that Tamed the Rains):
  mountain range in Sindan

mymyc: one of the kin, mymyc live and hunt in packs. From a
  distance, mymyc strongly resemble black horses

Nar Bedayyan: a sea to the west of Atualon

Nar Intihaan: a sea to the east of Sindan

Nar Kabdaan: a sea east of the Zeera and west of Sindan

ne Atu: member of the royal family of Atualon

Nian-da: a ten-day-long festival in Sindan. Any child born
  during this time is assumed to be fathered by a Dae man
  during Moonstide, and without exception is taken to
  Khanbul at the age of sixteen

Night of Sorrows: an historic uprising in Quarabala, brought
  about via political machinations by the Cult of Eth, which
  left the populace decimated and the ruling families nearly
  extinct

Nisfi: Zeerani pride

O'oraid: large, intelligent spiders used in divination by
Illindrists
outlanders: term used by the Zeerani to describe people not of
the Zeera

parens: heads of the ruling families in Atualon
pride: Zeerani clan. Also used to describe all prides as a single
entity

Quarabala (also known as the Seared Lands): a region so hot
that humans live in cities far underground
Quarabalese: of Quarabala

reavers: insectoid humans that have been modified by the
Araids. Their bite is envenomed
Riharr: Zeerani pride
russet ridgebacks: large spiders that live in underground
colonies. Harmless unless they are disturbed. Their eggs are
considered a delicacy in the Zeera.

sa: that half of atulfah which is known as the heart of the soul.
An expanded sense of empathy and harmony
Sajani (Sajani Earth Dragon, the Sleeping Dragon): according
to legend, Sajani is a diva (a female dragon) who sleeps
beneath the crust of the world, waiting for the song of her
mate Akari to wake her
Salar Merraj: city of the salt miners built upon the shores of a
dead salt lake. The Mer family stronghold
Salarians: citizens of the salt-mining city Salar Merraj
Saodan: capital city of Quarabala
sand-dae: shapes made of wind-driven sand
Shahad: Zeerani pride
Shehannam (the Dreaming Lands): the otherworld, a place of
dreams and strange beings
shenu: a board game popular in the Zeera

shofar (pl. shofarot): wind instrument made from the horn of
    an animal

shofar akibra: a magical instrument fashioned from the horn
    of the golden ram

shongwei: an intelligent, carnivorous sea creature

Sindan: empire that stretches from Nar Kabdaan in the west to
    Nar Intihaan in the east

Sindanese: of Sindan

Snafu: patron divine of fuckups

the Sundering: cataclysm that took place roughly one thousand
    years before the events of this story

surdus: deaf to atulfah

Tai Bardan (Mountains of Ice): mountain range in Sindan east
    of Khanbul

Tai Damat (Mountains of Blood): mountain range in Sindan
    on the Great Salt Road, north of Khanbul

tarbok: goat-sized herd animal, plentiful near rivers and oases

touar: head-to-toe outfit worn by the Zeerani wardens: head
    wrap and veils, calf-length robe, loose trousers, all blue

Twilight Lands: a land at once part of and separated from the
    world of Men; home of the Dae

usca: a strong alcoholic beverage popular in the Zeera

Uthrak: Zeerani pride

vash'ai: large, intelligent sabre-tusked cats. Vash'ai are kin,
    descended from the first races

Wild Hunt (also the Hunt): deadly game played by the
    Huntress, a powerful being who enforces the rules of
    Shehannam

wyvern: intelligent flying kin

yendaeshi: trainer, mentor, and master to the Daechen and

Daezhu

Yosh: a hellish place in Zeerani mythology, and of that wicked spirit or deity that rules it. Variously thought to be deep underground, hidden in the Jehannim, or on another plane of existence altogether

youthmistress/master (istaza/istaz): Zeerani adults in charge of guiding and teaching the pride's young people

Zeera: a desert south of the Great Salt Road, known for its singing dunes, hostile environment, and remote barbarian prides

Zeeranim: people of the desert

Zeeravashani: a Zeerani person who has bonded with a vash'ai

ACKNOWLEDGEMENTS

I would like to give a nod of thanks to...

My readers. I love you guys.

My rockstar agent, Mark Gottlieb of Trident Media.

My Dark Editorial Overlord, Steve Saffel of Titan Books.

Alice Nightingale, again, for initially acquiring *The Dragon's Legacy* and applauding my every success.

Nick Landau, Vivian Cheung, Paul Gill, George Sandison, Joanna Harwood, Hayley Shepherd, Julia Lloyd, Chris McLane, Lydia Gittins, Katharine Carroll, and Polly Grice of Titan Books, for believing in my story.

My high-school English teacher, Deane O'Dell, who against all odds kindled the love of literature in the heart of an ungrateful young barbarian.

Finally, I would very much like to thank the members of a certain speculative fiction authors' cabal, but I cannot— because such a cabal does not exist.

ABOUT THE AUTHOR

Deborah A. Wolf was born in a barn and raised on wildlife refuges, which explains a lot. As a child, whether she was wandering down the beach of an otherwise deserted island or exploring the hidden secrets of bush Alaska with her faithful dog Sitka, she always had a book at hand. She opened the forbidden door, and set foot upon the tangled path, and never looked back.

She attended any college that couldn't outrun her and has accumulated a handful of degrees, the most recent of which is a Master of Science in Information Systems Management from Ferris State University. Among other gigs, she has worked as an underwater photographer, Arabic linguist, and grumbling wage slave. Throughout it all, Deborah has held onto one true and passionate love: the love of storytelling.

Deborah currently lives in northern Michigan with her kids (some of whom are grown and all of whom are exceptional), an assortment of dogs and horses, and two cats, one of whom she suspects is possessed by a demon.

For more fantastic fiction, author events,
exclusive excerpts, competitions, limited editions and more

VISIT OUR WEBSITE
titanbooks.com

LIKE US ON FACEBOOK
facebook.com/titanbooks

FOLLOW US ON TWITTER AND INSTAGRAM
@TitanBooks

EMAIL US
readerfeedback@titanemail.com